THE VINE EATER

BOOK 2 OF THE MAGIC EATERS TRILOGY

CAROL BETH ANDERSON

The Vine Eater by Carol Beth Anderson

Published by
Eliana Press
P.O. Box 2452
Cedar Park, TX 78630

www.carolbethanderson.com

Cover Design:
Mariah Sinclair (thecovervault.com)

Map: BMR Williams

Paperback ISBN: 978-1-949384-06-2

First Edition

This year, I've focused on being grateful for every single person who reads my books.

Therefore, this book is dedicated to you, dear reader.

You bring your experiences, desires, and passions to my words . . .

and you make the stories come alive.

CHARACTERS AND PLACES

Characters

Zeisha Dennivan (ZAY-shuh DEN-ni-van)
Nora Abrios (AH-bree-ose), Princess of Cellerin
Krey (KRAY) West
Ovrun Kensin (OV-run KENN-sin)
Eira (EYE-ruh), trog
Isla (EE-sluh), Zeisha's friend
Sarza (SAHR-zuh) Phip, seer
Wendyn (WENN-din), trog
Ulmin (ULL-min) Abrios, King of Cellerin
Kebi (KEB-ee), trog
Osmius (OZ-me-us), dragon
Taima (ty-EE-muh), dragon
Hatlin (HAT-lin), New Therroan activist
Elo (EE-low) Golsch, Cellerinian spy
Brea (BRAY-uh), royal guard
Dani (DANN-ee), Nora's aunt and Ulmin's sister-in-law
Lars, Cellerinian soldier
Alit (AL-it), pub owner

Prime Minister Osk, leader of Cruine

The Anya (AHN-yuh)

Genta (JENN-tuh) Ril, preday newspaper columnist

Places

Anyari (ann-YAHR-ee), a planet settled by human colonists

Cellerin (SELL-err-in), kingdom centered around Cellerin Mountain

Cellerin City, capital of Cellerin, on the east side of Cellerin Mountain

Deroga (der-OH-guh), large, preday city

New Therro (THAIR-oh), province on the north side of Cellerin Mountain

Cruine (croo-EEN), nation east of Cellerin

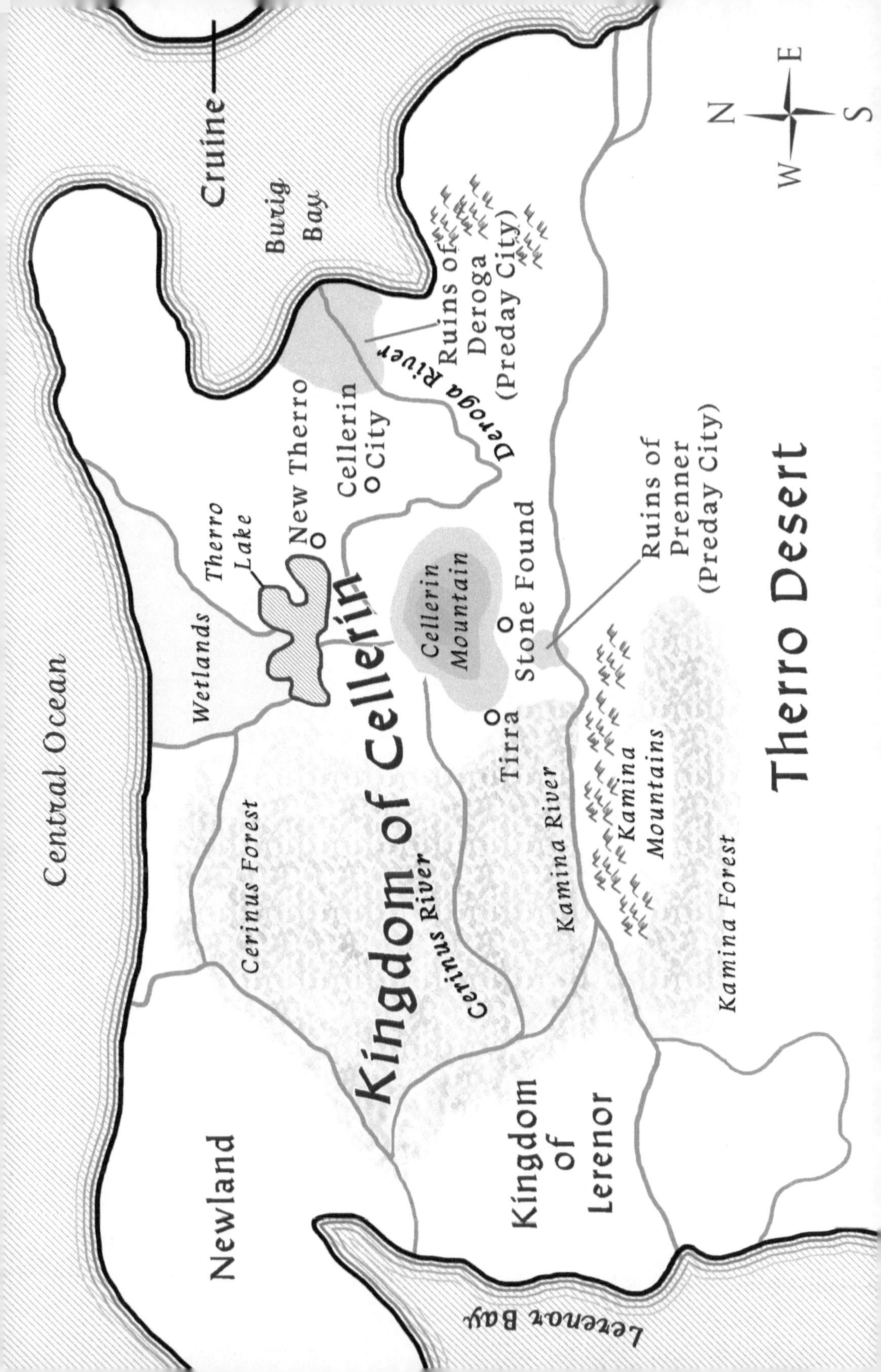

N
E
W
S
Central Ocean
Newland
Cruine
Burig Bay
Therro Lake
Wetlands
New Therro
Cellerin City
Cerinus Forest
Kingdom of Cellerin
Ruins of Deroga (Preday City)
Deroga River
Cellerin Mountain
Stone Found
Tirra
Cerinus River
Kamina River
Ruins of Prenner (Preday City)
Kamina Mountains
Kamina Forest
Kingdom of Lerenor
Lerenor Bay
Therro Desert

1

Our ancestors left Earth to colonize Anyari. Along the way, they lost all their technology. Over the next six millennia, their written communication progressed from cave-art drawings to digital documentation.

In our era of modern technology, The Derogan Chronicle *is the only newspaper on the planet that still prints a daily paper edition.*

Paper is our connection to the past. However, our newsorg must also remain future-minded. That's where our newest daily columnist comes in.

She writes under the pseudonym Genta Ril, and she is sixteen years old.

-*"Past and Future" by Chief Editor Laug Notol*
The Derogan Chronicle, *dated Quari 1, 6293*

A VINE BURST from Zeisha Dennivan's palm, shooting through the air. Just when she thought her strength would wane, it swelled, deep and full. She pushed more magic into her hand. The vine stretched longer, growing faster and farther until it threatened to pierce the orange sky above.

Movement caught Zeisha's eye. A girl, perhaps eleven years old, stood in the street a few mets away. The child's eyes, locked on Zeisha, were wide. Her chin trembled beneath tight lips. One foot was in front of the other, like she'd frozen mid-run. The girl's taut body screamed a single response: *fear.*

Zeisha's mouth dropped open. She halted her vine's growth, then scrambled backward as it dropped to the dirt street in front of her, collapsing in a tangled mess of strong, green coils. Dust clouded the air.

The girl spun and ran away, as if fleeing a monster.

Is that what I am now? A monster?

The buzz of creative magic still saturated Zeisha's hand. A moment ago, she'd savored the sensation. Now, she resented it. She wanted to run after the girl and assure her there was nothing to fear. But the girl had surely heard about Zeisha and the other magic eaters who'd fought each other two days ago, just blocks from here. She had reason to be scared.

Swallowing against the bile filling her throat, Zeisha tried to redirect her thoughts. She examined the vine where it merged with her palm. Her skin had lifted like an inverted funnel, forming the plant's cylindrical base. Over the span of several simmets, smooth, tan skin transitioned into tough, flexible, green plant matter.

Zeisha released her magic. The plant's base separated from her palm and slid to the ground. Her skin retained a bulge for a moment, then flattened. Zeisha reached forward and lifted several coils of the vine into her lap, her eyes widening at the weight. *So much magic. No wonder that girl was scared.*

A voice behind her asked, "How much fuel did you have to eat to create that vine?"

Zeisha turned. Standing behind her was a tall young woman with sleek, chin-length hair that shone in the sun. Like Zeisha, Princess Ulminora Abrios—who insisted on being called *Nora*—was seventeen. Yet she somehow looked like an elegant, sophisticated adult, even on this dusty street.

"I ate a few pieces of bark," Zeisha answered with a forced smile.

Nora walked around to face Zeisha. Her tailored, navy-blue pants looked terribly expensive. She didn't seem to care about that as she sat cross-legged in the dirt street. "Incredible. Could you do things like this before . . . well . . . you know, before?"

Yes, Zeisha knew what *before* meant. Before people who claimed to be recruiting magical apprentices had lured her from her hometown to the capital. Before she and other magic eaters had ridden in a dark, enclosed wagon which had at last released them inside a large building in an unknown location. Before a teenage girl called The Overseer had touched them all, mentally enslaving them and forcing them into a magical militia.

Zeisha shoved a black curl behind her ear. Like it had a mind of its own, the hair popped out and settled again in front of her left eye. "Back home, I could make vines," she said, "but they were very short."

Nora lifted one of the green coils. "This is impressive."

"I'm a fantastic learner when my mind isn't my own," Zeisha murmured. Fearing she sounded ungrateful, she smiled at the princess. "Thank you, Nora. For everything."

Two days before, Nora had killed The Overseer, freeing Zeisha and the rest of the militia from mental captivity. "Krey was behind the rescue plan," Nora said. "From the beginning, he was convinced you'd been kidnapped. He would've done anything to save you."

Zeisha nodded. Krey was stuck on a rooftop clommets away, keeping an eye out for danger. Everyone expected the king to retaliate for the loss of his militia. Krey's ability to fly made him the perfect lookout. Zeisha bit her lip, returning her attention to Nora. "Did you see Krey's neck after the battle?"

"Yes."

"I did that to him." Zeisha briefly closed her eyes, remembering the bruises and red welts on Krey's neck. Marks from the vine that had almost strangled him.

"You can't be sure it was you. There were other plant lysters in the militia. One of them might've attacked him. And whoever did it, the healer took care of him. He's good as new."

"It was me." The words made Zeisha's chest ache. "He would've told me if it were someone else. But he avoided my questions."

Nora placed her cool hand on top of Zeisha's. "Even if that's the case, it wasn't really you. It was The Overseer." She swallowed. "And my father. They're the ones who controlled you and the others."

Zeisha nodded, but the words didn't comfort her. Again, she dropped her eyes to the strong vine in her lap. A terrible question came to her, one that had been flitting in and out of her mind for the last two days. *Did I kill anyone during the battle?*

"Zeisha?" Nora's voice was gentle. "Are you okay?"

Zeisha almost gave voice to her question but couldn't convince her mouth to form the words. She forced a smile. "I'm fine. Did, uh, did you need something?"

Nora returned the smile. "Eira said if we're all staying here, we have to earn our keep. We had one day to rest. Now it's time to get our assignments."

Zeisha stood, gathering the heavy, green coils. She imagined—or remembered?—shooting a similar vine at Krey. Wrapping it around his neck. Tightening it until he couldn't breathe.

Shaking her head to rid herself of the thought, she walked to the side of the street and dropped the vine against a deserted building.

As they walked toward Star Clan territory, Nora took in her surroundings. The street was bordered by empty buildings. Ancient Skytrain tracks crisscrossed the sky. Crashed vehicles, dented from countless hailstorms and discolored by sunlight, created obstacles in the road.

Nora turned her attention to Zeisha, who was looking into the distance. Zeisha was beautiful, with her short, hourglass figure and that lively mass of glossy, black curls. She was also one of the sweetest people Nora had ever met. "What do you think of Deroga?" Nora asked.

Zeisha's eyes met Nora's. "I don't know what to think. I grew up hearing about preday cities, but I never dreamed I'd see one in person, much less live in one."

Nora laughed. "I know what you mean."

Deroga had once been a busy metropolis. Then came the apocalypse, an event known as *The Day*. Radiation from a mysterious stone killed nearly everyone on the planet of Anyari. The nearly half-million remaining humans gathered into new communities around the globe, rebuilding civilization. Few people stayed in cities like Deroga, which had been full of useless technology and rotting bodies.

Now, two centuries after The Day, six trog clans inhabited small sections of Deroga. Trogs were eccentric, to say the least. They lived in preday cities, shunning mainstream, postday society. Months ago, Deroga's Star Clan had made a deal with the king, allowing the magical militia to use one of their buildings.

By the time Nora, Krey, and their friend Ovrun had arrived in Deroga to rescue Zeisha, the Star Clan had grown resentful of the militia's presence. The trogs had agreed to join the fight to free the mind-controlled magic eaters and the city from the king's influence.

Nora's stomach cramped as she pondered that. It was bad enough for a country's king to steal the minds of his people. It was infinitely worse when that king was your father.

"I can't believe Eira is letting us stay here," Zeisha said.

Nora pulled her thoughts away from her father. "Neither can I." Eira was the unofficial leader of the Star Clan. "She knows her people are in danger now that they've made a stand against the king. The trogs need you and the other militia members to fight on their side. You're all so strong." Noting that Zeisha's full lips held no hint of her usual smile, Nora asked, "What is it?"

"I didn't want to hurt anyone." Zeisha's voice was soft. "I never wanted to fight at all."

Nora put an arm around the shorter girl's shoulders. "At least now you'll have control over your gifts. You don't have to do anything you don't want to do."

"I hope that's true."

Nora gave Zeisha's shoulders a squeeze as they turned the corner onto the busiest street in Star Clan territory. Streets like this one were easy to traverse, having long ago been cleared of preday vehicles. They walked to the high-rise building where, two nights before, the trogs had thrown a party.

Ovrun was waiting outside for them, his wavy, black hair ruffling in the breeze. Dark eyes sparkling, he raised an eyebrow at Nora. She couldn't hold back a grin. "Where were you at breakfast?" she asked.

"They told me to hunt for shimshims. There are only a few hundred people in the Star Clan, and now they've got three dozen extra residents. They said if we want to stay, we need to provide some food." He turned to Zeisha. "I think they're gonna ask you and the other vine eaters to help with their rooftop gardens."

Zeisha's customary smile returned. "I'd love that!"

"They're almost ready to start," Ovrun said.

All three of them walked into the building's former lobby, which the trogs now used as a community space. During the party, countless candles had brought flickering light to the room. Now, with daylight entering through glassless windows, it looked entirely different—especially the upper portions of the tall walls. Two nights ago, they'd been swathed in shadows. Today, Nora's jaw dropped as she took in the murals painted on them.

The art was unlike any Nora had seen, full of bold strokes and bright colors. Geometric shapes came together into pictures that grabbed her attention and wouldn't let go. Three of the scenes were of a bustling city, full of technology. *Preday Deroga.*

Nora was most drawn to the single rural scene. In it, a woman in a multicolored gown knelt over a dead child. The child's skin was stark white. Red circles, clearly representing blood, fell from its eyes, nose, and mouth. The woman's mouth was a gaping, black crescent. Nora could almost hear her wailing cry. Other dead bodies lay in the background. Green grass, distant trees, and a bright-orange sky gave the macabre scene an ironic beauty. It was the most incredible depiction of The Day Nora had ever seen.

"We better sit," Ovrun said.

Nora gazed at the mural a few seconds longer, then walked toward the center of the room. She, Zeisha, and Ovrun sat on a bench at a long table alongside other militia members and a few trogs who'd fought in the battle. Other trogs stood to the side, eyeing the newcomers warily.

Eira began the meeting. "New-city folk, each of you must tell us what you can do. We will give you work that suits you."

They started at the front of the room. As militia members disclosed their skills, the trogs assigned them jobs. When it was Nora's turn to speak, she was at a loss. Her ice lysting wasn't any use here, since the trogs didn't have any spare ice and the ground was free of snow. Her cheeks grew warm. "I'm afraid my practical skills are . . . limited."

Ovrun stood. "She's been learning archery. She could come with me."

"We need no unskilled hunters," a rough-voiced trog said. "If new-city folk do not know how to work, they should not live here."

"I'll get better the more I try," Nora insisted. "I also know how to clean shimshims. I'm sure I could learn to clean other animals too."

Eira pursed her lips, then nodded. "Ovrun will help you improve your hunting skills. You will clean the game."

Nora repressed a grin and sat down. She hated skinning and cleaning dead shimshims, but she'd do it all day if it meant roaming the streets with Ovrun. She caught his eye, and he winked at her.

Next to Nora, Zeisha stood. "I'm a vine eater, and—"

From behind them, a shouting voice interrupted her. "Eira!"

That sounded like Krey, Nora thought as she turned. Sure enough, he was flying through the room, his dark, shaggy hair fluttering in the breeze he created. When he reached Eira, he landed.

The elderly woman listened as Krey spoke in her ear. Her white brows lifted. She nodded once, and her voice rang through the open space. "The army is coming to Deroga! Star Clan, we will go underground!"

THE SEER: 1

Sarza Phip held her orsa's reins with one hand and covered her yawning mouth with the other. She'd been traveling for hours, and the beast's slow pace threatened to put her to sleep.

The previous evening, someone had come to her house and commanded her to go to the training grounds east of the city, along with the other members of the Cellerinian Army.

After she'd thrown on her uniform and tired herself out with a fifteen-clommet ride on a push scooter, she'd waited with her fellow soldiers for hours. Officers who couldn't tell their asses from their ankles tried to figure out what was going on. Royal messengers came and went. At last, the soldiers learned they were marching to Deroga.

Nobody seemed to know why. Sarza didn't care. She'd never dreamed she'd visit a preday city. She gazed at the skyline in the distance. How tall were those buildings—forty stories? A hundred?

All at once, her brain felt like someone had inflated it until it was too big for her skull. It wasn't pain exactly, just pressure. A feeling she knew well.

She swore under her breath. Of course this was happening now. She was sleep deprived, her daily routine thrown out the window.

Such circumstances tended to bring on visions. She bent low over her orsa, hugging its wide neck and clasping her hands. Just as she shoved her shoes deeper into her stirrups, images overtook her conscious mind.

Sarza saw a residential street. Based on the much larger buildings looming nearby, she assumed she was in Deroga. The homes appeared occupied, with chairs on porches and small, well-kept yards and gardens.

The only people on the street were soldiers like her, wearing Cellerinian blue and black. Sarza's vision zoomed to a gray house, then to its front window. Through it, she saw a tidy, furnished living room.

The vision ended. Sarza found herself leaning to one side, about to topple from her orsa. She blurted a curse and pushed herself upright.

The guy next to her chuckled. "Fall asleep?"

Sarza ignored him. Her head ached. Nausea gripped her gut. Visions often affected her in such ways.

Assuming the prophecy would come true today, the army would soon enter trog territory. That was undeniably cool. Why was the street empty though? Where were the backwards, violent people who lived among millions of bones in Deroga?

For half a second, Sarza considered telling an officer what she'd seen. She rejected the idea. Over the years, she'd used her visions to get ahead at jobs, score well on a test, and be the first in the kitchen when her father pulled a pie out of the oven. The one thing she never did was share her prophecies with others. Not anymore.

When she was very young, she'd been open about the things she saw. But nobody cared about a scrawny little girl who was the twelfth of fourteen kids. Her mama brushed off her confused babbling as an overactive imagination. And really, those early visions—an upcoming thunderstorm, a caynin running down the street—weren't impressive.

A month or so after the visions started, she'd seen something that had sent her to bed afterward, her head feeling like someone had run over it with a cart. "Mama," she'd moaned, "Ednin will die tonight." Ednin was her baby brother.

Her mother slapped her. When Ednin died in his sleep that night, Sarza's mother screamed that it was her daughter's fault. That was the last time Sarza had shared a vision. With anyone.

Her parents did take note of her occasional "fainting spells" and "fits." "Lie down if you feel one coming on," they said. Sarza obeyed, pretending the episodes didn't embarrass her.

There had been seers in preday times. The first time Sarza heard of the ancient prophets, she'd known that was what she was. What she wouldn't give to compare notes with one of them. But the seers, it seemed, were long gone. All but her.

Was it normal, she wondered, that sometimes her gift (or more like her curse) didn't manifest as a vision? At those times, she got urges to do specific things. She'd learned to heed such sensations. A couple of years earlier, she'd felt like she should learn to ride an orsa. She'd cleaned stalls at a stable in exchange for lessons. When she'd joined the army (the result of another urge), she'd gotten higher pay since she knew how to ride.

Maybe today, she'd have a vision or urge that would allow her to stand out from the other soldiers. What she wouldn't give to shout orders instead of taking them. Would the leaders give such power to an eighteen-year-old? Maybe, if she orchestrated events just right.

Ahead, an officer interrupted Sarza's musings. Thrusting his fist into the air, he shouted, "For Cellerin!"

"For Cellerin!" the army repeated.

"For the king!" the officer cried.

"For the king!"

Sarza fixed her gaze on the city ahead. "For me," she murmured.

2

The Teen Community Center in my neighborhood is being renovated for the second time in three years. Our city's leaders seem to think one more sports court will draw us to their shiny building. They don't understand why teens forgo expensive facilities to sneak into the dark, old tunnels under the city.

Adults, allow me to clear things up. We go to the tunnels for one simple reason: you're not there.

-"Burrowing Teens" by Genta Ril
The Deroga Chronicle, *dated Quari 2, 6293*

"UNDERGROUND?" Krey demanded. "What do you mean, underground?"

Eira pivoted away from him to speak to a trog who'd rushed up as soon as he'd heard the announcement. Krey stared at the old woman's long, white hair. She continued ignoring him, so he grabbed her arm.

"We can't hide!"

With surprising strength, Eira pulled her arm away. She fixed Krey with a heated glare. "Patience!" She returned her attention to the trog. Half a minute later, the man took off at a run.

Still, Eira ignored Krey. She turned to Nora, who'd come to the front of the room. "Do not call the dragons."

"Why not?" Nora asked.

"Today, we do not fight. The king should not know we still have dragons until we are ready to battle him." Eira shifted her attention to the entire room and shouted one word: "Silent!"

Every trog in the room repeated her. "Silent!"

"Trogs, go underground now!" Eira called. Trogs streamed toward the exits. "New-city folk, follow Wendyn." Eira gestured to a woman near her. Wendyn was both short and thin, but Krey had seen her fight fiercely in the militia battle.

Wendyn jogged toward the back entrance. Most of the militia members followed. Krey stayed rooted in his spot. "Do you want me to let the other clans know?"

"The other clans do not know you. They might kill you, and then we would lose our only flyer! I send a trog runner already. Word will spread quickly. Follow Wendyn."

Zeisha tugged at Krey's hand. Nora and Ovrun waited behind her, along with Isla, Zeisha's friend from the militia. Krey returned his attention to Eira, whose gaze, hard as the floor under their feet, was fixed on him. "It'll be hours before they get here," he said. "And we can't just hide. They'll get stronger and come back again."

Two steps brought Eira close enough that she had to tilt her head to look in his eyes. "What if they send scouts already, in the middle of the night? What if a flyer, like you, is coming now? We may have hours or only minutes. Everyone must go underground, lest they are seen. Today, we hide. Another day, we will fight. There is no time to discuss this. Go, or you put us all in danger."

Krey stared at her for a long moment, then released an angry sigh.

Whatever was going on here, he couldn't change it by arguing with the trog leader.

Nora stepped closer to Eira. "Are you going underground too?"

"No. I will watch from high windows."

"Let me stay with you. I know the king in a way no one else does. I'll watch and give you my input. Bring me with you, and Krey and the others will go underground." With a glance, Nora demanded Krey confirm. Rolling his eyes, he nodded.

Eira hesitated only briefly before saying, "Very well."

Krey, Zeisha, Ovrun, and Isla took off at a fast run. It didn't take long to catch up with the militia members.

Wendyn led the group through the streets into an abandoned four-story building. The lobby floor had been recently swept, but Krey's quick feet had to avoid a pile of fresh animal droppings as he ran through the room. A few hisses told him shimshims lived here.

Wendyn ran into a dark hallway. She lit a lantern and led the running group through multiple corridors.

Krey often took long runs, but back home in Tirra, Zeisha had never joined him. He touched her shoulder. "You okay, Zei?"

She laughed softly. "I think the militia must've required us to exercise a lot. I feel great."

"Stop!" Wendyn called. They all obeyed. She carried the lantern through a doorway. As the group followed her into a large room, Wendyn said, "You! Help me move this!"

A low, scraping sound followed. Several people gasped. Krey rose to his tiptoes but couldn't see past the others.

"I must know," Wendyn called, "if any militia members eat fuel today."

"I did," Zeisha murmured to Krey.

"Why are you asking?" Krey asked loudly.

"If the king comes to the city, he may control them," Wendyn replied. "This is worse if they have magic."

Krey cursed. He hadn't thought of that. The king had controlled Osmius without seeing him—but he'd known exactly where the dragon was. *How powerful is his talent? Can he use it to find people he's controlled in the past?* "Zeisha," he said softly, "do you know if Ulmin touched you and the others when he visited the warehouse?"

"I think he did. One of the ash eaters told me he's had dreams of the king controlling us all. "

"Anyone?" Wendyn asked. "We must hurry!"

Zeisha's voice carried over the small crowd. "I ate fuel this morning."

"I'll sit by her and restrain her if she loses control," Krey said.

"Very well," Wendyn said. "Now we descend. Wait at the bottom. Careful, the ground is not even."

The small crowd gradually thinned out. Krey grinned when he at last saw why. One by one, the group members were climbing through a rough-edged hole in the floor and descending a ladder.

Krey urged the others to go before him. Isla and Zeisha climbed down, but when Ovrun approached the hole, Wendyn held up a hand. "You go last. After me." She pointed at a large desk that still overlapped the hole. "The desk has handles underneath. You will pull it over the hole."

"Okay," Ovrun agreed.

Wendyn turned to Krey. "Go!"

Krey climbed down the ladder into a narrow, vertical tunnel. When he'd descended a few mets, he saw Wendyn following him, her lantern hanging from the crook of her elbow. Krey soon heard the scraping sound again as Ovrun pulled the furniture back across the hole.

The enclosed tunnel ended, but the ladder kept going, extending into open space. Krey breathed deeply of air that smelled and tasted stale. At last, he reached the floor. As Wendyn had said, the ground wasn't even. He nearly tripped over a hard, raised ridge. "Where are we?" he asked Wendyn as she stepped off the ladder.

"Underground."

"What does that mean?"

"I will tell you more soon." She lifted her voice so the group could hear her. "Follow! Careful!"

This time, Krey and his friends were at the front of the group. They followed Wendyn, whose light illuminated the way. They were in an odd corridor that was a few mets wide with a short, metal rail running down the center of the floor. That was what had almost tripped Krey. The sides of the corridor only came up to Krey's waist before leveling off into another flat surface.

"What is this place?" Zeisha murmured.

All at once, it hit Krey. "It's where the Extrain used to travel."

"Extrain?" Zeisha asked.

"I think it stood for *excavation*. It was an underground rail system. People called it *the Ex*. Skytrains eventually made Extrains obsolete." He shook his head in wonder. "This place is old."

He hadn't realized Wendyn could hear him until she said, "Very old."

After a few minutes of walking, Krey heard the slight murmur of voices ahead.

"Stop," Wendyn called. She turned to face them. "Beyond the next bend, we will join all the trogs."

"All the trogs?" a voice behind Krey asked. "Or just the Star Clan?"

"All of them. There is space down here for everyone. These are tunnels used by trains in ancient days."

"Extrains," someone said.

Krey smiled. Apparently he wasn't the only one who liked to read books about old cities.

"Wait a minute," a male militia member said. "If someone in our group knows about the Extrains, I'm sure the king does too. He probably knows how to get down here. You're telling me we're gonna all hang out down here, waiting for soldiers to come find us? Because I'm not letting someone take my mind again! I'd rather die! I—"

"Silence!" Wendyn commanded. When the young man complied, she said, "New-city folk may have old maps showing old

Extrain entrances. Trogs destroy those entrances many years ago. We make new, secret entrances inside buildings. We are safe." She turned again. "Follow me!"

As they walked, the murmuring they'd heard swelled until it became clear a large crowd was ahead. The tracks made a gradual turn. Golden lantern light bled into their path, and for the first time, Krey noticed that a parallel track ran to their right. When Wendyn's group rounded the bend, Krey's mouth dropped open.

The space they'd entered was massive. This must be where passengers had boarded the Ex. Countless trogs of all ages were streaming onto large platforms on both sides of the tracks. Other trogs waited on the tracks. "How many?" Krey asked, but all the voices swallowed his words. He tapped Wendyn's shoulder and shouted, "How many trogs? Total?"

"Nearly two thousand!" she yelled back.

The number shouldn't have been a surprise. There were a few hundred people in the Star Clan, and it was one of six such clans. Still, when Krey had read about trogs in the past, he'd pictured a couple hundred people broken up into small gangs. He shook his head, thinking about two thousand people living in this place, separate from the rest of the world.

In the Star Clan, he'd only seen a couple of children. Now he realized their parents simply hadn't brought them out to meet the scary newcomers. Here, there were kids everywhere, including multiple wailing babies.

Krey heard footsteps and voices behind them. He turned and saw more trogs traveling down the track. When several voices rose in anger, Wendyn wove her way through the group.

"What happened?" Krey asked when she returned.

"They are from the Hill Clan," Wendyn said. "They do not wish to be near new-city folk."

"What did you tell them?"

"I tell them they may return to the surface and fight the army alone." Lantern light reflected off her teeth when she grinned. "They say they will stay."

Trogs were still arriving when Krey heard the same call-and-response Eira had used. "Silent!" a few people called. "Silent!" voices of all ages repeated. After two more repetitions, the group was as quiet as a large crowd could be. A loud, male voice instructed everyone to sit and wait. He directed them to water and indoor outhouses.

Krey remained standing. Zeisha did too, slipping her hand into his.

"Wendyn," Krey said.

"Yes?"

"What's going on?"

Wendyn spoke loud enough for the whole militia to hear. "We wait. Trogs are watching from windows in all the clan territories. They will bring us reports. When the soldiers leave, we will go home." She gestured to the floor at their feet. "Sit."

Krey sat and leaned against the hard wall. Zeisha cuddled up next to him. He pulled her close, his arm around her shoulder, then turned to murmur in her ear, "You're beautiful."

She brought her lips to his ear and whispered, "We're sitting in shadows. You can barely see me."

He ran his fingers along her arm. "Yeah, but when it comes to discerning beauty, my hands are just as reliable as my eyes."

Laughing, she tucked herself closer to Krey's side. He closed his eyes, allowing the voices of thousands to flow over him, and tried to imagine what was happening in the streets above.

3

My school is eight stories tall. Between classes, chaos reigns. Today, administrators announced they're upgrading our lifts. The new models will move twice as fast.

They expected us to be happy about this, but none of us are. They're taking away our best excuse for being late to class.

-"Lift Me Up" by Genta Ril
The Deroga Chronicle, *dated Quari 3, 6293*

WHEN EIRA SAID they'd be watching from "up high," she wasn't exaggerating. After hurrying to a nearby building, she and Nora ascended flight after flight of stairs. The elderly trog had unbelievable endurance. Hand on ancient, metal handrails, she took one step after another. She stopped at every third landing to rest for about fifteen seconds, then resumed her steady pace.

Nora followed with a lantern, her legs burning. When the amber light illuminated a sign reading *Floor 34*, Eira at last entered a musty hallway. They made a few turns before she stopped, unlocked a door, and said, "Shutter the lantern." Nora obeyed, and Eira led her into an ancient office.

Sunlight and a cool breeze entered the room through a large window covered only by a thick, metal screen. Dust motes danced throughout the room. A desk sat in a corner, and two preday chairs were positioned in front of the window.

Eira pointed at a covered clay jar on the desk. "Drink some water, then sit. As your friend says, it will be hours before the entire army arrives. There are rooms like this on all four sides of this building. We will travel between them and keep watch."

When Nora was hydrated and seated, she asked, "Won't the soldiers notice the screen?"

With a soft sigh, Eira lowered herself into the other chair. "We have screens in many rooms and many buildings."

Silence fell. Nora's mind was too full to initiate small talk, and Eira wasn't exactly chatty.

After perhaps a quarter hour, they moved to a different room. From there, Nora could see the street where she and her friends had battled the militia two days before. As she stared at the area, her mouth went dry. That was where she'd faced off with Faylie, her friend who'd been turned into The Overseer.

I didn't have to kill her. I could've found another solution.

She replayed the scene in her mind, desperately trying to think of how she could've avoided killing her best friend. She shook her head and turned her attention to a different part of the city. Like a magnet, the warehouse drew her gaze again. Her mind agonized as she remembered.

Faylie.

The dagger.

The spike of ice.

Heart pounding, Nora suggested they move to the next room. But they returned to the second room again and again on their endless circuit. Every time they stepped through the door, Nora's stomach clenched in anticipation of the torturous memories.

A few hours after they'd come up the stairs, they spied a scout on orsaback. He wore the Cellerinian Army uniform: black pants, a blue shirt, and a black jacket. Nora knew she shouldn't fear one lone soldier. Nonetheless, she was short of breath. *They're coming. They're really coming.*

The quiet wait continued. It was late afternoon when Eira at last said, "Look."

Nora squinted, then drew in a sharp breath. In the distance, hundreds of soldiers marched in their direction, accompanied by a smaller group on orsaback. Within minutes, the army separated into six sections, each one funneling onto a different street. "Six groups for six clans," Eira said.

Eira and Nora returned to their original room, where they'd have the best view of the Star Clan. Dozens of soldiers soon entered their streets.

Nora pointed to about ten soldiers who'd broken away. "Where are they going?"

"They have entered our residential street," Eira said. "If they touch our homes . . ." She left the thought unfinished, the muscles of her jaw clenching visibly.

Most of the group of soldiers continued to the main street below Nora and Eira. They all gathered before one woman, who seemed to be their leader. After she addressed them, they gave a shout. A battle cry.

The soldiers spread out along the street. Several men and women ran into the building entrance below Nora and Eira. Nora's heart began beating as hard as it had while she was climbing the stairs. She knew the chances of anyone finding them in here were slim, but by the sky, she didn't like knowing their enemy was so close.

A soldier in the street pulled out a gun. A loud *POP* sounded, making Nora jump. The glass window of the butcher shop—one of the few such windows she'd seen in this place—shattered. The man and his companions kicked the rest of the glass out of the window, then went in through the door and returned with two wooden chairs.

The biggest of the group used his brutish strength to break apart the chairs. Each soldier took one or two pieces of wood then continued down the street. They used their improvised clubs to break door handles, destroy plants, and generally cause as much damage as they could.

"Are you watching this?" Nora murmured, pointing.

"I watch others," Eira said.

Nora followed her companion's gaze to a group of soldiers tossing furniture into the street. They formed a pile that dwarfed them all, then lit it on fire. "Oh no," Nora said softly.

"We can live without furnishings," Eira said. "Not without food." She pointed to the nearest rooftop garden. The soldiers atop it were ripping up plants and dropping them to the street far below. Their comrades on the main street threw smashed plants into the fire.

After a few minutes, Eira said, "We must see what they do in other areas. Come."

Moving from room to room, Nora watched frenzied men and women wreaking havoc. At first, all the violence was directed at the trogs' buildings and possessions. Then fights started breaking out between soldiers. A short, particularly brutal confrontation ended with a young man lying in the street, bleeding heavily from his head.

Nora had to look away. "I'm so glad your people aren't out there."

Eira nodded. A tear slid down her wrinkled cheek.

When they returned to their original lookout, they saw more bonfires. One blazed on the residential street. Nora could guess its contents: Clothes. Food. Furniture. Toys.

She shook with anger. Through his orders to his army, her father was destroying the trogs' homes. *How could you do this, Dad?*

Then her entire body stiffened. In the street below, as if he'd heard her silent question, King Ulmin had appeared.

He looked as regal as ever, wearing luxurious clothes and riding his gorgeous, brown orsa. The golden band encircling his head glimmered in the sunlight. Nora leaned forward, pressing a hand against the window screen. She gritted her teeth, trying not to cry. *By the stone, I miss you. I don't want to, but I do.*

More than ever, she wanted to separate him from the fuel that had poisoned his mind. He still had the capacity to be the father and king she used to know; she was certain of it.

Well, maybe not certain. But I won't stop hoping.

Her father proceeded down the street. As soldiers spotted him, they held their arms out and lowered their heads. He acknowledged their bows with nods. Smiling, he engaged them in friendly conversation, even as bonfires burned around them.

Desperate for air, Nora gulped in one breath, then another.

"The king?" Eira asked, her voice low.

"Yes."

"Why does he do this to us?"

"He's angry that the trogs helped bring down the militia." Nora didn't know how her voice could sound so calm while her insides twisted like brambles.

"I know that." Eira turned her whole body to face Nora, not speaking again until she held the teenager's gaze. "When I feel angry, I yell. I hold my hands tight so my nails cut my skin." She held out a tightly formed fist. "I do not destroy things. I ask you, why does your father do this?"

Nora opened her mouth. "I—" She bit her bottom lip. "I don't know."

"He is your father. When you ask to come with me, you tell me you know him like no one else does."

"I did tell you that." Nora pulled her eyes away from Eira, fixing them on the king below. "I know who he used to be. I think he's still in there. But the man we're looking at? I don't know him at all."

The hours passed slowly in the manmade cavern hosting all the trogs. At least Krey could chat with Zeisha, who remained cuddled up to him. *Could be worse.*

There were frequent lulls in their conversation, though. Zeisha was pensive, an unusual state for her. At one point, Krey felt her breaths turn quick, almost frantic.

"What's wrong?" he asked.

She didn't answer.

He tried again. "Do you miss your family?"

"It's not that. I do miss them, but that's not why . . . It's just—the militia battle. I can't stop thinking about it."

"You know what the battle showed me?" His lips brushed her ear as he spoke. "How strong you are. Zei, you're stronger than you've ever been. And now you're free. You can use your talents for good."

She stiffened a bit at that. He held her tighter. It was all he could do. His helplessness grated on him. When she remained silent, he whispered that everything would be okay.

But would it? He had no idea what she'd been through over the past months. She had little idea either, which made things worse. He wished she'd see herself the way he saw her—strong and talented and absolutely beautiful.

At last, the "Silent" call went out one final time. "The soldiers are gone," a trog announced. "Go home."

Most people rose to their feet, though Krey soon realized those who stayed seated were the smart ones. It would take time to move this many people. He turned to Wendyn. "You know the army will come back, right?"

She nodded. "We are not stupid. When they return, we will be ready. We will use our knowledge of our city against them."

Krey felt his own mouth widening into a smile. "Can't wait to hear more."

After a long wait, the track behind them cleared. Wendyn and her group began their return journey. By the time they reached the lobby they'd entered so many hours earlier, Krey's nerves were alight with anticipation. *Is Nora okay? What's waiting for us out there?*

A night sky, full of stars, was visible through the windows. After walking through dark streets, they approached the back entrance to the building where they'd met to get their assignments. Next to Krey, Zeisha breathed, "Oh no."

Others responded too, but all Krey could do was keep walking, right up to the door, his mouth agape. Inside, tables and benches were upended. Several had been thrown into a pile in the middle of the space. Flames consumed the pile. Smoke filled the room. The preday building was made of fireproof materials, but when the fire burned out, the room would be full of soot and ash. The Star Clan would need another community space.

Wendyn stood as tall as her small frame would allow. Flickering light from the flames reflected off her profile as she lifted her chin and spoke to the group of newcomers. Krey was close enough to see that the fire in her eyes was as hot as the one in the building. "We walk to the street," she said, pointing.

They circled around to the front of the building, where more bonfires burned. The breeze blew acrid smoke into Krey's mouth and nose. He coughed, waving a hand in front of him.

He didn't realize Nora had come up behind him until she spoke, her voice full of vitriol. "No, they'll never do that."

Krey turned. "What?"

She pointed at a building across the street. Flickering firelight revealed a message, painted in red:

TROGS: BOW TO KING ULMIN

Krey gritted his teeth. "Fat chance."

A male trog ran up to Eira, who stood next to Nora. He held out a sheet of paper. "This was left on a porch. It says, 'To the Trog Leader.'"

"That's my father's handwriting," Nora said as Eira took the paper.

"He was here?" Krey asked.

Nora was obviously trying to read the note, but Eira walked off to hold it closer to the firelight. "Yes," Nora said, sighing. "The king was here."

"That's good news." He explained Wendyn's concern about Ulmin controlling militia members. "Apparently he can't connect with their minds if he doesn't know where they are," he concluded.

"But he controlled Osmius before he saw him."

"I think that's because Osmius was chained up. Your father knew exactly where he was."

Nora nodded slowly. She looked exhausted. "I'm glad something good came out of today."

Eira returned. "Come," she said, beckoning Krey, Nora, Ovrun, and Zeisha. They followed her to a quiet spot in front of the neighboring building. She gave the note to Nora and held the lantern so the princess could read her father's words.

In a slightly shaky voice, Nora read aloud:

To the Trog Leader:

We have reason to believe you may be harboring the following Cellerinian citizens:

> *Princess Ulminora Abrios*
> *Kreyven West*
> *Ovrun Kensin*
> *Every surviving member of the militia which, until recently, trained in your territory*

The princess must be returned home for her own safety. The rest are fugitives and must be brought to justice in Cellerin City. You will

*immediately send each of these individuals to the palace, escorted by
your own armed guards.*

*When you meet this requirement, I will personally sign an agreement
to ensure the continued independence of Deroga's trogs.*

*If you choose to claim ignorance of the whereabouts of these
Cellerinian citizens or if you defy my order to return them, a larger
army will soon invade Deroga. We will fight until the city is part of my
domain.*

*His Majesty Ulmin Abrios
King of Cellerin*

Nora's gaze found Eira. "Will you accede to my father's demands?"

The old trog straightened her back and lifted her chin. "As Krey says, *fat chance.*"

"Even if it means he'll attack again?" Krey asked.

"Since The Day, trogs are independent. If we bow to the king's demands, he will require even more from us. An agreement from him is worthless. Just as he is worthless." Eira's eyes flicked to Nora, but she didn't apologize for the statement. "The king will regret the day his boots touched Derogan streets."

4

According to a new study, gardening is the fastest-growing hobby for teenagers.

People assume we want to connect to our planet. But that's not why I have a garden. I grow food because I don't trust the systems we have in place— big farms, transportation, distribution. What if it all breaks down one day? I want to provide for myself. Even if it's just a couple of salads a week.

-"Teen Gardeners" by Genta Ril
The Derogan Chronicle, *dated Quari 4, 6293*

"YOU ARE TIRED," the trog woman told Zeisha. "Eat more fuel."

Zeisha flinched. She was twenty-five stories above the city in a rooftop garden. *How long have I been staring into the distance— without even enjoying the view?* With a smile, she took a handful of rinsed plant roots from the bowl the woman held.

While Zeisha appreciated the fuel, her tiredness had nothing to do with magic. These days, life itself exhausted her. Yes, she'd been freed from the militia, but she couldn't go back to normal life. She couldn't even contact her parents; the king might've sent someone to watch them. And she had nothing in common with the other militia members. They all seemed to be energized by the possibility of battle. Was she the only one who didn't want to fight?

"Are you all right?" the trog asked. Her brown eyes were bright, the skin around them smooth. Zeisha guessed she was in her mid-twenties.

"I will be," Zeisha said. It was more a hope than a promise. "Let's get these plants growing." She knelt and dug her fingers into soil that still bore treaded boot prints from the king's soldiers.

Growing plants in the ground differed from creating a vine in her hand. She couldn't grow crops or trees from scratch; she had to start with a piece of the species she was growing. Thanks to the roots the Cellerinian soldiers had left behind, Zeisha could, in time, regrow this entire garden.

She released a soft sigh as the creative warmth of magic suffused her hands. A green sprout emerged from the dark soil, growing into a bluish-purple, flower-like collection of hardy, edible leaves. When the violitus plant was fully grown, Zeisha pulled her fingers from the soil and scooted over to start on the next one.

The trog woman knelt. Her medium-brown hair, short and curly, quivered as she harvested the violitus and moved it into a crate. "You save trog lives by doing this."

"Your own vine eaters are doing the same on other rooftops."

The woman smiled, and the sun reflected off her bright teeth. *Where do they get enough toothpaste for two thousand people?* Zeisha wondered. Realizing she was staring, she wiped her right hand on her pants and held it out. "I'm Zeisha."

"You live with trogs now. You must learn our trog greeting." The woman held up her left hand, palm facing Zeisha. "Fingertips only."

They pressed their fingertips together, then pulled their hands apart. "My name is Kebi."

"It's a pleasure to meet you, Kebi." Zeisha went back to work.

Minutes later, Kebi harvested the third plant Zeisha had created. She put it in the crate and stood. "Come. We must deliver these."

The statement broke Zeisha's concentration, and the plant beneath her fingers stopped growing. "We're done? I've got plenty of magic left."

"I know someone who needs food. We will take this, then return."

Kebi carried the crate to the edge of the roof. Zeisha followed. Kebi placed the crate in a large, wooden box attached to a pulley. As she pulled the rope hand-over-hand, the box descended. Halfway through, Zeisha took over.

"I wish we could use the same method to get down to the ground," Zeisha said as she finished. She and Kebi walked to the trap-door that led to the building's stairs.

As they descended, their way lit by a candle Zeisha carried, Kebi said, "You must have questions about trogs. Please, ask."

Zeisha asked the first one that came to her mind. "Have you ever left Deroga?" She'd heard that sometimes trogs left the city to purchase supplies.

"I am born in Deroga," Kebi said. "I live here all my life. One day, I will die here." She stopped for long enough to touch Zeisha's shoulder. "I am happy to meet a new-city woman."

"Am I the first non-trog you've met?"

"Yes." Kebi flashed her white smile again.

That answered Zeisha's question about how often the trogs welcomed outsiders. "Do you know people from the other clans?"

Kebi stood straighter, pride clear in her square shoulders. "I am from the Moon Clan. I live with my people until my marriage. My wife is from the Star Clan. She brings me here."

"What's her name?"

"Dera." Kebi's pace slowed. Her voice grew soft. "She dies from a fever ten moons ago."

"Oh, I'm sorry." Zeisha would have to get used to the trogs' unwillingness to speak in past tense. She'd assumed Kebi's wife was still alive.

"Zeisha, all people die. Dera is still here." Kebi placed a hand on her heart. "And beyond this building." She held both arms out. "Deroga is her home. That does not change."

For a couple of minutes, the only sound was their breathing, which got heavier as they continued to descend. At last, Zeisha said, "I thought the clans didn't like each other, but when we all hid underground, everyone seemed to get along. And you said you were born in a different clan. How does all that work?"

"Trogs change as time passes. The first trogs are violent, killing all intruders." Kebi's voice was soft, yet matter-of-fact.

"The first trogs . . . you mean the ones who lived here right after The Day?"

Kebi nodded. "Now, we rarely kill intruders. Usually, we scare them only."

Zeisha thought about a story Krey had told her, of a trog shooting arrows at him when he'd first visited their territory. Had the archer missed on purpose?

Kebi continued, "Trogs are strong. For some, to be strong means to fight. These trogs want to fight new-city folk, but new-city folk rarely come. So they fight trogs in other clans. Over trade, love, or territory."

"You said 'some.' Not all trogs are like that?"

"No. Many trogs say the clans should unite. We already trade with each other. That is how I meet my wife. My father makes bread. Dera's mother makes arrows. They trade. One day, Dera brings home more than bread." Her face softened into a smile.

When they exited the building, Zeisha blew out the candle and blinked at the sun's brightness.

Kebi picked up the crate they'd lowered. "Come," she said with a warm smile.

"I'll carry it," Zeisha said, reaching out.

"We will carry it together."

Each holding one of the crate's handles, they walked to the Star Clan's residential street. Everywhere, Zeisha saw evidence of the Cellerinian army's vandalism the day before. Front-yard gardens were torn up. Thin sheets of wood replaced torn-off shutters. Smoke still wafted from the blackened remnants of a bonfire.

Zeisha looked beyond the pointless damage, trying to see the homes like they'd been before. The walls were made of durable, preday materials in neutral shades of white, brown, and gray. The wooden doors, however, sported coats of paint in colors ranging from stark white to sunny yellow and bright red. *Not just toothpaste, but paint too?*

Kebi walked up a narrow path to a covered porch and knocked on the dark-blue door. A preteen girl opened it. Over the next few seconds, her face and voice underwent multiple transformations. First, she smiled shyly. "Hi, Kebi." When her eyes dropped to the crate, both her expression and her tone brightened. "Violitus!"

Then the girl's gaze found Zeisha. Her eyes widened. Her smile disappeared. She took a step back and grabbed the doorknob, like she might slam the door. Voice low and breathy, she asked, "Who is that?"

"This is Zeisha." Kebi didn't acknowledge her companion's status as an outsider. Instead, she said, "She is a vine eater. She makes this food for your family."

The girl blinked. Swallowed. After several long seconds, she stepped back, whispering, "Come in."

Kebi carried the crate so Zeisha could enter behind her. The girl led them to a room at the back of the house. A middle-aged woman opened the door. She smiled at Kebi and gestured for her to enter. Zeisha stood in the open doorway, waiting to see if the room's occupants would accept her.

A bed took up much of the space. Next to it sat an elderly woman. The bed's occupant was a girl who couldn't be older than sixteen. In her arms was a tiny, nursing baby.

Zeisha felt the stares of every member of the family except the distracted young mother and her hungry baby. Tension seemed to connect them all, like the taut lines of a stretched-out net.

In a voice flush with cheerfulness, Kebi said, "This is Zeisha, a new member of our clan. She is a vine eater. She makes violitus for your family."

The strained atmosphere abated a bit, but no one spoke. Then the girl in bed looked up, met Zeisha's gaze, and smiled. "Thank you. The army takes our food yesterday. Violitus is my favorite." Her face glowed with joy that Zeisha guessed was linked to the baby in her arms, not the vegetables in the crate.

The girl's smile and kind words sliced through the remaining unease. Suddenly, everyone was introducing themselves to Zeisha. She gladly touched fingertips with them all. The middle-aged woman gestured to the bed. "My granddaughter is born early this morning. She has no name yet." She gave her daughter a *hurry up and decide* look that almost made Zeisha laugh.

Zeisha walked to the bed.

"Would you like to hold her?" the girl asked.

Zeisha nodded. A soft smile found her lips as she cradled the infant. She was giving this baby health by feeding her mother. *Vine eating is a talent that brings life. This is how I want to use my magic.*

Zeisha and Kebi soon left. As they walked, Zeisha's heart was lighter than it had been since she'd woken from her slavery. The ancient city, with its crumbling Skytrain tracks and brightly painted doors, almost felt like home. For the moment, anyway.

Soon after the two gardeners got back to work, the wind picked up. A strange, clinking music rang through the air. Zeisha looked up, quickly finding the source: wind chimes hanging from a tall hook that rose from one corner of the roof. "That's nice," she said, pointing.

"Bone chimes," Kebi said.

Zeisha flinched. "They're made of bones?" Seeing Kebi's nod, she asked hesitantly, "Are they from trogs who've died?"

"No. We burn our dead."

Zeisha remembered the large, nighttime fire that had blazed in the distance the day after the militia battle. She could almost smell it now. She swallowed and tried not to grimace.

Kebi continued, "Bone chimes are from those who come before."

"Before?"

"Before The Day." Kebi placed a hand on Zeisha's knee and locked eyes with her. "Trogs have a purpose. We remember the *before*."

Zeisha nodded. It made sense—the murals in the community space, the chimes, even the trogs' insistence on living in buildings that were full of ancient memories. Such a focus seemed almost spiritual. "Are trogs religious?" she asked.

"Many are," Kebi said, returning to the plant she was harvesting. "We worship at home. We are not Rimorians, but we worship the same God."

That simple statement sent a wave of comfort over Zeisha. She missed the traditions she'd grown up with in Tirra—praying with her family and attending Rimorian chapel services with Krey. Zeisha had always yearned to know God.

Her ancient ancestors, she knew, had shared such a desire. Anyari's original settlers had represented various religions, but the details of their beliefs were lost over time.

The Rimorian religion was founded a thousand years after colonization. Rimorians had clergy, a book of scripture called the Sacrex, and prophets called emissaries. The religion's followers committed themselves to rediscovering and reconnecting with God.

Kebi interrupted Zeisha's thoughts, asking, "And you? Are you religious?"

Zeisha considered the question. At last, she looked up from the violitus she was growing and said, "I believe God is with me, and I seek to know him more."

"I am told new-city folk worship the stone," Kebi said.

Smiling, Zeisha replied, "A few do, especially in Cellerin City, since that's where the stone is kept. But most of us pray to God, not the stone."

Kebi gave Zeisha a smile. "We are more alike than I expect."

For another hour, the two of them worked and chatted. They'd filled several big crates with violitus when a loud *CLANG* rang across the roof. Zeisha jumped, then stood and looked at the metal trapdoor at the center of the roof. It was open. As she watched, Krey's head and shoulders emerged.

Zeisha's face broke into a smile. She dashed across the churned-up soil, stopping in the center of the roof, where nothing grew in a square about two mets per side.

"Hey," Krey said with a grin as he stepped off the ladder.

"Hi! What are you doing here?"

"We figured we should all talk."

"We?"

He gestured to the trapdoor, where Nora's head was now visible. "Ovrun's here too."

"I'd love to," Zeisha said, "but I should probably keep working."

"I need a break," Kebi called. "You take one too."

"How'd you get away from your lookout duties?" Zeisha asked Krey.

"They gave me a partner today. He's covering for me."

"And nobody knows Nora and I are taking a break," Ovrun said with a sheepish shrug. "We need to get back to hunting soon, since the soldiers stole most of the meat stores yesterday. We'll keep this short."

"Have a seat," Zeisha said.

When the four friends were seated, Krey spoke first, keeping his voice low. "I talked to Eira. The trogs are preparing for the next invasion, and they want to confirm that we're fighting with them. I told her yes—that's what we promised when they let us stay here. But we need to decide how long we're planning to stay. If this turns into an all-out war, will we stay involved?"

Zeisha's mouth went dry. *Don't ask me to fight.* Heaviness filled her chest.

"First of all, it may not turn into a war," Nora said, her voice steely. "If there's any way to get through to my father, I'll find it." Her sharp gaze moved between her three companions.

The statement allowed Zeisha's breaths to come easier.

Nora released a sigh. "But if he attacks the trogs again, then of course we'll fight with them. They helped us free the militia. We have to help them defend their independence."

All at once, Zeisha's heart pounded against her ribs. *I can't fight again.* Trying to keep her panic off her face, she glanced at Krey. He had his knees up and was tapping one boot against the roof, like he was ready to enter a battle right then.

Krey spoke up again. "Like Nora said, they're counting on us. And I know they're planning a defense. We need to make sure we're an active part of it." His mouth widened into a smile. "We have dragons on our side; that'll definitely help." He turned to Ovrun. "You're in, right?"

"We can't abandon these people after all they've done for us," Ovrun said. "I'll do whatever's needed to protect them."

Zeisha briefly closed her eyes. In that short moment, a snippet from one of her dreams the night before flashed in her mind. Her hand was stretched out, a strong vine extending from it. She'd wrapped the vine around the neck of a man in black—a trog. She pulled, tightening the magical noose. The man's eyes bulged. His mouth gaped in silent desperation.

When Zeisha opened her eyes to escape the image, she could still see it as clearly as if someone had engraved it on her brain. She drew in a sharp breath, released it, and gulped down more air. Her breaths kept coming, shallow and fast. Everyone stared at her.

Krey's arm, slim yet strong, slid around her shoulders. "You okay?"

The picture of her vine, tight around the neck of a man she didn't know, refused to fade. There wasn't enough air in all the world to fill her lungs.

"Breathe with me," Krey murmured in her ear, pulling her into a hug.

Zeisha felt Krey's chest swell slowly. She tried to convince hers to do the same. *In. Out.* Her lungs rebelled with a quick gasp. Krey murmured soft words of encouragement. After two or three minutes, Zeisha was matching him breath for breath.

Krey's arms released her. He cupped her cheek in his hand. "What is it?"

The words that came out of her mouth weren't the ones she expected. "Did I kill anyone during the battle?"

Even this close, she could see his eyes widen. He pulled back a bit and moved his hands to her shoulders. He was still so close that his breath warmed her face. "Zeisha, *you* didn't do anything in the battle. The king and Faylie did, using you and the others as weapons. I saw you, and trust me—it wasn't you at all. I don't even want you to think about what happened, because *it wasn't you.*"

"Did I?"

He opened his mouth, then closed it and licked his lips. A battle raged in his light-brown eyes. "Zeisha . . ." Apparently he couldn't think of a better answer than that.

"I wish you'd just tell me the truth."

"The truth is, you're literally the best person I've ever met. The truth is, you would never willingly hurt anyone."

That was exactly what he was asking her to do: hurt the king's soldiers. Willingly. She pulled away from him. *I was forced to be a weapon,* she wanted to say. *Don't ask me to choose to be one now.*

But Krey believed fighting was the only right thing to do. His passion was one of the things she loved about him. She couldn't bring herself to stomp all over it. Zeisha realized she was shaking her head slowly, her body betraying the hesitation her mouth refused to speak.

"Zei." Krey's voice was gentle, but when he took her hands, his fingers pulsed with restrained determination. "What is it?"

"I—" She took a deep breath, trying to slow her racing heart. The words she needed to say—*I can't fight again*—still wouldn't come out. Instead, she said, "The woman I'm working with took me to visit some trogs. There was a girl there, younger than me, who just had a baby. I gave her the violitus I'd just grown. Krey, that's what I want to be doing. Feeding people. Not . . . anything else."

"That's what I want for you too." Krey intertwined his fingers with hers. "By the stone, it's what I *love* about you! But when the army comes, you'll be using your magic to protect innocent people. We're all on the right side this time around. Your strength, it's . . . it's astonishing! You could—"

"Krey!" Nora interrupted, her voice loud enough to carry across the whole roof. More quietly but with no less vehemence, she said, "As usual, you're being an—" She halted, her gaze flicking briefly to Zeisha before returning to Krey. "You're being unreasonable. Let me talk to Zeisha. Alone."

Krey opened his mouth, like he'd argue with her. Then he looked to Zeisha, and his expression softened. "Would that help?"

"I think so."

Krey squeezed Zeisha's hands and stood. He and Ovrun strode through the garden.

Nora was already sitting across from Zeisha, but she leaned forward. Zeisha did the same.

"Do you know who Faylie was?" Nora asked softly.

Zeisha's eyebrows drew together. Of course she did. "The Overseer. She controlled me."

"Right, but did you know she was my best friend before my father turned her into a brain lyster?"

Zeisha's mouth dropped open.

Nora's face crumpled. She looked away, chin quivering. After taking and releasing two deep breaths, she turned back to Zeisha. "I killed her because it was the only way to save all of you—and myself. I . . . I don't think I had a choice. I also don't know if I can forgive myself." She blinked. A tear rolled down her cheek. It halted briefly in the thin scar that ran across her soft skin, before continuing its path to her chin. Nora ran her fingers along the scar. "Faylie did this to me. But I know it wasn't really her. And you know what? I'm glad the healer couldn't mend my skin completely."

"Why?"

"I want the physical reminder of my father's mistakes. Of how easy it is for those in power to hurt their people." She swallowed. "And maybe I think I deserve the scar after what I did."

They were both silent for several breaths. Then Zeisha spoke, her voice barely above a whisper. "I killed at least one person. I know Krey doesn't want to tell me the truth, but I dreamed about it last night."

The skin between Nora's dark brows wrinkled. "I'm sorry."

"So am I. About what you had to do and what I had to do. About all of this." Zeisha shook her head. "You did the right thing. And I know if I have to fight, I'll be on the right side, like Krey said. But I still don't think I can do it."

Nora grabbed both Zeisha's hands and squeezed. "You don't have to. Do you hear me? *You don't have to fight.* Krey feels the same way; I know he does. He's just stuck in justice mode right now. But if this turns into a war, I'm going to make sure we don't pressure any of the militia members to fight. If we do that, we're no better than my father."

Zeisha's breath escaped in a shuddering sigh. She pulled Nora into a tight hug. "Thank you. I'll support the rest of you the best I can, but I can't . . . that's not what my magic is for, Nora."

Nora spoke in her ear. "Leave Krey to me. We can plan a defense with one fewer plant lyster." She let go and smiled, despite her still-wet eyes. "Now go create some violitus. I want a big salad for dinner."

Zeisha laughed and stood. She looked to where Krey was sitting.

He raised his eyebrows and gave her a half-smile. She beckoned him over. "We'll talk later," she said when he arrived. She gave him a quick kiss. "Be safe out there."

"Always." He smiled and headed for the ladder.

5

Going downtown anytime soon? Don't be too shocked if you encounter a dragon.

Students around Deroga are studying ancient Earth myths. We've made hundreds of dragons from materials as varied as paper, bread dough, and polymus. The mythical creatures are waiting to greet you in restaurants, in stores, and on street corners. A few of them even breathe artificial fire.

I write under a pseudonym, so I can't tell you which one's mine. But trust me—it's fierce.

-*"Dragons Invade Deroga" by Genta Ril*
The Derogan Chronicle, *dated Quari 5, 6293*

"She's not going to fight?" Krey stopped on a landing and set down his lantern.

"No, she's not." Nora gestured to the many flights of stairs they still needed to descend. "Let's keep going. We all have to get to work."

Work could wait. Krey planted his feet. "Come on, Nora. Just tell me what you talked about."

Nora let out her breath and folded her arms. "Zeisha knows she killed someone, so you might as well stop hiding that from her. In case you've never noticed this about your girlfriend, she's an incredibly sweet, gentle soul."

"I know that," Krey snapped. "It's why I love her."

"Then you need to let her be the person she is! You can't drag her kicking and screaming into a fight!"

From a few steps above the landing, Ovrun spoke. "We should talk about this as we walk. That break was longer than we planned."

"I agree." Nora started descending the dark stairs again.

Krey huffed, grabbed his lantern, and followed. "I'd never force her to fight. Who exactly do you think I am, Nora?"

"I don't know! All I saw back there was a girl trying to tell her boyfriend that fighting is literally the last thing in the world she wants to do—and her boyfriend saying it'll all be okay because she's so strong! You were pressuring her to do the very thing that'll make her hate herself!"

"But it won't make her hate herself, don't you see?" Krey's lantern bumped against the wall at the edge of the stairwell. He moved it to his other hand. "Yes, I did see her kill a trog during the battle. Two trogs, in fact."

"Oh, Krey." Nora's voice was softer now. "That would break her heart—you know that, right?"

"Of course I know that." Krey's chest tightened. He didn't know if Zeisha would ever get over the guilt of killing innocents, even though it hadn't truly been her wielding that vine. "It's why I didn't want to tell her, though apparently that strategy isn't working. Listen, all this fighting is the last thing I ever would've wanted for her! But think about it. She knows she used her gifts for evil when she was controlled. By using them for good, she'll . . . she'll redeem herself. She'll be able to move on."

This time, it was Nora who halted on a landing. Krey almost bumped into her. She locked her eyes with his. Her tone was gentle now. "If you were in her shoes, you'd need that type of redemption. And I get that. It's what I need too, after what I did to Fay—to the Overseer." She let out a sigh. "I don't think it's what Zeisha needs. Redemption for her is making plants and bringing them to a hungry family. It's all about life, not death."

Krey stared at Nora in the dim lantern light. "You do realize you've known her for a few days, and I've known her for seventeen years, right?"

"Just think about what I said, Krey." Nora's voice hardened. "Use your brain, not your ego."

The words hit him harder than he would've expected. Probably because he suspected she was right. He squeezed past her, descending again.

"Will you consider what I said?" Nora's voice echoed in the stairwell.

She was gonna make him say it out loud, wasn't she? "Of course I will. I already am."

"Good."

They descended two flights in silence. From his spot at the back of their little group, Ovrun said, "I've got a question. Do you really think the trogs can defend their city against the king? There's only so many trogs, but Ulmin can keep drafting more soldiers if he needs to."

Krey silently thanked his friend for the change of subject. "I've been thinking about that too. We need to talk to Eira about tipping the scales. We need more people on our side."

"Like who?" Nora asked.

Krey smiled. "Like the New Therroans."

Nora grabbed Krey's sleeve. He stopped walking and turned to her. "You think they'd help us?" she asked.

"I think they have a heart for oppressed people."

"I agree. And there's one thing that might help convince them."

"What?"

Nora started walking again. Krey heard the smile in her voice as she answered, "Me."

The last time Krey had ridden a dragon, he'd just been woken from a brief stint of mental slavery and was desperate to find his girlfriend. Understandably, he'd been stressed out. Afterward, he'd convinced himself that if he was ever forced on the back of such a beast again, he'd be more relaxed.

His entire body was currently proving him wrong. He held to Osmius's scales with painfully tight fingers, his stomach alternating between agonizing cramping and gut-churning nausea.

"Osmius wants to know how you're doing," Nora called over her shoulder.

It was too dark to see her, but if her voice was any indication, she was actually enjoying herself. There had to be something wrong with someone who liked flying hundreds of mets above the ground on the back of an unpredictable beast. "I'm fine." Krey wondered if he was convincing anyone. Nora's chuckle confirmed he wasn't.

He'd been prepared for a solo, marathon flight into Cellerin City. He'd eat feathers along the way and stop to rest when he needed to. When Nora had offered to come, he'd assented quickly. He'd carry her on his back. It would be nice to have company.

Then she'd suggested Osmius take them. "It'll be so much faster," she'd said.

It was an easy argument to refute. "We can't fly a dragon into the capital city. Even at night."

"Of course not. He'll drop us off at the outskirts. You can fly us the rest of the way." Her voice had gotten softer. "The last few days have been tough. Osmius . . . he makes me feel strong."

How could he argue with that?

His stomach roiled, and he wished he'd tried harder.

Krey hated every second of the flight, but it only lasted an hour or so. Well outside Cellerin City, Osmius descended in a slow spiral and landed.

Krey and Nora slid off. He leaned over, hands on his knees, until his breathing slowed. His nausea would take longer to abate. When he straightened, Nora was standing before Osmius, her hand on his cheek. Moonlight reflected off the dragon's bulging, compound eyes.

Not for the first time, Krey envied her ability to speak, mind to mind, with dragons. *What are they saying to each other?*

Nora dropped her hand, and Osmius ascended.

"Did you and Osmius have a good talk?" Krey asked.

"Yeah," she murmured. "He told me I did the right thing." She let out an awkward little laugh. "Then he told me again. And again."

Krey didn't have to ask what *right thing* Osmius had been speaking of. Since the battle a week ago, he'd seen Nora's guilt over Faylie's death every time she pressed her lips together or stared off into the distance. "He's right, you know."

"He wants to be right, anyway." Nora took a deep breath. "You ready to fly?"

"I've gotta fuel up first." Krey sat in the dirt, pulled a bag of diced feathers from his coat pocket, and started eating. Nora sat next to him. Neither spoke.

After a few minutes, Krey rose to a crouch. Nora got on his back. When he lifted into the air and a frightened squeak exited her mouth, he let himself smile.

"Krey!" Hatlin's eyes were wide over his crooked nose. He pulled the pub's back door open a little farther, then stopped. "You brought someone else?"

Krey glanced at Nora. Her jacket hood was up, her head bowed. "I'll introduce her to you inside, if that's okay."

Hatlin narrowed his eyes, but beckoned them in. "Didn't know if we'd see you again."

"I still believe in your cause," Krey said.

He'd gotten involved with the New Therroan rebels two months ago because he'd suspected they were behind the militia. The province of New Therro had never had a good relationship with the monarchy. They could've used a bunch of mind-controlled magic eaters to fight for their province's independence. But the last time Krey had met with Hatlin and other New Therroan rebel leaders, he'd learned they'd never heard of the mysterious militia.

Krey looked around the empty room. Every Saturday night, a small group of rebels met here. When that meeting ended, an even smaller group of leaders remained. It was late; he'd expected to join that second group. "Where's Wallis? And T?"

"Before I answer any questions, you better introduce your guest."

"Right—sorry." Krey turned to Nora. "You can take the hood off." She did.

A lot of Cellerinians didn't recognize Nora at first sight. Most of them had only seen drawings of her in newspapers. But Hatlin's eyes widened as soon as the lantern light fell on Nora's face. "Princess! What are you doing here?"

"She's on our side," Krey said.

"I sure hope so."

Nora said, "A week ago, I played a major role in a battle against my father's lyster militia. Is that enough to convince you my loyalties aren't with the crown?"

Hatlin stared at her. "I suppose it is." He shifted his gaze to Krey. "Sounds like you have a lot to catch me up on."

"Can we have a seat?" Nora asked.

Hatlin's broad shoulders slumped as he let out a breath. "Yeah. I got a lot to tell you too."

Krey pulled out a chair and sat. "You go first."

Hatlin took a long drink from a beer mug in front of him, then leaned over the table, propping his elbows on it. "The king invaded New Therro."

Krey sat up straighter. "What? When?"

"Thursday."

Krey shook his head. That was two days ago, four days after the army's invasion of Deroga. He'd wondered why the army hadn't returned to the trogs yet. "By the stone . . . I'm sorry. How's the fighting going?"

"It's not."

"What?"

"Our people fought back, but the army caught us by surprise. There weren't even that many of them, less than a thousand. They're not very well trained. But neither were most of our people. The army stamped out our pitiful little resistance within hours. Yesterday, the king brought his own leaders into New Therro. He says they're *administrators*, but they're tyrants. We can't have our own governor or council anymore. They're arresting anyone who talks about New Therroan independence. And they've taken all our men who are sixteen-to-forty years old."

"Taken your men?" Nora asked. "Why?"

"They're all soldiers now. Forcefully conscripted."

"Damn," Krey said under his breath.

Hatlin continued, "After the army subdued us, they stuck around. About a hundred soldiers are staying in houses in the city. *Keeping order*, they say. The rest of them, including our guys, are in tents outside New Therro. They spend all day training. But nobody knows what for. I mean, who else would they need to fight? New Therro was the closest thing the king had to an enemy."

Krey sighed. The king had probably expected to achieve a quick victory in Deroga. When he'd arrived to an empty city, he'd realized how difficult urban warfare would be. If he had more soldiers, he'd be more likely to find, and defeat, the trogs. "So that's it?" he asked Hatlin. "You're not fighting back?"

Hatlin's tired eyes crinkled, and the corner of his mouth quirked up. "I didn't say that."

Krey returned his smile. "There's still a resistance?"

"A quiet one. But it's there. Ulmin made a mistake only taking our men. Our women are just as strong. They're looking for ways to communicate with the men in the army. We'll find some way to fight back. After all this, nobody in New Therro still wants to be part of Cellerin."

"So where are Wallis and T?"

Hatlin's face turned somber again. "In hiding, here in Cellerin City. Protection officers are looking for them—but the officers don't seem to realize I'm a leader in the movement too. They visited me and a bunch of others, warning us not to meet together anymore. I think they considered us pretty harmless though. They only knew about our big Wednesday meetings, not our Saturday ones. I came tonight, in case anyone showed up. Only a couple of people did." He shook his big head. "The New Therroans in the capital aren't as desperate for independence as those back home are."

"How are you getting information from New Therro?" Nora asked. "I'm sure the king's got sentries on the roads."

Hatlin chuckled. "We may not have many magic eaters in our city, but we do have a flyer. He carries messages back and forth."

"A feather eater?" Krey asked. "In New Therro?" Feather eaters were rare.

Hatlin nodded, then leaned back, clasping his hands behind his head. "Krey, I'm tired. What did you come here to discuss?"

Krey pulled water out of his pack and took a drink. "Last time we met, I told you about the magical militia. We found out the king was in charge of them. And we freed them."

"Please tell me that means you can join our cause."

"I wish I could. What I didn't tell you two weeks ago is that the militia was being housed in Deroga. Trog territory." Seeing Hatlin's wide eyes, Krey continued, "The trogs helped us free the militia. They're letting all of us live there for now. The king's not exactly happy about that whole thing. Turns out he was planning to use all those mind slaves to subdue New Therro."

Hatlin let out a low whistle. "No kidding."

"Yeah. Why endanger your whole army when you can send in a bunch of magic eaters to scare people into submission? We messed up that plan when we freed the militia. And we pissed off the king in the process." He updated Hatlin on the army's recent invasion of Deroga, concluding, "We keep expecting the army to return. We didn't realize they'd found another city to invade."

"You better keep preparing. Once the army trains all their new soldiers, I bet they return to Deroga." Hatlin shook his head. "What the hell is going on with the king? Until this week, the last time our army fought anyone was when they beat New Therro into submission fifty years ago. I never liked Ulmin—sorry, Princess—but I didn't expect any of this. It goes against everything our country has ever stood for."

Krey sighed and shook his head. He wasn't ready to tell Hatlin that King Ulmin was not only controlling others' minds, but also losing his own. "It's simple. Ulmin's gotten power hungry." He took a deep breath. "I came here to ask you if the New Therroan rebels would help the trogs defend their city. I knew you'd understand the importance of their fight."

Hatlin shrugged. "Sorry, man. The king's got most of our men. The rest of us are gonna fight until we get our home back."

"I know. But there's one thing you can do for us."

"What?"

"Send your feather eater to meet one of our people a couple of times a week. He can tell us what the army's up to. We can even meet him halfway."

"Wish I could, but we've got him flying too much already. Poor guy is worn out. And he's sick of eating feathers every damn day. He's gotta keep himself constantly fueled in case he needs to get somewhere fast."

Nora leaned forward. "He doesn't even have to go halfway. He just needs to fly far enough that no one will see him meeting me."

Face twisted in confusion, Hatlin asked, "You?"

She grinned. "I have an alternate mode of transportation."

Hatlin's expression didn't change.

Krey rolled his eyes. "She's talking about the dragon she's befriended."

Hatlin coughed and drew back sharply, like someone had punched him in the gut. "A—a dragon?"

Krey turned to Nora. "You sure he's willing to take you on a ride every week?"

"I just asked him. He said no problem. Using more formal words, of course."

"You—" Hatlin ran his tongue along his lower lip. His mouth opened and closed twice. "You asked him? Just now? You can talk to him?"

Nora nodded.

"Well, then." He cleared his throat and, with obvious effort, returned his face to an almost-neutral expression. "I guess our flyer could meet you once a week. Can't do it any more often than that. Every Friday, about three hours after sunset. Somewhere east of Cellerin City."

"Cellerin City? Not New Therro?" Nora asked.

"Yeah, he's based here. Flies in and out of New Therro."

Once they'd worked out a meeting location north of the Eastern Road, Krey opened his mouth to ask another question. He didn't get to speak a syllable. Loud, commanding voices sounded from the pub's front rooms. Hatlin leapt up and bolted the interior door that separated the room from the rest of the building.

The sound of running feet, approaching quickly, traveled through the interior door. Fists banged against it. "Protection officers! Open up! Open up now!"

"Let's get out of here," Hatlin muttered. He ran to the back door. Krey and Nora followed. Hatlin's hand was on the bolt when the knob started jiggling. The entire door shuddered as someone tried to force it open.

Hatlin cursed under his breath. The people on the other side of the interior door were still pounding and shouting.

Krey pointed at some shadowed stairs at the side of the room. "What do those lead to?" he whispered urgently.

"Upstairs hallway."

"Are there windows up there?"

"Yeah, but—"

"Come on." Krey grabbed his pack. As he ran to the stairs, he reached inside the bag, coming away with a handful of feathers. Chewing and swallowing, he took the stairs two at a time, followed by Nora and Hatlin.

They reached the second floor. Rooms lined both sides of a long corridor. "Get us to a window!" Krey said.

Hatlin tried the first door on the right, then the second. Both were locked. He threw his shoulder into the second door. Once, twice, again. The cheap wood of the door and frame cracked. The door swung open.

A woman huddled in a corner, holding up a hairbrush like a weapon. She screamed.

Hatlin ran up to her. He grabbed her brush with one hand and threw it on the bed. His other hand covered her mouth.

"We won't hurt you," Krey said, "as long as you stop screaming and stay still. Got it?"

She nodded.

Hatlin let her go. "What's the plan, Krey?"

He gestured to the large window. "I'm flying us out of here."

"Both of us?" Nora hissed.

"Don't be stupid!" Hatlin said. "You can't carry me!"

"I've carried someone larger than you." That might not actually be true. Hatlin was shorter than Ovrun, but he probably weighed more. Add Nora to the mix, and it would be dicey. Krey pushed every bit of doubt from his mind. He fumbled with the window locks. They didn't move. He cursed and pushed harder.

The locks popped out of place. Krey pushed on both halves of the window, swinging them wide open, then crouched. "On my back, Hatlin! Now! Nora, get on his back!"

"I don't think so." Hatlin shoved Krey out of the way, stepped on the windowsill, and leapt off.

Krey drew in a sharp gasp.

Hatlin didn't fall. He flew.

Nora cursed loudly, then leapt on Krey's back. The action was so sudden, it pushed him to his knees. He couldn't fly until he incorporated her body into his magic.

Footsteps and shouts in the hallway marred his concentration. He clenched his teeth, focusing his effort. In an instant, magic enveloped Nora. He felt her body as if it were his own. Tense muscles. Quick breaths. Pounding heart.

Krey stood.

"Stop!" someone shouted from the doorway.

Make that two pounding hearts. Krey leapt into the air and flew out the window. A hand grabbed his foot just as he exited. He kicked it off. Nora yelped.

But they were safe in the air. Krey looked down. He laughed at the half-dozen men at the pub's back entrance who were still trying to get in.

They flew quietly for a couple of minutes until both of them calmed down.

Nora broke the silence. "I guess we know who the New Therroan feather lyster is."

Krey laughed. "I always thought there was more to that guy than he was letting on."

THE SEER: 2

Sarza held the knife and went through her forms. Ten movements —slashes and thrusts, all at specific angles she'd learned from a neighbor years ago. After the ten forms, she took five deep breaths, then started the whole thing over. Again. And again.

Her family had thought it was funny that a skinny girl wanted to learn to fight with a knife. They didn't know about the prophetic urge she'd had, the one that wouldn't let her rest until she approached her eccentric neighbor and asked him to teach her.

The man was old and quiet. He stood in his front yard every day, practicing a series of exercises with a splintery wooden knife. He agreed to train Sarza three times a week. He didn't say more than a dozen words to her every session.

But he was an effective mentor. He demonstrated. Motioned for her to copy him. Nudged her arms, legs, hands, even her abdominal muscles. *Tighter here*, his calloused fingers would say. *Elbow up*. He taught her everything he knew. They started sparring together. After a few years, she could beat him in a fair fight. When she'd joined the army, her knife skills had impressed the officers and made the other enlisted soldiers jealous.

The movements were so natural to her that her mind could wander, even as her body moved and her tongue counted.

"One. Two. Three." Sarza had no idea why the king of Cellerin wanted to take over the city of Deroga. The why didn't really matter.

"Four. Five. Six." All that mattered was that *war* and *opportunity* went hand in hand. This was her chance to stand out. Get power of her own.

"Seven. Eight. Nine. Ten." But opportunity was useless if you didn't seize it. That was why she'd volunteered to stay in Deroga as a spy.

Five deep breaths. Sarza gazed out the window of the twenty-first-story office she'd called home for the last six days. It was midday, and trogs were going about their daily business. She watched, but there was only so much she could see from way up here. She kept hoping a vision would give her some indication of where she should go to get information that would help the army.

Spying kept her teetering on the border between fearful alertness and terrible boredom. So far, she'd left only at night, and only to steal food, clothes, and supplies. As a child trying to avoid attention, she'd gotten good at moving quietly and remaining unseen. In her brief career as a spy, not one trog had seen her taking the things she needed.

During the day, knife drills helped her stay busy, but she could only do them for so long. Today, she'd been repeating the same ten moves for at least two hours straight. Time for some rest.

A gust of cold, late-winter wind entered the room. Sarza wore only underwear and a sleeveless undershirt. Chill bumps rose on her thin, toned arms and legs. She stepped toward the stolen clothes she'd laid over an old chair.

Sarza was always glad when she got some warning before a vision. Today, she wasn't so lucky. One moment, she was fine. The next, her legs buckled. She fell to the floor.

An image entered her mind: a vast expanse of pale-orange sky.

Something was flying in from the distance. Something big. Maybe a carribird?

No, not a bird. A dragon. Tiny rainbows glittered off its iridescent, gray scales. Sarza's view shifted, bringing her closer. She could see the dragon's eyes, two great domes of faceted gold. A smiling girl with straight, chin-length hair was on the dragon's back, lying on her belly, holding on tight.

Sarza came back to herself. Her eyes were wide. A laugh burst from her mouth. Normally, she'd be annoyed to get such a seemingly pointless vision. But a dragon—with a rider? Well, that was awesome. Whether it was useful information or not.

She lifted her eyes to the sky, absentmindedly rubbing her hip where she'd fallen. She almost expected to see the dark silhouette of a dragon in the distance, but the only objects marring the sky's expanse were buildings and clouds.

Sarza sighed and got dressed. She'd keep paying attention—to the streets beneath her and the visions within her. Once she had information that would help the army, she'd sneak out of trog territory. A fellow soldier was holed up in a particular building in the city's western suburbs, waiting for her to come back and report.

Sarza would be the key to the army's successful invasion of Deroga. She didn't know how or when. But this was her time. She was certain of it.

6

I can't walk to school without seeing at least half a dozen signs with the flashing message, "SHIMSHIMS AREN'T PETS." I contacted Levey Rosh, president of the Derogan Animal League, to discuss their new campaign.

"Shimshims evolved as foragers," Rosh told me. "They're meant to spend all day searching for food. When we adopt them and feed them, they grow complacent. It shortens their life spans."

In other words, get a pet caynin like everyone else.

-"You're Killing Your Pet" by Genta Ril
The Derogan Chronicle, *dated Quari 8, 6293*

"CAN you tell me about your dad?" Nora asked.

Ovrun's footsteps slowed. When he didn't answer, Nora

56

wondered if she'd hit on a sore subject. "Sorry." She lifted her head to look at him. "You don't have to talk about it."

He met her gaze. "No, it's fine. It's just that I was thinking about where we might find a shimshim den. I didn't expect you to ask about my father."

"Really, forget I asked. I haven't known you long enough—"

He grasped her shoulder and put his opposite index finger to his lips. Nora halted. Ovrun pointed to numerous piles of what looked like tan pebbles in front of an office building. Nora had spent enough time hunting shimshims to know what she was looking at. *Where there's poop, there's prey.*

They entered quietly. In a back room, they found a lot more excrement, fresh this time, under an old desk. Shimshims liked to live in dark, enclosed spaces. But Nora didn't see any of the little reptids or hear their trademark hisses.

"They're probably outside, foraging," Ovrun said. Shimshims ate plants, and there was plenty of wild growth in Deroga. Between that and their frequent thievery of the trogs' food stores, the little reptids thrived here.

"Should we wait for them?" Nora asked.

"Yeah. We'll sit in the front room."

"Oh good, because this room stinks."

They walked back to the lobby of the small building. The couch was rotten, so after removing their packs, bows, and quivers, they sat against the wall, their knees touching.

Ovrun looked straight ahead at the open doorway. "So . . . my father."

"We really don't have to talk—"

"No, I want to. I trust you." He swiveled his head to give her a small smile, then returned his gaze to the door. "He was a traveling trader. He came to Cellerin City for about a month, enough time for my mom to fall in love with him. In fact, I used to sleep under a quilt he gave her."

Nora turned to Ovrun, though he still wasn't looking at her. "What happened?"

"He wanted to take her with him when he left, but she didn't think she'd like traveling for a living. So they broke it off. He told her he'd visit. After he left, she realized she was pregnant."

"Did he ever come back?"

A soft sigh slipped from Ovrun's mouth. "No. He'd given my mom an address before he left. Said it was his parents' house, and he visited them at least once a year. It was in some town south of Cellerin Mountain. My mom sent a letter after I was born, telling him he was a father. A year went by, and she didn't hear anything. She kept sending letters every few months. She held out hope for years, but about the time I turned five, she realized he was never coming back."

"Oh, Ovrun." Nora took his hand. "Your father is an idiot who doesn't know what he's missing."

Ovrun turned his head toward her and gave a helpless shrug. "Or maybe he died, or his parents moved and he never got the letters. I just wish I knew for sure, you know? And my mom . . . she deserves better. My sister's dad stuck around for five years after she was born, but he was a first-class asshole. We were all glad when he left." He blinked several times. "I miss them. My family. My mom's a good woman; she just hasn't had the best luck with men. Maybe someday you can meet her." He looked away again.

Nora waited for him to turn back to her. "I guess you got your goodness from your mom. Because you're a good man."

A short laugh escaped his mouth. "I'm not so sure. You remember when we were hiding in that old park? When we were traveling through Deroga together?"

Nora's neck grew warm. "How could I forget?" She hoped one day she'd experience kisses more perfect than the ones they'd shared under those trees, but she doubted it.

Ovrun squeezed her hand. "It was almost impossible for me to stop that night."

"Yeah." Nora laughed softly. "Honestly, I kind of wish we hadn't."

"That's the thing, though—what if we'd kept going? What if you'd gotten pregnant? I almost turned into my father that night, Nora."

"No!" Nora scooted to face Ovrun directly. She placed her hands on either side of his face. "You will never turn into your father. If I'd ended up pregnant, you wouldn't have left me. That's not who you are."

"But you don't know that." He lifted his hands and gently removed hers from his cheeks. "Maybe I wouldn't have been just like my dad, but think about what would've happened if you eventually went back to the palace. Your dad would never let me be king—and for good reason. It's not like it's something I'm prepared for or even something I want. I came so close to messing up your life the way my dad messed up my mom's. I should stay far away from you. But . . ." He trailed off, shaking his head helplessly.

"But what?" Nora whispered.

Voice low, he said, "But I'm drawn to you, Princess."

Nora swallowed. He hadn't called her that since his days as a palace guard. And while she didn't like being a princess these days . . . she liked the sound of that word coming from his mouth.

He wasn't done. "When I heard Eira was ready to give us assignments, I told myself I would make sure you and I were working far away from each other. And what happened when we got in the meeting? I immediately offered to take you with me so I could teach you archery."

"Why did you do it?" Nora breathed.

He reached up and traced her ears with his fingertips. He trailed them down her cheeks and her exposed neck, smiling when she shivered. His touch moved to her jacket-covered shoulders and continued its journey down her arms. Nora was far too happy when his fingers found skin again, this time on her palms, which he brushed so lightly, it made her shiver once more. He enfolded her hands in his and brought his gaze back up to hers. "Because no matter how much I try not to, I keep craving moments like these."

Nora rose to her knees. She leaned forward and grazed her lips against the skin of his cheek before bringing her mouth to his. As much as she wanted a replay of their previous kisses, she kept this one gentler, refusing to let herself lose control. That was harder than she'd expected, because, by the sky, he tasted and smelled so *good*.

And it was deeper than pure pleasure. Since the militia battle, what she'd done to Faylie simmered in her heart, repelling any hint of peace. She couldn't escape the sharp memories of cold ice and hot blood. But Ovrun's kisses pushed her torturous guilt to the side. For a few perfect moments, she could almost forget what she'd done.

Despite all that, she made herself pull away before it got out of hand. Ovrun opened his eyes and shook his head, smiling helplessly.

"No babies, I promise," Nora said. Those words elicited a deep laugh, and oh, was he *trying* to make her want him more with that perfect, rumbling sound? She resisted the idea of kissing him again, instead sitting back and asking, "Remember our conversation at the party last week?"

"Um . . . I remember our kiss at the party last week."

"Yeah." She let out a contented sigh as the memory filled her whole body. "Well, in case you forgot, we did talk that night too. I told you then, I don't know what my future is. These days, I don't want to be a monarch any more than you do. The only thing in my life I feel sure about is that I want you in it."

"Nora." His brow furrowed. "How are we supposed to commit to each other when we don't know what'll happen next week or a year from now?"

"Maybe we don't need to commit." The answer suddenly seemed so obvious. They were stuck in Deroga, among people they didn't know. They both needed companionship. And she had no idea what the future held, but she knew one thing: they were good for each other. "It's not like you need to propose to me," she said. "Although marriage would certainly have its benefits." She bit her lip and grinned.

Ovrun closed his eyes and ran his hand through his thick, wavy hair. When he looked at her again, he said in a low voice, "Maybe instead of making me think about those *benefits*, you should go on with whatever it was you were saying."

She stifled a laugh. "Okay. Let's focus on the basics. You like me. I like you. We'll keep ourselves under control, because we don't know what the future holds, and we're not ready to be parents. Do we really need to know anything else right now?"

"I don't think you get it," he said, his voice low. "I'm not looking for a casual relationship."

She digested that for a moment, then took his hand. Her smile was gone. "I understand. Does this feel casual to you?"

He licked his lips and swallowed. "Not exactly."

"Just because we aren't giving it a definition, doesn't mean it's casual." She let the tiniest smirk onto her lips. "I mean, I'm certainly not gonna drag another guy to this shimshim den to spend quality time with him. All I want is to keep the door open between us. To let this"—she pointed between the two of them—"be whatever it is."

"We shouldn't."

Nora looked down, releasing her breath.

Ovrun's hand tilted her chin up. "But I don't think I can say no."

Those words transformed her heart into a ball of soft cotton. She leaned over to kiss him, but for the second time that day, he held up his index finger. This time, he used it to cover her mouth. Then he pointed behind her.

Nora turned and saw a shimshim in the doorway, sitting on its hind legs, its long, blue body silhouetted against the bright sunlight. Apparently it didn't see them or thought they weren't a threat, because it dropped to all fours and skittered inside, running through the lobby and into the hallway that led to its den.

"Should we follow it?" Nora whispered.

"Not yet. Get comfortable and stay still."

Nora shifted to face the door again. Seconds later, another shimshim entered, then another. Within ten minutes, seventeen of the animals had darted through the lobby toward their den.

"That's probably all," Ovrun said. "It's a good-sized den."

Nora picked up her bow and stood, holding out a hand to help Ovrun up. "Let's go hunting."

Seventeen shimshims. Nora would've felt guilty for shooting them all in that enclosed space, if she didn't know how important the food was to their new community.

Field dressing them all would've taken forever. With this much game, they needed help. Carrying nine of the creatures in three overflowing sacks, they trudged to the butcher on the Star Clan's main street. The woman was pleased with the haul, especially when she heard there were eight more to come. She led them around the building to drop off the carcasses at the cleaning and skinning station.

Nora and Ovrun returned to the little office building and carried the remaining shimshims to the butcher. The three of them, together with the butcher's assistant, began cleaning the animals.

Nora found the whole process macabre, but she'd gotten pretty good at it during the weeks she, Krey, and Ovrun had hidden in a warehouse in a Derogan suburb. These days, with her memories of Faylie so eager to overwhelm her, she appreciated anything that kept her hands and mind busy. She chatted with Ovrun and the trogs to distract her from the yellow blood of the shimshims and the red blood of her friend.

As she was about to start working on her second shimshim, she held up the knife the butcher had loaned her. "This is much sharper than the one I usually use. The edge is holding up well."

"Good knives make good work," the butcher said with a smile.

Nora wiped the knife clean with a rag and examined the blade. "MADE IN CRUINE," she read aloud. Cruine was the country east of Cellerin. Burig Bay, which made up Deroga's eastern edge, separated the two lands. "Our chef back home only used Cruinite knives. He swore by them."

"My cousin lives in a little town called Emling, northwest of Deroga," Ovrun said. "There's a shop there that trogs sometimes visit. Is that where you get knives like these?"

The two trog women exchanged a quick glance. "Perhaps," the butcher said. "I do not buy knives."

"Someone else does the shopping?" Ovrun asked with a smile.

The butcher nodded, glancing again at her assistant.

Noting the looks the women gave each other, Nora examined the blade and handle more closely. She lifted her gaze to the butcher, her brow furrowed. "I thought when Cruine sent products to Cellerin, they had to mark every item with three letters: *CCE*, for Cruine-Cellerin Export. I guess they missed it on this knife."

"I have work inside," the butcher said. She gave Nora and Ovrun a quick smile before hurrying through the back door of her shop.

Nora dropped the subject but worked even faster. If the trogs had a relationship with a nearby nation, that could change everything. It was time to pay Eira a visit.

7

My family occasionally crosses Burig Bay. We've taken solarplanes, boats, and glidecrafts. In just four years, we'll have a cheaper transportation option: a Skytrain. The Derogan Skytrain Authority told me the track they're building across Burig Bay is the longest over-water track in the world.

-"Overwater" by Genta Ril
The Derogan Chronicle, dated Quari 9, 6293

As soon as Nora and Ovrun finished their task, they sought out Eira in her office. She was sitting at a dented, preday desk. *Has she always used such furniture?* Nora wondered. *Or did the army burn whatever she'd had before?*

At Eira's invitation, Nora and Ovrun sat. With no preamble, Nora asked, "Do the trogs trade with Cruine?"

Eira's sparse, white eyebrows rose. "Why this question?"

Nora explained what she'd noticed about the knife, then pointed at a pen on Eira's desk. It was carved of pale wood and had a fat bulb on the end, made to hold ink. A Cruinite design. "I'm guessing that doesn't bear the export stamp either."

"Are our trade habits important?" Eira asked.

Nora didn't miss the fact that the leader was asking, rather than answering, questions. "You heard the report Krey and I brought back two days ago. The New Therroans can't help us fight the Cellerinian army. If you have a good relationship with the nation across the bay, this would be a great time to turn it into a formal alliance."

Eira watched Nora for a long moment before at last saying, "We trade with Cruine."

"Do you think they'll help us defend Deroga?"

"I ask them," Eira said. Seeing the hope in Nora's expression, she clarified, "I ask last week. They respond yesterday. They refuse. Cellerin is their ally. They will not fight an ally."

Nora expelled all her breath in a sigh. She'd been afraid of that. She leaned over the desk. "Why didn't you want to tell me you trade with Cruine?"

"King Ulmin tells them not to trade with trogs. He wants us to remain isolated. Weak. Cruine does not wish to anger him."

"But they're willing to risk trading with you?" Nora asked.

"Cruine has few shimshims. The blue leather is valuable there. Trogs provide it to them, along with handmade goods. Cruine knows we will keep this secret." Eira tilted her head and examined Nora. "You ask me to ally with Cruine against your father. With how quickly you change your loyalties, I wonder if I can trust you."

Nora took a deep breath. "This may sound strange, Eira, but I'm not just doing this for the trogs. I'm doing it for Cellerin."

Eira squinted at her.

Nora tried to keep the tremble out of her voice. "Ten days ago, we freed thirty-three militia members—some of them as young as me. It should've been thirty-five people. The other two died, not knowing who they were!" Her voice was loud now. Unsteady. She didn't care. "Their families don't even know they're dead! And their leader—who was just as controlled as they were—I killed her. Her mother's out there somewhere, and she doesn't know her daughter is gone!"

Ovrun took Nora's hand and squeezed it. Neither he nor Eira spoke.

"Then what they did to you—and New Therro . . ." Nora took a deep breath. Tightness filled her throat. She pushed words past it. "When the army came here last week, I told you I don't know my father anymore. Well, I don't know my country anymore either. Cellerin doesn't enslave and vandalize and invade." Nora let go of Ovrun and grabbed Eira's wrinkled hand in both of her own. "The country I love is dying. I have to fight to save her. To return her to who she's supposed to be."

Eira's eyes fixed on Nora's. "Will you fight your father to save your land?"

Nora released Eira's hand, breathing hard. The best way to save Cellerin would be to save the king from his own addiction. *But what if I can't get through to him?* She gritted her teeth against the thought.

Lifting her chin, she drew in a deep breath. "Eira, I swear to you, I will do whatever is necessary to save my country. That includes preventing my father from taking Deroga."

Eira gazed at her with incisive, watery eyes. Nora sensed her credibility was on trial. She had to get this woman to trust her. "We stole four handguns from royal guards," she blurted. "We'll give them to you. Maybe you can use them."

Eira's brows lifted. She gave Nora a single nod. "At noon today, we will meet. Bring those who lead your people. It is time you know our battle plans."

Zeisha waited outside the building where Krey, Nora, Ovrun, and a few militia members were meeting with Eira.

Krey had invited her to the strategy meeting. She'd even

convinced herself to go. But when they arrived at the building, her hands started sweating. Her breath came in quick gasps.

She couldn't enter.

She couldn't hear about all the ways people wanted her to use her magic to fight. Again.

Krey had understood and even offered to stay with her. She'd seen the relief in his smile when she'd said no. He respected her desire to stay out of the fight, but he wanted to be right in the middle of it.

Even now, part of her wished she'd gone in. In their time together, Krey, Nora, and Ovrun had established a casual camaraderie. They'd welcomed Zeisha into their little group, but she felt like the new kid when they all spent time together.

It was different when she and Krey managed to snag time together, just the two of them. Then the world felt right again, even this far from home. Until the topic of fighting came up. Then, as much as Krey assured her she didn't have to fight—whatever Nora told him really had worked—she still felt disconnected from him. He wanted justice. She wanted peace. Was there any common ground between those goals?

Is this meeting ever going to end? Deroga had no working clocks, so Zeisha didn't know how long she'd been waiting. It felt like forever, though it was probably more like two hours. *Will Eira insist I fight?*

The doorknob turned. Zeisha stopped pacing. Isla and three other militia members exited the building, chatting easily with each other. Besides Isla, Zeisha couldn't remember any of their names. *I trained with them for months. And we're strangers.*

Isla stopped next to Zeisha while the other militia members moved on. "Why didn't you come to the meeting?" Isla asked. "They asked for militia volunteers."

Zeisha tried to shrug casually. "I don't consider myself part of a militia anymore. I've had enough fighting."

"But this is our chance!" Isla took Zeisha's hand, as she'd done so many times in the middle of the night in that dark room. Her long, black hair caught the sun's light as she spoke animatedly. "After what the king did to us, I can't wait to open up the ground underneath his soldiers!"

Zeisha bit her lip as she imagined Isla using her talent to do just that. This side of Isla hadn't come out when they'd had their gentle, late-night conversations. She squeezed Isla's hand and gave her a smile. "We need people like you. It's just—that's not who I am."

"Isla!" one of the other militia members called. "Let's go eat!"

Zeisha looked over to where Isla's three companions had stopped to wait for her. "Go ahead." She gestured to the building. "I had an early lunch with Krey before the meeting."

"Okay." Isla let go of Zeisha's hand, gave her a quick hug, and jogged off to join the others.

Zeisha's chest felt hollow. During their short conversations in the dark each night, she and Isla had encouraged each other. But they hadn't really known each other. Now that they were free, Isla was making new friends, while Zeisha reconnected with Krey and got to know Nora and Ovrun. The connection the two girls had formed through those lonely nights had met their needs at the time. Maybe that was the extent of it. They were both moving on, in their own way.

At last, Krey, Nora, and Ovrun exited the building. Nora and Ovrun said hi to Zeisha, then excused themselves for an afternoon of hunting.

Krey gave Zeisha a sweet smile. "Sorry that took so long."

"It's okay. I know we both need to get back to our posts, but can you tell me about the meeting first?"

"Of course." He took her hand. "Let's go to the park."

Those words brought lightness to her heart. They'd only been here a week and a half, but the Star Clan's small, well-tended park was already their special place. When Zeisha was there with Krey, she could almost imagine they were in a park in Tirra, before all this mess began.

They entered the peaceful space and strolled along a gravel-lined path. "When the army returns," Krey said, "we won't go underground. We can't use the same hiding place twice. Anyone who's not fighting will split into groups of ten or twenty. They'll hide in the upper floors of unoccupied buildings. The trogs keep the ground floors of all the buildings in the vicinity swept clear of dust, so invading soldiers won't notice footprints." He turned his head to smile at Zeisha. "I found out what your hiding place will be. Before we go back to work, I'll show you."

The space that had felt empty in Zeisha's chest filled with warmth. "Thank you for not pushing me to fight."

He pulled her close, his body heat banishing the chill of the shade they stood in. "Nobody's going to make you do anything you don't want to do."

She stood there for a few minutes, soaking in the security of his words. At last, they resumed their walk. "What about those of you who are fighting? What's your plan?"

He smiled. "We'll take advantage of the trogs' knowledge of this city. Some of them are magic eaters, and many are experts with knives and swords. They'll hide on the streets—in shadows, building lobbies, even under old sewer grates. The king's soldiers won't know where anyone is. The trogs will jump out and wreak havoc as the army comes through."

Krey was grinning; he clearly loved this. He continued, "Archers and magic eaters will attack from windows. All the militia members will stay hidden in case the king comes with his army. We can't risk him controlling them again. Osmius will help however he can, but he'll have to stay out of the king's sight too. Taima, on the other hand, has already told Nora she's anxious to join the battle."

"How many of the trogs will fight?"

"Most of the adults and quite a few teens. Remember I told you about that young trog archer who almost hit me when I first sneaked into the city? Well, it turns out a lot of the kids start training with weapons when they're eight or nine years old. Younger teens will be stationed in the safest locations, of course.

And they won't be forced to fight. But most of them want to do their part."

Zeisha swallowed. *Most of them want to do their part.* The phrase punched her in the gut. Teenagers would fight while Zeisha stayed as far away as possible. *But is it really right for thirteen-year-olds to fight? No matter how passionate kids that age are, should they be allowed to risk their lives?*

She tried to smile at Krey. "What about you? What will you be doing?"

He stopped at a smooth, wooden bench. "Want to sit?"

"Sure."

He sat in the corner. She settled next to him, and he pulled her close. "Every clan will have sentries stationed on rooftops," he said. "They'll have messengers at their disposal. If anything changes in their territory, they'll get word to the other clans."

"So you'll be on a rooftop again?"

He pressed a kiss into her hair. "No, I'll fly above it all. Provide a bird's-eye view. I'll travel between the rooftop observers to spread information between all the clans."

Zeisha pulled back far enough to look in Krey's eyes. She spoke through a broad smile. "That sounds like a pretty safe job. You can fly high enough to avoid arrows or bullets."

Krey's eyes dropped. He pulled his bottom lip between his teeth.

Zeisha knew all his expressions. Her smile faltered. "What are you not telling me?"

His gaze lifted to meet hers. "They need me to fight too, Zeisha. Not just watch. I'll throw ice on the enemy, and I'll carry another magic eater on my back—possibly Nora. She and I have already worked together so much. She's arguing against that, of course. She hates flying with me. So I might take a militia member. We'll make sure we don't get close enough to the king for him to recognize them."

She nodded, not sure why the thought of him carrying someone else bothered her so much. "Besides Nora, who are you considering?"

"An ash eater or"—he swallowed—"or maybe a vine eater."

"Oh." It was barely a whisper. She cleared her throat. "One of the other vine eaters from the militia is really good."

"Almost as good as you," he said.

She pulled back, like he'd burned her. Was he really going to pressure her, after all this?

"Zei—" He took her hand, holding it between both of his. "I didn't mean anything by that. Well, I meant it, but just as a compliment. I wasn't saying you should come with me."

She nodded slowly. She believed him. But she also knew him. And she was certain that underneath all his words of support, he was fighting an unspoken longing for her to fly with him and use her magic against soldiers below.

He watched her with his brows furrowed, the single sign of his internal battle. If he were a less honorable guy, he'd beg her to fly with him during that battle. But he respected her enough not to make that request.

Why, then, was a small part of her considering the question he would not ask?

There were a million reasons, she supposed. She wanted to see his face break into a smile when she said yes. And after all the time they'd spent apart, she didn't want to be separated from him, especially during a battle.

Besides, she was afraid Krey was right. She had a talent, one she'd honed to violent perfection. Now that she had such a powerful ability, did she have any right to refuse to use it?

Krey cupped her cheeks in his hands. "I don't know what's going on in that mind of yours, but you need to do what's best for you. The meeting today didn't change that."

"I know." Zeisha stood, trying to push away the arguments that were battling for prominence in her head. "You said you'd show me the building I'll be hiding in."

With a smile that wavered just a bit, Krey stood. "Let's go."

8

*I've avoided writing about the security breach in the Therroan govern-
ment's systems. However, the story isn't going away, so I'll (reluc-
tantly) address it.*

*My friends and I have grown up with devices in our hands since before
we could talk. Adults, here's the difference between your generation
and mine: unlike you, we grew up knowing privacy is an illusion. I
suggest you make peace with it, as we have.*

-*"The Pretense of Privacy" By Genta Ril*
The Derogan Chronicle, *dated Quari 12, 6293*

ZEISHA, Nora, and the other female militia members entered their
bunkhouse. Along with the rest of the Star Clan, they'd woken early
for a battle drill. They hadn't gone to their assigned locations in case
the king had left soldiers behind to watch them. Instead, they'd met
on the main street and reviewed their plans.

Zeisha crawled into bed but didn't try to sleep. The drill had interrupted a dream, and she didn't want to return to it. It was the same nightmare she had every night. She'd used her vine to strangle a trog. Watched the light go out of his eyes.

She'd stopped asking Krey if she'd killed anyone. She knew the answer. While the dream was always the same, the victim shifted. Over and over, she'd seen two distinct, male faces. She'd be willing to bet she'd killed them both.

When the sky turned from black to gray, she slipped out of bed and quietly exited the building. By the time she arrived at the rooftop garden where she'd been assigned to work, the sky was pale orange.

Zeisha worked in silence for an hour or so before Kebi joined her. They'd been gardening together almost every day.

As Kebi knelt, she yawned. She laughed when Zeisha did the same. "All of Star Clan is tired after the drill."

Zeisha pulled her hands out of the soil. She eyed Kebi, who would be stationed in a window with a bow during the battle. "Are you nervous?"

"Yes," Kebi said simply. She dug her spade deep into the soil and carefully removed a weed with its roots. She looked up.

Zeisha realized she was still staring at her friend. Well, not *at* her exactly. She was staring into space, and Kebi's face happened to be in the way. She laughed and returned to her work. "Sorry."

"Zeisha," Kebi said, "you should not fight."

Zeisha blinked. "I . . . don't know about that. Maybe I should."

"When you use magic to make food then give that food to others, your face fills with light." Kebi pulled another weed, gave Zeisha a smile, and dug her spade into the ground. "If you use magic to hurt others, you will hurt yourself too."

"But you're going to use arrows to hurt others."

"I know. I am trained to do this since I am a child. I am scared, but I am ready. If you fight, will you be ready?"

"I don't know." Zeisha let out a long sigh. "I think we should change the subject."

Kebi laughed softly.

At the end of the day, Zeisha was sore but happy. She joined Nora, Ovrun, and Krey for dinner in the small dining room where the militia ate their meals. Afterward, she returned to her room and lay down. Without meaning to, she slept.

For once, her rest included no torturous dreams. When she woke, it was dark. The room was full of deep breathing and soft snores. Zeisha shuddered. The darkness and sounds reminded her of waking every night in the militia warehouse.

She'd known she shouldn't lie down right after dinner. Now she was wide awake in the middle of the night. Like she'd done the morning before, Zeisha rose and quietly walked outside. Now that the trog guards knew who she was, it was pretty safe to be out after dark. The moon's round face gave her just enough light to navigate.

She found herself on the Star Clan's residential street. As she reached the last of the occupied houses, a heavy blanket of exhaustion fell on her body, weighing her down. A large evergreen tree, with lush branches that blocked out the stars, grew in front of the first of a long line of vacant houses. Zeisha sat, resting her back on its trunk. She pulled her legs up to her chest and closed her eyes.

Something woke her from a light doze. She jerked her head up. Moonlight outlined a man walking up to the last occupied house. The man was probably coming home after a late shift as a guard or something.

He stopped at the door but couldn't seem to get in. From her spot several mets away, Zeisha heard the knob rattle. Was his key stuck?

The door opened—but the man didn't go in. Instead, he turned and bolted away before the person on the other side could see him. Candlelight illuminated a young boy in the doorway. "Hello?" the boy asked softly.

The man fled into the shadows between the child's house and the one Zeisha sat in front of. Zeisha froze. She couldn't see him, but she heard him breathing.

"Hello?" This time, the boy shouted the word.

The man darted back to the door and grabbed the child. The candle fell and went out. A moment later, the man had dragged the child in between the houses. Muffled screams reached Zeisha's ears.

Coherent thought fled her mind, replaced by sharp panic. Acting on instinct, she pulled bark off the tree, shoved it in her mouth, and chewed.

The man spoke in a low, gruff voice. "I'm gonna let you go, and you're gonna go inside. I don't want to hurt you. I don't want to hurt anyone. But you can't tell your parents you saw me. If you do, I'll—I'll come back and hurt your family. Just—just go to bed, kid. Go to bed. Got it?"

He must've gotten the response he wanted, because he and the boy exited their hiding place. Moonlight revealed the large man in silhouette, his hand over the child's mouth.

"Go," the man said.

The boy was free, but he didn't run. He stood, limbs frozen, and screamed, "Ma—"

The man tackled him to the ground, stifling his cry.

Zeisha didn't consider her options. Didn't think at all. Her hand rose. A strong vine shot out, reaching its target in barely more than an instant. The end coiled around the man's thick neck. Zeisha drew her hand back, pulling the vine tight.

The man's hands rose to his neck. Loud sobs emerged from the boy beneath him.

"Get off him!" Zeisha screamed in a voice so loud and raw, it seared her throat. The man didn't move. She pulled the vine tighter. *"Get off!"*

The man tumbled to the side. The child scrambled up and ran inside, crying the whole way.

Zeisha screamed the word she knew would bring trogs running: "Intruder!" She grabbed the vine with her free hand, then released its base from her other hand. The skin of her palm shrank back into place.

Pulling herself along the vine as if it were a rope, she approached the man. She knelt next to him. "You try anything, and you'll never breathe again." She released the vine just enough to let the man gasp. "Got it?"

"Yes."

Running footsteps and shouts approached from all sides. Men and women knelt next to Zeisha. Some of them bore lanterns.

"He wears an army uniform!" one of them shouted.

"Spy!" another cried.

Hands grabbed the man. Zeisha let go of the vine. Trogs flung questions at her. She couldn't answer, couldn't even look at the trogs. Her gaze remained on the man's neck, covered with marks from her vines. *Not again*, her mind cried. *Oh, God, not again.*

THE SEER: 3

Sarza was in a different room tonight. The large office had probably been used by some bigwig in charge of . . . whatever preday bigwigs were in charge of. From the window in here, she could see a trog residential street. She'd been watching it all night.

A bunch of people with lanterns were moving about. Sarza was too far away to make out many details, but she knew exactly what was happening. She'd seen it the day before in a crystal-clear vision. Another Cellerinian spy, some guy she'd never even seen until his stupid face showed up in her head, had just gotten himself arrested.

Her vision had consisted of two scenes. First, she saw the hungry man leaving the building where he'd holed up. He tried to find food, but he got caught by a vine eater. Then an alternate scene had played itself out: she found the soldier and warned him not to go out that night. He remained hungry, but he was safe.

Sarza often saw unchangeable future occurrences. Like the vision of her little brother dying—she couldn't have stopped that from happening, no matter what she did. But when she saw multiple versions of a scene, it meant the future was unsettled. She had power. She could choose any of the options she saw.

Sarza could've saved the guy who was, at this moment, being led away by angry trogs. But what would've been the point? She would've revealed herself to a stupid, bumbling soldier who'd probably have eventually gotten them both arrested. No, she'd chosen the best option: he needed to suffer his own consequences instead of pulling her down.

At least that was what she told herself. She'd done the right thing.

But there was this part of her—a quiet-yet-persistent part—that argued, *You're selfish, Sarza. You didn't want to deal with the complication of working with someone else. But what if you could've helped each other?*

Sarza slammed the door on that line of thinking. Her life had given her zero reason to partner with anyone on anything. That idiotic soldier was in charge of his own future. She was in charge of hers.

She lay down on an old, stinky rug in the center of the room, pulling her jacket tight around her. Time to sleep, not think.

But her mind kept returning to the captured soldier's frightened face.

9

Today I'd like to tell you about a woman named Chara Rigget. When Chara entered one of Therro's largest prisons at age twenty-two, she thought her life was over.

That was ten years ago. Last week, Chara was released. She already has a job as an accounting assistant for a Derogan food-packing company. She learned all the skills she needed for her new career while she was incarcerated.

-"Education Doesn't Just Happen in Schools" by Genta Ril
The Derogan Chronicle, *dated Quari 14, 6293*

"A SPY?" Nora asked.

"Yeah." Ovrun kept jogging, his pace quick. "Zeisha caught him. She's really upset. Eira sent someone to wake up Krey. He figured it might help if you and Isla were there too."

Nora tried to keep up with Ovrun. The women's sleeping quarters weren't far from Eira's office, but her tired body protested every step.

Next to Nora, Isla said, "I'm glad you woke us." Like all the former militia members, she was in great shape. She wasn't even breathing hard.

When they entered the small lobby of the Star Clan's administrative building, Nora caught her breath as she took in the scene. Zeisha and Krey were on a couch. He was holding her tightly, her face buried in his chest. He was murmuring something into her ear. Isla sat next to them and put her hand on Zeisha's back.

Eira stood a short distance away. Slumped shoulders betrayed her exhaustion. The lines of her face seemed to have deepened in the last two weeks.

Comfort Zeisha or talk to Eira? Nora took one step toward Zeisha before deciding if she were upset, she'd want one or two people around her, no more. She altered her route to approach Eira. Ovrun followed.

"What happened?" Nora asked.

"People hear shouting on a residential street," Eira said. "They find a man in an army uniform with a vine around his neck."

"Dead?" Ovrun asked.

"No. Conscious." She reviewed what they'd learned from a trog whose son the spy had briefly taken.

"Why was Zeisha there?" Nora asked.

"We hope she tells us soon."

Nora took a step closer to Eira. "Where is this spy? I want to talk to him."

"This is trog business," Eira replied.

"We're honorary members of your clan now, remember?" Ovrun's low voice was friendly. "Who better to interrogate him than Nora? He's more likely to talk to the princess of his own land than to a trog."

"Please take me to him," Nora said.

Eira eyed Nora and at last nodded. "Very well."

"I'd like Ovrun to come too," Nora said. "He's trained as a royal guard."

Eira's gaze took in Ovrun's form. "A guard. This does not surprise me." She picked up a lantern. "Come. Both of you."

They walked to a small, squat building two doors down. A man holding a sword stood at the front door. He nodded at Eira as they entered. She led Nora and Ovrun into the tiny lobby and down a shadowy staircase into a stark, damp basement lit by hanging lanterns. A male guard, probably not out of his teens, stood watch at the entrance. He stepped aside, letting them pass.

Pungent body odor filled Nora's nostrils. A dirty man who looked to be in his mid-twenties was the source. He sat on the floor, his suspicious gaze darting between his visitors. His hands were behind his back, a chain connecting them to a metal ring on the wall. He wore part of a Cellerinian Army uniform: black pants and a long-sleeved blue shirt. His black jacket lay nearby. The man's thick hair was cut close to his scalp, and untrimmed whiskers speckled his cheeks, chin, and upper lip.

As Eira talked quietly with the guard, Nora watched the spy. Her breaths quickened, along with her pulse. A flush warmed her skin. *This man represents everything wrong with Cellerin.* From what she'd seen during the attack, the army wasn't mind controlled like the militia had been. She doubted even her father had the ability to control a thousand people. The man before her had chosen to join the army. He'd vandalized trog territory and tackled a child. Nora's pulse quickened, and she tried to tamp down her anger.

Eira moved between Nora and the spy, speaking quietly so only Nora and Ovrun could hear her. "You may interrogate him. Soft cloth lines his restraints. Long chains allow him to move."

"Okay," Nora said, not sure what Eira was getting at.

Eira captured Nora's gaze. "We do not mistreat prisoners."

Ah. "Of course not."

"Return to my office when you finish." Eira turned and left.

Nora caught the guard's eye. He nodded and gestured with his hand for her to proceed. She stepped forward. "What is your name?"

He didn't answer.

Her eyes narrowed. "Do you know who I am?" she asked in a low voice.

Again, no response.

She stood taller. "I am Nora Abrios, Princess of Cellerin."

That got a reaction. The man's chains clanked as he sat up straighter.

"Tell me your name!" Nora's words, spoken in a commanding tone she'd learned from her father, echoed off the hard walls.

Silence.

Nora's reason dissipated like hot vapor. "Do you know what you're doing to Cellerin?" she shouted. "You're making it possible for my father to destroy our nation!"

The prisoner's eyes widened, but his mouth remained closed.

Nora got on her knees, right in front of him. "Do you know why I left home?"

The spy smirked. "Because you got bored in your big palace? You're a poor little princess who couldn't stand her life of luxury for one more second?"

His utter disdain transported Nora back to her moment of greatest helplessness.

Faylie. Her face above mine. Begging her to stop cutting my cheek. Cold eyes. Cold blade. Unimaginable pain.

Lost in the powerlessness of it all, Nora released whatever tendril of control she'd been grasping. She made a fist and drew it back.

Before she could swing, a strong hand grasped her bicep. She turned. Ovrun's wide eyes stifled her rage.

Reason suddenly returning, Nora gasped and skittered back. Ovrun released her. *What am I doing? What's wrong with me?* Her gaze fell on the spy. For the first time, she noticed the red marks on his neck. *He's injured and shackled, and I almost hit him!* Nora turned to the young guard, whose eyes were wide. "Go—fetch a healer," she commanded.

"Eira tells me one is on the way."

"Go check!" Horror at what she'd nearly done lent urgency to her words. "Can't you see he's hurt?"

"I'll guard him while you're gone," Ovrun said.

After a moment's hesitation, the guard departed.

No one spoke. Nausea seared Nora's stomach. She stood and ran to the stairs. Halfway up, she sat, breathing hard. Would she have punched that man if Ovrun hadn't stopped her? Self-loathing twisted her insides. She buried her face in her hands.

Strong arms encircled her. "It's okay," Ovrun said.

Nora tried to slow her breathing. It worked, sort of. After a couple of minutes, she was reasonably calm, though her stomach ached, and she couldn't stop shaking her head. "I don't know what happened to me in there."

Ovrun was still holding her tight, his hand rubbing her back in slow circles. "Same thing that happened to me during the battle with the militia. Remember you had to stop me from strangling someone?"

Nora nodded.

"I guess I was returning the favor."

"Thank you."

They sat quietly. Before long, the guard arrived with a blood lyster, the same one who'd healed Nora after Faylie cut her. The healer finished a few minutes later. He stopped on a step below Nora and Ovrun. "I heal his neck," he said before continuing up the stairs.

"You need to go back in there," Ovrun murmured.

"That's the very last thing I need to do."

"You'll be fine. I'll be with you. If I see you losing control, I'll pick you up and throw you over my shoulder."

Despite everything, she grinned. "I might like that."

Ovrun rolled his eyes. "You're definitely back to normal. Come on."

Inside, Nora sat on the floor, a respectful distance away from the prisoner. She pinned the spy with her gaze. He didn't look up. "I shouldn't have gotten so angry," Nora said. "I'm sorry." She hadn't expected a response, and she didn't get one. She took a deep breath. "I left home because my father has lost control of his own mind."

Without disclosing the secret of brain lysting, Nora told the spy about the king's mind-controlled militia. About halfway through, he lifted his head and locked his gaze on hers. Gone was his derision; his mouth gaped as he took in every word.

When Nora finished recalling how she'd freed the militia, the man said, "I don't believe a word of that. You may not like your father, but he's a good king. He wouldn't abduct magic eaters to make some mind-controlled army. That's . . . that doesn't happen. Magic doesn't work that way."

Nora bit back the snarky remark she wanted to say. Instead, she said in a level voice, "Maybe you're right. The king you know wouldn't do that. Would the king you know invade the trogs and command his soldiers to vandalize the city?"

The prisoner didn't answer.

Nora continued, "Would the king you know attack New Therro with no warning and force all the men in that province to join the army?"

"We never did that."

"*You* didn't, because you're here," Nora said. "The rest of your army invaded New Therro four days after they left Deroga."

"Everything Nora told you is true," Ovrun said. "I was a royal guard. I lost my job because I was trying to help her track down the militia she told you about."

"If it's true," the spy said, "why would you tell me all this?"

Nora hesitated. She'd thought this man might switch sides if he realized his king was no longer worth following. *Probably messed that up when I screamed at him and nearly punched him.*

All she could do was respect him now. She spoke calmly, eyes locked on his. "I just wanted you to know the whole story. I think you deserve that." She drew in a deep breath. "Listen, what the army did to the trogs . . . I didn't realize how mad that made me until I came in here and saw you sitting there. What you did was wrong." Teeth clenched, she shook her head. "But I've done things I regret too. It's never too late to step off the path of injustice and choose another way."

The man watched her. Silence stretched so long, Nora gave up hope of getting a response.

As she and Ovrun walked toward the door, the spy called out, "My name is Elo Golsch. And the only reason I went to that house was because I'm hungry."

Nora turned. "We'll get you some food."

"Thank you."

Those two words sparked hope in Nora's chest.

Zeisha sipped tea from a clay mug. She'd reached the part of her story that she didn't want to tell, and she needed a moment to prepare.

The door opened to reveal Nora and Ovrun.

"Come in," Eira said. "Sit."

As they settled on the floor by the couch, Zeisha drew in a deep breath. Krey's warm hand was on her knee. She took it and held it tightly. In a shaking voice, she described why and how she'd attacked the spy, concluding, "I told him if he tried anything, I'd kill him. Lots of people came running, and, well . . . you know the rest."

"I'm sorry you had to do that," Nora said.

"Thank you," Zeisha whispered through a tight throat.

"I'm sorry too." Krey's voice drew her eyes to him. "But I'm also proud of you. You used your talent for good. You did the right thing."

His words were a salve to her heart.

"Zeisha," Eira said, "You may return to bed now, if you wish."

"I'd like to hear Nora and Ovrun's report." Zeisha managed a smile for her two new friends.

"Very well."

Nora recounted her conversation with the spy. "He wasn't sure whether to believe me," she concluded, "but he did listen. If you're kind to him, I think he'll keep listening. Maybe he'll even help us eventually. Oh, and he needs food. And a basin and sponge and some clean clothes."

"I already send someone to fetch all those items for him," Eira said. "Now, back to bed. All of you."

In the street, Krey quietly guided Zeisha away from the others.

"Where are we going?" she whispered.

"Our park."

She smiled and took his hand.

They walked along the park's dark path, laughing when they ran into errant tree branches. After a little while, they stopped. Krey leaned against a wide tree trunk and pulled Zeisha close to him. He kissed the top of her head. "You okay?"

She pulled in a deep breath. An image of the spy's neck flashed in her mind again. "I'm not sure."

"What you did tonight was good. Really good." After a pause, he added, "Did I mention I'm proud of you?"

She lifted her head, though she couldn't see him well in the darkness. "You did."

Krey brought a hand to her cheek, then slowly slid it into her hair. She let out a sigh. She needed him to kiss her, to smother this night's memories with his lips.

He didn't. She let some time pass—probably only a few seconds, though it felt like longer—then grabbed his face with both hands and pressed her lips to his. He let out a low laugh, one Zeisha felt more than she heard. Something about that laugh sent heat shooting through her. Her lips parted, and he responded with passion that matched hers. She pressed closer, relishing the rise and fall of his chest against hers. Her fingers dug into his hair.

Sooner than she'd have preferred, Krey released her lips and rested his forehead against hers. "You," he said, his voice low and a little growly, the tone that always threatened to buckle her knees.

She laid her head on his shoulder, trying to catch her breath. So much about her life recently had been all wrong. The king and his people had used her for her magic, stealing months of her life. She'd turned into a powerful, cruel magic eater—someone she no longer recognized.

But this—being here with Krey—this was right. With him holding her, the horror over her actions faded into the background. The way he'd looked at her, she could almost believe that what she'd done tonight was right. Krey's pride in her was contagious.

All at once, the fullness of his sacrifices for her slammed into her, renewing her breathlessness. He'd left home to live at the palace with a king he'd never trusted, just so he could find her. He'd gotten arrested, then gotten fired. He'd fled to an ancient city, where he'd fought a battle that could've killed him.

All for her.

Something in Zeisha's heart shifted in an instant, catching her off guard. Instinct told her to be cautious, but by the stone, she was tired of questioning herself. She needed to adjust to her new power . . . to her new life. It was time to push away her doubts.

Zeisha pulled back, took both of Krey's hands, and looked up at his face. Dawn must be on its way; she could make out his features now. "I'm going to fight," she said. "With you." When his eyes widened, she smiled. "You look as surprised as I feel."

"I told you—Zei, you don't have to do this."

"I know. I want to. I didn't think I would ever want to . . . but I do." She couldn't pinpoint why, but she knew it was true.

"Are you sure?"

She nodded, her heart feeling lighter by the second. "I'll be the vine eater on your back. You're gonna have to practice flying with me though."

He grinned. "You have no idea how much I've been looking forward to that."

"We could go now. Do you have any feathers?"

"A few, in my pocket. But—" He let go of her, ran his hands over his face, and chuckled. "I've told you what it's like for me. I feel the person who's on my book."

"I know. You incorporate them into your magic. You told me that."

"Yeah, but I'll feel *all* of you." He pulled her closer. She clasped her fingers behind his neck. His hands slid down her sides, coming to rest on her waist. "Every single part," he said, speaking in that low voice again.

Her breaths quickened again. Heat prickled the skin of her neck and ears. "Oh." It was more of a breath than a word.

His mouth found her ear. "I don't think I could handle that right now. As much as I'd like it."

She resisted the urge to kiss him again, knowing his lips would snip any thread of self-control she had left. Instead, she let out a soft laugh. "You're killing me, Krey. You know that, right?"

He pulled her into his chest and held her close as the sun rose.

10

Humans have been on Anyari for over six millennia. We've become so enlightened. We long ago left behind our lesser tendencies: inequality and injustice, scams and slavery.

Right?

Yesterday, I flew over Deroga in a glidecraft. I saw the fenced estates of our rich and the small houses of our poor. Sure, everyone has their basic needs met, but beyond that, only the rich enjoy the greatest privilege of all: unlimited options.

-*"Inequality in Equality" by Genta Ril*
The Derogan Chronicle, *dated Quari 15, 6293*

OVRUN APPROACHED the campfire where he'd agreed to spend the evening with his friends and several militia members. His stomach growled when he smelled bread cooking.

Krey stood as Ovrun approached. "Where have you been?"

"Exercising." Stalking shimshims through city streets didn't provide the level of activity Ovrun was used to. He couldn't let himself grow soft. He'd found a grassy area where he could do push-ups, planks, and other exercises to his heart's content. "Guess I lost track of time." He looked around. "Where's Nora?"

"She left a few minutes ago. She's about to go meet with Hatlin."

"Damn it, I forgot that was tonight!" Ovrun was sleepy, and he knew Nora was too. They hadn't gotten much rest the night before, thanks to their encounter with the Cellerinian spy. But sleep could wait. Tonight, he wanted to go on a dragon ride with her.

He ran toward the street where she'd told him Osmius would pick her up. It was too dark to see much of anything. "Nora?" he called.

From down the street, her voice rang out. "Ovrun, is that you?"

"Don't leave yet!" He sprinted down the middle of the street. Soon, in the light of a half-moon, he spied Nora and the dragon. He halted next to them.

Nora stepped close and lifted her face. "Came to say goodbye?"

"Actually"—he gave her a quick peck—"I came to see if I can come with you." He pulled his shirt away from his damp skin. "If you don't mind some sweaty company."

Nora wrinkled her nose. "I'm used to it. It's Osmius you should be worried about. If he's offended, he might incinerate you."

Ovrun laughed. "Sounds more like something Taima would do. Seriously, can I come?"

"Hang on." Nora paused, then said, "Osmius says it's fine. Despite your sweat."

She climbed up the dragon's textured scales, then lay on her belly, her arms and legs wide, knees bent. "Come on up," she said.

Ovrun climbed up behind her and assumed a similar position, though he had to hold his arms even wider since he didn't have a neck to hold. Once his fingers and the toes of his boots were wedged between Osmius's dark scales, he told Nora he was ready.

They took to the air. The only other time Ovrun had ridden on a dragon was after he, Nora, and Krey had rescued Taima, Osmius's mate. For the first leg of that flight, Ovrun was barely conscious, having sustained a gunshot wound. They stopped and visited a healer, but when Ovrun returned to the dragon's back, he was still in pain. He'd survived the flight to Deroga, rather than enjoying it.

Now, his arm didn't bother him beyond an occasional dull ache. He embraced the thrill of flying on a massive reptid's back. As Osmius spiraled higher into the cold sky, Ovrun laughed and called to Nora, "Tell him thank you for taking me!"

A moment later, she turned her head and shouted over the wind. "I told him! What made you decide to come?"

"Just wanted time with you!"

She smiled and turned to face forward again. It was hard holding a conversation while flying. Ovrun relaxed into Osmius's firm back and considered Nora's question.

He did want time with her, but a deeper desire, one he hadn't quite named yet, had driven him here. He pulled at the strings of his thoughts, trying to figure out what that desire was.

His eyes rested on the girl in front of him. She'd naturally become a leader in Deroga, but it was different from palace leadership. The trogs didn't care that the king of Cellerin was her father. Only occasionally did her role as a princess matter—like when she'd stayed with Eira during the invasion and when she'd interrogated the spy.

It mattered now too. She understood the ins and outs of government in a way no one else in Deroga did—not even Krey, with his head for strategy. Nora knew what questions to ask Hatlin and what to make of the answers.

Tonight, Nora was truly a princess. Ovrun wanted to know that part of her.

He and Nora had formed a shallow friendship at the palace but hadn't become close until she'd fled her home. Hiding in Deroga, she was just a girl, and he was just a guy. As much as he loved that, he knew it would eventually change again.

Nora would be queen.

She could argue that she didn't want power and that no one knew their future. But something told Ovrun Nora was made to lead their nation. This beautiful girl, whose long legs were currently holding tight to a dragon, would live in her luxurious palace again. He couldn't guarantee it, but he *felt* it.

If she married a man and became queen, her husband would be king. She was the heir, so she'd be in charge, but her king would still have power. He'd be expected to help lead.

Ovrun didn't want such a role. He'd never dreamed of leading the palace guard, much less the country. When Nora had asked him once what he wanted to do with his life, he'd painted an idyllic picture of being a quiet family man, living on a little plot of land, working hard and loving his wife and kids.

That was still what he wanted. Problem was, the more he got to know Nora, the more he wanted *her*. It went beyond physical attraction. He genuinely liked her—her laugh, determination, and unending quest for adventure.

Lately, when he thought about sitting on a quiet porch while several cute kids played in the front yard, he pictured Nora sitting next to him. He imagined that one of those kids would have her wide eyes, and another would have her glossy, straight hair.

If he could convince himself that scene was even a remote possibility, he'd succumb to his heart in an instant. For some time now, its rhythm had beat out an insistent message, telling him it wanted more than anything to fall in love with this passionate, funny, ice-making, dragon-speaking girl.

If he hadn't seen the downfall of thoughtless passion in his mother's life, he'd be giving his heart free rein. Instead, he forced himself to embrace logic, which told him Nora's path would soon veer far from his.

Unless . . . unless his own future could somehow line up with hers.

That was what this flight was about, he realized now. It wasn't about spending time with Nora, the girl he cared for. It was about spending time with Her Royal Highness Princess Ulminora Abrios. He'd experienced royal life as a guard. An underling. Today, he'd experience it at the princess's side. As an equal.

Was he trying to persuade himself he'd make a good king? Did he hope Nora's actions would prove she wasn't meant to be queen? Was he just trying to know her better, understand this girl he'd fallen for?

I don't know. I need to be here, but I'm not sure why.

Ovrun shook his head, rubbing his cheek against the dragon's smooth scales. All this introspection was getting him nowhere. Maybe he'd understand the trip's purpose more when it was over. For now, he could enjoy riding through the cold skies of Cellerin, warming himself by thinking about Nora. It wasn't too hard with her this close to him.

At last, they landed just beyond a little grove of trees, a couple of mets north of the Eastern Road that connected Cellerin City to Deroga. A man was waiting, holding a single candle. Nora and Ovrun slid off Osmius's back and approached.

"Hatlin," Nora said, her voice calm and confident, "this is Ovrun. He helped free the militia."

Hatlin shifted on his feet. He grunted something that might've been "Hello," but his eyes were fixed behind his visitors.

"The dragon won't bite," Nora said, laughter in her voice. "He also won't incinerate you."

"Well." Hatlin cleared his throat. An awkward silence fell.

"Would it help if the dragon wasn't here?" Nora asked.

"I, ah . . ." He seemed to have lost most of his ability to speak.

A few seconds later, Osmius flew off. "Better?" Nora asked.

"Better," Hatlin confirmed, his voice stronger now. "Listen, Princess, I don't have a lot to share today. The army's still training outside New Therro. They've recruited more soldiers. Good news for you is, I think it'll be a while before they're ready to fight."

Nora's brows lifted. "Why's that?"

Hatlin shook his head, chuckling. "Those soldiers have no idea what they're doing. You know how the Cellerinian Army has always worked. Weekend drills a couple of times a month. From what I've heard, a lot of those trainings got cancelled. And when they did meet, nobody learned much of anything. Hell, if my people knew how incompetent the army was, they might've done a better job standing up to them. It's scary when hundreds of people in uniform come at you with weapons. Guess they didn't notice the uniforms were full of idiots."

"Are they getting any more skilled?" Nora asked.

"Sure, a little. They're doing some serious training now. But word is, a lot of our guys, the ones who got forced into the army, they aren't trying real hard. They don't want to fight. We're trying to work out a way for them to revolt, but the planning's slow going." He shrugged helplessly. "Now, what's going on in Deroga?"

"I'd like you to get a message to the army's leaders," Nora said. "See if they're willing to talk to the trogs."

"They want to negotiate? After the army vandalized their city?"

Ovrun was as surprised as Hatlin. He hadn't heard about this request.

"Well, not negotiate, exactly." Nora sounded hesitant. "Between you and me, the trogs aren't willing to give up any of their freedom. They just want to convince the army this fight isn't worth it. Cellerin doesn't need Deroga. They don't need the space or the people, and it's not like the trogs would bring a lot of wealth to the country. Cellerinian citizens will die if they fight the trogs. It won't be worth it."

Hatlin let out a long breath. "I've been flying almost every night. Can we sit?"

"Sure," Nora said.

They sat in the dirt, facing each other.

Hatlin leaned forward. Flickering candlelight shone on his blood-shot eyes. "Here's the thing. One of my sources told me most of the officers agree with you—fighting trogs is pointless. But they're not the ones making the calls." His gaze didn't swerve from Nora's face.

"My father is," Nora said softly.

"Yep. The only person whose opinion counts is your daddy. And there's no way he's giving up on his plans. No way at all."

Nora's shoulders drooped. "That wouldn't have been the case in the past. Before he . . ." She trailed off.

"Before he what?"

Nora bit her lip and looked off to the side.

"Listen," Hatlin said, his voice now edged with annoyance. "I don't have the time to fly out here and meet with children every week, but I told you I'd do it anyway. You think I'm gonna share information with you if you're holding back? You tell me what you know. I'll do the same. Do we have a deal?"

Nora sat up straighter and met Hatlin's gaze again. In a calm, clear voice, she explained her father's brain-lysting capabilities. Krey had told Hatlin that the militia was mind controlled, but he'd never explained how that worked.

Hatlin's mouth dropped open within the first minute of Nora's explanation. When she finished, he licked his lips, swallowed, and shook his head. "Damn. I'm, uh . . . I'm glad to know that. Damn."

Nora nodded. "We probably should've told you before."

"Yeah, you should've. But at least I know now." One of his thick eyebrows rose. "I've got time to warn a New Therroan who's gonna start working in the palace tomorrow."

Nora leaned forward. "You're planting someone in the palace?"

"Yeah. She'll clean the offices at night." He tapped his temple. "She's sharp. And she's one of our few magic eaters. Dirt eater—good at it too. She's keeping her talent secret."

Nora spoke in a tense whisper. "She can't let my father touch her."

Hatlin nodded. "I'll tell her." He reached into his coat pocket and pulled out a handful of feathers. "I should go." He shoved the feathers in his mouth and blew out his candle.

They stood, said quick goodbyes, and agreed to meet again the next week. Hatlin flew off.

Nora's gaze lifted to the sky as they waited for Osmius. Ovrun watched her, admiring the way the moonlight outlined her profile. Her jaw was firm, her eyes focused and steady. He reached out and took her hand in his, lacing their fingers together. "You're so beautiful. And so strong."

She grinned, her face relaxing as she turned to him and wrapped her arms around his waist. "I could say the same about you."

She laid her head on his shoulder, and he stroked her hair. This Nora—relaxed limbs, her breaths timed to match his—she fit him perfectly.

The Nora who could easily negotiate with a trog leader four times her age or a man more than twice her size? Well, he admired her. To be honest, her confidence was a turn-on. Yet he still wasn't sure he *knew* her. And while she certainly fit in his arms, he wasn't sure he fit at her side.

He held her tighter, trying to find the words to express his concerns. *Do you think there's any way we can make this work? Give me some hope here, Nora, because my future is slipping through my fingers.*

He bit back the words. He'd felt the stress of Nora's responsibilities slide off her as soon as his arms came around her. No way was he going to throw another problem her way. *Hey, Princess, I know you're trying to keep your kingdom together, but can you also take a minute to figure out our relationship?* He couldn't do that to her.

"Osmius is coming," Nora murmured.

Ovrun let go of her. He couldn't help but feel this trip had been a failure.

11

Next year, Derogan schools will no longer have pallaball teams. I haven't seen students get so angry since our cafeteria stopped serving coffee.

My opinion on this matter won't make me popular, but I'm paid to be honest, so here goes. Every year, ten percent of student pallaball athletes are injured. It's time we move past such violent sports.

You know where no one gets injured? The library. Turn the old pallaball court into a second library, and we'll all be much happier.

At least I will be.

-*"Trade Sports for Books" by Genta Ril*
The Derogan Chronicle, *dated Quari 17, 6293*

"We are trogs!" Eira's voice filled the air over the Star Clan's fighting force of teens and adults.

The words made Nora shiver, which was odd, considering she wasn't a trog. But standing here, in front of the large warehouse where the militia had been housed, she could pretend she was truly part of this clan.

From atop a small platform, Eira cried, "Trogs are brave! Trogs are fierce!" The crowd cheered, but she held up her hand, quieting them. "Trogs remember." Her voice turned more thoughtful, just loud enough to reach those in the back. "We live in Deroga to remember those who come before. Those who live here when every street is full. The rest of Anyari may forget. Trogs remember." Again, she shouted. "Will we let anyone rule us? Turn us into those who do not remember?"

"No!" the crowd cried.

"Will we let new leaders force their new-city ways on us?"

"No!"

"Trogs, will we fight?"

"Yes!"

"Today, we train!" Eira shouted. "When they come, we will be ready!"

When the cheers died down, the white-haired trog directed people to their practice locations. Those who had experience with bows left for an archery field. Ovrun waved to Nora as he jogged away. Experts with knives and swords moved down the street to drill and spar. Nora watched them go, wondering if arrows and blades would be enough. *Too bad we don't have more guns.*

What they did have were lysters, both trog and former militia. Nora ran ahead and met them all at the warehouse's large, open bay doors. Eira had asked her to organize this part of the training. "There's fuel inside," Nora said. "There's even a bowl of shimshim blood for the healers, in case anyone gets hurt. Everybody eat up, then come back to the street to practice."

She smiled as they all rushed in. Traditionally, trogs practiced their weapons or magic individually or in small groups. After meeting with Hatlin two days before, Nora had encouraged Eira to start public training days. "There may be more spies out there," she'd said. "We want them to tell their officers just how capable trogs are. It may not keep the army away, but it'll mess with their minds."

"I know not if the army will hear of it," Eira had said, "but it will be good for us. It will bring us together." She'd even passed along the suggestion to the other clans.

Nora was about to enter when she realized Zeisha was still standing outside. "Is it tough, thinking about going back in there?" Nora asked.

Eyes wide as she gazed into the big space, Zeisha nodded.

A couple of the other former militia members in the room were hanging back, looking around with nervous expressions. Most of them, however, had rushed to a line of chests along one wall. "Check out all this fuel!" Isla cried. She was scooping soil out of a chest, shoving it in her mouth with a huge smile. Nearby, a trog watched her enthusiasm with a scowl.

Turning back to Zeisha, Nora said, "We came here because there's still a lot of fuel left from when . . . you were using it before. But we could always move the chests to another building for our next training session."

Zeisha shook her head, blinking rapidly. "It's . . . it's fine. I guess we should fuel up too, right?"

"Probably so." Nora smiled.

Zeisha returned the gesture, but it looked forced. They both walked in but didn't get far when Zeisha stopped. Her chest rose and fell rapidly as her head swiveled, taking in the whole room.

Ahead, Krey was approaching the fuel chests. Nora jogged up to him.

"I don't suppose we have any ice," he said.

"Actually, we do." Nora pointed at a chest that was smaller than the others. "Eira gave us some from the little icehouse at the butcher." Noting Krey's slight shudder, she suppressed a laugh. He'd made it clear many times how much he hated being around dead animals. He'd cook the meat, but he didn't want to be around when she was cleaning a shimshim.

But she hadn't approached him to talk about fuel or the butcher. She touched his arm. He turned. "Zeisha won't say it out loud," she murmured, "but she doesn't want to be here."

Krey sighed. "I should've thought of that myself. I'll talk to her. And I'll say it so you don't have to: I'm an ass." He gave her a rueful smile then stepped toward Zeisha.

Nora approached the ice chest. Four militia members and several trogs were already there, fueling up. "Do we have more than this?" someone asked her.

"No, but I'll get us more later this week." She'd already communicated with Osmius. He'd agreed to pick her up early on Friday, well before her meeting with Hatlin. He'd fly her to get more ice in the mountains.

Nora was almost done fueling when she noticed Zeisha and Krey kneeling next to a nearby chest. Zeisha was putting a piece of bark in her mouth, laughing at something Krey had said. Nora smiled and returned to fueling up. Before long, Krey joined her.

"Is she okay?" Nora asked.

"I think so. She's always loved using her talent, but it makes her nervous now. She doesn't get how the other militia members can be excited to be back here. She could barely walk in the building."

"I hope you told her everyone handles hard times differently, and it's okay that she's struggling."

"I did, or something like that. I'm not a complete idiot, you know."

"Just a partial one?"

He chuckled. After eating a handful of ice, he said, "I'm hoping today will be good for her. Nothing stressful, just having fun with magic."

Stomach full of ice, Nora moved away from the chest so others could finish fueling up. It felt good to get fuel back in her system, to feel the chill it sent through her body. At the same time, a seed of dread was growing in her gut as she thought about using her magic.

The last time she'd lysted, she'd formed a spike, hard as the stone itself. It had sliced her throat as she sent it toward—

No. We're here to have fun. I'm not going to ruin that with bad memories.

Over half the lysters had already gone outside to start practicing. Nora was waiting for Krey and Zeisha. But it wouldn't hurt to get a little head start, right?

She walked as quietly as she could, stopping just behind Krey. Dropping to a crouch, she catalyzed a little bit of fuel, forming cold, perfect snow in her throat. She opened her mouth and blew it on Krey's neck.

He yelped—complete with an adolescent-sounding voice crack—and leapt to his feet, pivoting to face her. "You suck," he said.

"Ooh, such an amazing insult."

In a flash, his hand came up, stopped in front of her neck, and sent out a cascade of tiny ice balls. Some bounced off her neck and onto the floor. Others slid into her shirt, tracing frigid, wet lines down her warm skin. Her squeal seemed to bounce off every surface in the big room.

Krey's uproarious laughter was interrupted when two vines grabbed his hands and pulled them behind his back. He swayed, nearly falling, and turned wide eyes on Zeisha, who'd sneaked up behind him. She gave him a big, sweet smile.

Nora snorted with laughter. "Well done." She draped an arm around Zeisha's shoulders and led her outside.

Krey followed, shouting, "Get these things off me!"

In the last couple of weeks, the trogs' reactions to the so-called *new-city folk* had varied. Nora and her friends had gradually gained Eira's trust. A few trogs, like Zeisha's friend Kebi, had reached out in genuine friendship. Many, however, were wary or outright hostile.

But as the lysters—trog and new-city folk alike—trained together, something changed. Nora, Krey, and Zeisha set the tone with their impromptu ice-vine fight. When they joined the others outside, they brought along an atmosphere of fun.

Streams of fire vaporized ice balls in mid-flight. Krey, the only feather eater, gave people daring rides that made them scream—some in fear and others in glee. Soil lysters like Isla softened and hardened dirt with precise timing, locking people's feet and ankles in the ground. Zeisha and other plant lysters kept their vines away from necks, instead tying people up or tripping them. Stone lysters sent clouds of tiny rocks into other lysters' hands, interrupting their magic. The whole time, there was plenty of laughter—and enough scrapes, bruises, and mild burns to keep the two blood lysters busy.

The trogs had good reason to be leery of the newcomers. During the battle two weeks ago, the mind-controlled militia had killed several members of the Star Clan. Since then, Nora had been relieved every time she'd seen trogs displaying any trust in their new neighbors.

Today's magical training was further shifting the dynamic between both groups. There was a lot of talent on this street. The eyes of magic eaters from both Deroga and Cellerin slowly filled with respect. People started asking for, and giving, advice. At one point, Nora saw a trog holding a militia member's hand, explaining his magical method.

Lysters gradually ran out of fuel. They left the street in groups containing trogs and new-city folk, their laughter ringing in the air long after their magic disappeared.

THE SEER: 4

Sarza lay on a dirty rooftop, waiting for stragglers in the street below to leave so she could stand and stretch.

She had to admit, the training she'd felt urged to watch was impressive. Some of those magic eaters . . . *wow*. How had trogs gotten so good at throwing vines and making fire?

One of the magic eaters was the straight-haired teenager Sarza had seen riding a dragon in an earlier vision. Despite her age, she'd led the training.

Then again, that girl hadn't been the only young magic eater in the street. A large percentage had looked like they were around Sarza's age. Had trogs given birth to a bunch of extra-talented babies nearly two decades ago? Or did they somehow recruit a bunch of crazy, young magic eaters to help them fight the king?

Now that was an interesting possibility.

Sarza rubbed her eyes. She'd gotten up before the sun to lie on this cold rooftop. When she saw a male feather eater flying low over the street, she'd crammed herself between two metal cubes that were bolted to the roof. They probably covered some sort of preday machinery. Then she'd covered herself in a blanket she'd brought, to make it less likely that the flyer would spot her. All wrapped up, she was a little too cozy. If she wasn't careful, she'd fall asleep right—

A brief sense of brain pressure alerted her to an incoming vision. She closed her eyes, and it began.

She was far above Deroga, watching Cellerinian soldiers advance on the city. It was dark, but she could see everything in perfect, grayscale detail. The army had grown. Its ranks appeared organized. Most of the soldiers didn't wear coats, and trees boasted plenty of fronds and leaves. *Springtime.*

Sarza's view changed, zooming in on trog territory, where residents moved through the dark streets quickly and with purpose. She soaked in every detail: archers ascended to the tops of tall buildings, teenagers with knives hid in shadowed areas, magic eaters fueled up and entered abandoned buildings. They were preparing for guerilla warfare.

Her focus shifted to a group of mostly kids and old people. In her mind, she followed them into a building. They navigated to a room that had a hole in the floor. One by one, they climbed down a ladder into an underground tunnel. They jogged a hundred mets or so, then ascended a ladder into another building. After climbing many flights of stairs, they huddled together in a big, windowless room, the elderly folks comforting the kids.

The vision continued, showing her more hiding places for civilians and combatants alike. At last, Sarza returned to awareness, every detail stamped on her brain.

She'd been considering leaving the city soon to meet with her contact in the suburbs. But she didn't want to go until she was sure she had some truly impressive information, enough for the army's officers to give her a ridiculous promotion and a life-changing pay raise. *This is that kind of information. I'll tell them I've been watching the trogs do battle drills, and that's how I have so many details. That's plausible.*

She couldn't leave the city until dark. Hell, she probably shouldn't even leave this rooftop until then. Might as well make the best of it and plan out what she'd tell her contact. Sarza opened her mouth, ready to practice her story in a soft whisper.

Her teeth snapped shut, clenching so tightly, she couldn't have pried them apart with a metal bar.

No! She tried to speak through her clenched teeth, but she couldn't get out any words about what she'd seen. All she managed to force out were several hissed curse words.

She stopped trying, knowing her efforts would be fruitless. She'd experienced this type of prophecy plenty of times. As a kid, she'd called them *super-secret visions*. A few years back, she'd taken off the *super* part. It sounded dumb. But calling the prophecies *secret visions* didn't make them any less annoying.

She was incapable of speaking a secret vision out loud. If she wanted to get it off her chest by talking to herself, she was out of luck. She'd tried journaling, but her hand cramped, not allowing her to write.

Now, after so many years, she finally had a vision worth sharing—and it was a secret vision? What was the point of seeing the future if she couldn't do anything about it?

Sarza let out a long sigh. Again, she closed her eyes, trying to block out conversations on the street below. Maybe if she was lucky, she'd have another vision up here—one she could actually use.

Or maybe she'd just take a nap.

12

People say my generation is complacent. We've grown up with incredible technology. They think we take it for granted.

Perhaps we do, but we still dream. Yes, I can control a flexscreen with my voice, but I dream of doing so with my mind. Yes, I can board a solarplane and fly across the world, but I dream of strapping on wings and soaring like a bird.

-"Dreams Haven't Died" by Genta Ril
The Derogan Chronicle, *dated Quari 18, 6293*

ALL AROUND, people were leaving the street in front of the warehouse, going back to whatever else they had planned for the sunny Sunday afternoon. Krey grinned at Zeisha. "How did that feel? Using your magic?"

"It was fun—really fun."

He took her hand. "I have an idea. I need to grab more feathers from the warehouse. You can wait out here."

"No, I'll come with you."

He raised his eyebrows. "If you want to."

Inside, Krey refilled the pouch of feathers he kept in his sleeve, then stuffed more fuel in all his pockets. The chest was nearly full and should last him weeks, if not months. It would be nice not to have to hunt for feathers anymore. He turned back to Zeisha. "Ready to—"

Her expression stifled his enthusiasm. She was somber, staring across the room. "Something tells me that's the room where we slept," she said, pointing at a closed door.

"Do you want to go in there?"

She turned her head sharply toward him, her eyes wide. "No!"

"Okay." He took her hand, and her fingers squeezed his so tight it hurt. "Let's get out of here," he said. As soon as they stepped outside, her grip on his hand loosened.

The street was mostly empty, though a few trogs and militia members lingered, chatting. Krey turned to Zeisha, relieved when she gave him a smile. "Guess what time it is?" he asked.

"Lunchtime?"

He laughed. "If you want. But I was hoping we could fly first."

Her smile broadened and her eyebrows leapt up. "Yes! What do I need to do?"

"After I fuel up, you'll hop on my back and hold on tight."

A few minutes later, Krey had eaten his fill of feathers. He turned and crouched. Zeisha got on his back, wrapping her arms around his shoulders and squeezing his waist with her knees.

He stood and activated his magic.

Then he stopped breathing.

Zeisha was the most beautiful person he knew. He loved her full lips, smooth skin, and hourglass figure. He'd seen that figure in clothes both baggy and snug. He'd kissed her hundreds, maybe thousands, of times. He'd held her hand and caressed her face.

But now—oh, by the very stone, she was part of him, enveloped in his magic, and he sensed every single bit of her. Not just the way her shirt and pants clung to her—something he'd always admired—but the skin underneath, mind-bendingly soft and curved. She had ripples and dimples and rolls, every one of them entrancing. She'd gained muscle during her time in the militia, and he admired those bands of strength beneath the flesh of her legs, waist, arms, and back.

But her muscles didn't snag his attention and imagination for long. His focus traveled, like an arrow, to the parts of her that were *hers* alone, places he'd never touched or seen. And as delightful as it was to be so suddenly introduced to the fullness of who Zeisha was, Krey felt like his magic had turned him into a voyeur . . . and quite possibly the biggest jerk ever. He forced his thoughts to move elsewhere.

Her neck. That was safe, right? But oh, had he ever noticed how the hollow of her brown neck was so perfectly rounded, how it could hold a drop of bollagrape juice in its soft little bowl? And if there were juice there, he could taste—

No, no, no, change direction. Her hair. Krey had always loved her shining curls, but now that he felt them as part of himself, he found their springiness extra delightful, their gloss even lovelier than he'd realized. And then there were her eyes, their enchanting hazel irises framed by long, beckoning lashes. Every time she blinked, those lashes seemed to point to her captivating lips.

He'd thought after all this time, he knew her lips, that he knew every bit of her mouth, but now—orange sky above, those damn lips were even fuller and softer than he'd realized, and would it be okay to put her down right now so he could kiss—

"Krey?"

He flinched, making her laugh. "Uh"—he cleared his throat—"yeah?"

"Are we gonna fly?"

"About that . . ." This felt weird, talking to her when he couldn't see her face. "I, uh . . ." *Out with it. She knows you better than anyone. Just be honest.* He kept his voice low, suddenly ultra aware of the other people in the street. "Zeisha, I told you when you were part of my magic, I'd sense every part of you."

"Yes, you told me that." There was a hint of amusement in her voice.

"Yeah, well, you're . . . I'm just really distracted because . . ." He turned his head as far as he could. She brought her chin over his shoulder and met his gaze. "The thing is," he breathed, "I knew I loved you, but right now, it's like I'm in a gallery, in front of the most incredible piece of art I've ever seen—but I'm not in front of it, I'm *part of it*, soaking in its colors and lines. Only it's not a painting, it's *you*. And your colors and lines—your everything—well, it's all so completely perfect, and I . . . I'm lost in it. In you."

He stopped, convinced he'd just made a complete fool of himself. *A gallery? Where did I come up with that?*

Her voice was hushed, but every word reached his ear. "That's the most amazing thing anyone's ever said to me. Maybe to anyone. Ever."

He couldn't help it; he laughed. "I don't think you get it. *All of you*, Zeisha. There's no part of you that isn't part of me right now. And the thoughts I'm having about you—well, I shouldn't be spouting off about art; I should be apologizing."

"Why?" Her breath was warm on his cheek. "Because you love me? Because you want me? Because right now, when I'm clinging to your back like a little kid, you're somehow making me feel more beautiful than ever?" When Krey didn't answer, she brushed his ear with her lips, whispering, "I want you too."

Krey let out all of his breath. His hands, holding her rounded calves, were damp with sweat. "That's all well and good, but if I can't get my mind in a different place, we can't fly. I have to focus to keep us both in the air. If I'm thinking about you—about your body that's so perfect it's torturing me—we're both gonna fall."

Zeisha laughed softly, which made her move in a way that ratcheted up his distraction. Then she started talking. Gone was the seductive whisper. Her voice was casual, informal, like they were chatting over a meal. "So, I've been thinking a lot about my mom and dad lately. And your aunts too. And my brothers. I wonder what they're doing right now. Maybe—"

Krey interrupted her with a loud groan. "Zei?"

"Hmm?"

"I didn't realize there was a switch, but there is, and you just turned it off."

"Oh good, because I was just remembering this time when my mom taught me to do laundry. We started with my brothers' socks—"

Krey leapt into the air, and Zeisha broke into peals of delighted laughter.

"More stories about your parents, less laughing," Krey said as he spiraled higher. But he was chuckling too, relieved to find that he could be aware of Zeisha's body, and even appreciate it, without being overwhelmed with desire.

They flew high over Star Clan Territory. The crisp, dry, late-winter air whooshed in their ears as Krey went faster and faster, urged on by Zeisha's frequent, gleeful shouts. He took them even higher. The city below turned into a child's playmat, with buildings made of blocks. The blue-gray river looked like a solid pencil line. Each of the city's occupants could've been a bug.

Zeisha's entire body shivered. Krey slowed so the breeze would caress them, rather than rushing over them. "So," he said, "you like flying?"

Zeisha's body quivered again with that distracting laugh. "Yeah."

"I know you've been nervous about being part of the battle. But today—well, I can tell you love your magic again. And I can feel how much fun you're having up here. I'm kind of looking forward to kicking some royal ass with you on my back." He laughed, but Zeisha was quiet. After some time, she drew in a deep breath and let it out slowly. "What are you thinking?" he asked.

He wasn't sure she'd heard him; the air up here swallowed up sound. He opened his mouth to repeat the question, but Zeisha answered, "This is the best day I've had since I left Tirra."

He squeezed her legs. "I'm glad."

"Let's not talk about fighting, okay?"

"Okay." Krey didn't want to feel disappointed, but he couldn't help it. He was buzzing with anticipation, and he wanted her to share it. It wasn't that he enjoyed hurting others. He'd love to avoid that part. What thrilled him, what sent life pumping through his heart, was the *meaning* behind the upcoming fight.

The battle to free the militia had been intoxicating. He'd risked his life to set people free. To set wrong things right. He'd do it again when the Cellerinian army returned. He'd take to the air to gather information, warn others, and rain ice on his enemies. Why? To protect the freedom of a community who'd done nothing to deserve the king's attacks.

When that day came—and it couldn't come soon enough—Krey would carry the girl he loved on his back. They'd fight together. They'd protect each other. What could be better?

But Zeisha, he was certain, didn't share his anticipation.

Did I pressure her into this? I told her she needed to do what was best for her. Did she believe me?

"Zeisha," he said, "if you change your mind—about the fight—it's okay. Really."

They flew for a good two minutes before she responded. "I love you, Krey."

He wasn't sure what that had to do with fighting, but he wouldn't push her to talk about it. This was the best experience he'd ever shared with her. He was as hesitant to ruin it as she was.

Again, Krey allowed himself to appreciate her perfect form, saturated with his magic. When that became too distracting, he shifted his focus to her hands, clasped over his chest. He lifted them both to his mouth and kissed her knuckles. "I love you too."

13

The whole world is talking about the archeological dig in the shadow of Cellerin Mountain. In case you've missed the most recent news, here's a brief recap. Archeologists, funded by tech giant Merak Technologies, are working to unearth an artifact that may date back to humanity's early days on Anyari.

The artifact's significance is both historical and scientific. Scientists have detected unique radioactivity at the dig. They believe the purported artifact is its source.

Yesterday, I spoke with Alvun Merak, owner of Merak Technologies. "We anticipate making major medical advances once we harness the power of this radioactivity," he said.

Sometimes it's not the future that's revolutionary—it's the past.

-"Let's Dig!" by Genta Ril
The Derogan Chronicle, *dated Quari 20, 6293*

Nora picked up the shimshim she'd just put an arrow through. Handing it to Ovrun, she said, "I'm sorry you have to clean this one."

"No, you're not."

"Okay, I'm not." Nora laughed and gave Ovrun a smiling kiss. "See you tomorrow."

"Have fun out there."

Nora jogged off, raising her eyes to the sky. After three weeks in Deroga, it still felt strange to depend on the sun alone for telling time. She kind of liked the challenge of it though. There were some high clouds, but the sun's rays extended beyond one of them. It was directly overhead. Osmius would be waiting.

Drawing deep, measured breaths, Nora ran through Deroga's streets. These days, running felt almost good. A few months back, she wouldn't have dreamed she'd ever think such a thing.

Osmius was waiting on a wide street. As he turned his head toward his visitor, his deep-gray scales shimmered with tiny rainbows. *Hello, Nora-human.*

Hi! Ready to get some ice?

Is your mate coming?

Oh, by the stone, Osmius, he's not my mate. He's my—I don't know what he is, but definitely not my mate. And no, he's not coming. He needs to hunt.

Osmius's deep laughter told Nora he'd been teasing. During her years being pampered in the palace, she'd never have dreamed a dragon would joke around with her. On a Derogan street. While she wore non-tailored clothes and zero makeup. Nora climbed up the beast's scales. *Life has gotten weird as hell, Osmius.*

He laughed again and lifted into the air. As they soared through the clear sky, Nora updated Osmius on the spy in Star Clan custody. According to Eira, Elo Golsch now lived in a more comfortable cell and seemed to be warming to the trog cause. However, he claimed not to know anything about the inner workings of the army. Eira made sure he was treated well, hoping that eventually, he'd play a larger role in the trogs' fight for freedom. Nora hadn't visited him since their first unfortunate encounter.

A few minutes later, Nora said, *I thought we were going to the mountains.*

We shall.

They're to the south. You're flying southwest.

Gathering ice will not take long. There are other things I wish to show you.

Other things?

Osmius went silent. Nora sighed. She was convinced he often adopted an air of mystery just to piss her off.

At last, the great dragon spoke. *You shall be a queen someday, Nora-human.*

She felt the muscles in her shoulders and arms tense. *About that . . . considering the current king wants to send his army into the place where I'm living, my future profession is up in the air. My future anything, for that matter.*

This is true. Still, you have the heart of a ruler. You should know the land you may rule.

He thought she had the heart of a ruler? Nora wasn't sure whether to argue, laugh, or be flattered. She mulled the words over in silence. Eventually, she asked, *Where are you taking me?*

To the places humans do not travel.

You're not gonna tell me more than that, are you?

There was that laugh again, sounding like it originated in the planet's core.

Nora sighed and tried to enjoy the ride. She supposed many humans would give anything to be in her position. In the early years after The Day, dragon sightings were common. These days, though, the great reptids mostly kept to themselves. Osmius probably knew the uninhabited parts of Cellerin better than any human.

Osmius, Nora said, *Why do dragons usually stay so far away from humans?*

You saw both Taima and me in chains. That was not the first time humans captured dragons. Need you ask why we lack trust?

Oh . . . right.

When I fly over civilized areas, Osmius said, *I fly high, so humans may mistake me for a bird.*

And so you're out of weapons range?

Yes. When men hired by the king captured Taima and me, we were in our den, not in the air.

The simmering rage in his voice took Nora's breath away. *I'm sorry, Osmius.*

You are not the one who hurt us.

It was her father, though. She couldn't help but feel somewhat responsible. *Why do you and Taima keep helping me? I'd understand if you wanted to fly off and never look at another human.*

You and your friends saved us, Nora-human. You earned our trust and our loyalty.

Nora squeezed his neck tighter.

They flew in silence for what must have been well over an hour, passing over the Kamina River and great swaths of uninhabited land. Frequent patches of green vegetation interrupted the brown dirt. Then the surface lightened to beige, as far as the eye could see. *We're over the Therro Desert, aren't we?* Nora asked.

We are.

The monochromatic, sandy dunes had a hypnotic effect. *I'm about to fall asleep, Osmius.*

That would be unwise. Look straight ahead, halfway to the horizon. What do you see?

She squinted. *Nothing. Your eyes are better than mine.*

Keep looking. Do not allow yourself to sleep.

After a couple of minutes, Nora saw a small, shimmery splotch. *Is that a mirage?*

It is not. Osmius covered the distance quickly and was soon spiraling down toward a bright-green pool. He touched down in the sand.

Should I get down? Nora asked.

Osmius turned his head. One of his golden, domed, compound eyes seemed to fix itself on her. *Have you heard the stories of when the land held the magic of the stone?*

Nora had been on her belly for the whole flight. She let go of Osmius's scales and sat up, stretching her arms above her head. *Do you mean all the strange things that supposedly happened after The Day? Rivers that parted, things like that?*

You have heard, then.

Heard, yes. Believed? I've never been sure.

Osmius stared at her. *Drop to the sand, Nora-human. Drink the water.*

She almost protested, almost asked a dozen questions about the safety of such a thing and why he'd want her to do it and what it would do to her—

But she trusted Osmius. Completely.

Nora returned to her belly and slid down the dragon's gray scales. The treads of her boots sank into the soft sand with a *shh* sound. She dropped her pack and started toward the pool. Walking through the sand required some effort, but it didn't take long to reach the water.

It wasn't like the pond back at the palace. There was no soggy ground leading to shallow water that gradually deepened. Instead, the ground stopped, and deep water began. The sand was like a wall, extending downward, visible through the water but not mixing with it. Despite the emerald-green water's stunning clarity, Nora couldn't see the bottom.

She'd almost think a human had made this pool and lined it with a thin, transparent preday substance. But something told her that wasn't the case. Perhaps it had never even been touched by human hands. And she was supposed to drink from it?

Do not fear, Nora-human.

She didn't know how he'd sensed her trepidation, but his words, simmering with the power of the stone, calmed her. Kneeling near the edge of the sand, she dipped her hand into the water.

But . . . was it water? It flowed like water, but it was far warmer than the cool weather should allow. A fragrance, sweet and calming, wafted from it. And it was smooth, so smooth, like it was woven with the finest fabric, or oil, or . . . magic.

Much of what she scooped up slid back into the pool, but a bit remained in her cupped hand. It glimmered in the sunlight, more than ordinary water would. She brought it to her mouth and drank.

It was like nothing she'd ever tasted. Sweet, but with a tingling bite on her tongue. She had seen no bubbles, but it felt like tiny bits of *something* were popping all over her mouth. The liquid warmed her as it traveled through the center of her chest and into her stomach.

All at once, the muscles in Nora's arms and legs came alive with joyful strength. She laughed aloud as desire filled her, an urgent need to dance, to run, to fly.

Like he'd tapped into her instinct, Osmius cried, *Go!*

Nora ran. The sand no longer bogged her feet down. It was like she was running on a springing surface, the ground itself propelling her forward. Grains of sand flew off her boots as she sprinted faster and leapt into the air. She landed farther away than should've been possible. Sand exploded around her like splashing water. It would've gotten in her eyes if she weren't already spinning and leaping past it.

She lost track of time, claiming the desert as her playground. She was one with the air and the ground, one with Anyari itself. The sun's rays, nearly blinding in their brightness, seemed to laugh with her. The sand rejoiced every time she sent it flying.

Finally, she felt drawn back to Osmius. After sprinting to him, she hurled herself up, grabbing his wide neck in her open arms and grasping his scales with clawed fingers. She reveled in the feel of her feet, dangling far off the ground. Dragon laughter resounded in her mind. Osmius's scent—musky with a hint of spice—filled her nose. It was usually so mild that she barely noticed it, but with her senses on alert, she thought she could've tracked him across the country.

Then, as quickly as it had filled her, the burst of magical strength and awareness disappeared. Nora realized she was hanging mets off the ground, holding on by nothing but her fingertips. She screamed. Osmius lowered his head smoothly, placing her back in the sand.

She sat, breathing hard, eyes wide. "What was that?" she asked aloud.

That, Nora-human, was magical water.

She switched back to telepathic communication. *Can I take it back to Deroga? Imagine the energy we'd all have during the battle . . .*

Is that the type of energy you need during a battle?

Oh. Maybe not.

Even if it were, the water quickly loses its power when taken from the source.

Why did you show me this?

Osmius paused before replying, *You are fighting for your kingdom. Your strength and courage shall be greater if you know what you are fighting for.*

Nora nodded. *Do you drink this water too, Osmius?*

I do. There is no other feeling like it. I would drink it now, but the effects on dragons are greater. I would be hopping about the desert for hours. His great head tilted to one side. *Do you want more?*

She almost said yes, then realized the experience had washed her in contentment. She felt alive and alert, yet relaxed. *No, but I hope you'll bring me back here.* She retrieved her pack and climbed up. Osmius rose into the air.

They spent the rest of the afternoon flying. Nora experienced her kingdom in a way she never had. Osmius took her over a great meadow, golden with winter-dormant grass, and directed her attention to an area that seemed to have a haze over it. *Anyone who walks there sleeps for three days. When they wake, they remember nothing of who they are.*

For a long time, they flew over ordinary land. *There were once many enchanted places,* Osmius explained. *When I was young, I saw things you could not imagine. A mountain's icy peak burst into flames during every full moon. Trees rearranged themselves, as if dancing with one another. Rivers flowed backward, including their waterfalls. Over time, the magic has faded from most of the land.*

Nora yearned to see such sights. But Cellerin held non-magical enchantments too. Osmius carried her in front of a massive waterfall, close enough for its mist to chill them both. It was as tall as Deroga's highest buildings and was tucked away within peaks so craggy, it would probably be generations before any human "discovered" it. They continued flying, passing over rushing rapids, rock formations that appeared sculpted, and a remote ranch with a large windmill and various animals grazing in huge fields.

Then Osmius showed her one more magical sight. Over the Kamina Forest, they dropped low enough to see a herd of seven sleeping unicorns. The sight of the wild beasts, with their shimmering silver coats and bone-white horns, made Nora shiver with awe.

As the sun set in the west, Osmius turned eastward toward the mountains where he and Taima lived. He soared first to the highest peak in the range, where he used his front claws to break off a piece of a glacier. The chunk was at least as big as Nora. She stood to the side, her hood up, and shuddered when Osmius broke the ice apart with his teeth. *I would not want to get on your bad side*, she told him.

He fixed her with a stare that made her back away. Then he laughed. Smoke puffed from his huge nostrils, filling Nora's nose with the scent of cooked meat—whatever the dragon had eaten for lunch.

When the ice pieces were small enough, Nora packed as many as she could in bags she'd brought. She used rope to tie them to Osmius, who only grumbled a little about being made into a pack animal.

That done, Osmius asked, *Nora-human, would you like to see my den?*

For a moment, Nora didn't breathe. *I would be honored to.*

He took her to a large cave, hidden among a mountain's sharp peaks. Taima waited there. She was standoffish, which was the norm for her. But as they walked through the cave, Nora could sense the huge female dragon's pride in the home she and Osmius had created.

They'd built up an impressive stock of dried mushu leaves, their fuel for the fire they breathed. In another corner, an immense pile of furs created a comfortable sleeping area. Nora considered how many wild animals the two dragons had killed to amass so many skins. They'd only lived in this place for a couple of weeks. Had they slaughtered so many in that time, or had one of them returned to a previous lair to retrieve what they'd had before? She didn't ask. Dragons hunted—for food and, apparently, to create luxurious beds. Who was she to question that?

Osmius used his fiery breath to cook some cervid meat for Nora. In Deroga, she rarely ate meat that didn't come from a shimshim. This meal was a nice change. As the sun set, Osmius offered her a few furs, and she curled up in them, falling asleep almost instantly. Her magical romp through the sand dunes had tired her more than she'd realized.

When she woke, the cave was as dark as the stone. The soft voices of Osmius and Taima reached her mind. They weren't talking about anything private—just the hunting they'd done that day—but Nora still felt like she was eavesdropping. The dragons usually shielded their thoughts from her. She sent out a *Hello*, and their conversation halted.

We must go, Nora-human, Osmius said.

I can't see a thing in here.

A moment later, the cave brightened with yellow-orange light. Nora found its source—a ball of fire flickering within Osmius's wide-open mouth. *Well, that's a cool trick.*

Osmius rose from his pile of furs, untwining himself from his mate. The sight sent an odd yearning into Nora's chest. She'd seen the depth of Osmius's devotion for Taima when he'd sent humans to rescue her. Taima had made her own passion known when she'd incinerated Cage, the dragon speaker who'd held Osmius captive. And just now, Nora had seen how comfortable the two huge reptids were as they discussed their day, their powerful bodies curled together.

Devotion. Passion. Comfort. It all added up to love.

Back in Deroga, Nora had the middle piece: passion. *I want the rest of it too.*

She pushed the thought aside, thanking Taima for her hospitality. Outside, Nora climbed on Osmius's back. He quenched the fire in his mouth, and they returned to the air.

Osmius, Nora ventured when they'd been flying a few minutes, *when did you fall in love with Taima?*

The question is wrong, Osmius replied.

What do you mean?

The dragon's flight curved smoothly—left, right, left again. Nora got the feeling he was pondering his answer. Finally, he said, *We did not fall into love.*

But you do love each other—I can see it.

We did not fall into love, Nora-human. We fought into love.

This time, she remained quiet. Waiting.

We were formed on The Day, Osmius said. *We woke with a dozen other small dragons in an empty building in Deroga. We were all in a room. The smell told us animals had lived there.*

Nora's mouth slowly widened into a smile. *You woke in an urban shimshim den.*

We did.

Does that mean the shimshims were . . . were they your parents?

We were not born. The shimshims who lived in that particular den became dragons—became us. Somehow we know this.

Nora pulled in a deep breath of cold air. Did anyone else in all of Anyari know how dragons had been created? *Osmius, thank you for sharing this with me.*

I trust you.

I'm glad. But . . . back to you and Taima falling in love. I mean, fighting into love. Can you tell me more?

We all lived together for a short time, but we grew rapidly. Within a week, the room was not big enough for twelve dragons. The strongest of the group began defending the den. She wanted it to be hers alone.

A guffaw escaped Nora's mouth. *I can guess who that was.*

I am sure you can. Gradually, the other dragons left the den. All but one.

You, Nora said.

Yes. I refused to leave. Every day, Taima and I fought. We were small, but our teeth and claws were sharp. Neither of us gave in. Every day, we grew. Soon, the room we'd woken in was not big enough for one of us, much less two. Nevertheless, we stayed.

Silence settled over them both, only broken by the occasional beat of dragon wings. Nora finally lost her patience. *You can't stop the story there. You told me the fighting part but not the love part.*

Nora-human, imagine it. Two dragons, grown into young adults, huddled in a room too small for them. They could not help but touch at every moment. Each learned the deep strength of the other. It was a small step from knowledge to admiration. Do you not think at some point, they would tire of fighting? His deep, smooth voice was a little condescending, but there was amusement in it too.

Nora wasn't sure if the warmth suddenly covering her was from an air current or her reaction to the story. *I suppose you would,* she said. *And once those two dragons realized they'd rather love each other than kill each other, I suppose they'd go looking for a home that could fit them both—maybe a cave?*

You suppose correctly.

Two centuries, Nora said. *Do you ever get tired of each other?*

Osmius angled his body, flying even higher. *On the contrary. A thousand years to love her would be too short.*

"The king locked down the palace," Hatlin told Nora. "The staff can't leave; they all live there now."

Nora stared at him in the light of his candle. "They're all living there? But a lot of them have families! How does he stop them from leaving? Even he can't control them all at once, can he? Besides, he has to sleep!"

"He doesn't control them constantly. But they never know when he's gonna do it. He takes over their minds at random times, then interrogates them. They know if they try to turn against him, he'll find out. It's a pretty foolproof way to get people to do what you want. One staff member tried to leave, and a guard shot him in the leg. They're all afraid of their king, and that's made them loyal."

Nora swore. "Not the kind of loyalty I'd want."

"Oh, and he fired all the lysters on staff. All except my contact. So far, she's managed to keep her dirt-eating talent secret. And she's avoided the king so he doesn't touch her, but she knows he gets to everyone eventually."

"How does she communicate with you?" Nora asked.

"The chapel is still open to the staff and the public. You know how religious your father is; I guess he doesn't want to stop people from worshiping. My contact leaves me notes under one of the chairs in there." He lifted his index finger, like he'd just remembered something. "Oh, and your aunt who lives there—what's her name?"

Nora froze. "Dani," she breathed. "Tell me she's okay. Please."

Hatlin's shoulders dropped, and his furrowed brow conveyed more empathy than Nora would've thought him capable of. "I think the king's got an extra-tight grip on her mind," he said softly. "She sits in her office each day, staring at nothing."

Nora's chest tightened and twisted with emotions she couldn't name. Dani had acted as a mother to her for ten years. "I can't—I don't—" She covered her mouth with both hands. "I have to go," was the only coherent sentence she could form.

"I'm sorry," Hatlin said.

Nora shook her head and turned away, calling Osmius back.

14

Therro hasn't had a monarch in six hundred years. The Return to Royalty Society (RRS) wants to change that. I attended an RRS meeting to find out why.

I'd love to share the Society's logic with you. Unfortunately, logic isn't their strong suit. The RRS yearns to return to ancient days of pomp and elitism. I sat in that musty conference room for an hour. When I got home, I felt like I needed a shower to wash off all the nationalist sentiments clinging to me.

-*"Practice Your Bows and Curtsies" by Genta Ril*
The Derogan Chronicle, *dated Quari 22, 6293*

Nora-human, I cannot take you.

Then ask Taima to do it. Please. I have to save my aunt. I have to confront my father. If I just talk to him—

NO! A wide stream of fire lit up the night sky, accompanying the silent exclamation.

Nora's body jerked with surprise. Her right boot and left hand lost their grip on Osmius's scales. She quickly shoved them back in place.

She wanted to give Osmius a telepathic lashing. Instead, she drew in a deep breath. She'd finally calmed enough to talk to the dragon carrying her; she couldn't mess it up. *Osmius, think about how much you love Taima. You'd listen to her. Even if you were in a bad place and didn't want to hear any reason, you'd hear her. My father . . . he'll listen to me. I know it.*

Osmius, too, had calmed. But his voice was all stony resolve. *You tried talking to your father on the day you freed the militia. He did not listen.*

The dragon was right, but . . . *How can you even compare that to this? I'd just fought a battle against his militia. He was angry! If I talk to him in his own palace, it'll be different. I know it will. And even if he doesn't listen . . . Osmius, my aunt! I've got to get her away from him!*

Listen to yourself! The dragon's words somehow made her chest quiver. *Once your father has rebuffed you, do you think he will let you rescue your aunt? Or will he imprison you in his palace? I cannot allow this, Nora-human! We shall speak no further of it!*

Nora ground her teeth together and remained quiet the rest of the trip. But her mind was racing.

Her father still existed. The real him, the one who would do anything for his daughter. And she was the only one who could reach him. She could remind him of everything he'd lost through his addiction and his quest for power. It wouldn't be easy for him to rebuild his life, to restore healthy rule in their nation. But he could do it, supported by his daughter. Nora was certain of it.

Almost certain, anyway.

When Osmius landed on the dark Derogan street, he spoke to

Nora's mind again. *I will help you fight, Nora-human. I will not help you lose.*

A rush of affection for the massive beast filled Nora, despite her anger. She kissed one of his scales, then sat up. *I understand.* And she did.

But did he understand how determined she was?

Early the next morning, Nora sat at the breakfast table with Zeisha, rubbing sleepy grit from her eyes. A few minutes later, Ovrun and Krey arrived. The four of them had a table to themselves.

Nora began sharing the information Hatlin had given her. Halfway through, Zeisha reached across the table and took her hand. Nora stopped talking. The words wouldn't travel through her tight throat. *Zeisha gets it.* Nora wasn't just sharing the story of a king going insane. She was living the tragedy of losing her father and, in a way, her aunt. She squeezed Zeisha's hand and sniffed loudly.

When she'd steadied her breathing, she continued her recap, then concluded, "I have to talk to my father."

"Like hell you do," Krey snapped.

At the same time, Ovrun said, "I'm not sure that's the best idea."

The table went silent. Zeisha was the one to break it. "Nora, why don't you explain what you're thinking?"

Nora liked this girl more every day. She gave Krey a sharp look. *You could learn something from her, you know.*

She'd had hours of sleeplessness to improve the arguments she'd tried on Osmius. After a deep breath, she presented her case. Her father, she explained, hadn't completely lost himself to his dark talent. She could bring him back around. No, it wouldn't be easy. Yes, it would take time. But think of the lives it could save. Shouldn't someone try to prevent war, even as the trogs and former militia continued to prepare for it?

"So," she concluded, again looking at Krey, "I need you to fly me there. Tomorrow night."

"Nora." His stubborn, sharp gaze sliced into her. "I can't fly you to the palace. We might as well offer to let your father start up another militia, right there, with you and me as the first two members."

"He wouldn't do that," she hissed.

"Maybe not to you. But he'd control me in a heartbeat. You know it as well as I do."

She opened her mouth but promptly closed it again. Her father had taken Faylie—Nora's best friend, her *only* friend—for his own purposes. He hadn't just controlled her; he'd turned her into a brain lyster. When Faylie had lost her very self to the sadism of dark magic, he hadn't let up. Now he had his grip on Dani, a woman he used to love as a sister.

Would King Ulmin snatch up the arrogant, talented lyster whose arrival at the palace had led to Nora's exit? *In a second*, Nora realized. "Then we won't let you get anywhere close to him," she said. "You can drop me off outside the palace grounds. We'll make another ice ladder. We'll—"

"No!" Krey interrupted. "If I thought this would work, I'd take you without hesitation! I'm saying no because it'll make things worse, not better. I'm saying no because I care about the nation of Cellerin as much as you do!"

"As much as I do?" Nora's voice turned shrill. "It's my land! I'm supposed to protect it!"

She realized the entire room had turned quiet. She looked down at her untouched food. She was so tired. Was she even making sense? Her eyes flicked up and found three concerned gazes. No, two concerned gazes. Krey was watching her from under angled brows, his jaw clenched, lips tight. *What did I say this time?*

"It's not *your land*." Krey's voice was low. "This nation doesn't belong to the royal family, Your Highness. It belongs to all of us. We're all supposed to protect it. Not you alone."

She squeezed her eyes shut. *He's right. Damn it. I hate that.* "Okay," she said, returning her gaze to his, "You're right, we all need to protect the kingdom. It doesn't belong to me. But I do care about it. More than I ever realized. And if anyone can reach the king and prevent war, it's me." She took a deep breath. "Osmius said he'd take me. I'd rather go with you, because my father will control Osmius if he realizes he's nearby. But if that's my only option, I'll make it work. We'll go at night."

Nora hadn't planned this lie. She was exhausted and desperate, and the false words came far too easily. Krey always wanted to be in the middle of things. If he knew she was going anyway, surely he'd insist on bringing her.

"If you're gonna ride a dragon, why not Taima?" Krey asked. "The king's never touched her. She's safe from his control."

For a split second, Nora froze. Was he calling her bluff? She recovered, the lies again sliding effortlessly from her mouth. "She's still healing from the militia battle. A wound on her side got infected. She can help us if the army invades. But she doesn't think she'd make it all the way to the palace."

Krey's eyes narrowed. Nora didn't flinch. He looked away, returning his attention to his food. Over the next few seconds, Ovrun and Zeisha did the same. Other than the scrape of metal forks on clay dishes, the table was silent. Nora was trying to convince herself to eat another bite of sausage when Krey at last spoke again.

"It's a bad idea." He took a sip of his water and set it down firmly. "But you win. I'll take you."

Krey shoved feathers in his mouth and picked up his pace. He needed to get to his assigned rooftop and relieve the night watch. He'd stayed at the breakfast table longer than he'd planned, thanks to Nora's terrible idea.

"Krey, wait!"

He turned to see Zeisha running toward him. When she caught up, she said, "I wanted to talk to you privately before we both go to our rooftops. I'll walk with you."

They set off together. Krey stuffed his mouth with too many feathers and started chewing.

"Do you really think you should take Nora to the palace?" Zeisha asked.

Krey pointed to his full mouth. Zeisha's dark eyebrows lifted. Her smile told him she knew he was avoiding the conversation. *It's nice to have someone in your life who knows you so well. Except when it's not.*

She walked quietly next to him while he continued chewing. If anyone else were questioning him, he'd take to the air. But he couldn't keep the truth from Zeisha. He swallowed. "I'm not going to take her."

Zeisha's head tilted to one side. The sun glimmered in her wide, hazel eyes. "You lied?"

He sighed. "Yeah."

"Why?"

"She lied to me first. Do you really think a two-hundred-year-old dragon would be stupid enough to take her to the palace? She's determined to get there no matter what. I'm just delaying her until I figure something else out."

Zeisha's voice was gentle. "Krey, you lied to your friend."

He stopped and faced her. "I lied *because* she's my friend." The words dredged up something in him, some anxious fire he couldn't explain. He resumed walking, faster now. Why did he care so much about the spoiled princess who'd brought him to her palace for her own entertainment?

But he knew the answer to that question. Nora had risked her future, her comfort, her very life, to save the militia. By the sky, the only reason Krey was walking next to the girl he loved was because Nora had killed her best friend. He hadn't wanted to give the princess his friendship, but she'd earned it. No way in hell was he going to let her return to a father who'd break her heart and ruin her life.

How could he explain all that to Zeisha? He wanted to assure her that Nora was only a friend. And that was true; Krey had eyes for no one but the girl at his side. But . . . *only a friend?* That term minimized what he, Nora, and Ovrun had forged in their few months together. Krey honestly believed he'd die for either of them. Would Zeisha understand that?

Her hand found his, and her mouth softened into the smile he loved. "These recent months have changed you," she said, "and I want you to know I love who you are."

The words were a breath of peace to his soul. He stopped for long enough to kiss Zeisha's temple. "I don't want Nora to get hurt," he said as they continued walking. "I didn't want to lie to her, but I . . . I needed some time to figure out how to stop her from sabotaging her own future."

"How will you stop her?"

The question, direct and simple, had an odd effect on Krey. An idea had been simmering in his mind—for how long, he wasn't sure. Certainly since before the battle for the militia. The notion had lurked in the background, so unthinkable that he'd barely been aware of it.

Until this moment . . . when he realized the reckless, stupid, horrible idea had somehow morphed into an actual plan.

Zeisha won't like this.

He considered hiding it from her, then chided himself for the thought. It was bad enough to lie to a friend. He wouldn't set that precedent with the girl he hoped to marry.

But he couldn't bring himself to come out and say it either.

For the first time since Zeisha had found him, Krey took notice of their surroundings. They were in an uninhabited part of the city, between trog clan territories. Their route formed zigzags around old vehicles. The empty buildings looked almost sad, their gaping windows and doorways reminding Krey of dead eyes. In the distance, the call of a feral caynin—*uh-uh-uh*—rang through the city air.

"Krey?" Zeisha asked.

He licked his lips and drew in a deep breath. "At some point, we gotta fight fire with fire."

She stopped walking.

He'd expected her to respond with questions. But when he halted and met her gaze, he realized she knew exactly what he was saying. Her eyes were wet, her chin and lips tight. She shook her head slowly and spoke in a choked voice. "Krey."

Oh, this had been hard enough when he was just *thinking* about it. Seeing Zeisha's face, her beautiful mouth twisting with dread . . . that made it ten times worse. She was as hesitant to speak the words aloud as he was. Neither of them wanted him to take the path he was now considering.

But what other choice did he have? Something in him had known it would come to this, to him returning to a time in his past he'd promised himself never to revisit. Better now than in the middle of a battle, with people already dying.

"I'll be careful," he said.

She was still shaking her head.

Would she tell the others? Expose the piece of his history that no one in the world except the two of them and Krey's aunts knew about? Would Zeisha do something to stop him?

If she asked him not to do it, he might not be able to. He could deal with Zeisha being angry with him, not that it happened often. Could he live with her disappointment? He brought his hands to her cheeks, wanting to comfort her, anxious to know what else she'd say.

She didn't speak at all. Just wrapped her arms around his waist and laid her head on his chest. He held her tight, appreciating her warmth and acceptance.

Then she walked away. When she was out of sight, Krey took to the sky.

15

Deroga's mayor, Mintin Shew, just celebrated his seventieth birthday by running from the western edge of the city all the way to Burig Bay.

I'm proud of the guy, really. But I'm embarrassed that I could barely complete the two-clommet run my school required last week.

-"Mayor Shew Wears out His Shoes" by Genta Ril
The Derogan Chronicle, *dated Quari 23, 6293*

ZEISHA DIDN'T KNOW how long she'd been lying awake, but it felt like hours. The sun had finally risen, and she heard a few former militia members quietly getting ready. She couldn't bring herself to climb out of bed. *Too anxious to sleep. Too tired to get up.* Covering her head with her thin pillow, she tried to drown out the reminders that daytime had arrived.

Krey had first told her of his plans—or rather, *not* told her of his plans—three days ago. She hadn't gotten any time alone with him since then. He'd ended up with extra guard shifts, thanks to a sick trog. When he wasn't working, he was sleeping. Yesterday, he'd finally had time off, but she was on a rooftop, growing plants.

Would he willingly return to one of the darkest times in his life? Should she ask him not to? She understood why he felt it was the only way. But the consequences . . .

"Happy birthday!" several voices shouted.

The sound made Zeisha jump. Whose birthday was it? And why couldn't they celebrate later in the day?

Someone pulled the pillow off her head. She groaned and opened the eye that wasn't smashed into her bed.

Krey stood above her, beaming. "Happy birthday!"

"Oh." Her voice came out rough. She knew it was the month of Wolf, but had the 26th come already? Was she really eighteen today?

Krey kissed her. "Kinda weird," he said, "kissing an adult."

She hit him with her pillow.

Zeisha didn't know why Eira had agreed to give her, Krey, Nora, Ovrun, and Isla the morning off. But she appreciated it. After breakfast, they'd all remained in the militia dining room.

Nora and Ovrun had strung together pieces of broken, multicolored polymus, then hung the impromptu streamer above the table they all used. The festive decoration reminded Zeisha of birthdays at home, when her mom decorated their dining room. She missed her family so much, her chest ached with it. With effort, she pulled her focus to the present, letting her friends' banter redirect her maudlin thoughts.

About half an hour into the party, Isla said, "I wish I could stay, but my team has a ton of buildings to sweep today, and I don't want to leave it all to them." She gave Zeisha a hug and jogged off.

Zeisha tried to smile as she watched Isla leave. Not many people understood what it had been like in the militia. She'd thought she and Isla could help each other through this strange, painful time. But unlike Zeisha, Isla seemed to be handling the transition from mental bondage to trog life with aplomb. She'd made new friends and was enjoying her life as part of the Star Clan.

Zeisha had made new friends too, but she wasn't really settling in. While Kebi was infallibly kind, they hadn't known each other long. Krey, Nora, and Ovrun were all wonderful, but their closeness and inside jokes often left Zeisha feeling like an outsider.

Isla's moving on. Everyone else is embracing trog life. Why am I the only one who feels so stuck?

"Zeisha?" Nora's soft voice brought Zeisha back to the moment.

Krey and Ovrun were standing. "Be back soon," Krey said.

"Where are they going?" Zeisha asked as they walked away.

Nora laughed. "You were in another world, weren't you? They have a secret mission. Very hush-hush. Ovrun wouldn't even give me a hint."

Zeisha's lips relaxed into a smile. Birthday surprises from Krey, just like old times. Maybe some things hadn't changed.

"While we're waiting, want to play some Skip Slide?" Nora asked.

"Sure."

Nora retrieved the game from a chest across the room. Back at the table, she unfolded the simple wooden board, which was covered in painted triangles. She distributed the carved game pieces—flat circles and crescents, representing suns and moons. "Birthday girl goes first."

Zeisha slid one of her pieces from one spot to another. Nora did the same. They quickly got into a rhythm. They'd both just learned the trog game, but it had simple rules, making it easy to talk while playing. Zeisha used a moon to skip over one of Nora's suns. She flipped her opponent's piece over, rendering it temporarily immobile. "Now that we have a few minutes alone," she said, "I want to know what's going on with you and Ovrun."

Nora countered with a move that trapped several of Zeisha's pieces in a corner. "He's a very, very nice guy." The corner of her lip twitched. "If he were just better looking, I might even be interested in him."

Zeisha burst out laughing. Her attraction to Krey never wavered, but Ovrun was the most objectively gorgeous human she'd ever seen.

Grinning, Nora said, "Your move."

Zeisha ignored the game and leaned forward. "I won't pressure you to talk about it, but I think sometimes it helps to be honest with another girl." The statement caused her a twinge of guilt. She wasn't being totally honest with Nora . . . but Krey's secrets weren't hers to tell.

Nora sobered. "He's . . . ." She sucked in a deep breath and groaned. "He's too hot for his own good. Or maybe too hot for *my* own good. If he were a jerk, it would make things a whole lot easier, but he's not. He's a genuinely good guy. We like each other a lot."

"But . . .?" Zeisha prompted.

"But he's focused on the future. We're trying to live in the present, but he keeps worrying about what comes next."

"What do you think comes next?"

Nora shrugged and laughed, though she sounded more frustrated than amused. "That's the difference between him and me. I'd rather not consider that question at all."

Zeisha made a move, then returned her attention to Nora. "You'll figure it out, you know."

"I hope so." Nora skipped over one of Zeisha's pieces. "Your turn."

Zeisha moved, though she didn't know this game well enough to tell if she was winning or losing.

Nora chuckled. "I just realized, I said, 'Your turn,' and you thought I meant the game."

"You didn't?"

"No. Your turn for girl talk. How are things with Krey?"

Now that was a loaded question. Zeisha's mind latched onto the secrets she couldn't share. Krey's lie. His plans. Her uncertainty.

Nora saved her by speaking again. "I know you've chosen to fight when the army attacks. I've been wanting to talk to you about that."

Zeisha tried not to make her exhale too obvious. *Now this, I can talk about.* "It's a relief, in a way. To have made the decision."

"Is it? A relief?"

"Yeah." Zeisha took in Nora's narrowed eyes. "I mean, it's scary too. Of course."

"We're all scared." Nora's smile was gentle. "But you—well, I was surprised. You didn't want to fight. Why did you change your mind?"

Zeisha looked down at the board, then realized it wasn't her turn. She gazed at her hands, like she'd find an explanation there. At last, she lifted her eyes. "I'm not sure. It felt like the right thing to do."

Nora made a move that didn't change the game much. Attention still on the board, she asked, "Did you change your mind because Krey wanted you to?"

"No!" The nearly empty room seemed to amplify the single word. "No, of course not. He wouldn't push me into fighting. I know you haven't known him that long, but . . . well, Krey has strong opinions, but he doesn't try to control me."

Nora's hand covered Zeisha's. Their eyes met again. "I know Krey's not a jerk. Most of the time." Her grin softened the statement. "I respect him. I also know his opinions outnumber the hairs on his head. And he never hesitates to share them. Am I on the right track here?"

Zeisha nodded. All strategy forgotten, she used her free hand to move a random piece.

Nora squeezed Zeisha's hand, then let go. "Think about this from my perspective. You insisted you wouldn't fight. Krey obviously hoped you would. You changed your mind. Doesn't it make sense that I'd wonder if he had anything to do with that decision?"

The question squeezed Zeisha's lungs. A sheen of moisture invaded both eyes. *What's wrong with me?*

"Want some juice?" Nora pointed at a table that held a pitcher and several cups.

Zeisha pushed herself into a standing position. "Yes—thanks." As she followed Nora, she filled her chest with cool air and slowly blew it out.

Nora poured the juice into two cups and handed one to Zeisha. "To the next year of your life."

They clinked their glasses together and sipped.

Zeisha coughed. "Is this wine?"

Nora's eyes were wide. A giggle burst from her chest. "I think so. I asked Eira for juice, and this is what she gave me. It tastes weak though. I don't think it'll affect us much. Besides, you're an adult, and I'm"—she took another sip and grinned—"thirsty."

There was a bowl on the table full of pepperins—small, spicy cookies the trogs had introduced them to. Zeisha snagged a few and popped one in her mouth. They walked back to the table and sat again.

"So . . ." Nora said, "about you fighting . . ."

Zeisha ate another pepperin. Her shoulders were tight with all the emotions she'd been holding in for weeks. She closed her eyes for a moment. *Talk. Whatever comes out, comes out.* "Krey didn't pressure me. I could see how hard he was trying *not* to pressure me. But I know he wants me to fight with him. He wants me to use my talent to help the trogs."

Nora put down the wine, which she'd been sipping. "I'm sure he does. But more than that, he wants what's best for you. I believe that."

"I do too. But he thinks I'm strong. Full of potential. He . . . well . . . the way he sees me? That's the person I want to be."

"Forget potential, Zeisha. You're strong already. Those food deliveries you make? You're building trust between us and the trogs. Your strength is the gentle sort, which might be more important than the fighting sort. Are you trying to change who you are?"

It wasn't like Nora had yelled at her or said something mean. But the question, spoken in a soft voice, slammed into Zeisha like a bullet crafted of words. There was no stopping the tears this time. They poured down her cheeks. She shuddered with sobs. Curls bounced into her eyes. In seconds, Nora came around the table and pulled her into her arms. Zeisha held onto her new friend and cried into her shoulder like she'd done as a little girl with her mother.

Nora whispered kindnesses in Zeisha's ear, assuring her it was okay to cry. After several long minutes, Zeisha's tears slowed. She pulled away, wiping her eyes and nose. Nora went to the drink table, returning with a cotton napkin and another cup of wine, though Zeisha's first cup was still mostly full.

Her body relaxing in relief and weariness, Zeisha wiped her cheeks and nose. She drank several large gulps of the tangy wine.

Nora again settled herself in the chair across from Zeisha. "We all need a good cry sometimes." She reached out and squeezed Zeisha's hand. "What brought that on?"

Zeisha pulled in a breath and blew it out, shaking her head to settle her thoughts. "You asked if I'm trying to change who I am."

Nora nodded but didn't speak.

"The thing is—" Zeisha's voice thickened with emotion again. "Back in Tirra, I knew who I was. I was a pretty talented magic eater. I loved my family. I loved Krey. I loved the outdoors. I used to tend our family's garden or hike on Cellerin Mountain, and during those times, I'd feel so close to God. Things weren't perfect there, but they were *good*. Then—" Tears tried to form in the corners of her eyes, but she denied their attempts, opening her mouth and letting the words rush out like the white flow of a waterfall. "Then someone stole me. My mind and my body. You and the others freed me. But I—I don't feel free. I remember doing terrible things. Things I can't take back. I know I killed people. Their faces are written in my dreams, Nora."

Chin trembling, Nora nodded. "I understand."

And Zeisha knew the princess did understand, at least in this one way. They'd both killed people. They couldn't recapture their innocence.

She swallowed and continued, "When I woke up and Krey found

me—that moment was magical. I really believed everything would be okay. But over the next few days, I realized something. Krey—he's changed as much as I have. Except somehow he's *more* himself, not less. He was always strong and brave and passionate, but now . . . he's a fighter. All his life, he's wanted to fight for what's right, and finally, he has the chance. He . . . he's so alive out here."

"None of us have come through this unchanged," Nora murmured.

"I know. But Krey knows who he is, and I don't. I have no idea who I'm supposed to be now! So when I stopped that spy and Krey told me how strong I was, I thought . . . well, maybe that's who I am now. Or who I need to be. Or . . . I don't know."

"Zeisha . . ." Nora's eyes traveled to some point on the other side of the room. She licked her lips, opened her mouth, closed it. At last, she fixed her gaze on Zeisha. "Krey is strong enough to take it when someone disagrees with him."

Zeisha sat up straighter. "But—" She halted. Krey never had a problem disagreeing with people. She loved that about him. So why did she want to argue the point?

Because I don't know if I'm strong enough to disagree with him.

The thought carved into her with its harsh truth. She grasped one of her cups and nearly dropped it bringing it up to her mouth. The wine threatened to come back up when she swallowed it. *Why did I tell Krey I'd fight? Is it because I'm strong? Or because I'm weak?*

"Zeisha Dennivan!" The booming voice belonged to Krey, though it was pitched lower than usual, like he was announcing a singer at a concert.

Zeisha turned. Krey and Ovrun approached, each carrying a plate covered in a napkin.

Krey was grinning. "I present to you . . . trog birthday bread!" He and Ovrun pulled the napkins off their plates. Underneath were round loaves of bread. Smaller pieces of dough had been used to form eyes, noses, and mouths. Steam rose from the golden faces.

"Trog birthday bread?" Nora asked.

Krey grinned. "Apparently it's tradition. Let's put these on the drink table."

As soon as the guys passed them, Nora took Zeisha's hand. "It's going to be okay."

Zeisha tried to smile. "I know."

But she didn't. Not really.

THE SEER: 5

*T*HIS IS *the reason I never spend time with people my age.*

In the middle of the night, Sarza had followed her urges to a particular building. When she'd entered the first-floor lobby, she'd found a bunch of tables and benches, plus a kitchen with a wood stove. She'd hidden behind a stack of furniture in a corner of the main room.

Peeking through a gap between a chair and a couch, she'd watched as people came in to cook, then as more arrived to eat. She recognized them as young magic eaters she'd watched during the recent training. *Who are these people?* she'd asked herself. But with so many conversations happening at once, she hadn't been able to pick up much information.

After breakfast, a small group had stuck around to celebrate a birthday. Now, only two remained—the birthday girl and the intriguing dragon rider. They were sitting halfway across the room from Sarza's hiding spot, talking and playing a game.

Sarza couldn't hear much of their conversation, but the parts she did hear seemed to be all about guys. She rolled her eyes so many times, her irises were dizzy. Through the years, Sarza had sat on the outskirts of countless conversations like this. When she was twelve or thirteen, she'd tried to participate in a few. But she hadn't known what to say. Sarza had no interest in romance. She'd always figured she'd grow into such feelings, but she never did. Love, at least of the gushy, toe-curling variety, held no appeal to her.

Oh, by the sky—now one of the girls was crying. Loudly. This was the other reason Sarza didn't hang out with other teenagers. Their emotions were incredibly annoying. *Come on!* she wanted to shout. *It's your birthday, for the sky's sake! Do something crazy. Eat some cake, if they have such luxuries in this awful city. Go find whatever guy it is you couldn't stop talking about. Whatever you do, dry your stupid tears.*

Why in the world was she here? Her urges had been strong and specific, leading her to this building. She always wondered if a deity of some sort was in charge of her visions. If so, was the nameless god playing a sadistic trick on her? That must be the case, because damn it, the girl was still crying.

At last, the sobbing stopped. The two girls moved closer to Sarza to pour some drinks. A few moments later, Sarza had to stifle a groan. The girls had just discovered they were drinking wine. *Here I am, parched after sitting here for hours. And those infuriating girls are drinking their troubles away.*

The girls returned to the other table. There was more quiet talking on their part, more eye rolling on Sarza's. The two guys came back. The four teenagers stayed in the room a couple of hours longer, talking and laughing. Sarza almost fell asleep.

Finally, the birthday girl left, along with one of the guys. Probably the one she'd been crying over. The dragon rider stuck around with a big guy whose muscles seemed to have a life of their own. They walked to the wine table, where Sarza would actually be able to hear their conversation.

Except the dragon rider and her friend didn't seem interested in talking. After they refilled their wine, they started making out. Sarza closed her eyes, but she couldn't block out the smacking, slobbering sounds. Her legs twitched with the urge to stand and walk away. That was how she always responded to public displays of affection—just get away. Don't look; don't think about it. This time, though, she was stuck. Her stomach tightened, and she realized she was clenching both fists and curling her toes. *Just end this. Please.*

Finally, they stopped. Sarza released her fists. Both her hands stung where her nails had pressed into her skin. She pressed her palms together.

In a low voice, the guy spoke one word: "Princess."

Sarza grimaced. Of all the terms of endearment in the world, *princess* was surely the worst.

"I like it when you call me that," the girl said with a little laugh.

Then there were more kissing noises, lasting even longer than before. Sarza's hands clenched again. She pictured a map of Cellerin, naming as many cities and towns as she could—anything to get her mind off the sounds traveling mercilessly to her ears.

When the couple halted at last, the girl spoke, her voice breathy. "Ovrun."

"Nora," he replied.

Sarza stopped breathing. Nora wasn't a common name. In fact, the only person she'd ever heard of with that name was Princess Ulminora, whose nickname was Nora. Sometimes there were drawings of her in the newspaper. She was a pretty girl with big eyes and chin-length, straight, dark hair. Sarza stared at the girl a couple of mets away, who was laughing and sipping her wine. Her hair was a little ragged, but with a trim, it would match the drawings exactly. Her eyes were large and animated.

Princess Nora Abrios is living with the trogs.

In an effort to calm her pounding heart, Sarza started breathing again. Now, this—this was information the army would actually want to know.

Maybe there really is a deity in charge of all these visions and urges. And maybe, by some crazy miracle, I'm on its good side.

16

Over the last few hundred years, Therroan society stabilized and substance abuse became less common. Then, fifty years ago, the percentage leveled off. Addiction rates have been low, but level, since.

It's 6293. We're an advanced society. Addiction is just a problem; shouldn't we be able to find a solution?

> -*"Can't We Beat Addiction?" by Genta Ril*
> The Derogan Chronicle, *dated Quari 26, 6293*

"I'LL TAKE you in five days."

That's what Krey had told Nora. "I'll try everything I can to convince you not to go," he'd said. "You have to actually listen to me. If I can't change your mind, I'll take you."

She'd agreed.

He hadn't really needed five days though. He'd needed four. Now that Zeisha's birthday had passed, he was ready to implement his own plan—which involved going to the palace alone. He knew the king might capture him. He might never see his friends again. *Before I leave, I have to give the girl I love a good birthday*, he'd told himself.

The morbid side of his mind had argued that if he died, he'd be ruining all of Zeisha's future birthdays. *God, keep me alive*, he'd prayed countless times.

It hadn't been a fun four days.

Now here he was, standing in a dark, dusty street. He'd fueled up with feathers. But he couldn't move as he considered one final question: should he tell Zeisha goodbye?

She didn't know he was leaving. In fact, she hadn't asked about his plans. That concerned him. In her position, he'd try to stop her. Just like he was stopping Nora. But Zeisha trusted him—a gift he didn't deserve. She honestly believed he'd do the right thing.

And I'm paying her back by doing this?

He took a good two dozen steps toward the building where she was sleeping. He'd tell her he was leaving. She deserved that.

He halted.

The little metal piece he'd used to break into a house in Cellerin City was in his pocket. Getting in wouldn't be a problem. But what if he accidentally woke Nora?

Zeisha trusts me. But Nora's not blind to my lesser qualities.

Krey pivoted and walked in a different direction. He'd left a note for Zeisha among his clothes. Someone would find it if he didn't return. That would have to be enough.

Decision made, he moved toward the one destination he needed to visit before he went to the palace. With every step, his feet got heavier, sodden by guilt and disgust and terrible memories. He kept walking anyway. It didn't take long to reach the Star Clan's butcher shop.

He'd avoided this place completely ever since coming here. Nora and Ovrun had teased him about his unwillingness to be around the dead animals they killed. What would they think of him when they knew why he'd really stayed away?

First, I'll check the ice storage. It would be nice to have access to all my talents. He walked to a side door and found it locked with a thick padlock. *Okay, no frost eating tonight.* With no other tasks to distract him from his real goal, Krey kept moving.

He had good reason to believe this quest would be successful. Ovrun and Nora had come to dinner flush with victory, having brought in twenty shimshims. *It almost seemed like God wanted him to do this,* Krey had mused. Then he'd tried to take the thought back, because he certainly shouldn't pin his own terrible ideas on God.

The moon was a tiny sliver in the sky, and the stars provided scant illumination. Krey lit a candle and examined the cleaning station behind the shop's rear wall. On the left was a tap, connected to an elevated water tank on the roof. Next to that was a sturdy table. The odor of Anyarian blood—sweet and harsh, like something fermented—hung in the air. But everything was clean and tidy. Too clean.

What was I thinking? Of course they'd clean up every day. How am I supposed to get what I need? I'm not a hunter—

There. Something he hadn't noticed, under the table. A chest. Krey opened it. The scent of blood and waste wafted up. This was it.

Trogs used most parts of shimshims. Pelts were dried into leather and traded or used to make clothing. They ate the meat, even some organs. Bones, once boiled, were used to make glue. But they couldn't use everything, and apparently this chest was where they put the extra animal parts before they buried or burned them.

Krey spotted the round, sac-like organs that stored shimshim waste. There was a heart, wrinkled and elongated, nothing like the human heart. His flame glimmered off a few round, faceted eyes. No use for those.

And there—looking dull in the dim candlelight—was a shimshim brain. It was small, about the diameter of a quid coin. Roughly spherical, it was composed of thin, overlapping layers. Almost like a head of lettuce. Krey knew it was a deep indigo color, though with the poor lighting, it looked black.

His heart went wild, its beat not just fast but frenzied. His mouth watered. Glee, disgust, and dread warred in his mind, building up with such pressure, he almost cried out.

Oh, God, no.

Oh, God, yes.

Oh, God, forgive me.

He picked up the damp, slick brain and put it in his backpack. Hand shaking, he rummaged through the chest and found two . . . three . . . five more. Nothing like the twenty-plus he'd feared and hoped for. Someone must've emptied the chest when most of the day's game had already been cleaned.

Six was enough. He hoped. They all went into the front pocket of his pack. He wiped his hand on his pants. Firmly fastened the buckle on the pocket.

The little brains, smooth and tempting, reached out to him, begging to be picked up. Devoured. Converted into the darkest talent of all.

The thrill of anticipation lit up his mind. He yearned to control someone, anyone. He tried to tamp down the urge, but it was frighteningly strong.

The intense craving brought him back to his childhood. Back then, it wasn't shimshim brains he desired; the little animals weren't common in Tirra. He'd eaten the brains of other creatures. They all had the same texture, though. The same smell. It had grossed him out the first time he'd held one. He almost hadn't taken a bite.

The first taste had changed everything. It was still disgusting; it always would be. But it was also divine. And as Krey's mind fixated with frightening intensity on the contents of his pack, he faced the fact that for the rest of his life, he'd crave Anyarian brain matter. If his desire hadn't fled after nine years, it never would. Staying far away from dead animals kept the urge under control, but it had been there all along, ready to spring up and bite him.

I can't believe I'm doing this again.

His hand reached toward the pocket of his pack. Just one taste . . .

He clenched his fingers so hard they ached, then grabbed the straps of his pack and swung it on his back. This wasn't about indulging his sick craving. It was about using a terrible talent to fight a terrible man. He'd wait to eat the fuel until he needed it. He'd be strong. He had to be.

Krey turned on his flight magic and jumped into the air.

He hadn't anticipated what it would feel like to incorporate the backpack into his magic. He sensed every element of the tiny, dark-blue brains. If he wanted to, he could count their layers. They swathed him in desire that dulled his other senses, warmed him in the cool air, teased him with sweet whispers.

Focus. Eat some feathers. Think about what's next.

He did eat feathers, but his mind didn't want to travel into the future. Instead, it slithered into his past.

He was eight years old. He'd recently quit his magical training classes, convincing his parents he could learn better by reading books at home. His reading was nothing short of voracious in those days. Aunt Min and Aunt Evie, who lived down the street, let him browse and borrow their tomes on magic.

Tucked between larger books on a bottom shelf, young Krey found a rare, handwritten book, dated just three decades after The Day. It had the most intriguing title a young boy could imagine: *Secrets of the Stone.* Krey's aunts didn't want him to take the valuable book. For weeks, he plied them with constant arguments about its educational benefits.

He convinced them, probably through annoying persistence, rather than his negotiating skills. Neither Aunt Min nor Aunt Evie had read the book. They sent him home with it and told him to report back after finishing it.

The handwriting inside was atrocious. Krey almost gave up on it. Then he found the passage on brain eating. His little jaw dropped as he read the author's story of how a magic eater had discovered that when he ate brain matter from Anyarian animals, he could influence others' minds.

That was the coolest thing Krey had ever heard. He'd immediately run to the home of a friend whose parents were hunters. His friend's dad was behind the house, cleaning the game he'd caught that day. Krey offered to burn the unwanted parts of the small animals. The man laughed. "Doubt your parents would want you doing that alone, but you can help me."

When Krey came across a brain, which the hunter had already removed from the skull, he slipped it in his pocket. A few minutes later, he snagged another. Claiming to remember an unfinished chore, he ran home.

Like most young kids, Krey thought himself invincible. Sure, he knew Anyarian brain matter was poisonous. But the book had convinced him magic eaters were immune. He hadn't read the rest of the passage in the book—the part where the author disclosed the darkness behind brain eating. Most magic eaters who ate brain matter died, just like any other human would. Those who didn't die grew addicted and eventually went mad. The author said he'd considered hiding the discovery but had decided future generations deserved a warning.

The next day, when Krey deciphered all those scrawled words, he realized how lucky he was. He was one of the few who could eat brain matter and survive it. By then, he'd already used his new gift on his parents.

He'd started small. Instinct had told him to touch his mother. He'd felt the connection with her mind immediately. It was like he was staring at an open door, but he couldn't see what was inside. Brain eating allowed him to influence minds, not read them.

Krey had convinced his mother to make a cake. He'd kept the link to her mind open until the cake went in the oven. Soon after, his fuel ran out. His mother shook her head and said, "I must really love you, Krey. I certainly didn't have time to make that cake today!"

In the coming days, Krey kept stealing fuel and experimenting. Unfortunately, the gig was up pretty quickly. A week after Krey first ate brain matter, his mother brought home a bowlbird for dinner. She left the room. When she returned, she found Krey plucking the bird's brain out of its skull and lifting the little organ to his mouth.

"Stop!" she cried, rushing to him.

He grinned and ate it.

The entire kitchen shook with Krey's mother's screams. She grabbed him, weeping, insisting they go to a healer to get the poison out of his system. He planted his feet. He had to shout, "I've been eating brains for a week!" for two minutes straight before his mother heard him.

The rest of the truth came out: the cake, the delayed bedtimes, all the other little indulgences Krey had convinced his parents to give him over the previous week. He didn't think to tell his mother about the addiction and possible madness. His young mind was convinced he was stronger than that. When his mother read the book for herself, her tears started again.

The next six months of Krey's life were hell. His parents didn't let him out of their sight. He slept in their bed, between them. His mother withdrew him from school and taught him herself. When he needed the outhouse, she walked there and stood outside while he used it. Worse yet, when she had to use it, she brought him in with her.

For the first day, Krey thought the new rules were pointless. He promised he'd stop eating brain matter. Then the cravings started. When he'd gone thirty hours without his new fuel, all he could think about was how to get more.

He attempted to sneak out of the house in the middle of the night. His parents caught him as he opened the front door. They installed padlocks. That didn't stop Krey from trying to sneak out windows when his parents turned their backs. They were too vigilant for him to succeed.

Nausea kept Krey from eating. He thrashed all night. He was full of energy one moment, exhausted the next, anxious always. The worst of the detox symptoms lasted a week. Then his body recovered, but his mind still fixated on one thing: *I need my fuel.* Not feathers, not ice. He didn't care about those talents now. He needed brain matter. Salivated every time he thought of it. Twisted his mind in knots trying to plan an escape attempt.

He was eight. His sense of strategy sucked. Every attempt to leave the house was stopped by his firm, loving, tired parents.

The cravings began abating after the first couple of weeks. But it was a slow decrease. Krey had been recovering for five months when he woke one day and said, in all honesty, "I don't want to see another animal brain in my whole life." It wasn't that he didn't desire them. He missed the texture, the taste. He missed the mental power most of all.

But at last, he could see it had cost him the small amount of freedom he'd had at that age. And he was finally convinced he'd go mad if he returned to his addiction. He was nine by then; maybe he'd grown up a bit.

His parents kept him home for another month. Gradually, they reinstated his privileges. He stayed in the house while his mother visited the outhouse. He played with a friend outside. In the last week, he slept in his own bed. After half a year of recovery, Krey went back to school. To his parents' relief—and his own—he never tried to steal animal brain matter again.

His parents kept the incident secret. They told the school some story about an illness he'd battled. Life returned to normal. Until a little over a year later, when Krey's parents died of orange plague.

Krey moved in with Min and Evie. He learned that during his mother's dying days, she'd disclosed his addiction to his aunts. During Krey's months of deepest grief, he was tempted to kill an animal with his own hands, crack open its skull, and indulge. He confessed the urges to Min and Evie. They helped him stay strong.

Years later, Krey and Zeisha became more than friends. In a rush of passionate trust, he told her the truth. She vowed to never tell a soul. She'd kept that promise.

But he'd made a promise too. He'd told her he'd never eat the brain of an animal again, never even touch one.

And here he was. Flying over the black wilderness between Doroga and Cellerin City. Mentally caressing the tiny brains in his backpack, like the depraved human being he knew he was. *I'm breaking my oath.*

He made it to Cellerin City, only stopping twice on the way to rest. Somehow, he kept the front pocket of his backpack closed during those stops.

Krey alighted in the street before a pub that had a very specific reputation. He'd never been there, but during his short stint living in the capital, a few of his fellow apprentices had gone there every weekend. Krey knew the place would have the item he was seeking.

The front and back doors were locked. Krey flew to the second floor and let out a relieved breath when he found a pair of open shutters on a bedroom window. Ten minutes later, he'd stolen what he needed from the pub below, and he was back in the air.

After another short flight, Krey dropped to the ground, allowing the trees of the woods outside the palace grounds to swallow him up. He opened his backpack. Fingers shaking, he unbuckled the front pocket too.

Water first, a few good gulps. Then—oh, by the sky, when his fingers brushed against the smooth little spheres in the pocket, when they felt the tiny ripple where one layer of brain matter overlapped another, it was all he wanted.

He lifted his hand. Opened his mouth.

His tongue got its first taste. His teeth bit in, and he groaned. In delight. In despair.

Krey reached for another.

Zeisha didn't claim to understand God. Lately, she'd had a hard time even talking to him, after what she'd done during the militia battle.

But she trusted him. And some knowledge, deeper than logic, told her he was with her, every moment.

She woke in a dark room. Such middle-of-the-night wakings usually gave her flashbacks of her nights in the militia.

This time was different. She didn't wonder where she was. She wasn't anxious or confused. A prodding urge overtook her: *I need to check on Krey.*

After her emotional chat with Nora, Zeisha had pondered whether she should confront Krey about his plans. Late last night, she'd concluded he would want her to be honest. She had to talk to him. A sense of urgency had squeezed her gut, but Krey had already gone to bed. It could wait until morning, she decided.

Now here she was, wide awake, certain she shouldn't have waited.

Minutes later, Zeisha stood at the door of the building where Krey slept. The room was probably locked, but she tried the knob anyway.

It twisted.

Something told Zeisha this was a bad thing.

She stepped into the blackness and reached down, touching the beds on the right. *One. Two. Three.* This was Krey's. She patted her hands along its length. Blankets. Sheets. Pillow. No Krey.

Zeisha's breaths quickened. She turned to the next bed. Her hand fell on a firm shoulder.

"Ovrun!" She shook his shoulder. "Ovrun, wake up!"

17

I've never eaten meat. None of my friends have either.

It's been forty-one years since the global passage of the Lab-Created Meat Statute, the law criminalizing hunting, meat sales, and meat consumption. However, last month, a Derogan family of four died after eating meat they purchased from a poacher. The cause of the family's death was announced today: ingestion of cervid brain matter.

You know what doesn't contain brain matter? Lab-created meat.

You know what else doesn't contain brain matter? The skull of someone who buys meat from a poacher.

-"Brainless" by Genta Ril
The Derogan Chronicle, *dated Quari 27, 6293*

Six tiny brains sat in Krey's belly, ready to be catalyzed.

Most of the time, he went days, weeks even, without dwelling on his desire for brain matter. But tonight, the forbidden fuel had quenched a thirst that had lurked in his subconscious for nine long years.

It felt amazing.

And torturous.

Krey swore to never look at another animal brain again. *If I manage to escape the king tonight.*

That was a big *if*.

Krey put on his backpack and returned to the air.

He flew straight up, so high that no one would be likely to notice his body against the stars. Then he leveled off and flew over the palace grounds.

Lights allowed him to see parts of the property. The difficult thing would be avoiding the attention of guard caynins. They knew his scent and voice—but before he got close enough for them to recognize him, they might sound the alarm.

After a few minutes, Krey got a good sense of where all the caynins were. Some patrolled with guards; others roamed the property alone. If he timed it right, he could drop on a rooftop without being seen.

Krey descended, slowly and smoothly, until another guard came into view—soaring through the air.

Oh, hell. I thought the king had fired all his magic eaters. He must've hired this one recently. Krey adjusted his strategy, even as he ascended. This could work. It would all be about timing, but he could deal with another flyer. He could *use* another flyer.

Krey watched the feather eater take the same route over the property twice. The predictability would make this even easier. Anticipation, ugly and thrilling, sent his heart pumping harder. It was time to use his terrible magic.

Krey confirmed that the guards patrolling outside the property weren't nearby. He dove, then pressed himself against the outside of the gold, stone fence, head even with the barbed wire at the top. The feather eater was flying his direction.

As soon as the flyer passed, Krey shot into the air and silently approached, praying the guard caynins didn't notice him. He had to make skin-to-skin contact with the feather eater. That would be tough, since the guard was bundled up—including gloves and a hat. *Come on, it's not that cold.*

Krey flew directly over the guard, whose gaze was on the ground. Not breathing, Krey descended. His hand came out. Cool fingers touched a warm neck.

The flyer jerked, crying out with a voice that sounded female. Her body started dropping, concentration clearly compromised.

Her fall broke their physical connection, but Krey had established a mental connection. Unlike the king, he could only control someone if he was touching them or keeping them in sight. There was enough light for Krey to see the flyer. "You're safe," he called softly. "You can fly."

It worked. The feather eater stopped falling. Krey swooped down to her, scanning for caynins the whole way. "Follow me."

She looked up with wide eyes. "Okay."

He zoomed higher. The woman followed.

Curses exited Nora's mouth, long strings of words she rarely gave herself permission to say. Ovrun took it in stride, but Zeisha's mouth hung open like someone had broken the hinge of her jaw. She'd probably never expected to hear a princess talk that way.

Deep breath. No time to be mad. Nora looked between Zeisha and Ovrun. The three of them were huddled around a lantern near the women's bunkhouse door. "I need to make sure I've got this right," Nora said, her voice hushed yet intense. "Krey's a brain lyster, and he's gone to confront my father?"

"Yes," Zeisha said. "I was going to talk to him and tell him he shouldn't go. I should've done it last night, but—"

"Okay, Zeisha, okay," Nora snapped. She took another deep breath. Yes, she was angry. Quite frankly, she couldn't believe Zeisha hadn't come straight to them when Krey had first disclosed his plans. But the last thing Zeisha needed was for someone to blame her for this. *It's not her fault. It's the fault of that massive ass who is at this moment on his way to get himself arrested or killed. Or turned into the next Faylie.* The thought sent painful cramps into Nora's stomach.

"We have to go there," Ovrun said. "Nora, can you call the dragons?"

Thank the sky one of them was thinking straight. Nora reached her thoughts out to the mountains south of Deroga. *Osmius! Are you awake? Osmius?*

No answer.

Taima? Osmius? Please! It's urgent!

Damn it, why did magical creatures have to sleep at all? Over and over, Nora pushed her telepathic messages through the air. She was almost ready to give up when Osmius's low voice reached her mind.

What do you need, Nora-human?

Osmius! Oh, thank the stone. We need your help.

Krey had never stopped craving the manipulative power of his magic. He'd known he'd take awful joy in controlling someone again.

Something in him, however, had changed over the last nine years. Touching this woman's mind, guiding her to agree with everything he said . . . yes, it filled him with an unnatural bliss. But it also felt wrong. Sick.

He pushed his emotional battle into the background. No time to deal with the psychological ramifications of brain eating tonight. That would all come later.

He and the woman were sitting in the dirt in the same wooded area where he'd stopped on his way in. He couldn't see her face in the dark, but he'd gotten a brief glimpse of it in the light of lanterns over the palace grounds. She was probably in her forties, with small features and bits of short hair sticking out from under a knitted cap.

Krey squeezed the woman's hands, which were no longer covered with gloves. In the dark, touching her was the only way to keep their connection active. "What's your name?"

"Brea."

"Brea. It's good to meet you. I need to reach the king. You're going to help me."

"How?"

"I'll tell you my plan. At the palace, you'll follow my lead, but you'll also take any steps that will help me complete my mission."

"Okay."

Krey explained his strategy. He and Brea refueled with additional feathers, then returned to the air.

They flew high and stopped directly over the administrative wing of the palace. "Drop to the roof," Krey said.

As they'd planned, Brea kept her body parallel to the ground. Krey hovered above her, using her as a visual shield in case anyone looked up. They began a smooth descent.

A caynin who'd been in the shadows came into view.

"It's me!" Brea called.

The animal kept running, ignoring them.

The two flyers alighted on the roof near the rear entrance Krey had used when he'd worked at the library.

"Go," Krey said.

Brea flew down and landed by the door guard. Krey leaned over the roof, watching in the light of the guard's lantern as Brea chatted with the man. With her in sight, Krey's control over her remained strong.

Brea's job was to get the man relaxed enough to walk away from the door, but they'd found a guard who was a little too diligent. Even as Brea backed up, chatting the whole time, he remained glued to the door. Krey's breathing accelerated. *Come on. Get him away so I can fly in behind him.*

Krey's power was nothing like Faylie's had been. He was most effective when giving verbal commands, but he could also send general ideas into someone's head. He pushed a thought toward Brea: *Get him away. Try something else.*

Brea gestured to the guard to come look at something. Still, the man didn't move his feet even a simmet away from the door.

I gotta improvise.

It came to him. An idea that just might work.

Brea was shorter than the door guard. The man was looking down at her. From above, Krey could see the man's bare head.

Please don't look up.

Krey lifted off the roof. He positioned himself with his head pointed to the ground, boots straight up in the air.

Keeping every action controlled, Krey glided forward until he was directly over the guard. Hands extended, he moved smoothly downward.

Brea looked up. The guard followed suit. "Hey!" he shouted.

Oops.

Krey shot down like a bullet. He grabbed the man's face with both hands and established a mental connection. "Silent," he said.

The man's mouth closed.

Krey let go of him and landed. "I have an important message for the king. Open the door."

The man complied.

Krey's chest ached with dread over what he had to do next. Controlling two people at once strained his mind and burned through his fuel. So he commanded the man to go to a nearby office. The guard obeyed. In the office, Krey compelled him to hand over his keys and explain which ones opened which doors.

After instructing the guard to sit against the wall, Krey opened his pack and retrieved the bottle he'd taken from the pub. It was a strong liquor, laced with an illegal substance extracted from the Anyarian vinnin plant. Everyone referred to the drug as *vin*.

In very small doses, vin sent the user into a state of deep relaxation. In slightly larger doses, it knocked someone out. While it was powerful, it was rarely toxic.

That fact didn't eliminate the twist in Krey's gut. This was the best way he'd thought of to put the guards out of commission, but that didn't make it okay.

He held out the bottle. "Drink," he said. "Four large gulps."

The guard obeyed. Within a minute, his mouth curved into a slow, intoxicated smile. Seconds later, Krey's connection with the man snapped. Krey gasped. He hadn't considered the possibility of drunkenness having such a result.

But the guard wasn't upset to find himself in a bathroom with two strangers. He simply took both their hands and slurred, "This is so very, very nice," before slumping into unconsciousness.

Krey used cloth to gag the man and rope to tie his hands and feet. He had to be sure the guard couldn't easily get free if he woke early. That done, he and Brea returned to the hallway outside the office.

The palace was silent at night. They traversed one corridor after another, carrying the guard's lantern. Before long, they reached the door leading to the hallway between the administrative wing and the residence.

After handing Brea the keys, Krey hid behind the door. Brea unlocked and opened it.

A male guard on the other side of the door said, "Who are—wait, are you that new flyer?"

"Yes, the guard at the door sent me with a message. But I saw something concerning on my way here." Having repeated the words Krey had told her to say, she backed away from the door and pointed.

The guard walked in. Krey touched him, established control, and whispered, "Tell your partner at the end of the hall that you need to check on something. Say whatever is necessary to keep them calm. Then come back here with me and remain silent."

Krey watched from the darkness beyond the lantern's light as the guard stepped into the hallway and said, "Hey, I need to check on something. I'll be right back."

"You know we can't leave our posts," a female voice said.

"It's just in this room. It won't take long." When there was no response, the guard walked around the door.

"I need you to sit over there." Krey pointed at a heavy armchair.

The man obeyed. It didn't take long to drug him into oblivion. Krey whispered instructions to Brea and hid behind the door.

Brea walked to the doorway, calling, "Something's wrong with your partner. He just fell over."

The female guard cursed. In seconds, she was within Krey's reach. Krey's breathing slammed to a stop. His hand halted halfway to the guard. He knew this woman. They'd joked around with each other when he lived here. Now he'd control her. His mouth grew dry with dread, even as his heart raced with anticipation.

She turned and squinted. "Krey?"

He grasped her hand and established control. "No talking. I'm genuinely sorry for what I have to do. It's nothing personal." It was a terrible, meaningless apology, but nothing he could say would make this right. A couple of minutes later, she, too was seated and unconscious.

Krey and Brea gagged both guards and tied them to their chairs. After taking the female guard's keys, Krey extinguished the lantern and set it down. He led Brea down the corridor, which was lit by electric bulbs.

"Unlock the door," he said, handing Brea the keys. She tried one after another, the jangling metal making Krey grimace. When the knob turned, he released a sigh.

They entered the dark residence. Krey remembered enough of the layout to get to Nora's quarters. He'd never been to the king's rooms though. He and Brea crept through the large home, groping along walls and bumping into furniture.

When they entered the home's main living room, the sweet, subdued smell of Anyarian brain matter reached Krey. Saliva flooded the space under his tongue. He swallowed. Could other people smell it too, or had his recent ingestion of the fuel increased his sensitivity to it?

He breathed through his mouth, trying not to take in the distracting smell. Crossing the room, he looked down the dark hallway that led to Dani's and Nora's quarters. Surely Ulmin slept somewhere nearby.

Krey knew Nora would want him to rescue her aunt. But he didn't have long. The guards would wake. One of them might even break free. The king was his top priority.

He kept walking. Ahead, a bit of light spilled from another hallway. Krey stopped and peeked around the corner.

Two guards stood on either side of a door. It had to be Ulmin's quarters. Krey turned to Brea, held a brief, whispered conversation with her, and watched her enter the hallway.

"It's Brea," she said quietly. "The feather eater."

Again, she said she'd seen something suspicious—and again, it worked.

She led the first guard out of the hallway, straight into Krey's influence. At Brea's insistence, the other guard came to check on his colleague. Both men were soon unconscious, gagged, and tied to chairs in the living room.

Krey wasn't usually superstitious, but something deep in his gut told him he'd pay later for how well his plans were going now. Or maybe that deep gnawing wasn't fear. Maybe it was guilt for all the people he'd drugged tonight. Five guards. Then there was Brea—she was conscious, but he was enslaving her mind. *Definitely including her on the list of people who have every right to hate me.*

And since he was making a list, he'd better add Nora. He'd outright lied to her. Ovrun wouldn't be too happy with him either.

Zeisha might accept what he'd done, but he suspected it would change things between them. Maybe irrevocably.

I've come too far to stop now.

Brea's hand in his, Krey flipped a switch on the wall. Darkness enveloped the hallway.

They walked to the king's door. Krey grasped the knob.

It turned.

18

Therro's biggest ad agencies have entire departments devoted to one audience: teenagers.

Let me tell you a secret: teens hate slick ads. You want to get us to do something, buy something, go somewhere? Persuade us it'll change our world for the better. And convince us it'll be fun.

Most of us aren't as selfish as you think we are. We want to make a difference. We just want to enjoy ourselves along the way.

-*"The Path to Persuasion" by Genta Ril*
The Derogan Chronicle, *dated Quari 31, 6293*

As Nora rode on Osmius's back, she tried to tune out Taima's disdainful messages—things like, *Humans should not be allowed to leave home until they're three decades old.* The female dragon thought

Krey was mad for wanting to confront an incredibly powerful brain lyster alone.

Nora agreed.

They'd been flying for over an hour—Ovrun riding Taima, Nora and Zeisha sharing Osmius's back. Both Nora's friends were quiet. Even Osmius seemed to sense that she wanted silence. She needed this flight to come to terms with what she'd learned about Krey. Her friend. The one she trusted.

The one she'd lied to.

So why am I so mad at him for lying to me? Whether it made sense or not, fury burned and bubbled in Nora's chest. Krey had spent days stringing her along, telling her he'd take her to the palace—all while he prepared to pop some brains in his mouth and fly off alone.

Krey West was a brain lyster. And he'd lied about it for months.

But was it a lie, when he'd simply neglected to tell the whole truth? Nora wasn't sure.

Maybe the only reason she was mad was because she felt so stupid. She should've figured out Krey's secret faculty a long time ago. Krey wasn't the type to get grossed out easily, yet he avoided dead animals. And he knew so much about brain lysting. She'd never questioned him when he said he'd read it in a book.

All this time, he'd stayed away from dead shimshims because he couldn't handle the temptation. He'd learned about brain lysting through personal experience.

Why was he going back to a practice that, according to Zeisha, he'd left behind nine years ago? *He's an idiot. It's that simple.*

A hand found Nora's ankle and squeezed. "Are you doing okay up there?" Zeisha asked.

Nora wanted to laugh. To say Zeisha was having a rough day was a massive understatement. She was ashamed of not confronting Krey. She was flying on a dragon for the first time, an experience that could be overwhelming. Despite her hatred of violence, she was prepared to storm into the palace to save the boy she loved.

And she asked if Nora was okay.

Did Krey understand what a jewel he had in Zeisha?

Nora turned her head. "I'm fine. Are you okay?"

"It's not as fun as riding on Krey's back, but I'm managing!" Zeisha's voice shook a bit.

Before Nora could respond, Taima's voice penetrated her mind. *I see the palace.*

Nora closed her eyes, releasing all her breath. She'd hoped that with the dragons' incredible speed, they'd catch Krey on his way to the palace. Either he'd had too much of a head start, or they'd unknowingly passed him.

Nora let the cool air wash away her anger. Time to focus. Time to save a friend.

Even if he was an idiot.

Brea's hand in his, Krey moved silently through a sitting room that was barely lit by glowing embers in a fireplace. The smell of brain matter was stronger in here. Desire rushed into Krey. He pushed it away. *Focus.*

They reached the door that Krey hoped led to Ulmin's bedroom. It creaked as he opened it. This room, too, was lit by a dying fire. A shadowed figure lay on the bed.

Still holding Brea's hand, Krey tiptoed to the bed. He placed a hand on the king's ear.

The king's mind felt like any other—open, receptive to Krey's control. Krey's response, however, was nothing like it had been with Brea or the other guards. Ulmin Abrios had given orders for Zeisha to be kidnapped. He'd enslaved her. Traumatized her. Now Krey was controlling the controller.

Gone was his guilt for taking over someone's mind. This felt amazing.

The king didn't wake. Krey backed away, stopping near the door.

At last, he let go of Brea's hand, whispering instructions to her. She walked to the bed and sat on the edge. Keeping his eyes on both the king and Brea, Krey turned on the light.

"Everything is fine," he said, repeating the phrase three times as the king sat up, blinking and rubbing his eyes.

King Ulmin's dark-brown eyes reminded Krey of Nora's. Gray streaked his hair—more than Krey remembered him having before. His skin looked more wrinkled too. But he still appeared powerful, his loose pajama shirt not hiding his broad shoulders.

"Hello," Ulmin said in a pleasant, level voice. "You're Kreyven West."

"I am."

"Do you know where my daughter is?"

"We aren't talking about that."

Ulmin nodded.

Krey had spent much of the previous four days considering what he'd do once he reached the king. The most strategic option was to assassinate the man. Without Ulmin, Nora could return, claim the crown, and bring the army home.

And she'd forever live with the grief of both of her parents being slain. Of knowing that one of her few friends had turned her into an orphan.

Perhaps that would be what was best for Cellerin. But God help him, Krey couldn't do that to Nora. Not unless it was the only option.

Ulmin, however, couldn't remain in power. Krey had to get him away from the palace. Lock him up somewhere remote. Keep him away from the fuel that let him control others.

Then Nora could talk to her father, just as she'd planned. But those conversations would happen far away from the palace. Away from the king's fuel and the people who might help him. Nora would have to lead Cellerin, at least temporarily. Maybe Ulmin could recover from his addiction, maybe not.

Krey knew Nora didn't feel ready to be queen. But she was more capable than she gave herself credit for.

"Ulmin," Krey said, "You're going to get out of bed and put on your shoes. Then we'll walk through the palace together."

"All right." Ulmin pushed his blankets off his legs.

"Brea," Krey instructed, "stay with him."

Ulmin and the feather-eating guard stood. The king walked straight to his shoes, next to the door. He sat on the floor to put them on.

Krey watched him. There were so many questions he wanted to ask, but they could wait. Right now, he had to stay focused. Clutching two minds strained his endurance. Sweat beaded on his upper lip and forehead. He begged his fuel to continue giving him power.

Nora wanted to fly Taima all the way to the palace. But it was one thing for Krey to attempt to fly in unnoticed. It was another thing entirely for a huge dragon to fill the sky, just begging armed guards to shoot her.

They'd have to do this the hard way. She, Ovrun, and Zeisha had come up with a simple plan as they'd waited for the dragons to pick them up.

They'd stop in the woods outside the palace. Zeisha would get them over the fence. Nora would escort them through the property, keeping caynins at bay. Ovrun would be ready for any surprises.

After an uneventful flight, the dragons landed in a clearing barely large enough for Taima's wide wings.

If you need assistance, call me, Taima told Nora as the humans dismounted. *I would like to encounter the king again.* Her tone was low and colored with cruelty.

Nora, Ovrun, and Zeisha hurried through the dark trees, getting scratched up along the way. Within a few minutes, the palace fence was visible.

"I fueled up as we walked," Zeisha whispered. "I'll get to work."

Time slid by. Nora bit back her desire to tell Zeisha to hurry. At last, she heard her friend scrambling down a tree.

"It's ready," Zeisha whispered.

Nora walked to the tree, followed by Ovrun. Zeisha had used her magic to create a ladder of branches on the trunk. Even in the dark, it was easy to climb.

At the top, Zeisha spoke softly to both of them. "The ladder arcs high into the sky. I didn't want any guards to spot us. It goes all the way into the wooded area inside the fence, the one Nora told me about."

"It can hold me?" Ovrun asked.

"Yes, it's very strong."

After the next guard passed by, they proceeded. The arched ladder was indeed stable. It was also scary as hell. As Nora crawled across, she feared a gust of wind would knock her off the edge.

From the rear, Zeisha said, "If anyone falls, I'll use a vine to catch you."

The thought wasn't all that comforting.

At the ladder's highest point, each of them had to turn and start crawling backward. Nora's knee slipped off the edge, but somehow she stayed on. At last, they passed over the fence and into the wooded area. When Nora's foot hit solid ground, leftover fear constricted her chest. She gulped air, only calming when Ovrun took her hand.

She led her friends through the palace grounds, greeting two caynins along the way. When the residence came in sight, Nora muttered a curse. Someone had installed electric lights at the gate.

After a quick huddle, the three friends approached the residence from the rear. Nora didn't have any fuel, so making an ice ladder wasn't an option. Once again, Zeisha would have to get them over the fence.

She created a long ladder, this one of vines. Ovrun coiled up half of it and hurled it over the fence. He held the ends of the ladder in place while Zeisha scrambled up it to cover the barbed wire with more vines. She descended and told Nora, "Be careful up there."

Nora climbed up. The vine ladder was floppy and awkward. At the top, barbed wire snagged her pants as she attempted to turn around. She broke free and climbed down the other side, quietly greeting two caynins. As she neared the bottom, the animals sniffed her and wiggled with glee.

When Zeisha and Ovrun joined her, they all walked to the icehouse. Nora put her key in the lock.

It didn't turn. Her father had changed the locks. Dani, now mind controlled, had probably told him about Nora and Krey's nighttime visit before the militia battle.

Nora cursed again.

Krey swallowed the vomit pressing at his throat. When he was eight, he'd held onto two minds only once. He'd needed to convince both his parents that he should get an extra slice of pie. That had been difficult, and he'd only done it for a couple of minutes.

How much longer can I handle this? I'm burning fuel too quickly. By the orange sky above, how long does it take to tie a pair of shoes?

Krey knew what he had to do; he just didn't want to. Brea had helped him get here, albeit unwillingly. She seemed so kind, someone he'd love to chat with about feather magic. And this was how he'd pay her back?

Ulmin stood, shoes tied.

If I can just hang onto two minds for a few more minutes.

Krey's roiling stomach told him that was too much to ask.

"Ulmin, don't move. Brea, please come sit on the floor next to me."

She sat, relaxed, as he instructed her to drink the drugged liquor. When his connection with her broke, his entire body seemed to sigh in relief. Just one mind to control. He could do this. Brea's eyes fluttered shut, and Krey laid her on the floor. No need to tie her up. He'd be out of here soon, flying away with the king.

"We're going to walk to the front door of the residence," Krey said. "You'll go in front of me. If we encounter any conscious guards, tell them I'm a houseguest and that we're going outside for some air. Got it?"

The king nodded.

Krey grabbed Ulmin's arm. They walked into the sitting room. Again, the scent of brain matter wafted into Krey's nose, making his mouth water. *I could make him tell me where it is. I could refuel.*

Just as he was about to obey that instinct, Zeisha's face popped into his mind. *You don't have time,* he imagined her whispering. *Those guards may be waking up right now.* Somehow, despite his craving, he listened.

"Run," Krey instructed. He held the king's arm as they jogged through the hallway and into the dark living room where Krey had left the two guards from the king's bedroom. They were halfway through the big room when Krey's knee slammed into the corner of a low table.

In a moment, everything fell apart.

With both hands, Krey grabbed his bruised knee. Ulmin kept running. In the moment it took Krey to realize he'd let go of his prey, the king disappeared into the darkness. Krey's connection with the man's mind snapped like a dry twig.

"What is happening?" Ulmin roared.

The room's electric lights came on. A guard, standing in the room's entrance, shouted, "Your Majesty! I found unconscious guards in the—who is this?"

Krey fixed his gaze on the king, who had dashed across the room. He tried to reestablish his hold over the man's mind, but his magic sparked on and off. He'd burned through nearly all his fuel in the panic and pain after his collision with the table.

Fury searing his mind, Krey floundered, trying to grasp the threads of his magic. The effort was pointless. His remaining fuel dissipated as soon as he tried to use it. Running was his only hope now. He pivoted, prepared to flee.

His path was blocked by yet another guard, a massive man who looked like he spent half the day working out and the other half eating raw meat. Krey tried to run past him. The guard leapt, tackling him to the floor.

Krey's breath exited his chest, along with his hope. Strong, quick hands flipped him on his belly and grabbed his arms, wrenching them behind him. Knees dug into his back. Gasping to regain his breath, Krey bucked and squirmed. His captor was too strong.

Then it hit him. He had fuel of another sort.

He lifted off the ground. The guard on his back cried out and tumbled off.

Krey bounced off the ceiling. His eyes found the king. Ulmin was pulling something from a box on an end table. Dread washed over Krey as he caught a glimpse of indigo, right before it entered the king's mouth.

The guard who'd tackled Krey recovered. He jumped up and snagged Krey's foot. Krey incorporated the man into his magic, pulling him off the ground.

"Catch him, but don't shoot him!" the king cried.

Krey flew toward the room's exit, shaking his leg. The guard held on fast.

Still kicking, Krey dropped low enough to go through the doorway. Halfway through, a handgun flew through the air and slammed into his forehead, breaking his focus. He dropped like a stone, landing hard on his hands and knees, right next to the gun. Krey reached for it. The guard was faster.

Krey scrambled to reactivate his flight magic. But too much was happening. A guard pinned him down again. His body cried out in pain. His talent wouldn't respond. *Come on, come on, come on!*

Two pajama-clad knees knelt in front of Krey.

A hand gripped his cheeks.

His mind went blank.

19

I went to a fire illusionist show last week. It was the most fun I've had in months—thousands of audience members, most of them around my age, watching someone play with fire.

I believe such shows are popular because our world is so safe. Hemmed in by precautions and certainty, we crave wildness. And what is wilder than fire?

-"On Fire" by Genta Ril
The Derogan Chronicle, *dated Quari 32, 6293*

Nora held her breath.

Zeisha was trying to slip a skinny vine between a window and its frame. Unfortunately, she was working in the dark. *She's good, but is she this good?*

"I got the vine in," Zeisha breathed.

"The latch should be right there," Nora said. "Catch it with the vine and pull it to the right." She'd already told Zeisha that, but she couldn't handle just standing here, waiting.

"I can't seem to grab it." Zeisha grunted as she kept trying.

Nora suppressed a frustrated moan.

"Got it!" Ovrun said, from a nearby window. He was trying the same thing, but with a knife.

Nora and Zeisha rushed up to him, greeted by the delightful, awful sound of a squeaky window opening. Ovrun boosted Zeisha through the window. He couldn't fit, so he and Nora rushed to the icehouse door. Seconds later, Zeisha opened it from the inside. Nora shoved a handful of ice into her mouth and grabbed two more handfuls to eat on the go. They all ran into Nora's bedroom.

A shout rang out from somewhere in the house. Nora sprinted through her dark bedroom and sitting room. A smidge of light glowed underneath the door that led to the hallway. She swallowed a mouthful of ice, then dropped the rest and opened the door carefully.

The light was coming from the living room at the end of the long hallway. "Wait here," Nora told Ovrun and Zeisha.

She continued alone. As she passed Dani's door, her body ached with the desire to grab her aunt and flee. But based on the shouting she'd heard, she guessed Krey was in immediate danger. *One thing at a time.*

At the end of the corridor, Nora peeked into the living room. *Oh no. No, no, no.*

Just inside the far doorway, Krey had been pinned down by a huge royal guard. Nora's father, clad in pajamas, was kneeling, touching Krey. Another guard stood nearby. Two unconscious guards were tied to chairs along one wall.

As Nora scurried back to Ovrun and Zeisha, she called Taima to circle high above the palace. Then, panting, she whispered to her friends, "If you hear a really loud noise, it's Taima. That's when I'll need you to come help."

"Do you want us to get your aunt?" Ovrun asked.

Yes! Nora's heart cried. But a deeper urge made her hesitate. Her father was awake. At any time, he could take control of Dani's mind. Then there would be one more person working against them.

"No," Nora said. "We'll come for her later." It was a promise—to her friends, her aunt, and herself.

Without waiting for more questions, Nora returned to the end of the corridor. Krey was on a couch. The king sat in front of him in a chair, talking softly. The two guards watched from a few mets away. It had been perhaps a minute since the king had touched Krey. How many secrets could her father have learned in that time?

Krey spoke, his voice louder than Ulmin's. "Nora is healthy," he said flatly. "She's been hiding with me and—"

"Dad!" Nora interrupted, stepping into the room.

Both guards jerked to attention, pointing handguns at her.

Her father stood, telling the guards, "Guns down. You will not touch her unless I instruct otherwise."

The guards returned to their previous stances—relaxed yet ready for anything. Her father was controlling them even now; she was sure of it.

King Ulmin Abrios turned toward his daughter. The coldness of habitual authority fled his eyes. They crinkled at the edges as his mouth curved into the smile Nora had grown up with—the one that told her he cherished her. "Come in, darling," he said.

Darling. The guards didn't need to shoot—that word was a bullet. "I won't let you touch me," she murmured.

He closed his eyes briefly, and when they opened again, she saw pain in them. He sat. "I don't want to control you."

His voice was gentle, but Nora took note of his words. He didn't *want* to control her. But he hadn't promised he wouldn't.

She entered and stood behind the velvet couch where Krey sat. Expensive furniture wasn't much protection against her father or the guards, but it was something.

She gazed at her father. He looked different. It seemed his wrinkles and gray hairs had multiplied. *Is the stress of driving his country into the ground getting to him?* Nora pushed away the sarcastic thought and gave him a small, sad smile. "Can we talk, Dad?"

"I'd like nothing more."

Taima's voice entered Nora's mind. *I am high above the palace. Out of weapons range.*

"What would you like to discuss?" Ulmin asked.

"Give me a minute, Dad. This is a lot to take in."

He nodded.

Nora told Taima her plan, instructing the dragon not to act yet. This was her chance to remind her father of the man he used to be. She turned back to him. "Dad . . ." She licked her lips, unsure what to say. If she pressed too hard, he might not talk at all. She settled on, "How does it feel, controlling people?"

His brows rose a bit. "It feels wonderful. But that's not why I do it."

"Then why?"

"Left alone, people make poor choices. They're selfish. Proud. Violent."

He'd saved *violent* for last, but something told Nora it was really first on the list. Maybe it was the only thing on the list. A violent woman had killed the queen ten years ago. Her father had been desperately trying to protect himself, his family, and his kingdom ever since.

"But right now," Nora said, "you're the violent one. You formed a militia of mind slaves. When that didn't work, your army attacked New Therro. This isn't you, Dad. Or at least it doesn't have to be."

"My goal is peace." Ulmin spread his arms wide, the picture of a benevolent leader. His gaze begged her to understand. "New Therro was full of angry terrorists. Now that I've subdued them, our nation is safer."

"Dad, you took away their rights. You forced their men into your army. Is safety worth it if your people lose their freedom along the way?"

His head tilted a bit, and she thought he was finally seeing her—

as she was, not as the little girl he remembered. After several seconds, the softness in his eyes turned to steel. "Anything worthwhile comes with a cost. Darling."

There was something foreboding about the way he said it. About his sudden tension, like he was getting ready to leap out of his seat and touch her. Control her.

For your own good, he'd say. *To keep you safe*, he'd say.

She should give Taima the signal. But she needed just a little more time. "How do you control so many people? How did you share your magic with . . . with Faylie?"

"I'm sorry, Nora. Some secrets are too dangerous to share."

One final plea. The words hitched in her tight throat. "Dad, just tell me you'll stop it. All the mind control and the attacks. Let Krey go. Give your guards their minds back. Do it now, Dad, and I'll come live at home. I swear to you, I'll never leave again. I'll help you heal. Please. Tell me you'll stop."

The emotion of her words hit him; she could see it. His brows furrowed, and he pressed his lips together. Oh, thank the stone, he was considering it.

After a long moment, his mouth curved into a sad smile. "If it were just you, sweetheart, I would. But I must stand up for my kingdom. Even if it means standing against you."

Nora's stomach clenched. The hope she'd arrived with—that her father would become her ally, not her enemy—dissolved. He might still choose to change. But not today.

Nora sent a message to Taima: *Now!*

Too late. Her father was done talking. She braced for him to attack her.

He sent Krey instead.

Nora's friend, who'd thrown snowballs at her and teased her and comforted her, stood and turned, fixing cold eyes on her.

She pivoted and ran. A scream pushed its way through her lips. She dashed toward the dark hallway. Hers were the only footsteps.

Maybe Krey wasn't chasing her; maybe he'd resisted the king's control—

Just before she reached the corridor, something slammed her into the floor. There had been no footsteps because Krey hadn't run—he'd flown.

Nora struggled against him. They were the same height, but Krey was more muscular. She twisted, struck him with her elbows, kicked her legs back. Other than soft grunts, he didn't react.

Then she heard the footsteps she'd expected before. Somehow she knew it was her father, even before he knelt in front of her. He would take her mind while she was pinned down. Just like he'd done to Krey.

"Sweetheart," he said again. He reached out a hand.

Behind him, fire exploded through the ceiling—just where Nora had told Taima to aim. East of the big skylight, where nobody in the room was standing. Wood and plaster fell less than a met from Nora. Heat flooded the room. The king scrambled to his feet, leaving Nora untouched. "Get her away from here!"

Though Nora had expected Taima's attack, its violence broke her focus. By the time she remembered she was supposed to be fighting, Krey was pulling her to her feet.

The fire spread quickly on the lush carpet. Ulmin ran along the room's perimeter toward his mind-controlled guards. Krey followed, yanking Nora by the arm.

"Get us to safety!" Ulmin commanded the guards.

Nora willingly ran with Krey for a short distance, having no desire to be charbroiled. When they were past the worst of the danger, she planted her feet and began struggling again. She catalyzed her fuel, shooting hard balls of ice at Krey. His grip remained firm.

"Get her over here!" the king yelled.

The huge guard ran toward Nora and Krey. Nora froze, squeezing her eyes shut, anticipating the man's crushing hands.

Instead, she heard shouts and grunts. She opened her eyes to find

Ovrun on top of the man, fighting him with frightening ferocity. Just as Ovrun landed a knockout punch, Krey's grip on Nora loosened. Yanking her arm away, she saw why. Zeisha's vine was wrapped around his waist, and she was pulling him back.

Her friends had come through.

At the doorway into the foyer, Ulmin turned, shouting, "Do you have—?" A vine, shot by Zeisha's other hand, captured his neck, cutting off his speech.

Next to Ulmin, the other guard lifted his gun.

Oh no, you don't. As Ovrun charged the man, Nora shot one ice ball after another, hitting the guard's torso, head, and arm. He got off a shot, but it went wide. Ovrun took him down.

Gasping frantically, Nora surveyed the scene. Two guards were still tied to chairs. One now struggled against his bonds. Ovrun had rendered both the other guards unconscious. Face twisted in a grimace, Zeisha held vines taut around Krey's waist and the king's neck. Both of them tried to pry off the plants.

"Zeisha!" Nora shouted. "A soon as my father passes out, let go of his neck!"

Ulmin continued to pull at the tightly coiled vine. His face turned deep purple, and at last, he collapsed, his eyes rolling back.

"Zeisha!" Krey shouted. "Are you okay?"

Zeisha released both vines and ran to him, falling in his arms.

Dani! Nora could get her now. The king couldn't control her when he was unconscious. She turned toward the hallway.

Dani was already in the corridor, mouth agape. "Nora!" she cried.

She was only a few mets away. But the carpet between them blazed with dragon fire. Hot fingers of flames taunted Nora.

There was no way to get to her aunt.

"Dani!" After crying her aunt's name, Nora drew in a lungful of smoke. She bent over, coughing.

"Go!" Dani shouted. "Be safe!" She turned and ran down the hall, away from the thick smoke.

"Wait!" Coughing overtook Nora again. She got past it and

shouted, "Meet us . . . in front!" The roaring fire devoured her message. Dani was gone.

Taima's voice entered Nora's mind. *The guards see me on the roof! They are running this way. We must go!*

We'll have to leave through the front gate! Nora replied. *Can you meet us outside? Keep the guards away until we get out there?*

I shall try.

"Let's go! Front door!" Nora called between coughs. "Drag the guards and my father . . . out of here. I don't want them to get burned!"

Before long, they were in the foyer, which was getting smoky too. Ovrun had pulled out the chairs holding two tied-up guards. Both were now conscious and grunting against their gags. Ovrun tried to calm them.

"Where's Krey?" Nora cried.

Then she saw him flying into the room, holding an unconscious female guard wearing a knitted cap. He set her down carefully, then grabbed Nora's shoulder, his voice urgent. "We have to take your father with us. Get him away from his source of fuel."

Her eyes widened, hope filling her chest. Yes—with her father unconscious, they could get him to safety. Help him through his addiction.

This was her chance to save Cellerin by saving the king.

"Ovrun!" she called. "Carry my father!"

Another voice shouted, "Stop!"

Nora turned. Three royal guards stood in the foyer, pointing weapons—two bows and a gun—at the group.

Nora held up both hands. "Don't shoot! It's me! The princess!"

"I know," the tallest guard said. "Stay away from the king."

"We need to take him with us," Nora said. "You know he's controlling everyone at the palace."

"I do know," the same guard said. "But he's my king."

"I am your princess."

"That's why I'm letting you leave unharmed. If you step away from the king."

Nora, Taima called. *I am holding them off, but we must go!*

Nora gave her father one last look, then turned to the guards. "My aunt fled through the icehouse. Please make sure she's okay." When the tall guard nodded, Nora ran to the front door, followed by her friends. Outside, she opened the gate.

Her jaw dropped.

Taima sat, regal and proud, on the lawn in front of the palace residence. She'd set fire to a large, semicircular line of grass, starting at one corner of the residential fence and ending at the other. White-hot streams of fire, extending from Taima's mouth into the dark palace grounds, kept the guards at bay.

Nora, Krey, Ovrun, and Zeisha mounted Taima. She took to the air, swathing the land in fire as she ascended.

20

Our nation's leaders brag that our mental health services are top notch. I agree . . . to a point. When I dealt with depression last year, I loved my therapist. Daily medication keeps me going.

But what about those who can't live independently? I visited a long-term inpatient facility yesterday. Do you know how many visits their average resident gets every year?

Two.

How can someone heal if we lock them away and forget about them?

-"Where's the Care in Mental Healthcare?" by Genta Ril
The Derogan Chronicle, dated Cyon 1, 6293

ZEISHA WANTED to hold Krey close and tell him how sorry she was that she'd wrapped her vine around him. But he was behind her, clutching Taima's scales just as she was. He hadn't said a word since they left the palace. She couldn't even hold his hand.

The wind brought her snatches of conversation from Nora and Ovrun, who'd mounted Osmius after Taima flew them back to the clearing. Their calm chatter contrasted with Krey and Zeisha's silence.

What will I say to him when we get back to Deroga?

She could tell him everything would be fine. But was that true? Neither of them knew what the coming weeks and months would hold. He'd recounted the recovery he'd suffered through at eight years old. Would it be easier or harder almost a decade later?

Maybe she could tell him she understood why he'd done it. Except she didn't, not completely. She knew he'd wanted to stop Nora from doing something stupid. But going off on his own, lying to Nora, not telling Zeisha when he was leaving or even asking her opinion on the whole thing—she didn't understand any of that.

He was acting like an addict. The thought entered Zeisha's mind, and she squeezed her eyes shut, as if that would make the truth flee. After so many years, just the thought of eating brain matter again had been enough to resurrect the worst of Krey's addictive behaviors. Lying. Hiding things. Taking unnecessary risks.

What would the coming weeks be like?

Krey's hand, warm and solid, closed around her ankle. "Zeisha," he said, his voice loud enough to carry over the wind, "I'm sorry."

"I understand." The words slipped out, replaced by immediate guilt. That was what she'd just told herself she couldn't honestly say. Well, he probably hadn't heard her anyway.

"We need to talk about what happens when we get back to Deroga," Krey said.

Zeisha turned her head and spoke louder. "I'll help you through the detox and the cravings, and I'll keep helping you after that."

"Zeisha." His voice sounded choked. "You don't understand. In a little over a day, all I'll be able to think about is getting more fuel. I'm afraid I won't let anyone get in my way."

"What are you saying?" she called over her shoulder.

"We need to tell Eira what I did. And she needs to lock me up."

"When you are a child, you eat brains?" Eira thrust a wrinkled finger at Krey.

Zeisha took in his defeated posture: head low, shoulders slumped, hands in his pockets.

"Yes," he said.

"When you arrive here, you do not think this is important to tell us?" Eira's voice bounced around her little office.

Behind Krey, Nora said, "Don't feel too bad about it; he didn't tell any of us either." They were the first words she'd said since they'd arrived back in Deroga. Her gaze was sharp enough to slice Krey to pieces.

Krey lifted his head with effort. Dawn sunlight streamed through the window, highlighting the redness of his eyes. "I should've told my friends. I should've told you. You'll need to lock me up until the worst of the cravings are gone. I'm fine now, but tomorrow . . . it won't be pretty."

"You forget," Eira said, "we trogs know how brain eating works. Come with me."

"Can I come too? Please?" Zeisha asked.

"As you wish."

Zeisha took Krey's hand. It was clammy. When she squeezed it, he gave her a sad smile. Eira led them out of the building that held her office. Nora and Ovrun followed.

After walking for several blocks, Eira stopped in front of a house on a seemingly deserted street. She pulled out a key but didn't use it, instead turning to face the four teens. "This location is not to be disclosed."

They all nodded.

Eira unlocked the door and led them in. It was cold in the house.

Eira explained that smoke from a stove would give away the location. They walked past a kitchen. A trog sitting at the table nodded in greeting. Eira took them through a living area and stopped at the entrance to a lantern-lit hallway where two trogs stood guard. "This place is guarded constantly," she said. "The trogs have knives and are trained to fight."

She paused briefly at the first door. "Elo Golsch is here."

Zeisha recognized the name of the spy she'd apprehended. The memory rushed back, squeezing her gut as tightly as her vine had squeezed the man's neck.

"As long as he cooperates with us, he will remain here," Eira said. "It is quite comfortable." She led them to the second door. "Krey, you will stay here." When he reached for the doorknob, she touched his wrist. "Not yet. I wish to introduce you to our last resident."

They walked to the final door. "How is he?" Eira asked the nearest guard.

"The same," the guard said.

Eira nodded once. "Unlock it."

The trog did so, and Eira opened the door. "Come in," she said. "All of you."

Inside, a young man sat in a comfortable, upholstered chair. He had shaggy hair and a dark beard and looked oddly familiar to Zeisha. He stared straight ahead, not turning his head when his visitors entered.

Eira walked up to him and put a hand on his shoulder. He didn't respond. "This is Girro," she said. "He is the brain eater who works with the militia for a time."

Black intruded on Zeisha's vision. Nausea twisted her stomach. Her knees loosened, threatening to collapse.

She must've made some noise, because Krey's head swiveled toward her. Eyes wide, he put an arm around her waist, holding her up. "You okay?"

The man's face churned up deep memories, but they refused to leave her subconscious. Painful pressure built up in her head. "I just

. . . need to sit." Besides Girro's chair, the only seat was the bed across the room. She didn't think she could make it there, so she lowered herself onto the floor. The cold floor made her shiver. Krey sat too, but she said, "I really am okay. You can stand."

He did, after confirming that she was fine. She'd have loved for him to sit with her, but he was the one who needed to hear what Eira was saying.

"Girro is a stone eater," Eira said, "and a hard worker. He can create fences and walls from stone. He also has a very strong body."

Zeisha looked up at Girro. He was pale, his clothes baggy over scrawny limbs. Eira was speaking of the man's past.

The white-haired trog continued, "Then Girro works for the king at the warehouse. He eats animal brains every day. When the king sends Girro home, he is different. Confused. Violent. We bring him here. Two weeks ago, the violence stops. Now, Girro sits here every day. He lets the guards bathe him. Clothe him. Feed him. Attend to his needs. He never speaks. We want to send him home, but his family fears his violence will return."

A sigh left Zeisha's chest. She didn't know what exactly this man had done to her. But she wouldn't wish this fate on him or anyone else.

"Krey." Eira stood directly in front of him, her hands gripping his shoulders. "You are talented. You have strength and purpose. If you cannot conquer your desire, he"—she pointed at Girro—"will be you." Her eyes, unblinking, remained fixed on Krey's.

"I know." Krey's words were barely audible.

Zeisha stood, certain her strength had returned. "I want to stay with Krey."

Nora's eyes widened. "No, Zeisha! He did this to himself!" She spoke in a harsh whisper, as if that would keep Krey from hearing her. "You don't deserve to be locked up with him!"

Yes, I do. Zeisha didn't say it aloud, but she wondered if the truth was written in her eyes. Maybe she could've stopped him if she'd confronted him. She couldn't change that now, but she could help him heal. "I want to stay."

Eira didn't respond, but back in the hallway, she called both of the guards over. "This man," she said, gesturing to Krey, "is your prisoner. He will be chained to his bed." She placed a wrinkled hand on Zeisha's shoulder. "This woman will stay with him. If your prisoner does anything against her, if he even yells, you will protect her."

Zeisha's breathing sped up. Krey would never hurt her . . . would he?

Next to her, Krey's shoulders slumped.

A loud, ragged gasp woke Zeisha. She sat up, disoriented. She was lying on a hard floor, wrapped in two warm blankets.

Krey's voice floated across the room to her, loud and low-pitched. "No. . . . no . . . no."

The doorknob rattled as someone unlocked and opened it. Lantern light filtered into the room. "Are you all right, ma'am?" a female trog guard asked over Krey's continued moans.

She stood. "I'm fine, but he's not. Please—can you get him some water? And can you bring me a lantern?"

"I will fetch water," the guard said. "The lantern . . ." Hesitation stiffened her expression.

"I'll keep it away from him," Zeisha said. "I promise." A padded shackle and thick chain connected Krey's left hand to a ring anchored to the wall next to his bed. The chain rattled as he brought his hands to his face and started sobbing.

The guard nodded. "You can have this one. Keep it in the opposite corner."

Zeisha thanked her, took the lantern, and put it on a table in the corner of the room. The guard left.

Krey had been fine the previous day—though he'd repeatedly

warned Zeisha about what was coming. They'd gone to sleep early. Now, as he continued crying, she approached the bed slowly. "Krey?"

"I need it," he wailed through his tears. "Oh, God, oh, Zeisha, I need it! Please, I need fuel!"

Zeisha knelt by the bed. He was so pitiful; he wouldn't hurt her. "You know I can't, Krey." She touched his trembling leg.

He lowered his hands and used both of them to grab her hand. He squeezed it tightly enough to make her wince. Even in the dim lantern light, his eyes were frenzied. "They trust you," he whispered, no longer crying. "They'll let you leave and come back. All I need is a little bit. A little now, and less tomorrow, and less the next day—and then I'll be fine. Just a bite, Zeisha. I can tell you where to look." He lifted one hand to point at the barred window. "It's dark; no one will be there. You just have to—"

"No!" When he kept talking, she spoke over him. "No, no, no, no, no!" Finally, he quieted. "I will support you however I can," she said. "But I won't make things worse by feeding your addiction!"

Krey released her hand and flipped over, facing away from her. His weeping resumed. Interspersed with his wracking sobs were five words: "I thought you loved me."

"That's why I'm saying no." Zeisha touched his back. He pulled away. She returned to her pallet on the floor, but she knew she wouldn't sleep.

"Please," Krey groaned again once he'd calmed.

"I love you too much to hurt you."

He raved, never letting his voice get loud enough to bring the guards. He begged. He cried. The sun rose, and his pleading continued.

Her response didn't change. "I love you too much to hurt you."

21

I'm making a glossary of phrases politicians use and what they really
mean. Here's what I've got so far:

- *"Unfortunate error" = "Oops, you caught us lying"*
- *"Leak of confidential information" = "We could've sworn*
  we'd get away with it this time"
- *"We deeply regret this mistake" = "We deeply regret*
  getting caught"

-*"Politician Glossary" by Genta Ril*
The Derogan Chronicle, *dated Cyon 3, 6293*

AFTER EATING AN EARLY BREAKFAST, Nora and Ovrun walked to
the prison house. The day before, Eira had taught them a secret
knock. She'd also written a note giving them permission to visit Krey.
"The first days without fuel are the most difficult," she'd said.
"Things are easier if the brain eater is with people who love him."

Nora had tried not to snort at those last four words: *people who love him.* Love was about the last thing she felt toward Krey right now. But when Ovrun had suggested they check on him, she couldn't bring herself to say no.

The scene in Krey's room was dismal. He was curled on his bed like a baby, facing the wall. Zeisha sat on a pile of blankets across the room. She was hugging her knees. Her eyes were red and utterly exhausted.

Nora knelt by her. "Are you okay?"

Zeisha shook her head.

"Come to the kitchen with me." Nora stood and extended a hand. "We'll talk."

Zeisha complied. On their way out, Nora turned to Ovrun. "Beat some sense into him, would you?"

Ovrun raised an eyebrow.

The guard who'd opened the front door for them was sitting at the kitchen table. When he saw Nora's pursed lips and Zeisha's bloodshot eyes, he left the room without a word.

"He was fine yesterday," Zeisha said, "but then in the middle of the night . . ." She shook her head. "He won't stop begging me to bring him fuel." She rubbed her temples, groaning.

"Is he hurting you?" Nora asked.

"No, but he's not exactly being kind."

If Zeisha would admit such a thing, Krey's level of assery—assishness? assination?—whatever it was, it must be in the stratosphere. Nora clenched her teeth to prevent herself from venting her anger on Zeisha, who looked like she'd crack into a million pieces if she heard an unkind word.

After a few moments, Nora was ready to speak without screaming curses. She was pretty impressed with the gentleness in her voice when she said, "Krey is an idiot."

Oops. That wasn't what she'd planned to say. Zeisha's squished-up forehead proved that it hadn't gone over well. "I didn't mean to say that out loud," Nora blurted. "I meant to say that you're amazing, and I'm so, so sorry you're going through this. You don't deserve it."

Zeisha let out a long sigh and leaned into Nora's open arms.

"Have you had breakfast?" Nora murmured.

Zeisha shook her head.

"Sit here as long as you need to. Then I'm gonna stay with Krey, and Ovrun will take you to breakfast. After that, you can take a bath and a nap."

Zeisha pulled back. "It's not my day for a bath. And I'm supposed to work at one of the rooftop gardens today."

Nora tilted her head and gave Zeisha a smile. "You're taking the day off. So are Ovrun and I, so we can sit with Krey. I already cleared it with Eira. And trust me, when they see you at the bathhouse, they won't be able to say no. Just make sure you look just as miserable as you did when I got here."

Zeisha actually smiled at that. Despite her lack of sleep and her red eyes, she was beautiful. *I'm going in there, and I'm going to make sure Krey knows what a jewel he has in her. And how incredibly, mind-bendingly stupid he is for not treating her like a queen.*

"Please don't be too mean to Krey," Zeisha said.

Nora let out a surprised laugh. "I won't tell him anything he doesn't deserve to hear."

Zeisha gave her a worried look but didn't argue. With a wobbly smile, she said, "I guess I'm ready to go."

Nora stood. "I'll get Ovrun."

When Nora entered Krey's room, Ovrun was sitting on the floor next to the bed, arms resting casually on his raised knees. He was talking, but his deep voice grew silent when Nora entered.

Krey turned his whole body toward Nora. A chain connected to his wrist rattled. His wide eyes were even redder than Zeisha's. "Nora," he said in a quiet voice that was nonetheless frantic, "the best way for me to recover is gradually. Cutting me off from my fuel will make everything worse. All I need is a bite, and then tomorrow, I'll need less. Can you help me out? Please?"

His pathetic desperation tamped down some of her anger, but it didn't come close to convincing her. Eira had warned them all that if Krey ingested any additional brain matter, it would make his symptoms worse, not better.

She put her hands on her hips. "Not gonna happen."

His face reddened, brows drawing together. "You're all the same!" he shouted hoarsely. "You're there for each other but not for me! To think I trusted you!"

A guard poked his head in the door. Nora waved him away. "Trust?" She crossed to the bed, grabbed Krey's shoulders in a fierce grip, and got right in his face. "You're talking to me about trust? I thought I could trust you until I found out you've been lying to me from the beginning! How dare you accuse me of not being trustworthy?" She shook him. "How dare you?"

His unchained hand came up and pointed in her face. "You lied to me! You told me Osmius was taking you to the palace!"

She shoved him back on the bed and threw her hands up. "Well, pardon the hell out of me, Krey! I told you one lie. You've lived a lie the whole time we've known you! So please, keep talking about how I'm not trustworthy!"

He sat up and grabbed her hand. "Please. You've gotta help me through this. You don't know what it feels like."

She pulled her hand away. "You're right. I don't. But I do know what it feels like for one of my only friends to betray me. So I'm happy to see you miserable, Krey! You deserve every bit of it!"

The words were only half true. Yes, his misery sent a vengeful thrill through her. It also made her heart ache. She turned away, lest Krey see empathy in her eyes.

Trying to distract herself from the pitiful sight on the bed, she knelt next to Ovrun. "I'll stay with Krey. Zeisha is in the kitchen, waiting for you. Can you take her to breakfast and make sure she gets to the bathhouse after? She shouldn't be alone right now."

"Yeah." He stood and walked across the room, beckoning Nora

close. "Be careful," he whispered. "He's not himself. I don't know what he'll do."

"Of course I'll be careful." She locked her gaze on Ovrun's. "But I won't coddle him."

The corner of his mouth twitched. "I'm sure you won't."

As Ovrun exited, Nora dragged a chair across the hard floor. She parked it next to Krey, sat, and folded her arms, watching him.

"Nora, please—"

"Shut up, Krey. Don't waste your energy. I'm not getting you more fuel."

He flipped over, back to Nora, with all the drama of a thirteen-year-old who's angry at the world. His lean, firm shoulders rose and fell with every rapid breath.

Nora said, "Since I have you as a captive audience—literally captive, I might add—I'm going to tell you what I think of you."

His only reply was a grunt.

Nora got comfortable, pulling her legs up and crossing them on the seat of the chair. She propped her forearms on her thighs. "You know what really pisses me off, Krey? It's not that you ate brains when you were eight. You're not expected to make wise choices when you're that age. I'm not even mad that you're an addict. We've all got our struggles, right?"

No response.

"What really pisses me off—" Nora didn't mean to stop talking, but a tight knot of emotion invaded her throat, cutting off her words. *What the hell? I'm not here to cry, I'm here to give him a piece of my mind!*

She swallowed and barreled on. "What really pisses me off—"A sob leapt from her chest, filling the space between her and Krey. With a groan, she gave in to her weeping. "It pisses me off that you're my friend—a real friend!" Her sobs came harder. "And you . . . you didn't trust me! Did you . . . did you think I wouldn't . . . wouldn't be there for you? I would've . . . damn it, I wanted to . . . to support you,

Krey! You could've . . . you could've told me! I care about you . . . and I'm so . . . so tired . . . of being betrayed!"

She was crying too hard to keep talking. Maybe that was a good thing. She'd meant to scream at him, giving him a guilt trip so fierce, it would tear a hole through his chest. She'd meant to tell him how terrible *he* was, not how hurt *she* was. She certainly hadn't meant to call him a friend, at least not in the present tense. And how could she have said she cared about him?

As her crying subsided, she saw that Krey had curled into a ball, his face pressed into his pillow. She knelt on the floor and, with a resigned sigh, rested a hand on his shoulder.

He grasped her hand. After a few minutes, he moaned, "Please. Just a little."

"No." Her voice was hard, but she didn't move her hand.

When Ovrun returned, he found both Krey and Nora sleeping. Krey was on his side in bed, knees pulled in tight, his back to the room. A chair sat next to the bed, but Nora was sitting on the floor, head resting on the mattress. Her hand was on Krey's shoulder, covered by his shackled hand.

Ovrun tried to sit silently, but the chair squeaked when his bulk hit the seat.

Nora's head lifted. She pulled her hand from Krey's and rubbed her eyes. "Hey," she whispered.

Ovrun stood and gestured to the chair. Nora got up, but she didn't sit. She took his hand and led him to a corner of the room, smiling as she pulled him down to sit on the floor. He wedged himself in the corner and draped his arm over her shoulder, drawing her into his side.

Nora let out a long breath and snuggled closer. "How's Zeisha?" she whispered.

"She's tired," he murmured. "I dropped her off at the bathhouse, and she said she'd take a nap afterward."

"Good." Nora yawned. "I guess we're all tired."

"How's Krey?"

Ovrun felt Nora shake her head. "He's desperate for more fuel. When he realized I wouldn't give it to him, he went to sleep."

"Did you lecture him first?"

"I tried. Ended up crying and making a fool of myself instead." Nora pulled away, sitting up straight and meeting Ovrun's gaze. "He betrayed us."

Ovrun lifted his eyebrows.

"Part of me wants to write him off completely," Nora said, "but I can't bring myself to."

Ovrun ran his thumbs along the swollen skin under her eyes. Her full lips curved up at his touch, and he dropped a soft kiss on them before taking her hands and saying, "He hid the truth from us, but I wouldn't call it a betrayal. He went to the palace for *you*."

Her forehead furrowed, and for a second, he could picture what her worry and laugh lines would look like when she got older. She'd be just as lovely as she was now. "What do you mean, for me?" she asked.

"When you were comforting Zeisha, he talked to me. He was trying to get me to bring him fuel, and I guess he wanted to justify what he did. He said you need to be able to lead the country, and it wouldn't be safe for you to confront your dad alone. He knew what he did was dangerous, but he wanted to protect you."

She blinked several times. Her tongue ran across her lips, and he cursed his body as it responded. *Now's not the time for that.*

At last, she said, "He wouldn't risk himself for me."

"Why not?"

"Because—because that's something you'd do for someone you care about. Our whole friendship has been a lie. He doesn't care about me."

"Nora . . . you lied to him too. You . . . you lied to all of us. Osmius was never gonna take you to the palace."

Her head dropped. She pulled her hands away. "I shouldn't have done that. I was just desperate, and I—didn't think it through. I—"

"I know," he interrupted. When her chin came up and she met his gaze, he said, "We all do stupid things when we're desperate."

"But he hid the truth from us for months! You're telling me he was desperate for months on end?"

"Sure! Desperate for something. Acceptance or safety or . . . something."

Her eyes darted off to the side, but not before he saw her thoughts churning in them. She nodded. "Maybe you're right. But I'm still mad."

Ovrun looked over at Krey, who appeared smaller than usual, curled up as he was. They didn't have time for this. They had a battle to prepare for, and now one of their fiercest fighters was detoxing. He'd also been touched by the king, which would limit his role if Ulmin came to Deroga. Ovrun released a deep sigh. "I'm mad too."

"You know what?" Nora whispered. "I'm sick of all this. I'm sick of *thinking*. I'm sick of planning." She locked her gaze with Ovrun's. After several seconds, her furrowed brow smoothed out, and her lips drew into a sly smile. She glanced at Krey, then climbed into Ovrun's lap and whispered in his ear, "It's enough to make me want to run off with you and live in the country like you talk about. Just me and you."

Ovrun took her shoulders in his hands and locked his gaze with hers. He tried to keep the hope out of his voice. "Is that really what you want?"

Still smiling, she bit her lip and released it. "You know my responsibilities, Ovrun." She brought her lips back to his ear. "But it's fun to pretend things are different, isn't it?"

Her flirtation didn't have its intended effect. That was his dream she was talking about, and she was throwing it out there like it might actually happen. His breaths came faster, not because he wanted her, but because he was, for the first time ever, angry at her. "Nora—" he said, his voice a low growl.

"Hmm?" She rested her forehead against his. Her hands reached for him. He caught them in his own before she could slip them over his shoulders.

She pulled her head away from his, her eyes sparkling with flirtation. "Krey was really tired," she said softly. "He's not gonna wake up."

"That's not why I stopped you."

His anger must've been obvious, because Nora yanked her hands away. She crawled off his lap and sat in front of him, knees pressed to his. "What's wrong?" Her low voice held more than a hint of challenge.

"Is this a game to you?" he demanded.

"Is what a game?"

"This." His hand pointed back and forth roughly between them. "You crawling into my lap and saying we might actually have a future, then reminding me it's all pretend. Is that fun for you?"

Nora blinked hard, then leaned forward, spitting vehement, hushed words at him. "No, it's not a game, Ovrun. I was just trying to enjoy our time together. Like we agreed on, remember?" Her arms spread wide. "We're in this stupid city, far from home, eating food we're not used to and using dirty bathhouses and outhouses. And sorry, but I wanted to enjoy one of the few good things I've got here. I just wanted to flirt with my boyfriend. Is that so bad?"

"Is that what I am? Your boyfriend?"

"Yeah." Nora's voice had lost its edge. She swallowed hard. "If . . . you want to be."

He grasped her shoulders. Hushed words scraped his throat as they emerged. "You know I want to be your boyfriend! That's not the problem! The problem is, I want more! I want you to be part of my future! We both know you can't, so why do you tease me by saying it's what you want too? Do you have any idea what that does to me, Nora? Any idea at all?"

Under his hands, her shoulders lost their tension, collapsing. Her head dropped. They sat for several seconds before she met his gaze again. "I'm sorry," she said quietly. "I was just trying to have a little fun."

Ovrun had a sudden urge to shake her until her teeth clacked together. Horrified by the thought, he let go of her shoulders and pressed his back against the wall, folding his arms across his chest. Every muscle in his arms remained taut. By the stone, what was wrong with him? This was the girl he . . . the girl he . . . *the girl I what? Like? Want? Something more? And if it's that, how the hell did I let myself reach that point?*

He spoke in a strained voice that held no hint of lightness. "Of course it's been *fun.* But there's a problem. The more time we spend together, the more I want from you. I . . ." Arms still crossed, he leaned forward, struggling to push words through the tightness in his gut, his chest, his throat. "I don't know if we should do this anymore, Nora. You mean too much to me. This is way more than *fun* for me, and you don't get that."

"What?" Nora's voice was shrill and explosive. She swiveled her head to look at Krey, who didn't even flinch. Nora locked eyes with Ovrun again, her chest rising and falling like she'd been running. "This is *way more than fun* for me too, and I am"—her breath came out in a frustrated, suppressed grunt of anger—"you have no idea how much it pisses me off for you to sit up there on a pedestal, like the high king of . . . of . . . righteous passion! Like you're the only one who feels deeply about this. Damn it, Ovrun, I want this to work too!"

He pressed his lips together, eyes still drilling into hers, daring her to convince him.

"You want the truth?" Nora continued in her whisper-scream. "I *do* want to run off and live on a farm with you and make gorgeous babies and forget about the palace! And I *also* want to go back to that same palace and rule the kingdom the way it's meant to be ruled! I hate wanting both of those things. I said it was fun to pretend, because I know full well that my future was set before I was born. I don't know if there's any way to change it. I don't even know if I want to. I don't know much of anything, except I honestly care about you! I'm willing to stay with you if there's just a little chance of it working out. And I sure as hell think we should enjoy ourselves along the way! Is that really such a bad thing?"

Nora's fury had an odd effect on Ovrun. It calmed him, mesmerized him—her flushed skin, passionate words, rapid breaths. She'd never be the type to give in and smooth things over, whether they were in their twenties or their seventies. He loved that about her.

And then he realized that despite him threatening to end things, despite her admission that she probably couldn't join in his dreams, he was still imagining a future—a full, lifelong future—with her.

Nora wanted to continue holding on to some slim hope that they could make this work. Could he do the same?

"Ovrun?" Her voice was suddenly soft. She never stayed mad for long. "Can I ask you something?"

"Sure."

"Is there any hope of you . . . becoming someone you never thought you'd be?"

He knew what she was asking. He'd told her plenty of times that he couldn't be king. But with her by his side . . . "Maybe," he murmured, even as he wondered if it was true.

Her full lips widened in an indescribably gorgeous smile. A moment later, her hands slipped inside his open jacket, wandering over his shirt, tracing his muscles.

"Nora," he breathed. His flare of anger was rapidly turning into a blaze of desire. Logic warred with his baser instincts. *We need to talk more. A lot more. We didn't resolve anything—*

Her lips found his. He responded, pulling her closer with one hand and digging the other hand into her hair. He forgot what he needed to say. His lips had more urgent needs. Nora answered with a hunger that threatened to devour them both.

Across the room, a groan rose from the bed. Ovrun and Nora

both froze, then pulled away from each other. In unison, they muttered, "Damn it."

Krey was still facing away from them. He might be sleeping . . . but he might not. Nora scooted back against the wall, her eyes on the bed, her breaths coming fast. Ovrun watched her as he tried to steady his own breathing.

Her eyes fixed on Krey, Nora whispered, "Will he be okay?" After a pause, she said, "Will Cellerin be okay? Will *we* be okay?" She shook her head hard, blinking rapidly.

For a long moment, Ovrun squeezed his eyes and his lips shut. He doubted he could fit into Nora's life in the long term. But he could fill the role she needed now. He slipped an arm around her and pulled her close again. With his free hand, he nudged her chin until she was looking in his eyes.

Thumb caressing the thin, pale scar on her cheek, he said, "Whatever you need from me, I'm here."

Her lips parted. All her breath left her body in a deep sigh that seemed to take all the tension out of her. He pulled her even closer.

"Thank you," she whispered.

Krey groaned again. This time, he turned to face them. "Please," he moaned. "Just one bite."

Ovrun and Nora walked to the bed, hand-in-hand, to tell him no.

THE SEER: 6

SARZA SHIVERED as she stood at the window of the ancient office building she'd lived in for over a month now. She'd been waiting for this night: the new moon. Clouds were rolling in too. *Perfect. The darker it is, the better.*

The dark night would protect her. It would also make it hard to navigate. *That means I need to get going.*

Using a single candle for light, Sarza descended the stairs on quick feet, wishing yet again that she'd gotten a vision to guide her tonight. Her mind stayed stubbornly in the moment, as it had been doing for over a week. *Guess I'll just have to use my wits.*

The trek down the stairs was a long one, but she'd gotten used to it. She went out a couple of nights every week to steal supplies and to let the breeze wash away the dank, old smell that seemed to coat her after too much time inside. The breeze wasn't the most effective shower, so she took cold dips in the nearby river when she felt especially gross.

Hopefully last night's bath and supply raid had been her final one. Hours from now, she'd report Princess Nora's location to her contact. With any luck, he'd insist Sarza return to the army, where accolades would be waiting. She tried not to think too much of the alternative: that he'd send her back to this stinking, creepy city to keep spying.

Sarza entered the silent streets. Several hours (and one near miss from a trog arrow) later, she at last reached the silent, dusty suburbs. The golden light of dawn illuminated layers of colorful graffiti, left behind by The Day's jaded survivors and their descendants. Plenty of preday artifacts still existed too. Several times, Sarza shook her head at signs for weirdly specific businesses. What the hell was a versabox, anyway? And why would someone go to a store that only sold lipstick?

At last, she arrived at the squat, black building she was seeking. Behind it was a large, open lot where hover scooters, glidecrafts, and solarcars were still parked after all these years. Even with broken windows and weather damage, they were still pretty cool-looking vehicles.

Sarza approached the back door. As instructed, she called out the passphrase. "Carribird here!" When no one responded, she went inside.

Musty hallways swallowed the open doorway's light. Sarza lit her candle and started exploring. When continued shouting of the passphrase didn't attract any attention, her stomach clenched with angry nerves. *Don't tell me that soldier left. Did he desert? Couldn't handle a few weeks alone? What a—*

Her light fell on smudges in the dust around a doorknob. Sarza opened the door, calling, "Carribird here!"

Nobody responded.

She stepped into the windowless room. Her light fell on a crumpled blanket on the floor and a few dishes sitting on a table.

In preday times, people had probably hated working in a dark space like this. Now, it was a decent place to stay warm on chilly nights. Unfortunately, the most recent occupant had liked the room so much, he'd used it as a latrine too. The stench was so strong, Sarza could taste it. *Disgusting, man. Seriously?*

The big question was, did the soldier still live here? He might be out hunting or something. Sarza knew how she could tell. The idea made her lips twist with disgust, but she went with it, following her nose to the source of the terrible smells.

Don't puke. DON'T PUKE. She obeyed her own instructions—admirable strength, she thought—and examined the human waste. The walls and floor were both stained with dried liquid. The crap in the corner looked dry too. Sarza groaned. That meant her contact—the guy she was supposed to report to, the one who could've brought her back to the army as a spy hero, worthy of a promotion and a raise—had been gone for some time now.

Sarza huffed and let a river of expletives exit her mouth in a toxic flood. She stomped out, slamming the door behind her. She'd grab a nap in another room. One that didn't smell like a soldier's stupidity.

22

Allow me to speak for all teens.

We know we should go outside. We know sunlight and green plants and human interaction are healthy.

But how do you expect us to drag ourselves out of our homes when you've put such exceptional entertainment at our fingertips? Adults, you designed flexscreens. You put them in our hands.

(And be honest. You're as addicted to your flexes as we are.)

-"I'm an Inside Girl" by Genta Ril
The Derogan Chronicle, *dated Cyon 5, 6293*

ZEISHA TRIED to put on her shoes quietly, but Krey woke anyway. After releasing a big yawn, he asked, "Where are you going?"

She knelt by the pallet on the floor where he'd been sleeping. A ray of dawn light, shining from between the shutters, cast a bright stripe on his hair. Touching the side of his face, Zeisha said, "We've got another magic practice today."

He absentmindedly rubbed the wrist that had, until a few days ago, been shackled. "I wish I could come."

"I do too." She kissed his cheek. "Soon, I hope. Why don't you take the bed? Get some more sleep?"

Krey stood and opened the shutters to let the breeze flow through the barred window. Spring had arrived, and the mornings were getting warmer. Lifting his arms, hands clasped, he grimaced as he stretched. "In the last couple of weeks, I've had enough sleep for a year. I'll run instead."

She laughed. "Don't go too far." Krey missed his frequent runs around Deroga. The last couple of days, he'd taken to running in place for an hour at a time in the middle of the bedroom that served as his cell.

It had been nineteen days since Krey's palace break-in. Zeisha had stayed in his room every night. At first, she'd slept on the floor, far from Krey. Everyone had feared he'd grow violent. That fear ended up being unfounded, but his constant wheedling and begging that first week had nearly driven Zeisha mad.

The next week, his craving for animal brain matter had remained strong, but he'd stopped asking for it constantly. He'd acted more like himself again. And two weeks after Krey had ingested six shimshim brains, his cravings had finally become manageable. Eira had told the guards to remove Krey's shackle. He was still, however, confined to this room. He'd started sleeping on the pallet on the floor, giving Zeisha the bed.

When Krey finished his stretch, Zeisha put her arms around his waist. He returned the embrace. "Have fun out there," he said.

"I'll try." She couldn't imagine enjoying it, though. Eira had recently told all the magic eaters and the trog fighters to get serious about their drills. They were preparing for war, she'd said. They should act like it.

With that admonition heavy in her chest, Zeisha made her way to the warehouse where she'd been held captive. Anxiety pressed against her mind, but she refused to let it in. Instead, she allowed numbness to swallow her as she entered the warehouse and fueled up with bark and roots. Back outside, she waited in the street for instructions.

Nora, who was leading the magic eaters' practice time, instructed them to get into pairs. "Practice hurting each other," she said, grinning, "without actually hurting each other."

Zeisha's numbness dissolved, making way for sharp dread.

A tall, muscular male dirt eater from the militia invited her to partner up. She nodded silently, and they found a wide space to practice in.

"You go first," Zeisha said.

"Don't worry; I won't bury you!" The dirt eater smiled, revealing dark soil stuck between his teeth and in his gums. Gaze fixed on Zeisha, he knelt and placed his hands on the dusty street.

The dirt under Zeisha's feet shifted. Small cracks formed. She held her arms out, swaying along with the ground. The cracks grew, and a cloud of dust enveloped her.

With a series of sharp *pops*, the hard dirt beneath her loosened into soft dust. Zeisha gasped as her legs sank down to her calves. She swayed, then fell, sinking into the ground. She tried to scream for the dirt eater to stop, but her breath caught in her throat. Her waist was level with the street now, her backside and lower legs buried, knees poking out of the ground like round stones.

Zeisha couldn't breathe fast enough. With every frantic inhale of air and dust, her panic grew. Her exhales were half coughs, half cries.

The dirt eater seemed unaware of her state. Zeisha sank farther, sucked into the soft ground. Through the thick dust, she couldn't make out the dirt eater's features. He was nothing but a blurry blob— a body, a neck, a head.

A neck.

Coughing, Zeisha surrendered to instinct. She raised one hand

and shot out a thick, flexible vine. Its tapered end snagged the dirt eater's neck.

The dirt stopped sucking her in. She released the vine from her palm and grabbed it like a rope, pulling herself hand-over-hand out of the soft pit. In seconds, she was back on solid ground, coughing violently.

Her eyes fell on the dirt eater. He was on his belly, hands on the tight vine at his neck. His tan face had turned dark red. His soft-brown eyes bulged. His mouth was open, like he was trying to gasp or scream. He could do neither.

The reality of what she'd done slammed into Zeisha like a club. "No!" she cried, releasing the vine from his neck. "Oh, I'm sorry, oh—no, no, no!"

Hands grasping his neck, he drew in rough, wheezing breaths. Zeisha tried to crawl closer, but he scooted away.

He's afraid of me.

Zeisha stood, horror widening her eyes and burning her cheeks. She ran through the other magic eaters. Seeing her face, none of them attacked. "Healer! I need a healer!" she screamed.

Someone directed her to a blood eater. Zeisha found him and brought him to the dirt eater she'd nearly strangled.

She sprinted away, gasping apologies into the cool air.

When Zeisha arrived at the rooftop garden, panting from her climb, Kebi was there. Her group, the archers, had drilled the day before. Kebi stood and rushed to her friend. "What is wrong?"

The story came out in a stream of self-loathing words. At some point, Kebi guided Zeisha to sit.

When she finished describing her experience, Zeisha was surprised to find she wasn't crying. She was numb, inside and out. "Apparently this is what I do now. They trained me to use my talent as a weapon. I did it when I saved that kid from the spy, and I did it today."

"You are panicked when the dirt eater uses his magic on you," Kebi said.

"Of course I was panicked! But I could've wrapped my vine around his waist." That was what she'd done to Krey at the palace. Why hadn't it occurred to her to do the same today? "I just needed to stop the dirt eater, not hurt him," she continued, "and I needed an anchor to pull myself out. So I went straight for his neck. Because that's what I do now."

"You say that twice."

"Huh?" Zeisha looked up and found Kebi's eyes waiting.

"You say that twice. That this is what you do now."

"It is."

Kebi stood and extended a hand. "Come."

Zeisha allowed her trog friend to lead her to a row of bollaberry bushes. When they were both sitting again, Kebi pulled a few leaves off the nearest bush and held them out. "Eat."

Zeisha obeyed.

"That plant," Kebi said, pointing at a bush smaller than the rest, "struggles to grow. What will you do about it?"

Zeisha raised her eyebrows but played along. She grew the bush until its thriving branches were heavy with ripe berries.

Kebi handed Zeisha a wooden box about the size of two fists. "We will fill this. Our young friend with the baby does not sleep well. This will cheer her up."

Half an hour later, they left the young mother's house, having delivered the berries. As soon as the door closed behind them, Kebi took Zeisha's hand. Eyes glued to her vine-eating friend, Kebi said in a soft, firm voice, "You grow things. You bring life to the hurting. *This is what you do.*"

Zeisha nodded thoughtfully. "Thank you."

Back atop the roof, they worked quietly. After some time, Kebi stopped what she was doing and looked up at Zeisha. "When the king comes, you do not have to fight. Do you want to change your mind?"

Zeisha couldn't answer that question. She pulled her hands from the soil and hugged herself, breathing deeply. "Do you have any idea how terrible it feels not to know yourself?"

"Who do you want to be?"

Zeisha yawned and lay back on the soft soil. "I want to be the strong person other people think I am."

"Other people? Do you mean Krey?"

Zeisha laughed softly. "Am I that transparent? Of course I mean Krey." She turned her head to gaze at Kebi. "He didn't pressure me, you know. He just . . . inspired me. To see more in myself."

"Hmm," Kebi said. She returned her attention to the soil, pulling a weed.

Zeisha's brows lifted as she watched Kebi. "Please tell me what's going on in your head."

Kebi's lips twitched. "New-city folk use odd phrases." She pulled one more weed then repositioned herself, sitting next to Zeisha's prone form. "Here is what is *in my head*, Zeisha. You say you do not know yourself. Then you say you want to be who Krey thinks you are. It is strange to look at yourself through another's eyes instead of your own."

Zeisha scooped up soil and filtered it through her fingers, watching it flow from one hand to the other. She couldn't argue with Kebi's words. Why did she feel threatened by them? She swallowed, eyes still on the soil she was sifting. "Of course I want to see myself through his eyes. He loves me. And I love him."

"This I do not doubt." Kebi laid a hand on Zeisha's shoulder. "But I must ask: do you love yourself?"

Zeisha squeezed her eyes shut and drew in a deep breath. Her exhale was shaky. She whispered, "How can I love myself when I can't stand myself?" After another few breaths, she spoke again, eyes still closed, her voice a little stronger now. "When Krey looks at me, he doesn't see a monster who murdered people. Of course I'd want to see myself the way he does. He sees my violence as strength, not . . . not wickedness."

"Sit up."

Kebi's voice was so stern that Zeisha's eyes popped open.

"Up," Kebi said. "Face me. Bring your eyes to mine." She held out a hand. Zeisha took it, pulled herself up, and lifted her wary gaze to Kebi's face.

Kebi took Zeisha's warm cheeks in her cool hands. Her expression softened, though she wasn't smiling. "You call it *your* violence. My friend . . . this violence is not yours. It belongs to those who force you to be the person you are not. If there is wickedness in your actions, it is not yours. It is theirs."

Zeisha felt herself nodding. The tightness in her heart released, just a notch.

"Some warriors are strong and good," Kebi continued. "If you become a warrior, I know this is the kind you will be. But open your ears to me, Zeisha. You are strong and good now." She removed one hand from Zeisha's cheek and gestured at the thriving plants around them. "You are strong now." She pointed down into the city, toward the home they'd just visited. "You are good now. You need be no one but the person you are."

Kebi opened her arms. Zeisha fell into them and held on tight. When she pulled away, her eyes drifted toward the city below. "I should go see Krey."

Kebi's eyes narrowed. "You spend all your time with him in his locked room, yes? Unless you are with me?"

Zeisha nodded. She'd told Kebi about Krey's imprisonment, though she hadn't given any details about why he was there.

"You need time by yourself," Kebi said. "In the sun, with spring green around you. You say you do not know yourself. We know someone by spending time with them."

"He needs me right now. More than ever."

Kebi smiled. "Krey will be fine. When you care for yourself, you are stronger for others. Will you do this? Spend time with yourself before you go to him?"

"Okay." The word surprised her.

As soon as she walked into the park she and Krey had claimed as their own, Zeisha felt lighter. She breathed the crisp air, listened to birds grumbling, and ran her fingers along green leaves. Prayers left her mind and her lips, whispers to a God she'd been too distracted to talk to lately. She'd expected to miss Krey. Instead, she found herself more content than she'd been since her release from the militia.

Before she left the park, she sat on a bench. After making sure no one else was around, she whispered to herself, "Hello, Zeisha. I don't know you anymore." She felt silly, but she kept going. "Maybe if I spend time with you, that'll change."

23

I'm tired of films about advanced technology. You know what I want to watch? Movies about pre-computerized societies. I want films with bladed-weapon combat, people lost in jungles, and spies infiltrating cities instead of databases.

-"Take Me Back in Time" by Genta Ril
The Derogan Chronicle, *dated Cyon 10, 6293*

KREY SAT on the edge of his bed, trying to read a book. His eyes kept roaming to the closed window shutters, where rain pattered in a steady beat. For once, his three friends all had the day off—and they were stuck in Krey's little room.

They'd planned to spend the morning wandering Deroga's streets. It was the first day they'd all had off since Eira had started allowing Krey to spend time outside. That was two weeks ago. In total, eight weeks had passed since he'd consumed shimshim brains. While he'd committed to never touching his dark fuel again, he still battled daily cravings. Any time he left the prison house, at least one friend had to accompany him.

When a rainstorm had ruined the group's plans, they'd settled for relaxing together. Lanterns and candles provided light, but the little room was still dreary. They'd talked for a while, until the rain's soothing sounds had lulled first Nora, then Zeisha, to sleep.

Krey read a paragraph for the third time and still had no idea what it said. The rain's steady taps against the shutters felt like a personal attack. *I just want to go outside.*

"It must be almost time for lunch," Ovrun said from the corner where he was seated.

Nora blinked and yawned, then cuddled closer into his side.

"Aren't we supposed to meet Elo?" he asked.

"Oh!" Nora sat up straight. "I forgot! We'd better get our shoes on."

Krey slipped a bookmark into his book. "You're meeting Elo Golsch? The spy?"

"Yeah," Nora said as she put her boots back on. She seemed to be avoiding Krey's gaze. "Eira's coming too. We're trying to figure out if we can trust him."

"Can I come? I'd like to be part of that conversation."

Nora slowly tightened the laces of her boots. "I've . . . been talking to him a lot lately. I don't know if I'm supposed to bring anyone else."

Krey set his book down. "You said Ovrun's going with you."

"Yeah, he . . . he comes along sometimes."

Krey stared at Nora. When she finished with her boots and met his gaze, he said, "I haven't seen Eira since the day she put me in this place. I haven't been part of any strategizing. Just say it, Nora. Eira doesn't trust me."

Nora pressed her lips together.

"Say it!" he demanded, standing and stepping toward her.

"Fine." She stood and lifted her chin. "Eira doesn't trust you. Neither do I."

Krey's jaw muscles tightened. His chest swelled as he drew in a deep breath. "I'm the same person I always was. I did one thing wrong. *One thing.* I've followed every one of Eira's rules. I wish she'd give me even a little bit of trust! I wish you would too, for that matter."

Nora looked to the side, muttering something under her breath. Krey wasn't about to let this go, though. Nora had spent plenty of time in this room. But since that first day, when she'd yelled at him about how she couldn't trust him, they'd both avoided talking about where they stood as friends.

Krey wasn't sure why he'd spent eight weeks not confronting her. He wasn't exactly afraid of conflict. Sometimes a good fight was what you needed to clear the air. He missed their old friendship, the one that was both deep and easy. It was still easy, but it was shallow now. They were dancing on top of everything they weren't saying.

"Krey." Nora cleared her throat; the word had come out as a croak. "Yes, you're the same person you always were, but Eira doesn't know who that is anymore. And you know what? Neither do I. I want to trust you, but I don't know what else you aren't telling me. Or what you'll hide in the future."

Defensive words sprang to Krey's tongue. He opened his mouth to spew every one of them . . . then closed it. Something told him he needed to be really careful here, or he'd screw things up. More than he already had. Though his muscles were still tight, he unfolded his arms. Once he'd taken a few deep breaths, he felt capable of speaking without making an ass of himself. Nora watched him the whole time, her brows furrowing.

"Listen," he said at last, "you're my friend." He turned to Ovrun, who was now standing behind Nora. "You too. Between the two of you and Zeisha"—he turned and, finding her awake, gave her a sad half-smile—"well, besides my aunts, you're the three people in this world I trust the most."

He spread his arms wide and said words he'd been wanting to say for some time now. He wasn't sure what had stopped him. "From now on, no more lies. I'm serious." His gaze locked on Nora, and his breaths came quicker. *Okay, maybe not all the anger is gone.* "But I haven't forgotten that I'm not the only one who lied."

Nora's shoulders dropped. "Can we sit?"

They all joined her on the floor.

"I lied," Nora said softly, "because I was scared. I didn't think you'd help me if I told you the truth. If I could go back and change it, I would. I'm sorry. To all of you."

Ovrun took her hand. Zeisha murmured words of acceptance.

Krey found her eyes. "Thanks." When she nodded, he said, "Ovrun and Nora, I didn't tell you I was a brain eater because I didn't want to lose your trust. Seems stupid now, since I ended up betraying you all. But that was it. Plus, I was embarrassed." He spread his hands wide. "But you've all seen me at my worst now. Ask me all the stuff you've ever wanted to know about brain eating. I'll tell you anything."

Nora leaned toward Krey, biting her lip. Unspoken questions danced in her eyes.

"Just ask," he said softly.

She swallowed. "Is there any hope for my father?"

All at once, she seemed different. Younger. It wasn't just her soft voice; it was her eyes, wide and vulnerable. Krey didn't look away from her, though he knew his words wouldn't be what she wanted to hear. "I don't know, Nora."

Gone was her girlish hope. Her brows drew together, and she thrust both hands out. "What do you mean, you don't know? You're the expert! Just tell me the truth!"

He didn't rise to her bait. "I am telling the truth. I don't even know how long it took the guy next door to go past the point of no return. And I certainly don't know how long it would take your father.

"He's been doing this for years. That shouldn't be possible. But we all know his magic is different somehow. He's way more powerful than he should be." Krey shook his head. "Nora, maybe he can still recover. But you told me you talked to him when we were at the palace. If there's any chance of him changing, he has to want it. And he clearly doesn't."

Nora's jaw clenched as she drew in a loud breath through her nose and blew it out. "What are you saying, Krey?"

"I'm saying I hope he recovers . . . but you should start thinking about taking him down."

"I'm not giving up on him!" she snapped.

"I'm not saying you should."

Nora sat up straight, pulling her eyes away from his. She swallowed. "Okay, another question. Why did you tell me you'd fly me to the palace?"

Krey sighed. As hard as it was to talk to Nora about her father, it beat talking about himself. "I just . . . I wanted to stop you from doing something stupid. And then . . ." He ran his hand through his thick, shaggy hair. "Once my plan was in place, I didn't say anything because I didn't want anyone to stop me." He lowered his head. "The cravings, they came back so fast. I wanted to . . . to taste it again. I wanted to . . . control people." He looked up, trying to read his friends' reactions.

"Do you still want all that?" Ovrun asked.

"Yeah. But not as much as I want to be free of it. And all of you—I don't want to control you. I'm telling the truth, okay? You're too important to me. I . . . I broke my parents' trust when I controlled them. Even when I imagine controlling people, it's never any of you."

"So you still imagine it?" Zeisha asked softly.

He took her hand and didn't shy away from her gentle gaze. "I try not to, but . . . it's been less than two months. I still want it, Zei. I don't want to want it, but I do."

Ovrun said, "If you can't stop thinking about it, tell one of us. If you admit it when it's just a thought, maybe it'll never be more than a thought again."

Krey groaned, his shoulders drooping. If there was only a way for all of them to forget this. *But there's not. So deal with it.* "This is gonna suck," he said. "But yeah—yeah, I can do that. When I can't get it out of my head, I'll tell you."

Nora rested a hand on his knee. "And we won't judge you."

He gave her a little smirk. "You sure?"

Her lips twitched. "Well, maybe I'll judge a little, but I'll hide it really well."

Krey laughed—a real, chest-shaking laugh. It felt good.

The door opened. Eira stood there, holding a bag and a large basket. Her white braids dripped rainwater. Despite being soaked, she looked somehow regal. "Nora and Ovrun, shall we go?"

They all stood. "I'd like Krey to come," Nora said. "Zeisha too, if she wants to."

Eira didn't respond, other than a slightly tilted head.

"Krey should be in on our plans," Nora said. "We can trust him."

Those four words pierced Krey's chest, then traveled to his throat. He swallowed to prevent himself from crying. Eira might not take him along if she thought he was weak.

Eira fixed her gaze on him for an uncomfortably long time, and he knew his attempt at hiding his emotions had failed. At last, she gave a slight nod. "Very well. Come along."

<hr>

Nora felt a new sense of lightness as she followed Eira to Elo Golsch's room. Yes, Krey still craved brains; her father was ruining their nation; and she was about to meet with a spy who had uncertain loyalties.

But her friendship with Krey was back on solid footing. Until this moment, she hadn't let herself admit how much she'd missed that.

Eira gestured for a guard to unlock Golsch's door. Nora wiped the smile off her face. Time to act like a princess.

Golsch was standing by the window. His hair, which had been very short upon his arrest, now stuck out straight in all directions. His lips were curved in a tight, tentative smile.

Nora stepped forward, holding out her hand. "Elo, it's good to see you again."

"Your Royal Highness." Rather than shaking her hand, Golsch bent both arms, holding his hands straight in front of him, and lowered his head briefly.

Nora almost laughed. "You know you don't need to bow. Or call me that." *And I know you'll do it again, no matter what I say.*

Eira took the room's single chair, while everyone else sat in a circle on the floor. Zeisha distributed food, not giving any to herself or Krey, since they'd been last-minute additions to the meeting. "We'll grab lunch after this," she said.

Nora ate her sandwich, chatting easily with Golsch. Even after several meetings, she was surprised he had anything but contempt for her. After she'd screamed at him and nearly punched him the first time they met, she figured she'd ruined any chance of connecting with him, one Cellerinian to another.

A month ago, Eira had told Nora that Golsch didn't seem interested in talking any longer. Nora had offered to try speaking with him again, though she'd doubted it would help.

Golsch had seemed genuinely touched when the Princess of Cellerin apologized—again—to him. After begging her forgiveness for the sarcastic words he'd spoken to her, he talked to her like he'd known her for years. Her position as a Cellerinian royal instilled trust in him. Beyond that, she was his connection to home.

Eira asked Nora to continue meeting with Golsch. Over the last month, he'd opened up about his army experiences. He'd listened with genuine concern when Nora told him about her father's faltering leadership. Yesterday, Nora and Eira had agreed it was time to ask for his help. They both thought he'd react better if Nora led the discussion.

After a casual lunch with no topics more serious than the weather, Nora rested her elbows on her crossed legs and leaned forward. "Elo, you and I have discussed our concerns over what's happening to our nation. As you know, I'm trying to turn things around. Our first step is to ensure that the trogs remain free. From there, we can tackle other issues, like the army's occupation of New Therro."

He nodded. "We should all be free, Your Highness."

Nora locked her eyes with his. "We could use someone on the inside to help make that happen."

He sat up straight, swallowing hard. "You want me to turn against Cellerin."

"No, Elo. I want you to fight *for* Cellerin."

After a long pause, he asked, "What . . . what would that involve?"

Eira opened the bag at her feet and handed Nora a stack of papers from it.

Nora held up the papers. "These are diagrams of the Derogan Extrain tunnels." Seeing Golsch's blank stare, she described the old method of transportation. "Last time the army came," she said, "the trogs hid in these tunnels. We want you to tell the military leaders you stole these papers."

While the diagrams she was giving him were real, they didn't show the trogs' current Extrain access points, nor the tunnels they used. This was worthless information, and Golsch probably suspected that. What he did with these papers would show where his loyalties lay.

"When you give this to them, it'll build trust," Nora said. "Then you can gather information to help us defend the city." *And we'll hope like hell my father doesn't have time to interrogate you,* she added silently. At least Golsch didn't have any information of real value, except that Nora lived with the trogs—and the king already suspected that.

"How would I communicate with you?"

"Someone will be in touch," Nora replied. Hatlin and his people would help with that part of the strategy if they got that far.

Golsch picked up a piece of fruit he'd left on his plate. Eyes lowered, he took a bite. The rain had finally stopped, and his chewing was the only sound in the room.

Nora watched him, wishing she knew where he really stood. She wanted to tell him about the army uprising Hatlin, Wallis, and T were working on. A successful rebellion would force the army out of New Therro. Hopefully the chaos would also delay the army's attack on Deroga.

If Elo Golsch truly wanted to stand against the king, he could help facilitate the uprising from within the army. But Nora would leave it up to New Therro's rebel leaders to determine if Golsch was trustworthy enough for such a position.

Golsch ate the whole piece of fruit before he returned his attention to Nora. He held his hands out and bowed his head, then said, "I'll do it, Your Highness. For Cellerin."

24

*I recently met an elderly couple who married young, at twenty-one.
I've talked to other sixteen-year-olds about this, and none of us can
imagine marrying in five years. Sure, we'll fall in love, but marriage?
We'll be too busy living to think about that.*

-*"Love Without Marriage" by Genta Ril*
The Derogan Chronicle, *dated Cyon 12, 6293*

OVRUN HELPED CLEAN up the rest of the lunch food, but he barely saw the sandwich crusts he was tossing back in Eira's basket. His mind—and his eyes—kept drifting to Nora.

He hadn't said a word during the meeting. He'd been too busy watching the girl next to him. Once again, she'd gone into princess mode. And damn, she'd done well. Ovrun loved the take-charge confidence Nora put on as easily as a hat.

Since their quiet fight in Krey's room, Ovrun had spent way too much time considering Nora's question. Could he become the person she needed him to be?

Could he be a king?

He'd always assumed the future king should be an amazing leader. An expert strategist. A shrewd negotiator. But Nora herself was developing all those qualities. Did she really need a king with strengths she already had? Maybe all she needed was a partner by her side, someone—

Eira's firm voice drew Ovrun's attention back into the room. "Tonight," she told Golsch, "you will leave when it is dark. You must act as if you are sneaking out, in case other spies are watching you."

"But nobody will stop me?" Golsch asked. "Even in the other clans' territory?"

"I will give you directions to avoid them. They know to ignore you if they see you." Eira turned to the teens who'd joined her in the meeting. "You may go. I will talk to Elo alone."

In the hallway, Zeisha said, "Krey and I need to eat. Want to meet back in his room later?"

"Sure," Nora said.

Ovrun slipped his hand in hers, and they left the prison house. The rain had finally stopped. They strolled down the street, breathing in the fresh, damp air. "You were amazing in there," he said.

"All I did was talk to him."

"That's not all you did. You put him at ease, and he responded to that." His eyes narrowed. "Do you think he's really on our side?"

"I don't know. That's why we didn't tell him about the New Therroan uprising." She shrugged. "If he's on our side, he'll be a spy for us. If he's not, he can tell his leaders every detail of his experience here. All the ways the trogs tortured him, like giving him a comfortable bed, blankets, and plenty of food."

Ovrun laughed. "Good point." They turned a corner. He halted, pulling Nora close. When she slid her hands over his shoulders and smiled up at him, he surrendered to a plan he'd been considering for weeks now. "There's somewhere I've been wanting to take you."

"Oh? Where?"

"It's a surprise."

He led her through Star Clan territory. When they left the inhabited portion of the city, Nora said, "We've hunted over here. You know I'm not gonna scope out shimshim dens on my day off, right?"

"I promise I won't even say the word *shimshim*."

"You just said it."

"What, *shimshim*?"

She let out a half-groan, half-laugh. "Lead on."

He draped his arm around her shoulder. She responded by sliding her hand around his waist. By the sky, she fit him so well. Could there be a better feeling than holding her close to his side like this?

Yeah, idiot, there could be way better feelings. A quiet laugh shook his chest.

Nora looked up again. "What?"

"Nothing. You're just the best."

One dark eyebrow lifted. "And that's funny?"

"No, I was just—thinking about things that'll get us in trouble."

"Oh." She gave him a flirtatious smile. "I like getting in trouble."

"Believe me, I know."

With the mood they were both in, it might not be the best time to take her to the place he'd found, but Ovrun couldn't make himself turn around.

After several minutes of comfortable silence, Ovrun led Nora into a green, overgrown area. "We passed this place when we were hunting last week," he said. "It reminded me—"

"Of the first place we kissed." Nora's voice was soft.

He looked down and found her smiling in a way that made him melt. "Yeah," he said. He led her to a large tree. Rainwater dripped from its lush fronds. They took off their jackets and laid them on the damp ground.

"You"—Nora sat, pulling him down next to her—"you, you're so . . ." She completed the thought with a kiss that left him breathless.

"Glad you like this place," he whispered in her ear.

She laughed and moved as if to kiss him again, but he lifted his finger and put it on her lips.

Nora grinned, opened her mouth, and bit his finger. A raindrop plopped on her nose, and they both laughed.

Taking one of her hands, Ovrun slowly wove their fingers together. "I didn't just come here to relive our first kiss."

"No? You had more in mind?" She leaned forward. The fingers of her free hand trailed down his neck, then his chest.

He captured her hand. "Yeah, but not in the way you're thinking." His heart pounded, and not just from the excitement of her touch. *I didn't expect to be this nervous.* When her eyes lifted to meet his, he licked his lips and spoke again. "Nora, I need to tell you something."

She stiffened, her sly grin disappearing in an instant. "Please don't leave me, Ovrun."

His chin dropped. "You really think . . . you think I'd bring you to a place like this to break up with you?"

"I—" She pulled her hands from his and covered her cheeks, which had turned a deep red. "Of course you wouldn't. I don't know why I said that." Her gaze dropped.

All at once, it came together in Ovrun's mind. Faylie, Nora's first friend, had left. Maybe it hadn't been Faylie's decision, but Nora hadn't known that at the time. Later, Nora had learned of her father's lies and Krey's secrets. Life had taught her that the people she cared about betrayed her.

"Hey." Ovrun nudged her chin higher, then used his thumb to wipe a raindrop off her cheek. "I'm not leaving you."

"Good." It came out as a squeak.

He grinned at the sound. His voice didn't waver as he said, "I wanted to tell you—I *needed* to tell you—that I love you."

She blinked. Then blinked again. Her lips parted. "What?"

"You—you didn't hear me?"

"I did, but I . . ." Her eyes were wide, like a trapped shimshim. "What do you expect me to say to that?"

"Shh." He put his finger on her lips again. "You don't have to say anything."

"But if I don't say it back, that makes me . . . it makes me an asshole! I thought we'd agreed we couldn't commit to anything long term, so I haven't even let myself consider—I mean, why would you put me in this position?"

He lifted both hands in a gesture of surrender. "I didn't tell you I love you so you could say it back. I told you because it's true."

She turned her head away, fixing her eyes somewhere in the distance. He could barely hear her next words: "I can't give you what you want, Ovrun."

"Nora, I'm serious, I didn't expect you to say it back." *Hoped for it, but didn't expect it.*

"That's not what I mean!" The words came out shrill. She faced him again and grabbed his hands, holding them in a desperately tight grip. "You want to live in the country, with open land and kids who can run free. You want a life that has all the normal problems everyone deals with—not all the problems royals deal with. I don't think I can give you that, Ovrun. As much as I've imagined escaping from this place and forgetting about the trogs and the crown and my father . . . I also *can't* imagine doing that." She let go of one of his hands and ran her fingers through her hair, groaning. "I'm not making sense."

He took the hand back in his own. "You are. And when I say I love you, I mean it." He licked his lips, swallowed, and pushed his next statement past an odd resistance in his throat. "I love you more than I love my dream of living in the country."

Again, her mouth gaped. "What are you saying?"

"I . . . you heard me."

"Ovrun." Nora leaned forward and took his face in her hands.

She didn't look angry. Panic and hope warred in her eyes. "Don't lie to either of us, okay? Have you really given up that dream?"

He covered her hands with his own. His eyes fell closed. He pulled up a mental picture he'd been imagining lately: the two of them standing in front of the palace.

Without his permission, the image shifted. Now they were on a farmhouse porch, surrounded by fields, watching the sun set.

He pushed his mind back to the original scene. From the palace, they could see the same sunset, even if trees and buildings covered parts of it. In this version of his vision, he was with the same Nora. She was just wearing nicer clothes.

She's what's important.

He fixed his will on that thought, opened his eyes, and smiled at her. "You're the only part of my dream that matters, Nora. Not the location."

Nora pulled her hands off his face. Her eyebrows drew together. "Be honest, Ovrun."

"I am being honest. With you and with myself." His heart ached as he said it, but he barreled on. "Nora, I've told you a hundred times, I don't want to be a king. I don't have what it takes to lead a country. But you do! All by yourself. So I'm not offering to lead the country; I'd botch it up. But I want to be with you. If the only way I can do that is by wearing a crown, well . . . I guess I can deal with that."

"So"—her eyebrows rose, along with the corners of her lips—"Are you offering to be the hot figurehead while I do all the hard work?"

He shrugged and let out a short laugh. "I'd be happy to earn my keep. Chopping wood or something."

Nora's gaze drifted to the side for several long moments. Ovrun cleared his throat, and she brought her attention back to him, a mischievous smile on her lips. "Sorry, I was just imagining watching you chop wood on a hot day. Pretty sure I wouldn't get any actual work done."

He rolled his eyes, but they were both laughing.

Silence fell. It was Ovrun who broke it. "I know I'm not what you're supposed to look for. Even if your dad recovers, he'll never approve—"

"I don't care what my father thinks." Her eyes flashed. "I'm not letting him or Dani make this decision for me. I wasn't ready to stand up to them a few months ago. I am now."

"Good. But still . . . I'll understand if what I'm offering isn't what you want."

Nora took a deep breath. "You are . . . incredible. You just offered to give up a dream to be with me. I don't care if you meet all the 'king standards' I grew up with. What I do care about is whether I love you or not. And I . . . I want to say it, I do—"

"Not until you can say it honestly," he said. "If that ever happens."

"If," she whispered.

The word cast a shadow on his bright enthusiasm. But he nodded, not letting go of her gaze. "If."

Her eyes were full of moisture, though none of it escaped. She released a frustrated groan.

"I love you," Ovrun said, emphasizing every word. "Even if you can't say it back. And I'm not going anywhere."

He expected a kiss or sweet words. Instead, Nora covered her face with her hands, shaking her head.

"What is it?" he asked. When she didn't answer, he pulled her close. She let go of her face and buried it in his chest. "What is it?" he asked again.

"You love me." She pulled back. Her lips were pressed together, and her brows furrowed, but she didn't cry. She shook her head again, releasing a long breath. "My mom loved me, and she died. My dad loved me, and he . . . he might recover, but for now . . . well, he's gone, and thanks to him, so is Dani. And then there was Faylie. Oh, Ovrun —" She took his hands again. She swallowed hard, and her lips broke into a bittersweet smile. "I've missed . . . being loved."

She brought her lips to his and kissed him gently. "Thank you," she said, before drawing him into a tight hug.

He rubbed her hair and her back. A thought popped into his head, so clear, he could see the words written on his mind.

I'm helping her reframe her past. She's helping me reframe my future.

He held her even tighter as his heart tensed with an emotion he couldn't name.

THE SEER: 7

Sarza's eyes popped open. She squeezed them shut again, bringing her hands up to her head and stifling a groan.

Where am I? Why does my head hurt?

She pried her eyes open. She was outside, in the dark, lying on cool dirt. Her head rested on the sharp edge of . . . something.

Some distance away, a dim light, filtered by a curtain, caught her eye. She'd seen that before. It anchored her in the present. Memories rushed in.

She'd run out of food and water earlier that day. As always, she'd waited until most of Deroga was asleep before exiting the office building with several empty water bottles and a bag. She had this down to a science. First, she'd sneak into a trog storehouse for food. Then she'd refill her water bottles at the river. In less than an hour, she'd be back at her temporary home.

Except everything went wrong this time around. There was now a padlock on the storehouse. So Sarza had crept to the Star Clan's main residential street. She'd found a dark house with a tended garden. *Perfect.* The garden meant it was occupied; the darkness meant everyone inside was asleep. She'd sneak in, take some food from the kitchen, and leave.

As she'd approached the stairs leading to the back porch, a vision, sudden and powerful, had literally knocked her off her feet. It seemed she'd hit her head on the bottom step.

She wasn't sure if the head bump or the intense vision had stolen her consciousness. Maybe a combination of both. It certainly wasn't the first time she'd hurt herself when a vision sent her to the ground. It was, however, the first time it had happened when she had no access to doctors or healers.

Sarza gingerly reached for the wound on the back of her head, gasping when her fingers touched it. It was bleeding quite a lot, but it was less than a simmet in length. She blew out her breath. It might keep her awake tonight, but it wouldn't kill her.

As she stood, memories of the vision flooded her mind. She grasped for the handrail over the steps.

She'd hardened herself to the shock of disturbing visions a long time ago. This one hadn't even been that awful—but for some reason, it bothered her. Maybe because after months in this damn city, she felt like she knew some of the people in the vision.

Sarza gritted her teeth, let go of the handrail, and marched toward the river. Food could wait; she needed water. Needed to clean her wound too. *Focus on that, Sarza. Get to the river.*

But she couldn't get the vision out of her mind. It was one of those two-part prophecies, the kind that gave her options. Something bad was happening soon. She could stop it.

No. I don't stop things from happening. Terrible stuff happens to me too, and no one's there to rescue me. That's life. Not my job. Not my problem.

But the people in the vision . . . despite herself, she felt—what was that, empathy? Yeah, that had to be it. Stupid emotion, empathy. But she couldn't seem to banish it. Things would be bad if she didn't intervene. *Which I'm not going to do.*

Sarza had been beyond pissed to find her army contact had fled.

But once she'd gotten her head on straight, she'd realized maybe staying in the city was for the best. She could spy on the princess and her friends until the army returned. Then she'd give her superiors so much information, the army would easily win their battle over the trogs. The king would give her a medal, her own orsa, and a raise. (And really, she'd settle for just the raise.)

Watching the group of teens became easier when one of the guys the princess hung out with got imprisoned in a house with windows and no exterior guards.

She'd started spending hours near the window leading to that guy's room. When the shutters were open, she had to huddle out of sight behind some nearby bushes, listening to conversations that drifted her way. But when the shutters were closed, which they often were on cooler days or when it rained, she stood at the window, peeking through a crack.

The prisoner was named Krey. His girlfriend, Zeisha—the one who'd cried through her own birthday party—stayed with him. Princess Nora and her pushup-doing boyfriend, Ovrun, stopped by almost every day.

Standing by that window, Sarza had learned about the disgusting, intriguing practice of brain eating. She'd also heard all the reasons Princess Nora was rebelling against her daddy. If half of it was true, the king was off his rocker.

She'd gotten to know these four friends too. Krey thought he was funny and smart, but mostly he was just arrogant. Nora laughed too easily. Despite that, Ovrun couldn't keep his eyes off her. Sarza was tempted to throw a handkerchief through the window with a note: *For your drool, Muscle Man.* And Zeisha—well, she clearly had some sort of ulterior motive. Nobody was really that sweet.

Sarza was content to sit outside the window, judging the people inside. Until one day when she'd felt an uncomfortable tightness in her chest as she'd watched the four friends laughing. It had taken a full week for her to identify the strange emotion.

Jealousy.

She'd never had real friendships. What she wouldn't give to be in the room with these four people, joking around with them. Because as obvious as their faults were, well . . . Sarza liked them.

What was wrong with her?

She liked these annoying people, and now she knew some of them would soon be in serious trouble. She'd seen what would happen, how scared they'd be, how unjust it was. On top of that, she knew how to stop it.

No.

She broke into a run. The wound on her head throbbed as her pulse picked up. She focused on the pain, trying to get her mind off the vision.

Not. My. Problem.

25

Therro is now the only nation in which possessing a firearm carries the same penalty as shooting one. Yet we still hear about people getting caught with an old handgun, claiming they couldn't give up something with that much sentimental value.

Here's a tip to keep you out of prison: hang onto Grandpa's old scarf or coffee mug instead of Grandpa's old gun.

-"Use Your Brain, Not Your Arms" by Genta Ril
The Derogan Chronicle, dated Cyon 14, 6293

ONCE AGAIN, Zeisha put her shoes on as quietly as she could.

Once again, Krey's sleepy voice reached her ears. "Hey, beautiful."

She tiptoed to him, kneeling by his pallet on the floor. "You know, I left that shutter cracked open just right so the light would fall on me, not you. You weren't supposed to wake up."

"C'mere." He grabbed her hand and tugged her down until she was lying next to him. "You could send a message to Kebi. Tell her you're sick."

"What, sick of you trying to keep me from my work?"

He chuckled and pulled her closer. "I think you're more sarcastic than you used to be. I like it."

She thought of asking him if he'd like to come to the rooftop garden. He'd happily help her and Kebi with pruning or weed pulling. Sometimes, though, it was nice to have girl time. Just like sometimes it was nice to have alone time.

I never used to feel that way.

She'd changed—much of it due to the solitary walks she'd taken almost every day for the last month and a half. She liked the person she'd become. *Or the person I'm still becoming.* Every week, she felt further removed from the girl who'd grown up in the shadow of Cellerin Mountain. She was both stronger and more empathetic. She hadn't known those two things could fit together.

"Sorry you have to stay in here alone." Acidic guilt burned her insides as she said the words. Maybe she should ask him to come with her after all.

"It's okay, I've been looking forward to reading the book you brought me yesterday."

She smiled. "Perfect." After a quick kiss, she was out of bed and out the door.

Halfway down the street, Zeisha heard rapid footsteps. Turning, she saw a man barreling toward her from in between two houses.

Zeisha froze, her mind racing. Who could be running to this street? Most people didn't even know about the prison house. Maybe Eira had sent someone to tell them the army was attacking. She opened her mouth to ask the man if that was it.

He spoke first, as he skidded to a halt. "Excuse me, are you Zeisha?"

She took in his appearance. His medium-brown, curly hair hadn't seen scissors or a brush in a long time. An equally wild beard stuck out from his face and neck. His eyes, surrounded by a few lines, were hazel like hers.

He didn't look like a trog. His shirt was navy blue, rather than one of the neutral colors trogs preferred. And trogs bathed regularly. If Eira saw this man, she wouldn't even let him visit a bathhouse. She'd send him straight to the river.

Zeisha's perusal of him took only an instant. *Get away!* her instincts screamed. A burst of warning energy sent her feet running, churning up the dirt of the street.

The man's weight slammed into her back. Her knees, chest, and cheek hit the ground. He grabbed her wrists and yanked them behind her. Gripping them in one strong hand, he slapped his other hand onto her mouth. "Don't say a word."

He was sitting on her waist. All she could think to do was press her legs together. Like that would stop him if he—*Oh God, no!* Sobs pushed themselves from her nose and her covered mouth.

She squirmed, but he was too heavy. Her cries became more frantic. She tried to bite him, but his hand was pressed too hard against her mouth. He tasted like dirt and onions and smelled like he hadn't bathed in weeks. Gagging interrupted her crying.

"Stop!" he commanded. "I don't want to hurt you! Just be still, damn it! Listen to me!"

She forced herself to stop fighting. Her sobs kept coming.

"I'm gonna let go of your mouth," he said. "We're too far away for people to hear you scream, so don't try. Got it?"

She nodded. Her lips rubbed against his calloused hand.

He let go of her mouth.

"Please." She tried to keep her voice quiet, but the sobs made it impossible. "Please let me go. Please—"

Her pleading stopped when, out of the corner of her eye, she saw the gun he'd pulled out. Frantically, she shook her head. Pebbles dug into her cheek and ear. She barely noticed. Her body started fighting again, like it had a mind of its own.

The man's voice pitched up. "I said, I don't want to hurt you. You gotta calm down!"

She stopped fighting, but her whole body was shaking. Desperately, she gulped in air, one breath after another. Her sobs halted, but she was lightheaded now. *Oh God, oh God, oh God, don't let him hurt me.*

"If I get off you, will you just sit? And calm down?"

She nodded her swimming head.

He climbed off her. She rolled onto her side and tried to sit up, then fell back down. "I'm gonna pass out," she moaned. She raised her eyes to his and found restrained fury there. His muscles were coiled, alert.

This guy might not *want* to hurt her, but he would if he had to. If she kept panicking, his finger might find the trigger of that gun.

Zeisha tried to slow her breathing. After a minute or so, she was able to sit and yank her knees into her chest. "What do you want?"

"I want to do my job."

"What job?"

"I'm a soldier in the king's army."

"You don't have jurisdiction here. Deroga is independent."

"I'm not here to talk politics." He gestured with both hands.

Zeisha's eyes darted to the gun he still held. "Just let me go." She swallowed, determined not to cry again. "I won't tell anyone I saw you."

"Don't be stupid, you know I can't do that. Just do what I say, and I won't have to hurt you. But if you try to run—" He pointed the gun at her, and his voice took on an ominous tone. "Just don't."

Zeisha's breath came faster. She hugged her knees tighter.

"We're gonna travel to the king," the man said. "He wants to talk to you. You, Krey, Ovrun, and Nora."

Zeisha froze. *He can't take them too.*

The man continued to talk, his voice low and steely. "I know Krey is in that building. I know you were just there. We're gonna find a place to wait until Nora and Ovrun come to visit."

"They won't come." The lie flowed smoothly from her mouth.

"I know they visit almost every day. My contact told me."

"You mean Elo Golsch?" Funny how her mind was sharp, even as her heart raced.

His eyes widened, and he stiffened, confirming her suspicion. Apparently the spy had heard more from his room than they'd realized.

Zeisha drew a deep breath. "That man left here a week ago. He doesn't know what happened since then. Monday, Nora told Krey she was done visiting him. She doesn't trust him anymore because of —of what he did. Ovrun does what Nora does. We can wait if you want, but they're not coming."

She'd always been a terrible liar. Apparently, desperation changed that. She had no problem staring into this man's eyes and telling him a story that might save her friends.

The man swore. Zeisha could see the storm of uncertainty in his fidgeting fingers and tight mouth. She didn't dare flinch.

At last, he said, "We'll wait until nightfall. If the princess and Ovrun don't come by then, I suppose two's better than none."

"Okay." *That gives me time to figure out . . . something.* But who was she kidding? She wasn't like Krey, Ovrun, and Nora, who thrived under pressure. She'd never get away from this guy.

The man led her across the street and behind the houses there. They entered an abandoned house that smelled of shimshim waste. From the large, glassless window in the front room, they had a perfect view of the prison house. The man dragged two old, sturdy chairs across the room, settling them in the shadows, a few mets from the window. "Sit down."

When they were both settled, the man tucked the gun in his jacket pocket. He folded his arms and leaned forward, watching Zeisha with cold eyes.

After tackling her, he hadn't hurt her further, which told her he had some measure of self-control. But Zeisha knew the army leaders would've chosen someone capable for this mission. She'd seen the anger in this man's gaze when she'd panicked. If she tried to run, he'd stop her with whatever force was necessary.

From one of his jacket pockets, the man retrieved a small, glass water bottle. He offered it to Zeisha.

"No, thanks."

He rolled his eyes, then drank and offered it to her again. "It's safe."

The offer told Zeisha something else about this man: even though he was capable of violence, he hadn't lost his humanity.

She took the bottle and sipped. The glass smelled like him, but the water tasted good. She handed it back. "Thanks." Strange to thank this guy, but a new strategy was entering her mind. She had to build trust. Get his guard down. "What's your name?"

"Lars."

"Lars. It's nice to . . ." She let out her breath and shook her head.

He ran a dirty hand over his filthier face and let out an exasperated grunt. "I know it's not nice to meet me."

After a long pause, she asked, "Will you tell me about yourself?"

He frowned. "What the hell, you trying to make friends?"

"If we're going to sit here for hours, I'd like to distract myself," Zeisha said quietly.

Lars nodded slowly and crossed his arms again. Then he told her how fighting in the army gave his life meaning. How glad he was that the king had brought those "damn New Therroan terrorists" under control. He oozed patriotism and loyalty.

True to his word, Lars didn't hurt Zeisha. When they both started squirming from the effects of the water, he led her outside, keeping his back to her while they took care of business. She considered attacking him then, but he was still holding the gun. She looked around for a leaf, a weed—anything she could eat for fuel. But she was crouched in the dirt, and the nearest plant was at least a dozen steps away.

Back inside, hours passed. Zeisha's stomach shrank into a dense, twisted ball of hunger and anxiety. Lars was right; Nora and Ovrun visited Krey nearly every day. She prayed they'd make an exception today or come well after nightfall.

Nora brought her dinner plate to a table in the militia dining room. Ovrun was already there. "How'd hunting go?" she asked as she sat.

"Not bad. Thirteen shimshims."

"Nice!" Nora said.

"Did you enjoy sleeping the day away?"

She scowled. "I only slept half the day away, thank you very much." She usually slept in on Saturdays instead of hunting. Her Friday-night flights with Osmius wore her out. "Hatlin gave me bad news last night."

"Again?"

"Yeah." Nora sighed. Her information-gathering meetings with Hatlin hadn't been encouraging. Almost two months ago, he'd told her that the king had touched the New Therroan palace spy. While he hadn't immediately interrogated her, she'd known it was coming. She'd fled, using her soil-lysting faculty to dig an escape tunnel.

Another week, Nora had learned that the king had secretly fired all his ministers when he'd locked down the palace. They were the people most likely to talk sense into him, and now they were gone. He'd paid the former ministers to stay quiet and bribed the newspaper not to report it, but word had eventually reached Hatlin.

And week after week, the New Therroan flyer had described the army's increased size and organization. The soldiers were undergoing ruthless training, focused on teaching them to obey orders without question. That made planning an uprising difficult. Hatlin thought the army might now be disciplined enough to carry out an effective attack on Deroga.

Nora took a drink of water, then said, "The army has been recruiting lysters. They've gotten a few dozen of them by promising double the normal pay."

Ovrun's eyebrows leapt up. "Another militia?"

"No, just regular soldiers. I think my father learned his lesson the first time, when his entire militia switched sides because I killed the Overseer." She took a bite, trying not to surrender to the emotion that was always close at hand when she thought of Faylie. "Plus," she said after swallowing, "finding an Overseer can't be easy. Most lysters die if they ingest brain matter." She'd often wondered how many people her father had sacrificed before recruiting Faylie.

Ovrun let out all his breath. "Feels like the odds are getting worse every week."

"Yeah, it does."

After dinner, Ovrun said, "It's still light out. Want to walk to our spot?" He gave her a sweet, hopeful smile.

Nora laughed. It had been eight days since Ovrun had told her he loved her. During that time, they'd gone back to the wooded space twice. It was always romantic, though they'd avoided any serious discussions. "As great as that sounds," she said, "I haven't seen Krey since yesterday afternoon. We should stop by."

Ovrun's laugh floated on the air, finding Zeisha's ears. She froze. Lars was talking and didn't seem to have heard.

Her mind raced. Ovrun was coming, probably accompanied by Nora. Once the two of them entered the prison house, Lars would go across the street to abduct them and Krey. He'd warned Zeisha that he'd have a gun trained on her the whole time. With her life on the line, he figured the guards would do whatever he asked. She was afraid he was right.

I can't let Nora and Ovrun go in that house.

But if she did anything, Lars would shoot.

Or would he? He'd let slip that the army leaders wanted Zeisha and her friends alive. And while his ability to embrace violence was written all over his thick arms and meaty hands, she thought he'd rather subdue her with strength than with a weapon. This was a guy who got into bar fights, not someone who executed people with firearms.

That was what her instinct told her, anyway. Was she willing to risk her life on that gut feeling?

Ovrun laughed again. Lars stopped talking. He pulled his gun out and stood next to the window. Holding his free hand out toward Zeisha, he commanded, "Stay there."

Her joints froze. Every instinct told her to obey the man with the gun.

But my friends! Zeisha dug inside herself for strength. Heart racing, she tiptoed toward Lars.

He spun to look at her. "I said stay there!"

"I just want to see which guards are coming. It's time for a shift change." Again, the lie emerged with casual ease.

Lars peeked outside again. "That hair—that's the princess!"

Zeisha darted the last few steps to the large window. Sure enough, her two friends were strolling down the road. The sight of them injected her with a dose of sudden courage. "This man kidnapped me!" she screamed, the words ripping at the tissues of her throat.

Lars grabbed her and pulled her against him, her chest against his. His gun was in the hand that held her to him. While the muzzle wasn't pointed at her, she felt the cold metal shape pressing through her shirt.

Nora and Ovrun had heard her—they'd stopped walking. Lars tried to grasp Zeisha's mouth. She shook her head hard, avoiding his hand. "Get help!" she shrieked. "He'll take us all to the king!"

Lars's dirty hand found her mouth. Grunting, he gripped it hard. As he struggled to pull Zeisha away from the window, she saw Nora and Ovrun run to the side of the street.

Lars was breathing hard. He held Zeisha so tightly, she couldn't move her arms. She kicked with her booted feet. He just grunted when they contacted his shins. His hand on her mouth squeezed painfully.

"Damn it!" Lars grunted, for no apparent reason. He adjusted the gun, pressing its metal muzzle into her side.

An electric buzz of panic permeated Zeisha's body. She stilled and saw what had made Lars curse. Two guards had exited the house across the street. They ran into the dirt road, looking around frantically. One of them brought his gaze to the window where Lars and Zeisha stood. He sprinted toward them. The other guard followed.

"I have a gun!" Lars shouted. "Stop, or I'll shoot her! Hands up! Get on the ground!"

The guards complied.

Zeisha heard footsteps. Someone was approaching—from deeper in the house.

Lars heard it too. In one strong motion, he lifted Zeisha over the windowsill, setting her on the ground outside. She tried to pull away, but he held her arm in a bruising grip. He joined her outside the window and pressed the gun to her head.

The footsteps behind them stopped. Zeisha swiveled her head to look.

Ovrun stood in the living room.

"Stop right there," Lars said.

Zeisha's gaze found Ovrun's. "I told you to go."

"Release her." Ovrun's voice was low, calming. "You're surrounded."

He can't see the gun, Zeisha realized.

Lars had positioned himself with his gun hand visible to the guards. He pivoted so Ovrun could see the weapon too. "Get your hands up and climb out the window!" he shouted at Ovrun. "I'll shoot her if you don't obey!"

Zeisha's knees weakened. Just moments ago, she'd told herself this man wouldn't pull the trigger. With the metal muzzle pressed hard against her head, she had no such confidence.

Ovrun's gaze darted to Lars and Zeisha, then to the guards.

"Now!" Lars shouted.

Slowly, Ovrun lifted his hands and climbed out the window. His expression was bland, nonthreatening, but his limbs were taut, ready to act. Behind his calm eyes, Zeisha knew his mind was racing, seeking any opportunity to turn things around.

"Ovrun," Lars said, "lie on your belly. Face to the ground. Hands behind your head."

All the air left Ovrun's chest. Resignation weighed down his shoulders. He obeyed.

"Zeisha," Lars said, "lie next to him. Feet even with his head."

He kept his gun trained on her as she followed his commands. At every second, she expected a bullet. As she drew in gasping breaths, dirt entered her mouth. She spit and coughed.

Lars spoke again. "You. Pull those shackles off your belt. Put one side on the girl and the other on the guy. On their right hands."

Murmuring apologies, a guard locked a cool, metal shackle on Zeisha's wrist, then did the same to Ovrun. The chain rattled as Ovrun's warm hand found hers and held it tight.

Next, Lars took the guards' knives. He pointed at the house where he and Zeisha had hidden. "You guards, hug those columns!" he commanded, pointing at two narrow columns on the front stoop. "Shackle your own wrists together!" He stood back far enough to keep his eyes and his gun trained on all his captives. The guards had no choice but to comply. Lars retrieved their keys to the prison house and to their shackles.

"Zeisha and Ovrun, stand," Lars commanded.

They obeyed. With the shackles on both their right wrists, there was no way to stand that wasn't awkward. In order to face the same direction as Ovrun, Zeisha had to stand with her right arm across her body. "Put your left arm around my waist," Ovrun said. She did, and it helped.

Lars led them to the prison house, where only one guard was left inside. After knocking, Lars shouted, "I have a gun on Zeisha and Ovrun. "I'll kill them both if you don't let us in!"

The door swung open.

Lars was quiet and efficient. Within three minutes, the remaining guard was shackled and locked in Krey's room. Krey's left hand was shackled to Ovrun's left, making it even harder for the three captives to move.

Zeisha listened for rescuers. But as Lars ushered his three captives out of the house and into an unfamiliar part of the city, she realized whatever help Nora brought would come too late.

Lars kept his gun trained on them as he led them through deserted streets. The only sounds were their footsteps and frightened breaths, murmured instructions from Lars, and the far-off calls of feral caynins.

<h1 style="text-align:center">THE SEER: 8</h1>

SARZA WATCHED the street from the second-story window of an old, abandoned house. She'd seen Zeisha walk out the front door of the prison house, then watched a man attack her. From a rear window, she'd seen the man take Zeisha to another house. Now, after a confrontation in the street and a quick trip inside the prison house, the man had his three victims: Zeisha, Ovrun, and Krey.

Three people Sarza felt like she actually knew. By the stone, she'd wanted to cheer when Nora ran off.

What a pathetic thought. But hey, spying was lonely. Other spies probably developed fake connections with people they'd never met. Right?

The still street below grew blurry. For one illogical second, Sarza thought it was raining. She blinked and realized there were tears in her eyes.

Damn it, this has gotten out of hand.

Why had she come here, anyway? She'd seen all those dramatic scenes already. Several intense visions had given her a front-row seat to Zeisha's frightened face, Krey's angry shouts, and the Cellerinian soldier's gun. Why had she watched it all again, in person?

I should get out of this city. Sneak back to the capital, find out where the army is, and join them. I'm getting soft.

But it all felt so pointless these days. What was waiting for her in the army? A promotion and more money, maybe. But what good was money when you didn't have any friends to enjoy it with?

Sarza huffed and shoved away the thoughts. *This place is messing you up. Look at the street, the buildings, the sky—anything. Stop thinking about people who have no idea you exist.*

Stop thinking about how guilty you feel for not stopping this.

JUST STOP.

She gritted her teeth and brought her eyes to the sky. It was actually worth looking at. There was a gorgeous sunset she hadn't noticed until now. Purple and deep orange and pink, the whole works. Sarza tried to let the sun's dimming rays bring her peace.

It didn't work. This sunset was just like the pay raise she'd been working so hard for. Pointless if she couldn't share it with others.

26

The median age of digital forgers is now nineteen. Fifteen years ago, the median age was twenty-nine. In another fifteen years, will nine-year-olds be running the world . . . or at least the digital underground?

-*"Conned by Kids" by Genta Ril*
The Derogan Chronicle, *dated Cyon 15, 6293*

NORA SPRINTED to Deroga's residential street. Panting, she knocked on the door of the first house.

No one answered.

She darted to the next house. A man, bleary eyed and unshaven, opened the door. A baby on his hip was wailing.

Nora spat out words between gasping breaths. "Someone attacked—the prison house!"

"Prison house? What is that?"

Oh, yeah—the prison house was a secret. A curse flew from

Nora's mouth. The man in front of her blinked. "It's a few—streets away," she panted. "We just have to—get some people—"

She halted. Get some people to do what? Confront a man with a gun? Ovrun had done that, but he was Ovrun. Most people, even trogs with combat training, would freeze or run when they saw a gun. She couldn't ask this young father to risk himself.

"Never mind!" Nora shouted as she spun and sprinted again. The gorgeous sunset seemed to mock her desperation.

Gun—gun—gun—need a—gun. The chant, timed with her racing steps, took Nora all the way to Eira's office. The elderly trog's assistant waited in the small lobby.

"Where's Eira?" Nora demanded.

Eira's assistant stood, eyes widening. "She is out. What do you need?"

Nora's gasps threatened to turn to sobs. She refused to let them. No time for that. She bent over and propped her hands on her knees, trying to get air into her lungs. By the stone, she thought she was more fit than this. "We need a gun—and someone who—can use it!" Her breathing grew more controlled as she explained what had happened.

"Come." The assistant led Nora into Eira's office, then used nimble fingers to insert a key into a locked cabinet. "Take one." She gestured at five guns inside. "I know nothing of guns, but I will take you to two men who do."

Nora took two of the four guns she and her friends had stolen from the men guarding Taima. The assistant took the fifth gun. It was a preday relic, probably the one Eira had threatened them with the first time they'd met her. Nora grabbed a handful of bullets from a clay bowl and put them in her pocket. She shoved the guns in her waistband, under her light jacket. They dug into her skin, cold and deadly.

The assistant locked the cabinet. "Let's go!"

"We need to run!" Nora said.

They stopped at a tannery a few doors down. Behind the small building, Eira's assistant gave a brief explanation to two men working there. The assistant gave her gun to one of the men, and Nora handed over the bullets. He loaded it. The other man told Nora that the bullets she'd grabbed wouldn't work in her guns—and that both were empty. She cursed again. She was doing a lot of that today.

They all ran, eliciting stares from trogs in the streets. The two men sprinted ahead, one of them wielding the loaded gun. Apparently at least one of them knew where the prison house was.

By the time Nora turned onto the proper street, the men were standing at the house across the street from the prison house. Two guards were shackled to the columns on its porch. Nora rushed forward and grabbed a guard's shoulder, squeezing it hard. "Where are my friends? Tell me!"

Nora paced in Eira's office. A few steps away, the yawning assistant slouched in a chair. *Of all the times for Eira to be visiting other clans,* Nora thought for the hundredth time.

The assistant stood, stretching. "If Eira is not back by now, she will not return until morning. We must sleep. You will come to my house. Your friends may tell the man where the bunkhouse is."

"What if the searchers find my friends?" The assistant had sent out several search parties. She'd refused to let Nora go.

"If your friends are found, someone will wake me. I will wake you."

That made way too much sense for Nora to argue.

The assistant's extra bed was comfortable, but Nora couldn't do more than doze. She kept in close contact with Osmius and Taima, who'd left their mountain den to fly high above Deroga, searching. But they'd had no luck finding Nora's friends. She guessed the group had hunkered down in a building for the night.

At daybreak, Nora returned to Eira's office and sat on the porch, jacket hood up, knees pulled into her chest.

The assistant arrived before long. Seeing Nora, she shook her head and sighed. Nora paced the front room for an hour until Eira finally arrived.

The elderly trog walked past Nora. "Come in."

Nora dropped into a chair in front of Eira's desk and let the whole story tumble out.

Eira wasn't one to overreact, but her thin lips pursed a few times. When Nora finished, Eira said, "I assume you have an ill-considered plan to rescue your friends?"

Nora bristled but responded, "The dragons are flying above the city and beyond it, looking for them. We've got to get to them before my father does." She lifted her chin. "And yes. Assuming one of the dragons finds them, I do have a plan to get them back."

Eira's brows rose.

Nora was about to defend herself when Taima spoke into her mind. *Nora.*

Suddenly breathless, Nora pointed to her head and blurted, "Hang on—dragon." Silently, she asked Taima, *Did you find them?*

In response, Taima sent Nora an image. Four people who appeared no larger than bugs had exited Deroga's suburbs and were walking in the dusty wilderness.

If I fly in quickly, Taima said, *I can burn the man who took them.*

We've talked about this, Taima. You'd have to get close to aim properly, and that man could shoot you—or my friends. Stick to the plan.

Very well. The beast's disappointment was clear in her tone.

Nora met Eira's gaze. "The dragons have agreed to the plan. Are you ready to hear it?"

Hours later, Nora and Eira brought a male militia member to a street where Taima, reclined and regal, waited.

The young man was equipped with an envelope in his pocket

and detailed instructions on his role in the rescue effort. An additional three militia members were currently traveling toward the city on Osmius's back, prepared to assist in their own way.

After Nora gave the young man several dragon-riding tips, he climbed on Taima's back. He let out a short, high-pitched cry when she leapt into the air.

Watching them leave, Nora felt a tingle in her legs, an illogical urge to run after the soaring reptid. It felt wrong, sending other people to rescue her friends. She'd wanted to go to the city to help, but Eira had insisted it would be too unsafe. Nora knew she was right —the princess of Cellerin was more likely to be recognized than anyone else. Besides, the militia members all had better magical skills than she did. But she didn't have to like it.

She turned to Eira. "What do we do now?"

"We wait." The trog let out a low laugh when she saw Nora's dismayed expression. "You cannot do everything, Princess. Waiting is part of life."

27

Derogan school officials just announced they're increasing physical education requirements by fifty percent. Pardon me while I throw my skinny arms in the air and stomp around using the underdeveloped muscles in my legs.

Some people improve society through physical strength, others through mental acuity. I think we all know which type I am. Every extra hour I run or do pushups is an hour I could've spent discovering world-changing new truths. (Or, you know, reading a good novel.)

-*"My Brain Is My Favorite Muscle" by Genta Ril*
The Derogan Chronicle, *dated Cyon 17, 6293*

ZEISHA'S EYES swept over her surroundings.

Focus on the beauty. Those trees in the distance have such bright leaves. The sky is a nice shade of pale orange today. I see a bird of some sort flying way up high. Also, there's a gun pointed at my back.

Zeisha's breath caught. She couldn't see the gun, but it intruded every time she tried to distract herself. *I don't need pretty skies; I need to run away!*

But even if they hadn't been guarded by an armed man, running would've been difficult. Zeisha and Krey walked on either side of Ovrun, whose arms were crossed, his hands shackled to theirs. His muscles must be cramping after walking like that for hours. He didn't complain.

From the other side of Ovrun, Krey spoke up. "Lars, you can unshackle us now. It's not like we can outrun your bullets."

"It better be the last time you ask me that," Lars snapped. After a pause, he said, "We need to eat. Let's stop here." Lars walked around to face them. "Anyone need to use the facilities?"

If Zeisha hadn't been so stressed and tired, she would've laughed. The only *facilities* were shrubs and trees. During the trek through Deroga, she'd endured the humiliation of squatting against buildings while shackled to Ovrun. Today, they were sweating out all their water. No one needed to "use the facilities."

Lars gestured to the dirt. "Sit down."

Zeisha scanned the ground. It was free of any plant life, and she groaned inwardly. Lars had successfully kept her away from her fuel this whole time. As they'd traveled through the city the previous night, he'd steered them away from wild plants. When Zeisha had tried to reach out for a tall weed, he'd threatened to shoot her hand. And nothing but stinky mold grew in the abandoned building they'd slept in.

"One. Two. Three. Sit," Ovrun said. He, Zeisha, and Krey lowered themselves to the ground smoothly. They were getting good at this.

Lars passed out dried fruit and meat. They all shared a bottle of water. The lukewarm liquid tasted heavenly on Zeisha's dry tongue.

She considered striking up a conversation with her abductor, like she'd done the day before. But he'd now held her captive for over a day. Her friendliness had expired hours ago.

Krey, however, chatted with Lars like they were old friends. The soldier had been tense during most of their journey, but now, he relaxed. He spoke of his job, renovating preday homes. Zeisha mostly tuned it out, but her ears perked up when Lars said, "Yep, for every ten homes I work on, I do one for free. Someone who can't afford it. I like to give back, you know?"

Zeisha cocked her head and stared at him as she chewed a tough bite of meat. The man who'd kidnapped them at gunpoint regularly engaged in charitable work?

Lars's gaze drifted to her. "Everything okay?"

No, she wanted to say, *I'm eating with my left hand, which I'm terrible at. Ovrun is lifting my right hand up and down over and over so he can eat. My wrist just started bleeding, but I don't want to complain, because I know both his wrists probably hurt worse than mine. And—oh, yeah—you abducted me so the brain-eating king can control my mind.*

She stifled the words and nodded instead.

Lars lifted his pack in one hand and his gun in the other. He stood. His voice turned gruff. "Enough talk. Let's go."

As they again walked through the dry dirt, Zeisha pondered the man behind her. He gave his time to help the needy. Yet over the last day, he'd abducted innocent teenagers and threatened repeatedly to shoot or otherwise injure them. And all because someone told him to. He believed he had no choice in the matter.

But he does have a choice. Unlike you, he could refuse. That's the difference between you and him.

This dusty wilderness was nothing like the beautiful park Zeisha frequented in Deroga. But a strange peace filled her as she listened to the part of her she'd chatted with for weeks now. The part of her that spoke truth. The part of her most connected to God.

Yes, he has a choice, she responded. *When I killed during the militia battle, I had no choice.* She let the truth travel from her mind to her gut, let it warm her down to her sore toes and chafed wrists. *I'm not the one who shot those vines. It was the person controlling me.*

The truth spoke to her again, so loud, it was a wonder Ovrun and Krey didn't hear it: *Then let it go.*

She filled her lungs with air, and as she blew it out slowly, she released her shame. Her guilt over actions she hadn't chosen.

A sense of stillness and acceptance filled the places she'd emptied. She smiled, despite her aches and fear.

The next steps she took felt a little easier.

———

Ovrun rolled his aching shoulders. The chains connecting him to Zeisha and Krey rattled. He suppressed a groan, unwilling to give Lars the satisfaction of complaining aloud. But damn, his shoulders and wrists hurt.

The journey had been mostly quiet. Lars didn't want them talking, afraid they'd somehow share coded messages with each other. Ovrun didn't mind the silence. He was busy brainstorming ways to break free. That morning, he'd seen Lars move the shackle key to the front pocket of his pack.

All I gotta do is get that key.

Easier said than done. When they'd stopped to eat, Lars had kept his pack well out of his captives' reach. *Maybe we can rearrange ourselves so I have more mobility. With my arms crossed, I can't do anything. If Krey and Zeisha moved—*

His thoughts ground to a halt. Sure, if he, Krey and Zeisha could sit and brainstorm, maybe they'd find a way to attack Lars. But what were they supposed to do, ask him for some privacy? Lars wasn't stupid.

I'm crap at strategizing. It wasn't like that was news to Ovrun; his best weapons had always been his instincts and physical strength. Maybe making a plan was useless. Or less than useless. His brain was spinning in such tight circles that if an opportunity presented itself, he wouldn't be ready for it.

I'm relaxed. Alert. Despite this resolution, his thoughts continued to churn to no effect. Trying to form a plan with no resources was like trying to bake bread with no ingredients.

By the stone, bread sounds good right now.

Movement ahead caught his eye. It was far enough away that he couldn't hear anything, but something or someone was up there.

On Ovrun's right, Krey's shoulders stiffened. He'd seen it too.

Behind them, Lars said, "Stop walking. Sit down."

They did. Lars crossed in front of them, gun in his right hand, eyes fixed on the horizon, where shadowy shapes hinted at the city ahead. The figure was slightly larger now. It was coming their way. Lars walked forward, then stopped and turned so he could watch his prisoners and whoever was coming. "Don't get up," he said gruffly, aiming his gun at them.

The approaching figure soon revealed itself as a person on an orsa. A little closer, and they saw it was a man. Closer still, and Zeisha drew in a soft breath. Ovrun didn't gasp, but he'd seen the same thing she had: the rider was one of the former militia members.

The orsa halted several mets from Lars, whose gun was raised and steady. The militia member held up both hands, one of them still gripping the orsa's reins. "I'm here at King Ulmin's command. I have a message to deliver."

"A message? How did the king know where to find us?"

The militia member pointed at the orange sky. "He wanted to know how your mission went. He dispatched a feather lyster to locate you."

"Why didn't the feather lyster bring us the message?"

"Because you probably would've shot a man diving down from the sky at you. The king said you might feel less threatened if a rider came." He gave Lars a nervous smile. "Listen, the letter is in the front pocket of my jacket. I can get it, or you can."

Lars paused, then said, "You get it. Move slow."

The former militia member nodded and slowly lowered a hand to his front-left pocket. He inserted two fingers into the pocket and pulled out an envelope.

"Drop it on the ground," Lars said. "Then back up your orsa. Sorry to be so careful, but I wasn't expecting to meet someone."

"Believe me, I understand. I'd do the same. Can't be too safe." It took a few tries, but the young man convinced his orsa to step back. "Sorry; I'm usually on a push scooter when I deliver," he said with an awkward laugh.

Ovrun gritted his teeth. *Believe him, Lars. Please.* His next thought was directed toward the young man. *And when Lars bends down, it would be a great time to pull out a weapon or attack with magic.*

But Lars kept his gun and his eyes trained on the supposed courier as he squatted and retrieved the note. "Does His Royal Highness expect a response?"

"No response, just obedience."

Lars's matted curls vibrated as he nodded. "Then you can head on back to the city. I'll obey the king's orders."

The militia member's eyes briefly found the captives before he turned his orsa. In seconds, he was trotting back toward Cellerin City.

When the messenger was too far away to do them any harm, Lars turned to face his captives. He sat a few mets in front of them, laid the gun in his lap, and lifted the envelope.

Ovrun tried to determine if he could somehow scoot close enough to kick the guy. But there was too much space between them.

Lars tore open the envelope and pulled out a folded note. His thick brows rose as he read. After a wait that felt interminable, he looked up. "Seems the king's gonna be away from the palace for a couple days. He doesn't want you there until he's ready to see you himself. So we get to wait at a house in the city." He held the note up, shaking it. "It's weird, though. A house? Why not a jail?"

"He probably wants to keep all this quiet," Krey said.

Lars stroked his beard with one dirty hand. "Yeah. Maybe that's why he told us to travel through the city late at night. Which means we've got a few hours to kill." He pulled his pack off his back. "Anyone hungry?"

"Starving," Ovrun said. It was a lie, but he had to keep his strength up. He ate dried meat, tuned out Krey's conversation with Lars, and watched for an escape opportunity that never came.

28

Human rights activists have long opposed the use of physical restraints when someone is arrested. They argue that even flex restraints (known as eights), are cruel.

Researchers have developed a nasal mist that renders someone temporarily semiconscious. They claim it has no side effects and is the most humane way to restrain someone.

Am I the only person who thinks this is ridiculous? If I've committed a crime, by all means, tie me up! Use coarse ropes or thick chains if you need to! But don't take my mind. If I'm going to jail, I want to remember the experience.

-*"Show Some Restraint" by Genta Ril*
The Derogan Chronicle, *dated Cyon 19, 6293*

Cellerin's quiet, dark streets brought up plenty of memories. Nora figured into all the best ones. Ovrun missed her, but he couldn't be happier she'd run for help and avoided getting caught.

Was she behind the faked message and the rescue attempt he was certain was coming? Probably so. He smiled into the darkness. *She's capable as hell.*

Walking was a little easier, now that his arms were uncrossed. To give him a break, Krey and Zeisha had offered to walk with their shackled arms stretched across their bodies.

"I've been in this part of town," Krey said, his voice quiet and casual.

Behind them, Lars said, "Thought you weren't from the city."

"I'm not, but I lived here for a little while."

At once, Ovrun realized why Krey had made the statement. This was the neighborhood where they'd twice stayed in a stinky, abandoned house. Nora was sending them to a place they knew. Someone would be waiting there to rescue them; Ovrun knew it. He let a grin spread across his face.

Sure enough, Lars led them to the tiny, boarded-up home where they'd stayed before. He brought the group to a halt and, in the light of a streetlamp, checked his note one more time. "I don't like this," he said. "I understand the king wanting us to be private, but I don't think he'd send us to a place like this."

Ovrun's breaths were shallow. *Just take us in there.*

"This place gives me the creeps," Lars said. He again pointed the gun at his captives. "We're not going in this place unless I confirm that note was from the king. Turn around."

Ovrun tried to keep his expression placid, even as his jaw clenched.

Lars led them farther into the city and onto a quiet street, full of businesses that were closed for the night. "I know a guy who owns a restaurant over here. He lives above it. He won't like getting woken up, but he owes me a favor. He'll bring a message to the palace for me."

A lamppost down the street shed dim light where they stood. "Sit," Lars said. "I gotta write this note."

We can't let him send that message to the king. We have to act, whether I have a good plan or not.

Aloud, Ovrun said, "One. Two. Three. Sit." But he didn't sit, he squatted—feet flat on the ground, knees up, weight forward. Like a predator ready to pounce. Gaze flicking to Ovrun, Krey did the same. Zeisha sat on her backside, legs folded, her body angled toward Ovrun to relieve her stretched arm. Ovrun tapped her knee, hoping she'd see his position and mimic it. All she did was give him a weary smile, before dropping her eyes to the ground.

Lars sat in front of them. Still holding his gun, he wrestled with the big buckle on his pack. At last, he put the gun next to him so he could undo the buckle.

Ovrun almost leapt forward then, but instinct told him to wait. His heart pumped wildly. He opened his mouth, trying to keep his breaths deep and quiet.

Lars reached a hand into the pack, muttering, "I swear I had a pencil." He used both hands to hold the pack wide open, repositioning it to bring it into the lamp's wide pool of dim light. His head dipped as he searched deeper inside the pack.

Krey's elbow caught Ovrun in the ribs, but Ovrun didn't need anyone to urge him on. His leg muscles, strengthened by hours of calisthenics, kept limber by his walks and runs while hunting, were already springing to life. At the same time he leapt, he pulled forward with both his arms. Krey was already jumping with him, but Ovrun was forced to yank Zeisha forward by the hard shackle on her wrist. She shrieked in pain.

He didn't have time to regret the action. Tackling someone while shackled to two others felt awkward. Unnatural.

And absolutely fantastic.

Just as Lars looked up, Ovrun's chest slammed into the man's legs. A split second later, his shackled arms connected with Lars's gut, shoving him down. From the corner of his eye, he saw Zeisha pick up the gun with her free hand.

But this clearly wasn't their captor's first fight. With one hand, Lars tried to shove Ovrun off him. With the other, he yanked his gun from Zeisha's grip.

Ovrun pushed himself forward, bringing more of his weight to bear on Lars. Zeisha and Krey pulled at their shackles and, in turn, at Ovrun's hands. His instinct was to pull his own hands back, but when his gaze flicked to Zeisha, he saw her again grabbing for the gun, with both hands this time. On Ovrun's other side, Krey was trying to capture their abductor's other arm.

Roaring in frustration, Ovrun gave Zeisha and Krey control of his hands. Zeisha's grip closed on the gun barrel. Krey grabbed Lars's arm.

Even as Lars fought for control of both the gun and his arm, he continued bucking and squirming beneath Ovrun. With a growl, he wrested his right arm from Krey. His hand scratched Ovrun's face, then caught his hair, ripping out a clump of it. He pulled at Ovrun's ear. It felt like he was ripping it off.

Ovrun shook his head hard, breaking loose from the man. "Krey!" he shouted.

Lars continued to claw at Ovrun's face until Krey grabbed his arm again. This time, Krey brought his knees down, pinning the man's muscular arm to the dirt.

Ovrun took a half-second to assess. Zeisha was still fighting for the gun. He felt a pulling movement under his belly. Krey was using both hands to retrieve the pack that had been on Lars's lap.

"Key! Front pocket!" Ovrun shouted. He left Krey to that task and returned his attention to Zeisha. He tried to use his shackled hand to grab for the gun. In that moment, Lars nearly threw him off.

Ovrun forgot about his hands and focused on one thing: keeping this guy down so his friends could fight. Both his wrists scraped painfully against the shackles as Zeisha pulled at the gun and Krey searched for the key.

Using the strength in his core and his legs, Ovrun pushed himself farther up onto Lars. His big chest pressed against the fighting man's chest, then against his face. Maybe he could smother him.

But Lars was big too, and he still had plenty of energy to thrash around. Without control over his arms, Ovrun slipped farther down again.

Then, above the sounds of groans and loud breaths, Ovrun heard metal scraping against metal. The shackle that had captured Krey's hand was suddenly hanging off Ovrun's wrist. Krey had retrieved the key.

Ovrun swung the newly released shackle into Lars's face. The big man cried out. Swinging the shackle again, Ovrun shouted, "Krey! Gun!"

Krey leapt up, which freed their enemy's left arm. Lars reacted with swift strength, grabbing the shackle and ending Ovrun's attack.

Zeisha was still fighting for the gun. Krey joined her. Within moments, he had the weapon. But Lars's gun hand was now free. Quick as a blink, he grabbed Zeisha's hair and yanked her toward him.

That didn't go over well with Krey. His boot slammed down on the man's bicep. With a cry, Lars released Zeisha.

Krey unlocked her shackle. Heavy chains and shackles hung off both Ovrun's wrists now. He tried to hit Lars with the shackle on his right hand, but the man had learned his lesson the first time. He grabbed the heavy metal as it swung toward him.

Lars kept thrashing. Ovrun struggled to free his arms and hold the man down.

But Lars was outnumbered and disarmed now. Krey fell to his knees next to their abductor's head. "You'll regret ever touching her!" he growled, smashing the gun into Lars's face. Blood poured from the soldier's nose. Shoving the muzzle of the gun into the man's forehead, Krey said, "Give me one reason not to shoot you right now."

Lars stopped fighting and released Ovrun's shackles. Tense silence fell over the group. Lars broke it by gasping, "I didn't want to hurt you at all. I could've killed you, all of you; I wouldn't have even gotten in trouble. Please—don't shoot me."

In the dim light, Ovrun saw Krey's trembling finger find the trigger.

"Wait!" The cry came from Zeisha. She'd been huddled in the dirt nearby. Now, she leapt forward, grabbing Krey's shoulder. "He's right," she said. "He could've hurt us. He didn't."

"He abducted you!" Krey's eyes, dark with murder, remained fixed on Lars. "He attacked you! He deserves a bullet!"

"Please," Zeisha said, her voice soft but desperate. "We can . . . we can take him back to Deroga. Hold him captive. But don't —please—"

Ovrun couldn't watch his friend kill a man in anger. "Give me the gun, Krey," he said. He was willing to kill if necessary, but at least he'd think it through first.

Seconds passed, each one interminably long. Below Ovrun, Lars's chest rose and fell with panicked breaths.

At last, Krey held the gun out to Ovrun. "Take it."

Ovrun did. Krey scampered back, breathing heavily.

Lars squirmed. Ovrun used his knees to pin the man's arms, then aimed the gun at his head. The heavy shackles hung above Lars's neck.

"Please," Lars said, suddenly still. "Don't kill me."

Ovrun's mind raced. Lars was subdued. Ovrun and his friends had won this fight. A killing now would be in cold blood.

But a prisoner would complicate everything. Traveling would take longer. It would be tougher to get rest, which they all needed. If Lars somehow escaped, he'd tell Ulmin about the failed abduction. The king would send someone to find them . . . sooner rather than later.

We can't let him go. Ovrun didn't see a way around it.

Despite his disgust at what he was doing, Ovrun pressed the gun's muzzle between the man's eyes. His chains clanked in the night air. One of the shackles knocked against Lars's ear, the other against his cheek.

The man's chest shook with sudden sobs. "I just—I only did it because—don't! Don't shoot! I'll tell you—I'll tell you everything!"

Ovrun's breaths were coming almost as quickly as his captive's. He pushed the gun down harder. "I'm listening."

Lars spoke between his sobs. "The army—they're marching—in ten days. They're marching—to Deroga—in ten days."

Ovrun's eyes widened. *Ten days.* With knowledge like that, they could actually prepare. Have everyone ready. Days of notice instead of hours . . . It might make all the difference in the world.

And no matter what his logical brain told him to do, he couldn't stomach the thought of killing Lars now. Not after he'd given them information they desperately needed.

Ovrun looked up at Krey and Zeisha, silently asking them if they agreed with him.

That moment of distraction was all Lars needed. He heaved and twisted his body, throwing Ovrun off him. Ovrun let out a shout as he landed hard on his side. The gun flew from his hand and into a shadowed gutter at the edge of the street.

Krey dove to the ground, groping for the gun. Lars and Ovrun were right behind him.

One thing Ovrun had learned in his guard training was that no matter how prepared you were, every fight included an element of luck. Three people searching the darkness for a gun? That all came down to luck.

Lars went still, crouching low over the ground. Ovrun could think of only one reason the man would've stopped: he'd found his weapon.

Luck had favored the wrong person.

In his gut, Ovrun knew another fight over this gun would result in someone getting shot. After nearly losing his own life, Lars wouldn't take any more chances.

Plus, lights were on in two nearby businesses. People lived in some of these buildings. This fight had been loud. Someone might come outside at any time.

Ovrun grabbed Krey's arm, yanking him to his feet. His other hand found Zeisha's arm. "RUN!" he shouted.

Thank the stone, they did.

Shots followed them. One—two—three earsplitting pops. But in the chaos, their former captor's aim was off.

Ovrun, Zeisha, and Krey sprinted into the darkness.

SARZA WOKE with pressure in her head. "No," she groaned in a hoarse, exhausted voice. "Not another—"

The vision began. It was a simple scene, just a few trog children playing a game with a ball. Nobody died; none of the kids needed rescuing. All they were doing was playing and laughing, looking remarkably cheerful despite their dull, neutral-colored clothes.

In no time at all, Sarza came back to herself. "Listen," she said aloud to whatever mysterious power might actually be paying attention to her. *In other words, no one.* She spat out the words anyway. "I'm sick of all this. All I want to do is sleep. Can't you just let me sleep?"

She wadded up the dirty jacket she was using as a pillow and squeezed her eyes shut. It was no good. Her mind was racing too fast for her to relax.

Sarza was desperate for rest. Two nights ago, she'd lain awake, dreading the abduction she knew was coming. Last night, she'd tossed and turned, fighting regret over not stopping it.

Why couldn't she let it go? She'd never be friends with those people in real life. So why had she held out hope her vision would somehow be proven wrong? Why had her stomach twisted when she'd watched that man take them away?

And the biggest question of all: after living eighteen years with a blissfully stunted conscience, why was Sarza now tortured by the double-bladed sword of guilt and regret?

All that stress and sleeplessness had led to way too many visions—several every hour, starting before sunrise. It was now the middle of the night, and the visions hadn't stopped. About half were scenes of trogs living daily life—playing, grieving, working, and arguing. Being normal people, in other words.

The remaining visions had shown her glimpses of the army she was part of. These scenes, too, took place in Deroga. Sarza had watched her fellow soldiers setting fires, shooting fleeing trogs, and taking children prisoner.

She was doing her best not to care about the people of this city, but her visions made such a resolution impossible. In fact, she found herself drawing one highly uncomfortable conclusion:

I've been on the wrong side.

A full day of quick, frequent visions had left her a wreck. Her head was pounding, her stomach empty from vomiting.

I'm so ready for this to be over.

Like the giver of prophecies had heard her and wanted to dig the knife deeper, another vision took over her mind.

This one was longer, consisting of two detailed, contrasting scenes. They offered her a choice: help the people you've been living among, or let them suffer.

She came back to herself and vomited before she could grab the bowl she used as a chamber pot. Wiping her mouth with the back of her hand, she started crying. "I don't want to help!" she wailed. "I just want to go back to my life! I'll find a job; I don't have to be in the army. I get it, okay? The army is doing bad things. I'm not trying to get a promotion anymore. But I'll never get to go home if I change sides!"

Her crying turned to laughter. That argument—that she'd never get to go home—couldn't be more ridiculous.

Sarza hated her home. She hated her parents. Her siblings.

She hated the little store on the corner with the clerk who always stared at her. She'd once been overtaken by a vision in his store and had knocked glass jars off a shelf. He always said she'd done it on purpose.

She hated the kids she'd grown up with, who'd laughed at her "fainting spells" and accused her of faking it. Who'd called her weird or stuck up when she spent all her time alone.

She hated her neighborhood and Cellerin City and maybe the whole country, come to think of it. And she was whining about wanting to go home?

"Okay," she whispered. "I'll consider helping these people. But I'm not promising anything."

She used a towel she'd stolen to clean up the mess she'd left on the floor. Then she rested her head on her jacket-pillow.

At last, she slept.

29

Flexscreens are robbing teenagers of their sleep. According to a recent study, teens today get an hour less sleep, on average, than teens who lived before the invention of handheld devices.

Parents are banding together, encouraging each other to take away their teens' devices at night. My question is, why? We teenagers are achieving greater goals than ever before. Sure, we're tired . . . but that's what coffee is for.

-*"In Your Dreams" by Genta Ril*
The Derogan Chronicle, *dated Cyon 21, 6293*

KREY HEARD RAPID, heavy steps. Lars was following them. The soldier was in good shape. Would he catch up? Did he have more ammunition? Would he shoot if he got closer?

We've gotta lose this guy.

Ovrun was in the lead. Krey took Zeisha's hand and forced more power into his legs. When they pulled alongside Ovrun, Krey said, "Turn! Here!"

They all turned right at an intersection. "Come on!" Krey said again. He led them into the shadowed space between two buildings. "Shh," he said. "Walk."

Their steps were silent and painstakingly slow. Krey had hoped to reach the rear of the building before Lars turned onto the street. No such luck. He heard the soldier's pounding steps approaching. "C'mere!" he hissed, darting to crouch behind a trash can shoved against one of the buildings.

Zeisha and Ovrun crouched next to him, pressing their backs against the wall. Their panting breaths, along with his own, sounded as loud as a thunderstorm. There was no way Lars wouldn't hear them . . . unless he was making enough of his own noise to drown out their breathing. Krey allowed himself a smidgen of hope.

The footsteps got louder . . . closer . . . and passed by. *Thank the sky.*

Krey jumped up and led them into the alley behind the building. "We have to go back to that abandoned house," he whispered. "I'd be willing to bet someone's waiting there to help us."

"We can't!" Ovrun said. "Lars knows just where it is!"

"Yeah, but he'd never expect us to go there, for the same reason you just said. We gotta go now, before he figures out he's lost us."

He turned and sprinted, not waiting for approval from Ovrun and Zeisha. They all clambered over a short fence. The house was about a clommet away. They jogged, their gasps bouncing off the surrounding buildings.

After a run that consumed whatever energy Krey had left, they reached the house. It was unlocked. Inside, it smelled stronger of animal waste than it had in the winter.

"It's Krey, Zeisha, and Ovrun!" Krey called in a low voice as they searched the dark house, bumping into walls and doorframes along the way. "We're alone! Anyone here?"

There was no response.

They entered the back yard. Krey again called out, with the same results.

"Please!" Zeisha said. "We escaped! If someone's here . . ." Her voice turned pleading. "We need to go home."

From the rear of the yard, a male voice called, "Come into the trees!"

There was no moon. Krey took Zeisha's hand. Along with Ovrun, they hurried into the darkness, toward trees they could barely see.

"Here," a female voice said softly.

They followed the voice. A hand grasped Krey's arm. He pulled away, muscles clenching, ready to fight.

"It's me. Isla."

Zeisha gasped and drew Isla into a tight hug. Once again, they were comforting each other, like they'd done for months in that awful warehouse.

As much as he wanted to let Zeisha enjoy the moment, Krey wasn't about to risk their lives for it. "Lars might be following us," he said.

"Then let's get out of here," Isla replied. She took off at a run. The rest of the group followed.

Krey had been a runner for years, but after a few minutes, his body refused to keep up with the rescue team. He'd gotten little sleep the previous night and none tonight. He feared he'd collapse. Zeisha's and Ovrun's breaths sounded as labored as his.

"We have . . . to stop," he gasped.

Everyone halted.

Krey bent over, gulping in air. Zeisha and Ovrun did the same. After several blissful breaths, Krey looked up.

"Let's get out of the street," Isla said. She led them between two buildings. Once they were huddled together, she said, "We can take a couple of minutes to recover, but we've got to get you three back to Deroga."

"Lars will tell the king we've escaped," Ovrun said, still breathing heavily. "I don't know if we can beat his people to Deroga. We know he has at least one flyer on staff. She could find us and shoot us down."

Krey had been thinking through this as they ran. "I need to find a place that sells feathers," he said. "I'll break in and take enough to fly me and Zeisha to Deroga. The rest of you can get orsas. If you don't have money to rent them, you'll have to steal them."

One of the male militia members laughed. "We don't need orsas or feathers. We've got a much faster option waiting outside the city."

Krey's shoulders fell. "You're gonna make me ride a damn dragon again, aren't you?"

"You don't like dragons?" Isla asked.

Krey's only response was a groan. Zeisha coughed, and he was pretty sure she was covering up laughter.

"Let's go," Isla said. "We can walk for a few minutes so you can catch your breath, but we have to keep moving."

As they walked at a quick pace, Krey scrambled for a way to avoid flying on a dragon. He knew it was a stupid phobia, but he could fly himself, if he just got some fuel—

He stopped walking.

"What is it?" Zeisha asked, halting next to him.

He forced his tired feet to move again. "I just had an idea." It was a good one, too. It would keep him off the dragon. More importantly, it might make a difference in the upcoming battle. "I need to find Hatlin."

"Hatlin? Why?"

"I have to tell him to move forward now with their army uprising. That might be the only way to prevent Deroga from getting invaded."

Zeisha slipped her hand in his. "What's gonna happen when you're alone?" she asked softly. "Will you be able to resist your cravings?"

He cursed. *My failure has to screw up everything, doesn't it?*

"How are you doing with all that?" Zeisha murmured.

They touched base like this at least once a day. Every time, Krey had to fight his natural defensiveness. He sucked in a deep breath, then blew it out. "The cravings are worse when I'm tired like this. I've been trying to ignore them, but . . . the desire is right there, waiting to leap out and grab me."

She squeezed his hand. "Thanks for being honest." She didn't admonish him. She just accepted his words and loved him.

God, you know I don't deserve her.

Krey pondered his quandary. Could someone else contact Hatlin? Ovrun had met the New Therroan flyer. But even if he could track down Hatlin, how would Ovrun get back to Deroga? If he walked, the king's people might catch up with him.

Krey's plan had been to go to the pub where the New Therroan League used to meet. The owner was sure to know where to find Hatlin. Maybe the entire group could go instead of just him.

He discarded the idea. It would take at least half an hour to get to the pub. Every minute was important right now. If Krey delayed them, he'd be putting everyone, including the dragons, at risk.

"Let's run," one of the militia members said.

Krey groaned but released Zeisha's hand and broke into a jog. He allowed his mind to drift to the shimshim brains he'd eaten almost two months ago. The thought of them made his mouth water.

It also made his brain light up with warnings—warnings he'd actually listened to lately. Yes, he wanted his fuel. But he also felt sick when he considered consuming it again. The cost was too high. More than he wanted the taste of the fuel and the thrill of controlling minds, he wanted his friends. His mental freedom.

He turned to Zeisha. She was panting but handling the run well. "Someday, I have to be able to resist it all by myself," he told her quietly. "I can't guarantee that I'm ready to do that. But I think I am."

Zeisha came to a halt. Krey did too. Everyone else was in front of them, and no one seemed to realize they'd stopped. Light from a street lamp reflected in Zeisha's wide eyes. She nodded slowly, then said, "If you believe you're ready, I believe it too. And if you're going, you should do it now." She stood on her tiptoes. Her lips, warm and soft, pressed firmly to his. "Be careful, Krey. I love you."

"I will. I love you too."

"Go. I'll tell the others."

And with that, she turned and sprinted ahead. Krey gave himself a few seconds to admire her departing form. He shook his head, laughing softly. Where had her new strength and decisiveness come from? Half the time lately, he felt like he didn't know her. But he loved the person she was becoming.

He turned and forced his feet to run again. Every few minutes, he took walking breaks, just to catch his breath. At last, he arrived, exhausted, at the pub.

It was locked, as he'd known it would be. Krey's knuckles were sore from knocking by the time the heavy, wooden door at last swung open. A bleary-eyed man holding a candle glared at Krey. "Something better be on fire."

Krey recognized Alit, the owner, but they'd never spoken. "I'm looking for Hatlin."

"Hatter? Never heard of the guy."

That was definitely a lie, though Krey had to give Alit credit for his quickness. "I used to meet with him, T, and Wallis."

"Must have the wrong place. I haven't heard of any of them." Alit slammed the door.

Krey's tired mind scrambled and landed on one fact he figured Hatlin didn't share with many people. "He's afraid of dragons!" he shouted.

The door swung open. After a long, torturous pause, Alit smirked and said, "Maybe I recognize you after all."

Krey let out a sigh. "Can you please tell me where Hatlin is staying?"

"Yeah. He flew back to New Therro yesterday afternoon."

Krey blinked. Exhaustion from the last two days, threaded with sudden disappointment, nearly pushed him to his knees. He forced himself to stay upright. "Any idea where he might be in New Therro?"

"I know a pub he frequents there."

That gave Krey a little hope. "Last question. Where could I steal a bunch of feathers?"

It took Krey three hours to steal all the feathers he needed. He had to break into four different stores. At the final one, he almost got caught by the owner, who lived upstairs.

The quest left him twice as exhausted as he'd been when he'd left Zeisha. So exhausted that putting anything in his mouth, even fuel, made him want to gag.

He did it anyway. *Just need enough to get out of the city before daybreak.*

When he couldn't force another feather in his mouth, he hopped up and down a few times, trying to convince his body he was awake. Then he took to the air.

Krey hadn't yet exited the city when he did something he'd never done before. He dozed off while airborne. His swift plummet woke him, and he barely turned his magic on in time to avoid a rooftop. The incident scared him enough to restore his alertness.

A few minutes later, he left Cellerin City behind. He landed next to a small copse of scraggly trees and closed his eyes. Instantly, he was asleep.

A sharp pinch on his arm woke him. Krey yelped and flicked a bug off his skin, cursing it.

The sun was barely above the horizon. If he closed his eyes again, Krey suspected he'd sleep the day away. He stood and shook his head and his limbs, trying to rid himself of grogginess. Even an additional half-day's notice might be what the New Therroans needed to launch an army rebellion in time.

Krey took a sip of water and ate a bit of dried meat, all stolen from shops. The hydration and protein gave him a little more energy and a lot more confidence. He fueled up with feathers and pushed himself into the air, heading northwest toward New Therro.

He expected the trip to feel similar to his flights between Deroga and Cellerin City. It was about the same distance. Once again, he'd fuel on the go and stop when necessary for short rests.

It was different in one vital way, however. Despite his short nap and his snacks, Krey was unspeakably weary. His thoughts drifted to animal brains. Temptation, wheedling and insistent, whispered dark possibilities to his weakened mind. *I could hunt from up here. Dive and catch an animal. Tear it open—*

He swallowed and forced his thoughts elsewhere. *Zeisha. Think of her.* His chest warmed as temptation of another sort overwhelmed his weakened body. *No, not that.* He tugged his thoughts away from Zeisha's perfect curves, instead considering who she was.

In the early days after the militia battle at the warehouse, guilt had overwhelmed Zeisha. She'd seemed so vulnerable as she grieved her lost innocence.

It struck him now that they hadn't discussed her violent actions in weeks. Something fundamental had shifted in Zeisha, so slowly that Krey couldn't pinpoint when it had started—or even exactly what had changed. She was more confident, but in a soft way that seemed to fit her perfectly.

I wonder what's going on in her head these days. His chest tightened with uncertainty, realizing how little he understood this new Zeisha. *When I get back to Deroga, we'll have a long talk. Just the two of us.* The resolution felt right, giving him just enough of a mental boost to keep flying.

As he continued, however, his stress and sleeplessness combined to make his normal pace impossible. He stopped more often—fueling up, eating, drinking, pinching himself. Anything to stay awake. Hours passed. He started talking out loud as he flew, just to keep his mind from shutting down.

At last, he saw something in the distance. Tiny specks, like insects. As he got closer, he became certain of what it was. *The Cellerinian Army.* North of that, he could make out the outline of a city.

New Therro. Thank you, God. Thank you. Krey ascended higher, above the sparse clouds, ensuring that anyone who saw him would think he was a bird. He approached, then flew in a huge circle over the area, trying to determine the best way to enter the city without being seen.

According to Hatlin, soldiers were stationed within New Therro. Likely, sentries also patrolled outside the city, keeping their eyes out for unwelcome visitors and preventing the men of the city from deserting and returning home. Krey saw villages east of the city; an army to the south; and green farms, spotted with windmills, on the west side. To the north were steep, uninhabited hills. That looked like the best direction to approach from.

I'll fly up there and descend just low enough to spot any lookouts. When I know where they are, I can plan a route into the city.

Alit had given Krey directions to the New Therroan pub Hatlin frequented. Krey was confident he could get there—if he could avoid the attention of soldiers both outside and inside the city.

He flew north until New Therro was behind him. Far below were clommets upon clommets of grassy hills. They were lush and green. Beautiful.

Mesmerizing.

Krey blinked, trying to keep his eyes open.

He'd love to lie on that grass with Zeisha. Hold her. Let the sun warm their skin. Close their eyes together . . .

Krey's eyes popped open. Panic filled his chest.

He'd fallen asleep. Approaching him at a truly terrifying speed was the bright green of a grassy hill. The leaves of a nearby tree were crisp and clear.

Krey was about to crash.

Forgetting his desire to remain unnoticed, he screamed, begging his magic to turn on.

It did—soon enough to keep him from striking the ground at terminal velocity. But not soon enough to keep him in the air.

He tried to tuck his legs so he'd roll. It didn't work. His hip and shoulder slammed into the grassy ground. An instant later, his head hit a jagged rock.

Darkness teased the edges of his vision, then took over completely.

30

At the Cellerin Mountain archeological dig, radiation levels continue to rise. The dig's organizers say workers are safe, since they're all equipped with personal-sized antiradiation devices called antirads.

I'd be nervous if I were out there, though. How can you be sure an invisible shield is working? Would you know if it suddenly broke?

-"You Sure About Those Shields?" by Genta Ril
The Derogan Chronicle, *dated Cyon 22, 6293*

ZEISHA SAT with Nora and Ovrun at the breakfast table—though today, it was more of a brunch table. They'd slept longer than any of their bunkmates, but it didn't seem to have done much good. Nora, who'd waited up for her friends' return, had bloodshot eyes. Ovrun had propped his chin in his hand and was barely touching his food.

Do I look as tired as them? Zeisha blinked, and it felt like there was grit under her eyelids. *Pretty sure I look worse.*

"We should go," Zeisha said, her voice low and a little hoarse. The night before, as a blood eater had healed Ovrun's and Zeisha's minor injuries, Eira informed them there would be a battle drill the next day. They all needed to prepare for the army's invasion in nine days.

"I'm sure Eira would understand if you skipped the training," Nora said. "You look like you need some rest."

"I won't be able to sleep, and I can't just sit around worrying." Zeisha's eyes slid to the door. Krey didn't fly as fast as the dragons, and he'd probably needed some rest before he left the city. She couldn't calculate how long all that would take. Her heart kept insisting he should already be here.

"Did you sleep at all?" Ovrun asked Zeisha.

She pressed the heels of her hands against her eyes briefly. "Not enough." She'd thought she was fine leaving Krey behind, but her subconscious had tortured her with disturbing dreams.

"We should get started; we're already late," Nora said.

They returned their plates to the small kitchen and exited the building. As she walked, Zeisha shook out her limbs. *If I'm this tired, what does Krey feel like? And if he's even worse off than me, will he be able to resist his cravings?*

A short walk brought them to the street where the militia warehouse, huge and foreboding, waited. Zeisha's heart rate accelerated the second she saw the building. Memory fragments sliced into her mind, each one too small to grasp. Without meaning to, she halted.

Nora and Ovrun stopped too. "You okay?" Nora asked gently.

Zeisha nodded.

Trogs and former militia members grappled and sparred with one another in front of the warehouse. A stone eater sent a barrage of small rocks at an armed trog. Across the street, a dirt eater shook the ground under a man and woman who were wrestling.

This was the third time Eira had scheduled a mixed drill, involving both magic eaters and nonmagical fighters. The Star Clan had invited the other five clans to drill with them, but no one had accepted. They'd fight a common enemy when they had to, but on a daily basis, old rivalries were hard to overcome.

"Let's fuel up," Nora said. Fierce excitement had replaced the sleepiness in her eyes.

Will I ever feel that way? Zeisha wondered as she trudged toward the warehouse.

When they were fueled up, Nora trotted up to Zeisha. "Ready?"

"Go ahead; I'll be out soon." Seeing Nora's eyes narrow in concern, Zeisha forced a smile. "I just need to figure out what I'm doing out there. I thought next time we trained, I'd be flying with Krey."

Nora bit her bottom lip. "He'll be back soon. I'm sure he will." But Zeisha heard doubt in her voice.

Nora jogged outside. Zeisha told herself she should follow. Yet ever since her fight with the dirt eater, she'd hated every training day more than the last. Now here she stood, short of breath before even entering the fray.

If Krey were here, he'd pick me up and say something about how distracting it is to fly with me. I'd still hate the thought of fighting . . . but at least his voice and the feel of his hands on my legs would keep me calm.

He wasn't here, though. There was no guarantee he'd be here on the day of the fight either. Zeisha needed to practice battling alone. She dragged herself to the doorway. From there, she watched the fighting, half-impressed and half-horrified.

There was a new level of fervor in the air today. A wooden knife flew toward Zeisha. She lifted a hand and shot out a short vine to bat the weapon away.

I need to step out there.

Her feet wouldn't move. When she went outside, it would only be a matter of time before her instincts sent her vine to someone's neck.

Her gaze caught on five trogs at the edge of the street. They all held practice swords and heavy, metal shields. They moved as though they were one organism, standing shoulder-to-shoulder, shields out, forcing their way into the crowd. Then, at some signal Zeisha couldn't see or hear from where she stood, they stepped apart and began fighting.

Something about the scene tickled her mind, like there was an important idea she was supposed to grasp.

Shields.

That was it. Could she create a shield with her vines? Maybe, but it wouldn't be very practical. She squinted and furrowed her brow. What was the significance of those shields?

An idea hit her, a way of using her magic she'd never considered. *Defense, not offense.* The thought was so delightful, it made her laugh. She gripped the new concept with the claws of her imagination, turning it one way, then another, fleshing it out.

I don't have to become someone else's idea of a warrior. I don't ever have to choke someone with a vine again. I can help the trogs in a different way. Threads of tranquil confidence, full and bittersweet, wove through Zeisha's weary mind.

Nearby, Nora was shooting ice balls at a woman holding a sword. When the woman fell, Zeisha called, "Nora!"

Nora ran over, her bright eyes scanning in every direction as she moved.

"Come inside for a sec," Zeisha said. When they were both safe in the warehouse, she took Nora's hand. "I'm leaving the fight. I didn't want you to worry."

"Leaving? Are you okay?"

"Yes . . . yes, I'm good." Oddly enough, it was true, despite her continued worries for Krey. "I just had an idea. I'll update you later."

"Okay." Nora's bright smile further boosted Zeisha's spirits. The princess ran outside.

Zeisha rushed through the warehouse, looking for a back door. She hated this place and its memories, but excitement overcame her disgust. Soon, she found a rear exit. Less than half an hour later, she emerged onto the rooftop garden where Kebi, who wasn't scheduled for today's training, was working.

"Zeisha!" Kebi rose and approached. "Did Krey arrive?"

"No." Zeisha's shoulders drooped. "But . . . that's not what I came to talk to you about." She took Kebi's hands. "When the army comes, I want to help your people. But I'm not a sword. I'm a shield."

Kebi's mouth curved into a confused smile. "What does that mean?"

"I'll explain. And I'm going to need your help, because you know way more than I do about Deroga's plants—and Deroga's people."

The next morning, Zeisha and Kebi sat in the street in front of one of Deroga's many overgrown, preday parks.

Zeisha knew they should discuss their plans for the day, but her focus was elsewhere. She turned to Kebi, who was already watching her. "On my birthday, Krey brought me birthday bread. Do you think I could get some for tonight?"

"I'm sure one of our bakers will make it for you. Who has a birthday today?"

Zeisha swallowed. "Krey. I'd like to have it, in case . . ."

"You want it for *when* he returns." Kebi reached out an arm and pulled Zeisha close. "Perhaps he is simply tired, and it takes longer for him to fly here."

Zeisha pulled away. A tight hug would just make her cry. "No matter how tired he was, he should've been back by yesterday after-noon at the latest." She blew out all her breath and drew in more, trying to keep her emotions in check. She fixed her gaze on the end of the street. "We'd better stand up. Someone's coming."

Over the next half-hour or so, the street in front of Zeisha and Kebi filled with people. Zeisha shook her head in wonder. She'd never considered herself a leader, but she was about to direct a team of twenty vine eaters, including representatives from each of the six trog clans. In less than a day, Kebi, who was a member of both the Moon Clan and the Star Clan, had brought Deroga's trogs together in a way even Eira rarely managed.

Now all those trogs were watching Zeisha, like they thought she knew what she was doing. *Let's hope they're right.*

She smiled, reached into a bucket, and grasped a thick, waxy leaf. When she tugged it, the leaf came free. She grasped the branch the leaf had been attached to, wincing when a small thorn pierced her thumb. "This is what we're looking for in that old park," she said, holding up the plant. "You all have knives and buckets; harvest as much as you can find."

"That is a Derogan thornbush," a man said.

"In the Hill Clan, we call it a waxen plant," a woman said.

A brief debate on terminology broke out. "Excuse me," Zeisha called. Miracle of miracles, they listened. "Today, we're calling this a thorn plant. We don't have time to argue about it."

"And today," Kebi said, "we are one clan of trogs, preparing to fight for our independence."

"What will we do with the thorn plants?" a teenage boy asked.

Zeisha smiled. "We're making shields."

About an hour later, Zeisha and half her team spread across a quiet street, from one building to another. The rest of the team did the same, several mets away.

Each of the vine eaters held a cutting from a thorn plant. Their goal was to grow the cuttings into tall hedges that would connect to become fences.

Once they proved the concept on this deserted street, they'd grow fences around the trogs' residential streets. When the army attacked this time, thorny shields would protect the trogs' homes.

During the battle, soldiers might cut or burn the brambles. Zeisha's team would travel through the Extrain tunnels, emerging to check their shields and repair any damaged ones. Kebi had maps of the tunnels and had already started studying them.

Excitement fluttered in Zeisha's chest. She squatted in the center of her line of vine eaters. Together, they'd make a huge, interconnected, impassable hedge.

"You ready?" Zeisha called.

"Yes!" twenty vine eaters shouted.

"Great! Press your branch to the dirt. Create roots first, then work on the fence."

Zeisha extended her power through the prickly branch and into the earth. She sensed the roots growing deep into the dirt. When she was confident the plant was well rooted, she encouraged it to grow above the ground.

Sprouts burst from the cutting she held, quickly thickening into branches with sharp thorns and smooth leaves. Zeisha cast a glance around and saw that others were finding success too.

"Tangle them!" she shouted. She let her instincts take over—instincts honed during her forgotten months of slavery. She encouraged the branches she was growing to twist, not only with each other, but with the ones growing on either side of her. The plants grew into a glorious, knotted web.

Anxiety over Krey's absence still ate at Zeisha's gut. Despite that, the joy of cultivation brought a broad smile to her lips. Her eyes remained fixed on the section she was growing. *If I were standing, it would be as tall as my hips,* she marveled. *No—my waist!*

She felt her magic waning. Apparently she wasn't quite ready to make a fence taller than a soldier, but for her first try, this was pretty great. She burned up the last bit of her fuel, pouring magic into the strong, forbidding shield.

Letting go of the branch she'd been holding, she stood. "That was —" She was about to say *amazing,* but once her eyes took in the rest of the thorn-shield, her mouth faltered. Only two of her ten team members had grown their portions of the fence more than knee-high.

And those two were shorter than Zeisha's. Her eyes found the other line of vine eaters. They hadn't done any better.

She fought an uncharacteristic urge to scream. *We've only got a week to figure this out!* Instead, she adopted a cheerful tone. "I guess we all need to refuel! Remember, we're more efficient when we relax. We've got time. Have fun with it!"

None of them looked like they were having fun as they stared at their "shield"—which any soldier could easily step over.

If Krey were here, he'd help Zeisha see the humor in the situation. Right now, all she could do was grit her teeth and try to keep believing her idea was a good one.

A hand found her shoulder and squeezed. Zeisha looked over. It was Kebi. Her empathetic eyes did more good than she knew.

"Let's try again," Zeisha called, her voice steadier than before.

31

A Derogan company claims they've created the smoothest-tasting beer yet. I asked my mother to let me try it. I think she was afraid I'd love it and start drinking every weekend, but she finally agreed I could have a little—for journalism's sake, of course.

I put my lips on the mug, sipped a bit of the amber liquid . . . and promptly spat it out. I don't know if it was smooth or not; I only know it tasted rank.

Is it possible all beer drinkers suffer from mass psychosis? It's the only logical explanation.

-*"Sickeningly Smooth" by Genta Ril*
The Derogan Chronicle, *dated Cyon 24, 6293*

KREY WOKE AND IMMEDIATELY MOANED.

The impossibly bright sun shoved daggers of pure pain into his brain. It must be mere simmets from his face.

He shut his eyes. The pain remained. He flipped onto his side. "My head!" he moaned, bringing his hands up. His fingers found dried blood on the back of his skull.

He stopped protesting out loud, only because the sound hurt his head too much. He lay there, trying to think of something besides the pain. The effort was akin to reaching into a burning fire to find a stone. Just thinking was agonizing.

He forced himself to do it anyway.

I'm on the grass. I was flying to New Therro. I fell.

When?

When . . . when . . . oh, God, it hurts! Help me, it hurts!

Stop. Think.

It was morning. But then I woke up. Yes—a few times. It was light . . . then dark . . . then light again.

I've been here over a day.

A curse flew from his mouth, the word searing his parched throat. He needed water, but that wasn't his most urgent craving. No, his mind brimmed with desire for the indigo flesh of Anyarian brain matter; for those beautiful, soft layers and that terrible, sweet flavor.

"No!" he cried, pushing himself into a seated position. Pain, shocking and cruel, exploded in his head. "I need food! And water!" His scream was hoarse, not nearly loud enough to drown out his darker craving.

Hands pressed to his pounding head, he looked around. Every movement of his neck made him want to vomit. He forced himself to take in his surroundings. He was on a hill. Based on the sun's position, it was early afternoon. New Therro, he knew, was somewhere beyond the hilltop.

"Oh, God, I want fuel!" Saying it out loud seemed to break loose a logical thought: yes, he craved brains, but he *needed* feathers. He had to get past the sentries and into New Therro. If he stayed out here in the wild, he'd soon be looking for animals to kill.

He wanted that, desperately, but he also hated himself for the desire. *No,* he told himself, letting go of his head. *No. Feathers.*

When he'd fallen, he'd dropped his bag. He didn't see it anywhere nearby. Maybe an animal had picked it up to eat the food inside. The only feathers he had were the ones in the pouch in his sleeve. He pulled out a handful.

Nausea and a terribly dry throat made eating torturous. He shoved the fuel into his mouth. Forced himself to chew and swallow. Over and over and over.

Just one brain. A tiny one. One bite, one taste—

"No!" he cried, lifting into the air.

The sudden movement was a bad idea. Pain ravaged Krey's entire body. He lost his magic a few mets up and dropped, barely recovering in time to prevent another collision with the ground. He slowed both his speed and his ascent. But even gentle movement was torturous. He vomited, every coughing heave causing fresh agony. The feathers he'd just eaten were now scattered over the ground below.

Krey landed. As he sat in the grass, eating more feathers, he realized he still had no idea how far away the city was. He hadn't even looked behind the hill on his short flight. His mind was too fixated on his pain and forbidden cravings. Krey tried to think of something else —the feel of dampness seeping through his clothes, the warmth of the sun, the slightly bitter taste of feathers.

It worked, somewhat. When he returned to the air, he was ready to survey the area. To his relief, the city wasn't too far away. It would be a short flight. Painful, but short.

There were no sentries between him and the city. Odd. He rose higher and realized why. To the south of the city, the entire plain where the army had camped was empty.

Krey screamed a curse, the volume of his own voice almost causing him to throw up again. He shut his mouth, gritting his teeth against the persistent nausea and cravings. Eyes fixed on the city of New Therro, he flew.

It turned out the army leaders had left a few sentries behind. Krey spotted them from above. He chose a path into the city that appeared unguarded, then flew low to the ground. When he got close to the city, he started walking. New Therro had few magic eaters; he didn't want to catch anyone's attention.

Walking was more painful than flying, which had in itself been torturous. Every step sent solid, sharp agony into Krey's head.

As he'd surveyed the city from high above, Krey had gotten his bearings. He'd found a large hotel Alit had told him was near the pub Hatlin frequented. If he travelled on minor streets, maybe he'd be less likely to encounter soldiers.

Krey had only walked a couple of blocks through New Therro's outer streets when he realized two things: his bloody head was catching too much attention, and he'd never make it to the pub without collapsing from pain and weariness. *I have to get help.*

Not two minutes later, he saw a kind-looking woman gardening in her front yard. Krey approached but didn't get too close.

"I know this is weird," he said, "but I need to get to the Green Brick Pub. Do you have any sort of . . . transportation?"

He must have looked even worse than he thought he did, because her brows drew together in pity. A pang squeezed Krey's heart. Her expression was the same one Aunt Evie wore when she encountered anyone—friend or stranger—who was hurt.

Krey was soon sitting in the woman's kitchen drinking water that tasted better than anything he could imagine—except brain matter. He still craved that with terrifying ferocity. The woman cleaned his wounds. That introduced a new type of torture to his aching head. When she was done, she gave him bread and sausage. Then she walked him to a small carriage and drove him to the Green Brick Pub.

They talked very little. She didn't even introduce herself. Krey didn't blame her. *When your city's been invaded, it must be hard to trust strangers.* She was kind, however, and that meant more to Krey than it ever had before.

"Thank you," he said as he descended from the cart, every step feeling like a hammer in his skull.

"Stay safe," she replied.

Krey tried to smile, though it felt more like a pained grimace. The woman responded with an empathetic expression that again reminded him of Aunt Evie. She set off down the street.

Krey took a minute to evaluate himself before walking in. His craving for brain matter had settled down somewhat, now that he'd eaten. He was still weak and in terrible pain, however. *Can't do anything about that now.* He entered the pub.

It was empty. Too early for the dinner crowd. Krey sat on a stool at the bar.

A woman emerged from the rear. Her eyes flicked to the cloth wrapped around his head. "Bad day?"

"Yep."

"You visiting New Therro?"

"Yeah." Krey's head wasn't feeling any better. Stringing polite words together seemed like more trouble than it was worth.

"Where from?"

He took a deep breath, forcing words past his pain. "From the city. Sort of. I need to see Hatlin, please."

"I used to know a man named Hatlin. Haven't seen him in years."

By the sky, Hatlin's friends were good at lying. "Tell him it's Krey." He leaned in close, though they were alone. "Tell him Alit sent me."

When the woman heard the name of the pub owner, the corner of her mouth rose. "Why didn't you say so? I'll get him."

"Is it safe for him to come here?"

She laughed. "He stays upstairs. Come on, you can meet him in the back room."

Krey followed her, trying to ignore his increasing nausea. Maybe he shouldn't have had so much food at that house.

The woman sat him at a small table, then left the room. Within a minute, the heavy tread of boots on stairs reverberated through the pub.

Hatlin entered. He shook his head when he saw Krey and released a big sigh as he sat. Turning to the woman who'd fetched him, he said, "Can we get two beers? Think we're gonna need them." He returned his attention to Krey. "Oh, I forgot, you never drink. Want some juice?"

In that moment, something occurred to Krey. He let out a short laugh that hurt like hell.

"What?" Hatlin asked.

"It's my birthday. I'm eighteen. I just remembered."

Hatlin chuckled. "You're legal, huh?" He turned to the woman. "One for each of us."

The drinking age in Cellerin wasn't always enforced, and Krey could've gotten drunk every night he'd lived in Cellerin City if he'd wanted to. However, he hadn't touched alcohol since he was fifteen and got into his aunts' bollaberry wine. His sickness afterward had taken away his desire to indulge.

Despite his birthday, he knew he probably shouldn't drink, not after lying outside without any water for a day and a half. But he'd hydrated pretty well at the woman's house. Maybe the beer would dull his pain, even a little.

"What happened?" Hatlin asked Krey.

"I was flying here, but I was too tired. I crashed."

The big man's thick eyebrows rose. "You coulda died!"

Krey squinted. "It feels like I did."

"We'll get a healer for you."

"New Therro has healers?"

"Just one, and he's not very good. But he might take the edge off."

"I'll take what I can get."

The woman returned with their beers. Hatlin asked her to fetch the healer. She nodded and hurried off.

Krey sipped the beer. It was bitter and strong. *I'd better pace myself.* He took one more swallow, then said, "Hatlin, where's the army?"

Hatlin put down his clay mug. Krey didn't think the big man had swallowed more than three times, but half his beer was gone. "That's why I figured you'd need a drink," Hatlin said. "The king himself arrived yesterday. Marched off with the whole army today. Looked like they were headed to Deroga."

Krey swallowed to keep from puking. He knew, instantly, why Ulmin had come yesterday. Lars had made it to the palace to update the king. Honest guy that he was, Lars had probably told the whole story—including how he'd given his former captives information on the coming invasion. Not willing to enter a city that was expecting him, the king had moved up his plans.

Krey couldn't prove it was true, but the timing was too perfect to be coincidental. The army was on its way to Deroga, and it was only because of his and his friends' botched escape. A string of curses tumbled from his mouth. He took a big gulp of beer. It wasn't helping with the pain, but it did loosen his tongue. "I came to tell you the attack was coming soon. Wasn't supposed to be this soon, though. I was hoping you could bump up the New Therroan uprising. Maybe stop the invasion from happening at all. I guess it's too late for that."

"Wouldn't've worked anyway," Hatlin said, frustration written all over his creased brow. "Two days ago, the army caught a couple of our soldiers talking about their plans. They're watching all the New Therroan soldiers closely now. Our whole rebellion fell apart overnight. Oh, also—that guy Golsch that Nora told me might help us? Pretty sure he's loyal to the king."

"Yeah, we figured that out." Krey groaned. He closed his eyes briefly against his pain, then returned his attention to Hatlin. "I have to fly to Deroga. Maybe I can give the trogs a few hours extra to prepare."

"No offense, Krey, but you don't look like you got the strength to fly next door, much less to Deroga."

"I know. I'll do it anyway."

"Figured you would." Hatlin drained the last of his beer. "Need feathers?"

"Yep."

"I don't think I have enough."

Krey almost laughed. Of course Hatlin didn't have enough. It would be asking too much for something to actually go right today. He picked up his beer, then immediately set it back down. If he was going to fly, he needed to be sober. "I'll take whatever feathers you've got. And . . . can I get some juice?"

32

Deroga's electrical outage last night, caused by a computer glitch, lasted three minutes. When it happened, I was in a glidecraft with my father. We'd been admiring the city lights, which are stunning at twilight.

Then the electricity went out—and the city became even more lovely. Buildings were reduced to sharp, angled shadows. Skytrain tracks looked like line art drawn on the darkening sky. Deroga was a grayscale wonderland, a place of unsettling, alien beauty.

I was disappointed when the lights came back on.

-*"Lights Out" by Genta Ril*
The Derogan Chronicle, *dated Cyon 25, 6293*

THROUGH THE DARKNESS, Krey could barely make out the city of Deroga. He was at last flying over its suburbs.

All at once, the city lit up.

Once-dark skyscrapers came to life, bright lights shining through the perforation of uncountable windows. Solarcar and glidecraft headlamps streaked through the streets and the air. A Skytrain traveled in the distance, its many windows appearing as a flowing ribbon of white light.

He laughed in wonder, and the sound seemed to trigger something. The air filled with voices from the city's millions of inhabitants. Derogan citizens called out to Krey, entreating him to make something great of his world, just as they had done with theirs.

Then, in a blink, it was dark and still again.

Krey cursed, his head suddenly clear. This wasn't the first hallucination he'd had tonight. His weariness and concussion made it impossible to stay anchored in reality.

The New Therroan healer had, quite frankly, sucked. He'd managed to relieve Krey's pain just enough to convince him he wouldn't die, but not enough to make him happy he was still alive. Still, the man's assistance, paltry though it was, had made it possible for Krey to get this far.

His body dipped a bit, and he reached into the pouch in his arm. After digging around for a full minute, his fingers emerged with one small piece of diced feather. The pack on his back, supplied by Hatlin, was empty too.

Great.

He ate the feather and flew lower. Squinting, he tried to find a major road that would take him all the way into trog territory. *There*—a wide street he was pretty sure he recognized. He flew over it. Within a couple of minutes, his magic started popping on and off. He took the hint and landed. The action jarred his head yet again.

The army was behind him. How far, he had no idea. He knew he'd flown over them at some point before it turned dark, but his addled mind couldn't guess how long ago that was. He did know there were many clommets between him and his destination. If he wanted to give the trogs enough warning to make this trip worthwhile, he'd have to travel fast.

Despite his suspicion that his legs would collapse or disintegrate if he quickened his pace, Krey broke into a jog. His stomach rebelled with instant nausea. His head screamed in pain.

He kept running.

Zeisha walked toward the Star Clan park, having been woken by a trog runner minutes earlier. The runner was supposed to fetch Nora and Ovrun too, but neither of them were in their beds. Zeisha had offered to find them. She yawned and stretched as she walked. She'd hoped to truly catch up on sleep last night. At least there was a beautiful sunrise.

She wasn't surprised to see the couple sitting on a park bench, eyes on the eastern sky. Ovrun's arm was around Nora, and they were talking softly. "Good morning," Zeisha called.

Nora and Ovrun turned and greeted her.

"Eira sent a runner to wake us all up. There's someone in her office she wants us to meet."

As the three of them walked toward Eira's office building, Ovrun asked Zeisha, "How did your experiment go yesterday? With the thorn shields?"

Zeisha released a long sigh. "We made several fences that would barely keep a caynin from running down the street. We're all struggling to grow them as tall as they need to be, even when we're fully fueled."

"I'm sorry," Nora said. "At least you've got a week to master it."

"I hope we can," Zeisha said, her voice laced with weariness.

A few minutes later, they stepped into Eira's office building. The lobby was empty, so they went straight into the office. Eira was sitting at her desk, looking remarkably alert for this time of the morning. Her long, white hair was pulled back into a neat braid.

A bulky trog, probably in his mid-twenties, had a tight grip on the arm of a tall, slender young woman whose hands appeared to be shackled behind her. She was wearing a cream-colored shirt and tan pants. It was typical trog clothing, but Zeisha didn't recognize her. She had messy, short hair and deep-brown skin. Her big, dark eyes were bloodshot, her jaw clenched. Her smooth skin looked like it belonged to someone in her late teens, but there was a hardness to her expression that made Zeisha wonder if she was older.

Eira didn't greet Zeisha, Ovrun, and Nora. Instead, she turned her sharp gaze on the prisoner. "All the people you ask me to fetch are here. I suggest you talk, and quickly. My patience is limited."

The young woman lifted her chin, not a bit intimidated. "My name is Sarza Phip. I'm a Cellerinian spy. I'm also a seer. And I might know how to win the battle that's coming."

"This new-city man says he is part of the Star Clan." The trog who was speaking, a Tree Clan sentry, squeezed Krey's arm, deepening the bruises he'd already put there. "Does he tell the truth?"

Krey recognized the Star Clan sentry they'd approached, but the man looked him up and down like he'd never seen him before. After hours of running through the city, Krey was barely upright. He'd sweated out the last of his patience hours ago. "Come on, man. Let me in."

The Star Clan sentry finished his perusal of Krey. He let out a loud guffaw, then slapped Krey's shoulder. "I know him. I only want to scare him a bit."

The Tree Clan sentry didn't laugh. "That is not what I hope to hear. If he tells the truth about his identity, perhaps he also tells the truth about the army."

In a split second, the Star Clan sentry sobered. "What about the army?"

"They're on their way," Krey said. "Today, tomorrow at the

latest." He had no idea how fast the army was traveling and how often they were stopping to rest.

"Spread the word!" the Star Clan sentry told his counterpart. He turned to Krey. "You must run to tell Eira."

Krey set off at a shuffling jog, every step torturous to his whole body. *I can sleep soon,* he assured himself as his heavy boots stirred up the dust of Deroga's streets.

"We should all sit," Eira said.

Zeisha sighed in relief as she dropped into a chair in front of Eira's desk. Two days of waiting, worrying, and attempting new magical feats had exhausted her.

Eira leaned forward, propping her elbows on her desk. She turned to Sarza, who was sitting in a wooden chair, her arm still gripped by the trog guard. Eira said, "It is many decades since I have heard of a living seer."

"Decades?" Nora blurted. "I didn't think we'd had any since Rona, the seer who tried to stop the apocalypse. That was two hundred years ago!"

Eira's eyes, always watery and always incisive, found Nora. "We trogs have a seer when I am young. He dies forty years ago. His guidance helps us keep our independence as new nations rise around us."

Nora's mouth gaped. "And here I thought seers were relics of the past. Like computers and reliable birth control."

A chuckle rumbled in Ovrun's chest.

"Well, here I am," Sarza said. "Not extinct."

"Why haven't we ever heard of you?" Nora demanded.

Sarza's hard gaze found Nora. "Sorry, Your Highness, but I never felt the need to tell you or anyone else about my curse."

Zeisha's brow creased. What had happened to this seer that she'd consider such a gift to be a curse?

"Why do you tell us now?" Eira asked.

Sarza tried to stand, then growled as her guard pulled her back down. Her reddened eyes turned fiery. "You think I want to be here? I never tell anyone my prophecies! Never! But I'm tired of not sleeping at night! I'm tired of all these visions showing me I'm on the wrong side of this war. I've tried to ignore it all. I even tried to leave the city in the middle of the night last night—but I had another vision, of Nora and Ovrun on a park bench, watching the sun rise. It's like the whole universe wanted to remind me that you're good people! I couldn't leave you here to lose this war!"

Eyes wide, Zeisha turned to Nora and Ovrun, whose mouths had dropped open.

"You saw a vision of us in the park?" Ovrun asked.

"Yeah, I don't know when it's going to happen. Obviously you'll consider it a self-fulfilling prophecy. I don't expect you to believe—"

"It was this morning," Ovrun said. "This morning, while you were sitting in this office, waiting for us."

Sarza's eyebrows leapt up. "Oh." Her gaze swept across Ovrun, Zeisha, and Nora. She swallowed, and her voice was a little softer when she spoke again. "I feel like I know the three of you. Krey too. I know I sound like a stalker. And, well, maybe I am, but—if you don't do what I'm telling you, you might not live through the battle that's coming. And honestly, you might die even if you do listen to me. But I think I can at least give you a chance. And"—she shrugged one shoulder—"I already hate myself enough. I'd hate myself even more if I didn't tell you."

Eira's businesslike voice cut through the confusion and wonder that had overtaken the office. "Tell us the prophecy."

Sarza pulled in a deep breath. "It's simple," she said. "We're supposed to fly across the bay to Cruine. On dragons. We have to ask the prime minister for his help. I don't know what he'll say, but it'll make a difference."

Multiple questions filled the room. "Cruine?" "Who's supposed to go?" "When?"

Eira lifted a wrinkled palm, bringing silence to the room. "I write letters to Cruine, asking for their help. Other clans do the same. Cruine says no, every time. They are at peace with Cellerin. They will not break such an alliance."

"We still have to go," Sarza said.

"Who is *we*?" Eira asked.

"Me," Sarza answered, "and you, Nora, and Zeisha." She nodded at each of them in turn.

"Me?" Zeisha asked. "Why?" Everyone else made sense. Sarza's gift might help guide them. Eira should be there for diplomatic negotiations. Nora was the only one who could communicate with the dragons carrying them. *Why would anyone want me there?*

"I don't know why," Sarza said. "I just saw you there."

Zeisha's logical side told her that no matter what the seer said, she should stay in Deroga, working on the thorn shields. But something deeper—the same instinct that had driven her to work on those shields in the first place—whispered that her path had shifted, for reasons she couldn't imagine. "I'll go," she said.

Eira declared, "None of us will go. We have no reason to trust you, Sarza Phip. Perhaps you do see a vision of Nora and Ovrun in the park. This does not mean you see a true vision of us going to Cruine. We will place you in a cell. I will talk to you over the coming days. Then we will decide."

Zeisha's eyes had remained fixed on Sarza the whole time Eira spoke. It was like the elderly woman's words had heated a pan of water inside the young woman. With every passing second, Sarza had gotten closer to boiling. When Eira stopped talking, Sarza exploded. "You can't wait!" she yelled, leaping out of her chair. When her guard tried to pull her back down, she yanked her arm away. "Just let me talk to these people!" she screamed.

Eira gestured to the guard to let Sarza speak.

The seer directed her shouted words at Eira. "Listen to me! I've been in your city since the army first attacked! I've had to steal water and food and clothes. I've had to sleep with my own stinky-ass body for months. I've been alone"—she choked up on those words—"completely alone, for so long! And somehow I know the reason I'm here at all is for *this moment.* If you wait to go to Cruine, it may be too late! I don't know when the army is coming, but something tells me you need to hurry! Please, just—"

Sarza's screaming diatribe halted, her attention captured by something across the room. Following her gaze, Zeisha saw that Eira's office door was opening. She expected it to be Eira's assistant, making sure everything was okay. Instead, she saw a dusty boot, followed by dirty pants, a sweat-stained shirt, and a head covered in shaggy, tangled hair.

Krey.

He was injured, a white cloth tied around his head . . . but he was alive.

Zeisha had never moved—or started crying—so fast in her life. She jumped out of her seat and rushed to Krey, throwing her arms around him. He stumbled backward, his chest shaking with laughter even as hers shook with sobs. She kissed his cheek and aimed for his lips, but he turned his head away. "Hold on," he said.

He spoke to the whole room. "The army is coming. They're marching now."

"How do you know—" Eira began.

She didn't finish her question, because Krey's legs buckled. He fell heavily to the ground.

In an instant, Zeisha was kneeling next to him. "What's wrong?"

He grimaced, his hand rising to rub the back of his head. "I just . . . I need a good healer," he said. "And . . . a nap. . . but can I have that kiss first?"

Zeisha touched his chapped lips, then kissed him as if no one were watching.

33

Yesterday, Mayor Shew invited me to his office. He wanted to meet the youngest reporter in town.

I was caught off guard by how ordinary he was. Sure, he leads a city of millions, but he sits behind a regular desk and wears normal clothes. He even had a few hairs out of place.

You know what wasn't ordinary? The snack he served me. Mayor Shew, those cookies were the best I've ever tasted. Invite me back any time.

-"Ordinary" by Genta Ril
The Derogan Chronicle, *dated Cyon 27, 6293*

KREY'S FACE WAS PLACID. His chest rose and fell in a slow, even rhythm. Zeisha wanted to crawl in bed and nap alongside him. But she had a dragon ride coming up. Krey had made her promise to wake him before she left.

She kissed his cheek. His mouth curved into a slight smile, but he didn't wake until she said his name several times and shook his shoulder.

His eyes fluttered open, his sleep-smile widening into a real one. "Hey," he said in a drowsy voice. "You gotta go?"

"Pretty soon." Zeisha was glad it had taken a few hours to prepare for the trip. Krey had needed the sleep. As he sat up, yawned, and stretched, he looked nothing like the half-dead guy who'd walked into Eira's office. "You don't need to get up for me," she said.

"If my head is on the pillow, I'll go right back to sleep." He patted the bed next to him. "Have a seat?"

"Krey, you *should* go right back to sleep. For as long as you can."

"I'm feeling way better already, thanks to the trog healer. My head only hurts a little. Come on, let me give you a proper goodbye. Then I'll nap like a good boy, I promise."

Zeisha smiled and sat, facing him. "Since you're awake, we should talk," she said softly.

His grin disappeared. "Okay?"

She drew in a deep breath. "Krey . . . I can't fly with you when the army comes."

His internal battle was clear and fierce. His mouth gaped and shoulders drooped in momentary disappointment. Then he caught himself, squaring his shoulders and smiling again. "That's okay. I've always told you it's okay. I know you hate fighting, and I'm glad you'll be safe with the other—"

"That's not it," she said, taking his hand. "Yes, I hate fighting, but . . . I love these people. I don't want to hide. I want to protect them. And I love flying with you—you know I do. But I can't use my magic in violent ways. I need to use it to protect the trogs instead."

His head tilted to one side. "How?"

She told him all about her dream to make thorn shields. "Don't be too impressed," she said when she saw his smile. "We tried, but it didn't work. Maybe if we had a week to prepare . . ."

"So what's your plan?"

"I don't know." She shook her head hard. "The shield idea . . . it felt so right. I thought maybe it was from God, not from me . . . you know?"

He squeezed her hand. "And now you don't know what you're supposed to do?"

She shook her head. A curl bounced into her eyes, and he tucked it behind her ear. "I hope I figure it out before the army gets here," she said. "All I know is, I can't fly on your back and kill people with my vines. I'm sorry."

"It's okay. Really."

"It doesn't feel okay. When I got this shield idea, I thought I'd finally figured out who I was—at least when it came to how I should use my magic. Now I'm lost again."

Krey pulled her into a tight hug. "I know who you are," he said into her hair. "I love who you are."

The words rang strangely hollow to her. A year ago, in Tirra, they would've been exactly what she needed to hear. What had changed?

It's not enough. I need to know myself. I need to love myself. She'd thought she was getting there, but yesterday's failure had torn up her self-confidence, as if the thorns she'd grown had somehow gotten tangled in her spirit.

Zeisha clung to Krey, letting his warm arms distract her from her confused thoughts. At last, she pulled back. She needed to go, and she couldn't leave without a kiss, not when Krey might be waging war by the time she returned.

He must've been thinking the same thing, because he brought his warm lips to hers. Their mouths fit together as perfectly as ever, and the kiss brought her the exquisite mixture of comfort and passion that characterized so much of their time together.

This was the same boy Zeisha had grown up loving. These were the kisses they'd shared for years. But in a way, it felt like she was kissing a different person—or like *he* was.

A strange thought slipped into her mind. *Maybe we aren't just kissing each other goodbye. Maybe we're kissing our old selves goodbye too.*

Zeisha pulled back. "I have to go. And you need to sleep before the army gets here."

"You're doing great," he said.

"Maybe I'd believe you if I knew what I was doing at all."

"You'll figure it out. I know you will."

She gave him a tight hug, then left.

It was late morning when Nora finally told the dragons it was time to go. Eira had spent the last five hours preparing her people for the upcoming battle.

Eira and Nora climbed onto Osmius as Zeisha and Sarza mounted Taima's broad back. "Are you okay?" Nora asked Eira.

The elderly trog turned her head. "Of course."

Well, then. Nora had envisioned having to support a frightened woman throughout the long flight. *Good thing Krey's not here; I'm not sure his sanity could survive a two-hour dragon flight.* She didn't realize she'd shared the thought with Osmius until his rich laughter filled her mind.

They rose into the air. Taima, who always took too many risks with her passengers, flew upward at a sharp angle. When Sarza cursed loud enough for all of Deroga to hear it, the female dragon shifted to a more gradual ascent.

It didn't take long to exit trog territory. Nora marveled as they flew over a great swath of wild land that had probably once been an urban park. As they neared Burig Bay, she saw massive warehouses, ten times bigger than the one that had housed the militia.

Boats and ships still inhabited the docks at the edge of the bay.

Once-bright surfaces were discolored, and a few masts had broken. A tree grew from a small boat that had been pulled onto shore.

Past the docks, a Skytrain track sloped down from above the city and ran through a large building on the shore. Where the track exited the building, ancient scaffolding held up a small section, extending over the water. Apparently it had been under construction on The Day. All Nora could think was that if she had a choice of how to cross the bay, she'd ride a dragon over a train any day.

Soon, the only thing Nora could see was pristine, blue water, sparkling with sunlight. The unending expanse lulled her into a near-trance. It felt like they'd been traveling forever when Taima's rich voice jolted her back to alertness.

The new human insists she must speak with Eira.

Sarza? Nora and Osmius asked in unison.

Yes. The pushy one.

Nora laughed.

I shall fly under you, Taima, Osmius said. He accelerated to catch up with his mate, then swooped down to fly beneath her. He positioned much of his body under Taima's right wing. Sunlight shone through the translucent skin of the great wing. Where the light hit Nora, she glowed, like someone had brushed gold dust on her skin. *Now that's an effect I wish I could use for parties,* she thought.

Taima's wing didn't cover Eira, who was in front of Nora. The trog lifted her head, her white braid falling to the side. "What do you need?" she called.

Nora couldn't see Sarza through Taima's wing, but she heard her shout, "I had a vision!"

"While in the air?" Eira asked.

"Yes! When we talk to the prime minister, we have to ask to meet with—" The wind swallowed the rest of Sarza's message.

"Who?" Eira called.

"Anya!" Sarza shouted even louder.

"Who is that?"

"I have no idea!"

"Very well!" Eira said.

Osmius dropped a few mets, slowing to again fly behind his mate. *Nora-human*, he said, his deep voice resonating in her mind, *Look ahead.*

She did. The water of Burig Bay no longer extended to the horizon. A land mass, gray and shapeless from this distance, awaited them. The nation of Cruine.

Preet, the Cruinite capital, sat on the shore of Burig Bay. A river ran through the city. Not too far north was another river, along which sat the ruins of a preday city. It was smaller than Deroga, but Zeisha still found it impressive from above.

Eira had assured them that the Cruinite government was peaceful, almost to a fault. She and other trog representatives had visited years ago to conduct trade negotiations. She seemed certain no one would shoot down the dragons as they approached. Still, Zeisha's pulse quickened as they descended toward a large, green lawn in front of the nation's rather modest capitol building.

No one attacked, but guards in dark uniforms shouted warnings as the massive reptids landed.

"We are trogs," Eira called as soon as the dragons had touched down.

"Please hold your hands up," a female guard shouted from several dozen mets away. They all complied.

"May we dismount?" Eira asked.

The guard gave them permission to do so slowly.

Taima and Osmius settled in the grass as their passengers approached the guard. After a short, animated conversation, the guard gestured for one of her colleagues to join her. When he arrived to keep an eye on their visitors, she ran toward the capitol building.

The male guard carried on a polite conversation with them while they waited. Cruinites had a slight accent that Zeisha found elegant. *I wonder if they feel the same about the way we talk?*

After at least half an hour, the female guard returned to escort them inside.

The capitol building was constructed of dark-gray stone. Just before the group reached the plain, wooden doors, the dragons rose into the air, their wings snapping.

"I wonder where they're going," the guard said.

"It was a long flight," Nora said. "They'll get water and hunt for some food."

The guard turned sharply to her. "Hunt? What do they eat?"

"Wild animals," Nora assured her.

"Oh . . . and how do you know that's why they left?"

Nora grinned. "They told me."

The guard's eyes grew rounder than Zeisha would've thought possible.

The guard led the visitors through the capitol's corridors, passing dozens of busy staffers along the way. She stopped at a single door that, like the rest of the building, was plain and functional. "Wait here." She went inside and soon returned. "The prime minister is ready for you."

They followed the guard into a waiting area. A smartly dressed young man with very short hair held open an inner door for them. Passing through it, they found themselves in a good-sized office with bookshelves lining three of the walls. The fourth wall held a lit fireplace.

A short, bald man was standing in front of a blocky, wooden desk. He introduced himself as Prime Minister Osk, then shook his guests' hands as they told him their names. "Make yourselves comfortable, please," he said, gesturing to a seating area in front of the fire.

Zeisha sat next to Sarza on a couch upholstered in smooth, black fabric. Nora and Eira took two stuffed chairs. Eira perched at the edge of hers, like she feared getting lost in it if she sat back. The prime minister sat in a wooden armchair with pads tied to the back and seat.

"I suppose you'd like sustenance after such a long trip?" he asked. Then he cocked his head with a half-smile. "Or perhaps it wasn't long at all, since you came by air?"

Eira's stern voice answered, "We will have water only."

The prime minister gestured to the young man who had let them in. Moments later, they were all holding well-made glasses full of clear water. The assistant left the room, shutting the door softly behind him.

"I did not expect trade negotiations today." The prime minister's smile was casual, but Zeisha saw keen intelligence behind it.

"We are not here to negotiate trade," Eira said. "As my letters say, the Cellerinian king wishes to take Deroga as his own. Even now, his army marches to the city."

Osk's brow furrowed with empathy that appeared genuine. "I am sorry. However, we cannot interfere. You know how much we value the peaceful relationship we have with the Kingdom of Cellerin. Our small army is only to be used for defense, and only as a last resort. I have sent letters to King Ulmin, asking him to reconsider his actions. They remain unanswered. I'm afraid that is all we can do."

Eira opened her mouth to speak, but Nora's urgent voice was the one that filled the room. "Prime Minister Osk, the king is my father."

Osk sat up straighter.

Nora continued, "My father's mind . . . he's not all there anymore." She swallowed. "I'm afraid we're headed toward civil war, with him on one side and me on the other."

"However," Eira said firmly, drawing all eyes to her, "we know you cannot send your army to help us. That is not why we come." She gave Nora a short glance that seemed to say, *Focus, Princess.* "We come here," Eira said, "because Sarza tells us to. She is a seer."

The prime minister blinked and turned to Sarza. "A seer."

"Yes," Eira said. "Sarza says we must request an introduction to someone named Anya."

The revelation about Sarza's ability had barely made Osk flinch. The name *Anya*, however, elicited a sharp gasp.

Sarza spoke, her voice sharp with impatience. "Obviously you know this Anya person. Where are they?"

Osk licked his lips and clasped his hands. His mouth opened twice, but no sound emerged. At last, he spoke directly to Sarza, his voice strained. "There is no reason you should know of him—unless you are what you claim to be."

"So Anya's a guy? Where is he?" Sarza demanded.

Osk's throat throbbed visibly as he swallowed. "He is a man. However, Anya is not a name. It is a title."

They all stared at him.

"The Anya," Osk said, "connects us to the Well."

34

Did you hear about the man who lived in a closet?

No, it's not a joke. Last week, a seventy-four-year-old man was found living in a two-by-two-met storage closet in a large office building. His sleeping area took up the back half. He had a comfortable chair and stacks of books in the front half. The man fed himself at night from left-over food in the building's kitchens. He claims he lived there for twelve years because he "wanted some peace and quiet."

I've lived in crowded Deroga all my life, and I feel bonded to this man I've never met. If journalism doesn't work out for me, maybe I'll become an eccentric hermit instead.

-*"The True Tale of a Happy Hermit" by Genta Ril*
The Derogan Chronicle, *dated Cyon 28, 6293*

OSK OFFERED to escort his guests to the Anya's home. It wasn't too far, he assured them. Traveling by wagon, they'd likely arrive by the next afternoon.

When they insisted on riding on dragons instead, the prime minister's intense fear of massive reptids became obvious. Zeisha's companions argued vehemently that they didn't have time to travel by land.

While she agreed, she felt no need to engage in the conversation. When Osk had first spoken of the Anya, a strange peace had settled on her. It seeped into her stomach, her heart, and her very joints. *I'm where I'm supposed to be.*

At last, Osk agreed to fly with them. They ate a quick lunch, provided by the in-house kitchen, then walked out to Osmius and Taima. Zeisha was quiet through lunch, and as she mounted Taima, she felt lighter than she had in years.

Osk rode with her and Sarza, since Taima's back was larger. Zeisha spoke quiet words to the prime minister, giving him tips on how to stay secure and assuring him that the dragon would keep him safe. As she spoke, some of the panic left his eyes.

The flight was longer than their trip across Burig Bay. It was late afternoon when they flew over a small forest and at last hovered above a house set in a clearing at the base of a mountain range. There were no other homes in sight.

The clearing was small, and one of Taima's wings clipped the roof of the house on her way down. Her passengers dismounted, then moved out of the way so Taima could fly away and Osmius could land. Zeisha laid a hand on Osk's arm. "Are you all right?"

He turned. "Yes. Your assurances helped." His eyes narrowed, and his head tilted just a bit. He examined her closely. "Why did you come on this trip?"

She couldn't keep a small smile off her lips. "I'm not sure. Why are you asking?"

He gave her an enigmatic smile. "No reason."

Osmius landed, and soon, all five humans stood before the stone house. Osk knocked on the narrow, wooden door.

At least three minutes passed, during which Osk knocked two more times. Zeisha's companions shifted on their feet. She stood still, feeling even more tranquil than before.

The door opened on smooth hinges. Before them stood a man who looked older than any person Zeisha had ever met. Despite his stooped back, he was of average height. He leaned heavily on a cane. His muscles appeared to have wasted away, but his shoulders were still broad. His clean-shaven face was so wrinkled that Zeisha had a fleeting thought that if someone stretched his skin out, it would measure three times as large as the area it now covered. Most of his head was bald, but long wisps of snowy-white hair hung from the back of his head. His skin had so many age spots that Zeisha struggled to determine what the original tone had been. Light-brown eyes, bright and intelligent, peered at them all. "Hello," he said.

"Our Anya." Osk bowed his head low.

"You know I need no such honors," the Anya said in a voice that wavered with age. "Please, come in." He turned, the movement painfully slow.

Zeisha's peace remained, but it was colored with anticipation. After Osk's comment about the Anya connecting them to a well of some sort, he'd refused to explain what he meant. This elderly man was clearly important. But how?

The Anya's tiny living room held only one piece of furniture, a small couch. He sat on it. "Would anyone like to sit with me?"

Zeisha found herself walking that direction. After taking two steps, she stopped. *What am I doing? If anyone's going to sit, it should be Eira. Or maybe Osk.*

The Anya smiled at her, an expression that was charming, despite his age-darkened teeth. "Please." He gestured to the seat.

She looked to Eira, who said, "After the long ride, I wish to stand."

When her eyes shifted to Osk, he said, "I'll stand too."

Zeisha sat.

The Anya's eyes swept over his guests. "Why are you here?"

Osk replied, "I brought them, because this young woman"—he gestured at Sarza—"said they should visit you."

The Anya's expression remained as neutral and pleasant as ever. "How wonderful. How may I help you?"

Sarza spoke, her voice seeming too loud in the small room. "Yeah, I'm the one who said we should come here, but I have no idea who the hell you are. So let's start with that."

Nora and Eira fixed Sarza with glares as sharp as swords. Zeisha, for some reason, found herself grinning.

The Anya laughed. The sound, full of joyful freedom, took decades off his age. "It is a worthy question." He spread his wrinkled, liver-spotted hands wide. "Our planet is full of magic. So full, it nearly bursts at times. You all know this, to a point." He gestured to Nora. "If I am not mistaken, you are an ice lyster. You also talk to dragons."

Nora's eyes widened.

"Your ice-lysting capabilities are generally quite average," the Anya told Nora, his voice gentle. "However, at your strongest, you used them in an exceptional way. In doing so, you saved others. You should know you did well."

Nora's chin quivered, and she didn't seem to be able to speak. Zeisha knew her friend still thought of Faylie daily. She'd needed those words.

"You, of course," the Anya said, shifting his attention to Sarza, "are a seer. I have never met a seer. I want you to know how honored I am."

"Um . . . okay," Sarza said, her cheeks darkening a bit.

The Anya continued, "Prime Minister Osk, your fire-lysting capabilities continue to grow, do they not?"

"They do."

"And you." The Anya turned to speak to Zeisha. "Your plant-lysting faculty is impressive, my child. And there is . . ." His lips curved into a smile, and she immediately wanted to adopt him as her grandfather. "There is more," he said.

"More?" Her voice was little more than a whisper.

His wiry, white eyebrows lifted. "You have a gentle heart. I saw it when you walked in. That is a gift." Seeing her smile, he winked, then returned his attention to the group. "I am sure you have all heard the legends of Anyarian planet magic."

"You mean weird magic that happened after The Day?" Sarza asked. "Rivers parting and stuff like that?"

"Yes." The Anya's eyes fixed on Nora. "You have seen it, have you not?" he asked.

A slow smile spread across Nora's face, and she nodded.

"What did you see?" the Anya asked.

Nora gestured to the front door. "The gray dragon showed me parts of Cellerin I'd never known existed. I drank from a magical pond that gave me energy. We saw a field that makes people fall asleep and forget who they are. He told me there used to be other places, but the magic has faded." She shifted her gaze to Zeisha. "I'm sorry I didn't tell you. I didn't tell Krey or Ovrun either. It seemed—"

The Anya interrupted her. "The dragon did well to tell you, Princess. You did well to honor the secret." He gestured to the wood floor. "Please, sit. I will tell you what I know. Then we will discuss what comes next."

Zeisha wanted to stay close to the Anya, but if they were going to be here longer than a few minutes, she couldn't keep the only comfortable seat in the room. She offered her spot to Eira, who took it. Everyone else sat on the floor. Prime Minister Osk's knees crackled as he lowered himself.

"After The Day," the Anya said, "many travelers came across various types of planet magic. Half a century after The Day, a woman from the area we now call Cruine learned to control such magic. She even gave it a name: the Well.

"The woman found that where the Well was evident, she could strengthen and direct the magic. She then discovered that the Well was not restricted to those places. The Well is everywhere; it is simply dormant in most locations. She learned to awaken it wherever she chose. The nature of the magic changes from one place to another, and she took joy in discovering its various expressions.

"After a time, the woman chose four lysters—for only those who already have a magical faculty may connect to the Well—and bestowed her gift on them. They became known as the Anyas."

"She shared her magic with them?" Nora asked. When the Anya nodded, she prodded, "How?"

The Anya lifted a gnarled finger. "That, I will not tell you. You see, the first Anya had chosen protégés she had every reason to trust. She taught them to listen. To only use the Well in ways it is meant to be used."

"Listen to who? Or what?" Sarza's cynicism rang in every syllable she spoke.

"Some Anyas say they listen to the planet itself; some believe it is the stone communicating with them."

"What do you think?" Zeisha heard herself ask.

"I think it is something bigger. Some*one* bigger." The Anya gave Zeisha that gentle smile again. "Someone who speaks to many people, not just Anyas." He held his hands wide. "Regardless of who or what was speaking, one of the four new Anyas chose not to listen. He drew forth magic from the Well and used it to wreak violence and benefit himself. The first Anya wished to bring him back to the path she'd taught him. She set off to meet with him. He caused a river to flood over a bridge as she crossed it, and she drowned."

"Damn," Sarza breathed.

The Anya continued, "The remaining three Anyas attacked and killed their rogue brother. They spent the rest of their lives traveling over as much of the planet as they could. They listened to fellow travelers who told of magical locations. The Anyas put the Well to sleep in those places so its power could not be used for evil.

"That is why humans rarely encounter the Well now. The magic has not faded; it is merely dormant. There were only three Anyas, however, and our world is large. They could not find all the areas where the Well was active. I am certain every continent still has such places.

"As the three Anyas grew older, they agreed not to pass on their magic to anyone, lest it again be misused. Then a seer arose."

"Another seer?" Nora blurted.

"Yes, a century ago, shortly after the nation of Cruine was established. She was very young when her visions began, and she died of a fever at the age of ten. While she lived, she told our nation's leaders that after decades of traveling the world, only one of the three remaining Anyas would come home. She said this Anya must pass his gift to his daughter, who still lived in Cruine. She was the only one of his children who was a lyster.

"Though that Anya never met the seer, he did as she'd instructed. His daughter was my great-grandmother. The gift became our family legacy. We, and Cruine's prime ministers, have faithfully kept our secret. Since the days of my great-grandmother, we Anyas have used our connection to the Well only rarely and only when it will bring peace and safety."

"Have you shared the gift with your child?" Nora asked.

The Anya's smile carried more than a hint of sadness. "My wife and I had no children."

"You're the last Anya?" Zeisha asked.

"Things do not always happen as we wish them to."

The room fell silent. At last, Sarza spoke. Her voice had lost its demanding edge. "How did you know about our talents? Are you a seer too?"

He smiled softly. "I am not. I merely listen. After many decades, I hear more than I used to. All magic is intertwined." He lifted his hands, weaving his fingers together. "My knowledge, however, is limited. I do not know why you are here or what you want from me." He turned expectant eyes on Eira.

"We live in Deroga," Eira said. "Cellerin's army is marching now to invade us. We need help to save our city."

"What kind of help?"

Eira shook her head. "I do not know."

Zeisha didn't feel any such confusion. "We need shields."

"Shields?" The Anya brought his warm gaze to her.

She knelt before him, taking his hand in both of her own. It was an intimate gesture, but it felt right. He responded by squeezing her hand, his wise eyes still fixed on her. She said, "We want to keep the army away from the areas where we live. I tried to use my talent to make walls from thorn plants, but it didn't work. If you could use the planet's magic to protect us . . ." She trailed off, inexplicable emotion taking over her voice. "Please," she managed.

The Anya smiled widely at her, delight dancing in his eyes. He leaned close and rested his free hand on her cheek.

"Of course I will," he said.

35

A woman who lives near me turned 103 years old yesterday. At her party, she told me she's writing a novel.

"I've met nearly all my life goals," she told me. "Only one remains."

"To publish a book?" I asked.

She gave me a bright smile. "No. To ensure I am not underestimated."

-"Centenarian Novelist" by Genta Ril
The Derogan Chronicle, *dated Cyon 29, 6293*

"WE'VE BEEN HERE at least two hours," Krey said to Ovrun, "and you still look like a kid who climbed a tall tree for the first time."

Ovrun laughed, getting closer to the edge of the rooftop where they were both acting as lookouts. "I love the view."

Krey followed his friend's gaze. The sun was setting, but there was still enough light to make out city streets and clommets of open land beyond. The area west of Deroga was mostly wilderness, with occasional patches of trees and bushes to break things up. Based on Ovrun's expression, you'd think it was a paradise.

The former guard pointed at the Deroga River. During the day, the banks were green, far more lush than the surrounding land. In tonight's dim light, the foliage looked gray. "Just think about it," Ovrun said. "You could start a farm along the river. Put a windmill on one of the hills. The soil's so fertile by the water, you wouldn't even need a vine eater to help things grow. It would take less than a day to drive a wagon to Deroga or the capital. You could live there in peace, growing crops, trading with Cellerinians and trogs."

"Trading with trogs is illegal," Krey said.

Gaze still on the river, Ovrun grinned. "When the king's that far away, you really think he's gonna care?"

Krey chuckled. "Maybe not. Though you keep saying *you*, and obviously you mean . . . *you*. Not me. Because no offense, man, but that life sounds dull as hell." He expected his friend to laugh.

Instead, Ovrun crossed his arms and coughed. "Yeah, well . . . I used to think that's what I wanted. Things change as we get older." He looked over at Krey and smiled, but his furrowed forehead ruined the effect. "I've been thinking lately about how it wouldn't be so bad living near a city."

Krey nodded slowly. "I suppose a princess can't live in a perfect little farm halfway between the trogs and the capital."

Ovrun shrugged. His smile was resigned now. "No, she can't."

After eyeing his friend for some time, Krey asked, "Is she worth it?"

"Absolutely."

"Then I'm happy for you two."

"Thanks, man."

Ovrun's words led Krey to consider his own future. He shifted his view from the open land in the distance to the shadowy city of Deroga.

His vivid hallucination of preday Deroga returned to him. It had been similar to dreams he'd had since moving to Deroga. Humans on Anyari had created a truly wondrous world before The Day. Krey's heart yearned to build something just as spectacular. Maybe in the coming years, he'd start that library system he'd always dreamed of, or establish a university or magical research center.

"Krey?" Ovrun said.

Krey flinched, but he was thankful for the distraction. Thinking so hard made his still-injured head ache. He turned. "Sorry. I was . . . somewhere else."

"Thinking how cool it would be to build your own farm?"

That made him laugh. "Hopefully something way bigger than a farm." Krey sat, his gaze sweeping the landscape. The day's light was nearly gone.

Something caught his eye—a darkening on the horizon. It was the type of thing he could've dismissed as a trick of the fading light . . . except he'd seen this type of shadow before. His eyes narrowed. "If I were a general," he said quietly, "I'd save the final leg of my trip for nighttime. I'd travel in the dark, hoping any lookouts wouldn't see me coming. Around dawn, we'd arrive, ready to fight."

"What're you saying?"

Krey pointed north. "That's an army." He sighed, grabbed his pack, and shoved feathers in his mouth. His breaths quickened, along with his pulse. It was almost time to fight for the city below. "Give me a minute to fuel up. We'll fly to the other clans to make sure they know, and then we'll start knocking on doors. When the army gets here, we'll be ready."

Ovrun pounded on the door of yet another house with a light shining in the window. "Get to your stations!" he shouted. "This is not a drill!"

A man opened the door. The candle he held shone on his exasperated face. "We are coming. We have time."

Ovrun wasn't easily angered, but after hearing that same message from people all over Deroga, he wanted to throttle this guy. Three months ago, when the trogs had all been told to rush to their hiding spots underground, they'd had to wait for hours before the army arrived. Many of them assumed they'd have that much time again.

"The army might be moving faster than we expect," Ovrun said. He spied a teenage girl standing in the shadows behind the man. Next to her was a middle-aged woman. "Don't you want to get your family to safety?"

"My family will fight!"

"Then you all need to get to your stations! Now!" Without another word, Ovrun left the porch, running down the Star Clan's main residential street to look for any other stragglers.

Ovrun turned at the sound of footsteps. After warning the other clans, Krey had asked a young trog to watch the street where the dragons were expected to land. Now, the girl was running their way. "They're back!" she gasped.

Within minutes, Krey and Ovrun arrived at the wide street where the dragons always landed. Taima and Osmius were already there, their passengers having dismounted. In the light of his and Krey's lanterns, Ovrun saw Nora, Zeisha, Eira, Sarza, and one extra person: a stooped, elderly man leaning on a cane.

Nora ran up to them, followed by Zeisha. "We flew high over the whole area," Nora said. "Dragons can see a lot more in the dark than we can. The army's coming."

"We know," Ovrun said. "Most of the people are at their stations. We hope it'll be a few hours—"

"We don't have a few hours!" Nora gripped his arm. "A hundred soldiers or so rode ahead on orsas. They've almost reached trog territory!"

Next to Ovrun, Krey said, "Eira, I'll fly and spread the word." He turned back to Nora. "Could you tell if the king was with them?"

"I don't think he was in the first wave," Nora said. "I know he wouldn't travel without guards, and the soldiers on orsas were pretty spread out. If he came, he must be with the main army."

Krey kissed Zeisha's cheek. "Be safe," he said, before jumping into the air and flying away.

Zeisha turned to Ovrun. "Do you know where Kebi is?"

"I saw her with that team of vine eaters yesterday," he said. "They couldn't get the thorn shields to grow large enough, but I think they're still planning to work together during the battle."

Her eyes brightened. "Can you find them?"

"I'll ask around. What do you want me to tell them?"

Zeisha gave him directions to a nearby building where they could meet. "Oh, and Ovrun?" she added. "We need you to stay with us during the battle."

"Okay . . . why?"

"I'll explain when you get back."

Ovrun nodded, then ran off in search of Kebi, his stomach tightening with every step. *They're here . . . and we don't have any help.*

It wasn't for lack of trying. Krey had done his best to ally with New Therro, but they didn't have any help to give. When Sarza had shown up, Ovrun's hope had bloomed again. But apparently the only assistance Cruine had provided was one elderly man.

Beating the king might be impossible . . . but I'll do whatever I can to protect the trogs and my friends.

Ovrun ran faster.

Zeisha, Sarza, and the Anya huddled in the lobby of a building just outside Star Clan territory. In a nearby room, they could access the tunnels under the city. Those tunnels were vital to their plan.

But to navigate the tunnels, they needed maps. Kebi had those; she and Zeisha had planned to use them during the battle to check on the thorn shields. *Maybe some good will come from that idea after all.*

Zeisha smiled at the thought. She caught the Anya's eye, and he smiled back.

Zeisha fueled up as she mentally begged Kebi to come quickly. Once they had maps, they'd travel through trog territory. The Anya would use the power of the Well to shield important streets from the Cellerinian army.

Sarza had offered to stay with the Anya. She hoped she'd have visions or general feelings—*urges*, she called them—that would help direct him. Knowing the importance of protecting the Anya, she'd also convinced Eira to return her weapon, a knife.

Zeisha, too, would stay with the Anya during the battle, by his request. When he'd asked, she couldn't imagine why he wanted her there, but she'd said yes. She'd also offered to bring Ovrun along to carry the Anya.

When Zeisha heard that Kebi had kept the vine-eating team together, she'd realized what her role must be. Along with the other vine eaters, she would protect the Anya. She despised the thought of using her magic in violent ways again, yet she knew in her gut she was where she was supposed to be.

A cool hand rested on hers. "It will be fine," the Anya said softly.

Her eyebrows rose. "What will be?"

"Not everything, but many things."

She flipped her hand over to squeeze his.

They'd been waiting about twenty minutes when they heard running feet in the street beyond. Zeisha and her companions stilled.

Ovrun and Kebi entered. Both had bows strapped to their backs. "I have our vine-eating team," Kebi said, ushering them all in the building.

"Great," Zeisha said. "Let's get away from the street."

Once the Anya was on Ovrun's back, the group made its way into a nearby hallway. Kebi lit a few torches and handed them out. As they rushed through the building, Kebi told Zeisha that she'd seen three orsa-riding soldiers in the distance as they'd rushed to meet Zeisha.

They reached the room leading to the old Extrain tunnels. Ovrun helped the Anya dismount next to Zeisha. She realized everyone was watching her expectantly. *Once again, they think I know what I'm doing.* She managed not to laugh at that. *Guess I'd better give them instructions.*

"We all want to protect trog homes," Zeisha began. "Our thorn shields didn't work out, but our mission hasn't changed." She placed her hand on the Anya's shoulder. "This man will raise shields for us. I don't know exactly what'll happen today, but I know this: we're all going to see things we can't explain. Our job is to protect this man . . . and protect his secrets. Can you commit to that?"

They all responded affirmatively.

"Are you fueled up? Extra fuel in your pockets and packs?"

Again, they said yes.

Zeisha scanned the group. They looked a lot more ready to fight than she was. She told Kebi what part of the city they wanted to travel to first, and they descended into the Extrain tunnels.

36

The Prime Minister of Therro made an eloquent speech yesterday about how proud he is of his people, who display friendliness, openness, and trust to all.

Then he returned to his home, hidden behind a tall, guarded fence.

-"Fences" by Genta Ril
The Derogan Chronicle, dated Cyon 30, 6293

"YOU DOING OKAY?" Krey asked Nora.

He didn't miss the tightness in her voice when she said, "I'm fine."

They were flying low over the dark city of Deroga. Neither of them was totally happy with the arrangement. Krey wished Zeisha were with him, and Nora still hadn't gotten over her fear of flying with a non-reptid. She'd argued against partnering with Krey, but Eira had told her to get over it.

At least I'm flying with a friend, not a random militia member, Krey thought. And Nora truly was the most practical choice. She could communicate with the two dragons who were also flying over Deroga. They were using their superior vision to monitor the situation below. When they saw anything the trogs needed to know, they'd tell Nora. Krey would then fly through the city, acting as a messenger.

From the air, it had quickly become clear that the mounted soldiers were there to gather information and to intimidate the trogs. Armed with guns, they rode swiftly through the streets, often drawing attacks from archers, magic eaters, and even Taima.

The black dragon's fire had consumed two mounted soldiers in the early minutes after their arrival. But to avoid burning entire streets, Taima needed to get close before attacking. Both times she'd flown in for a kill, she'd been shot at. One bullet had grazed her leg. Nora and Osmius had insisted that Taima stop attacking.

Krey hovered over a street where he could barely make out the outline of a soldier on an orsa. "Let's take him down," Nora murmured in his ear. She was handling herself with remarkable calmness, considering the fear she must be feeling as they flew. Even her heartbeat, which he could sense more clearly than his own, wasn't totally out of control.

He and Nora both loosed hard balls of ice at the still-mounted soldier. Despite all her practice, Nora only worked about half as fast as Krey, and her icy ammunition was smaller than his. Her aim, however, was top notch. Both of them hit the soldier. He wobbled in his saddle but remained mounted.

BANG!

The shot sounded close. Krey zoomed off, not about to stick around long enough to find out how well Cellerinian soldiers could aim.

BANG! BANG!

Krey cursed, flying erratically to make himself a difficult target.

"Feather lyster!" As Nora's voice reached his ear, he realized her pulse had doubled its speed. "To your left!"

He cursed as another shot rang out. The feather eater was barely a shadow in the dark sky. Krey's instincts took over. He flew upward at a steep angle, belatedly warning, "Hang on!" He needn't have said anything. Nora's thighs were so tight around his waist, he knew he'd be bruised later.

His mad flight must've been successful; no more shots rang out. However, he'd also lost sight of the feather eater. He scanned the sky, flying in wild spirals and dips. With one hand, he held Nora's leg, with the other, her arm. *Don't have a heart attack on me, okay?* he silently begged.

Another gunshot sounded. This time, Krey saw the accompanying flash of light. A wild grin stretched his mouth wide as he shot two huge balls of ice at that position.

The ice plummeted to the street below.

A half-second later, Nora shot ice missiles of her own, aiming them in two different directions, mets away from where Krey had seen the gunpowder flash.

"*Oof!*" The grunt, probably male, came from one of the places Nora had targeted. Krey laughed, shooting two more icy spheres. He was burning fuel—both ice and feathers—at a terrible rate.

It was worth it. His ammunition found its target.

Krey dove toward the grunts he heard. When he got close, he saw the soldier was falling, having lost control of his magic. Krey couldn't give him the chance to recover. He shot more ice at the man. Nora followed it with a ball of her own.

They kept at it until the magic eater hit the ground with a squishy *thud* that told Krey he was unlikely to ever get up.

Krey ascended again. The thrill of victory shot through his core, twined with the sickness of regret. Somewhere in the nation he called home, a family had just lost one of its members. It might be days or weeks before they learned of it.

As Krey, Nora, Ovrun, and the former militia had prepared for this battle, they'd discussed the terrible necessity of killing citizens of their own country. Nora had begged Taima not to burn the approaching army to a crisp. Protecting the trogs of Deroga was one thing. Purposefully massacring Cellerinians was another.

Krey focused on what was next, shifting his mind away from the smashed body beneath him. "Fuel!" he shouted. "I gotta find a place to stop; I burned too much in the air!"

"Okay—hey, what's that?" She was out of breath from their fight, and he could still feel her racing heart, but her voice was steady. "Look—to the right!"

He turned his head. Something orange was glowing a few streets over.

"We'll go to a rooftop and check it out while we refuel."

A few seconds later, they landed on a flat roof.

"What *is* that down there?" Nora asked as she dismounted.

"Fuel first. Then we'll check it out."

She sighed, and he heard her pulling off her backpack. She handed him a bag stuffed with feathers. There was a soft *thud*, the sound of her setting their block of ice on the roof. They'd wanted to bring crushed ice, but in this warm, late-spring weather, it would've melted too quickly. Krey chewed feathers while Nora attacked the ice block with a small hammer and a pick. The sound reverberated in his aching head.

Krey ate, but his focus wasn't on the feathers. It was on a particular spot down the street. He suspected Nora's eyes were wandering that direction too.

All was dark—except three tall streams of what appeared to be molten lava, shooting straight up from the side of the road, just past the first occupied house.

As Krey watched, another spurt of orange joined the others. Then another, and another, forming a deadly line across the street.

Krey's chewing slowed. Nora had stopped hammering too. She crawled up behind him, breathing softly.

"What . . . what am I looking at?" Krey murmured.

"It's the Well." She sounded as awed as him.

Immediately, he knew she was right. In the moments between

battle action, she'd told him briefly about the Anya and the Well. But she'd been too distracted to go into detail. Now, he asked, "How exactly is the Anya supposed to help us?"

"He's making shields, just like Zeisha wanted to do. Kebi is leading him through the tunnels. Zeisha, Ovrun, and Sarza are guarding him, along with Zeisha's team of vine oysters."

Krey's mouth curved in an admiring smile. "That beats the hell outta fences made of thorns."

Nora laughed. He heard her scoot back and return to her hammering.

Oh yeah. Fuel. He ate more feathers, then offered to take over the hammering. His eyes kept wandering to the line of lava fountains. They extended halfway across the street now. Krey was confident that by the time the man was done, no one would be able to access the residential district.

When the hammer bounced off his finger, Krey forced himself to focus on his task. But even without his eyes on the spectacle below, his smile remained. *Zeisha must be having so much fun down there,* he thought, wishing he could share her front-row seat.

Hours later, dawn's red-orange light painted the sky. Nora held onto Krey as tightly as ever, pinching her left hand with her right to stay alert. She was exhausted, physically and magically. She knew Krey must be in even worse shape, considering the head injury he was still recovering from.

They'd been in the air so long, she hardly felt afraid now. She hadn't thought that would ever happen.

Between fuel stops, she and Krey had killed another feather lyster; shot ice at mounted soldiers; and flown to all the clans to share information about what they and the dragons were witnessing.

The Anya had completed the huge lava fence around the Star

Clan's homes. And in the morning light, Nora and Krey saw tall jets of thick steam protecting another clan's residential street.

Hopefully the Anya had shielded some of the other clans' homes too. Krey and Nora couldn't fly over those areas, as the army had now entered them. Krey wouldn't go near the thousands of incoming soldiers until he knew where the king was.

Movement caught Nora's gaze. "Soldiers!" she hissed. "On the right!"

Gunshots rang out from two men on orsas below. Krey made a tight turn—and slammed into an upright pole extending from the roof they were flying over.

The shock of it must've snapped his connection with his magic, because he fell hard onto the flat roof. He rolled, crushing Nora. She screamed and let go. Krey kept rolling, stopping several mets away— at the edge of the roof, in view of the armed soldier.

Nora leapt to her feet. Krey's expression was empty, stunned. "Move!" she cried, grabbing his arm. "They'll see you!"

Another gunshot sounded, sending a shard of the roof's edge flying. Panic filled Krey's eyes. He scrambled to his hands and knees and crawled. Nora ran the same direction. When they reached the center of the roof, they lay on their bellies, panting hard.

That's when Nora realized her back was on fire. A moan slipped from her mouth.

"What's wrong?" Krey asked.

"My back!"

"Can you take your pack off?"

"Yes."

He helped her pull it off. Nora couldn't see his expression, but she heard his sharp intake of breath. "How bad is it?" she asked.

"When we fell, the pack must've gotten pushed to the side," he said. "Looks like you scraped up your back on the roof. The blood's coming through your shirt."

Through tears, Nora said, "It feels deeper than a scrape. Oh, by the stone, Krey, it hurts!"

"Can I look?"

"Okay."

She untucked her shirt, then eased it up her torso.

"Damn," Krey said. "I can't believe I fell—I—I'm sorry, Nora. It's a big abrasion, and it's also gonna bruise . . . a lot. But I don't think you broke it. Can you move okay?"

She pulled her knees up, curving her back. It hurt, but she could move. She pushed her legs back down, taking a slow, deep breath. "I'll be okay. Are you hurt?"

"No, I'm fine. We should get out of here." He started to push himself up, then froze, his face twisting into a pained grimace. "I'm . . . not fine." Loud groans exited his mouth as he turned onto his back and sat up. He grabbed his right leg.

Nora pushed herself up to sit next to him, her back rebelling against every movement. Krey pulled up his right pant leg, then unlaced his boot and started pulling it off. A grunting cry escaped his mouth.

Nora lifted her eyes to his face. His skin was pale and sweaty. "Let me help," she said.

She loosened his laces further and carefully pulled at his boot. By the time she got it off, he was screaming. When she slid his sock off, he was reduced to begging. "Stop, please!"

His ankle was swollen wider than his foot. The skin was stretched and glossy, the color mottled, bruises emerging. Nora cursed.

Krey took several deep breaths. "It might be broken," he said.

His obvious statement elicited a hysterical laugh from Nora. Krey brought confused, pained eyes to her. "I'm sorry, it's not funny," she said. "I just . . ." She swore again, then suddenly remembered they knew where a blood lyster was hiding. "We need to get you healed."

Krey nodded, grimacing. "Lemme . . . eat some feathers first." His mouth twisted, and he swallowed, holding a hand to his stomach. "I hope I can keep them down."

Taima's rich voice entered Nora's mind. *Listen, human!*

Nora stiffened, sensing urgency in the dragon's tone. *Yes?*

Drop out of sight. Now!

"Krey, lie down!"

He did, with a pitiful cry.

Lying next to Krey and trying to ignore her back pain, Nora asked, *What's going on?*

The king is close to trog territory, guarded by two dozen people.

Nora cursed. She'd held out hope her father would stay far away from the fighting. Now Krey would have to do whatever was necessary to stay out of the king's sight. Osmius, who'd landed before sunrise, might not be able to fly at all. He was too big to navigate easily through city streets like Krey could. *Where is my father?* Nora asked.

A picture entered her mind: King Ulmin, at the back of the army. He was talking with someone in an army uniform, but the men and women surrounding him wore the uniforms of the royal guard. Of course he'd choose protectors whose minds he controlled, people who wouldn't hesitate to give their lives for him.

Nora also saw why Taima had warned them to drop so quickly. The king was nearing the top of a hill. In seconds, he'd be at one of the highest points in the city. From there, he'd have a good view of much of the inhabited city—including the rooftop where she and Krey now lay. "We have to go now!" Nora said. "My father will see you!"

Faster than Nora would've thought possible, Krey pushed himself up to his hands and knees. "Get on!" he said.

She straddled his back and had barely gotten her arms around his neck when he took to the air. "Fly low!" she said.

"Where to?" His voice was strained with pain.

"Go south until I have more information."

Taima's voice reached her mind again. *The army is splitting up to cover more of the city. You must fly low and spread the word so the trogs are prepared! I shall send images to your mind.*

Nora cursed under her breath, then told Krey, "I know you need healing, but Taima has urgent messages for us to deliver. Can you keep flying?"

She felt Krey's body stiffen, but he answered with a single word: "Yes."

There are at least five thousand soldiers, Taima said. *Many have guns.*

Nora's heart dropped. They'd known that the trogs, who numbered less than two thousand including the old and young, were gravely outnumbered. But she'd hoped the foot soldiers would only be equipped with blades and bows.

People were dying down there—innocent trogs who just wanted to protect the city they'd always called home. And not just them, but Cellerinians too. Yes, Nora was fighting the army, but she didn't forget for a moment that they were her people. If the trogs didn't win this battle, all those deaths would be pointless.

A gunshot popped nearby. An agonized cry followed.

Nora's heart cried out for her father. He could stop all this with a word. He was near—but as unreachable as ever.

37

Medical researchers claim their latest bone-regeneration technology will facilitate even more rapid healing, with broken bones returning to full strength in hours instead of days.

My young cousin has the unfortunate combination of high energy and poor judgment. I'm guessing he'll find a way to test these claims before too long.

-"Building Bones" by Genta Ril
The Derogan Chronicle, *dated Cyon 31, 6293*

ZEISHA, Sarza, Kebi, Ovrun, and the Anya stood in a small room in Silver Clan territory, along with fourteen vine eaters. They'd all climbed up from an Extrain tunnel just minutes before.

A single vine eater ran through the door. "The residential street is in flames. Many soldiers patrol in front of this building. We cannot go outside."

Zeisha squeezed her eyes shut briefly. The Anya had successfully shielded five of the six clans' primary residential streets. It was too late to save the Silver Clan's homes.

Zeisha's team had reached the other five clans in advance of the main army. Along the way, they'd encountered several armed soldiers on orsaback. The vine eaters, plus Ovrun, Kebi, and Sarza, had defended the Anya as he created shields. However, gunshots had killed two vine eaters and forced three who were wounded to withdraw.

The team watched Zeisha, awaiting her orders. But all she could think of was what they'd failed to achieve. She'd hoped the Anya could shield not only the trogs' homes, but also their businesses and public buildings. Were soldiers even now destroying meeting halls and bakeries?

Next to her, the Anya spoke, his quiet voice full of authority. "The Well has more to give us. I know it."

Squaring her shoulders, Zeisha forced her attention to the elderly man from Cruine. "Where do we go next?"

The Anya pivoted to face her, his cane tapping the floor as he did so. The wrinkles of his face had rearranged themselves, twisting in confusion. "I do not know."

"I think I know," Sarza said.

"Did you have a vision?" Zeisha asked.

"No, just . . . an urge. We need to go back to the tunnels. Hopefully I can direct us from there."

Zeisha looked to the Anya, who nodded at Sarza, a small smile on his lips. "Please. Lead the way."

A strong vine eater lifted the Anya onto Ovrun's back. The group climbed down the ladder they'd just ascended.

In the tunnel, Sarza walked fast enough that Zeisha's shorter legs had trouble keeping up. They hurried down one tunnel after another, guided by lanterns and Sarza's quiet certainty. The vine eaters, including Zeisha, fueled up as they jogged.

Krey and Nora lay facedown on the roof of a three-story building. Below them, the Tree Clan's main street was host to hundreds of Cellerinian soldiers. With organized efficiency, they drew out hidden trog fighters, then killed or captured as many as they could. Some soldiers had guns. Others carried blades or bows. Well-fueled magic eaters wreaked their own sort of havoc.

Krey's ankle was killing him. He also had a burn on his arm from an ash eater's fire. And he had no idea when he'd manage to see a healer. He and Nora had approached a building outside trog territory where a blood eater was taking care of wounded trogs. It had only taken seconds for them to realize they were in far better shape than those waiting to be treated. They'd returned immediately to the fight.

Now he wondered if they'd made the wrong choice. Pain and weariness combined to make him lightheaded and shaky. Depending on sheer momentum to keep him going, he chewed feathers and ice, frequently aiming frozen spheres at soldiers below.

Nora lay next to him. Pus and blood had glued her shirt to the large abrasion on her skin. She was probably as exhausted as he was. Still, she fought. He watched her aim a ball of ice at a stone eater. It hit the woman's eye. *Where's that spoiled princess now?*

Movement drew Krey's gaze to a preteen trog boy slipping out of a sewer-access hole. Knife in hand, the boy rushed toward a male soldier who was finishing reloading his handgun. Even from above, Krey could tell the kid's movements were clumsy. Loud. The soldier turned, lifting his weapon.

Ice shot from Krey's hands at a dizzying speed. It found its mark. The man fell, his gun flying from his hand.

A female soldier who'd seen the whole thing looked to the rooftop, her eyes locking on Krey and Nora. She lifted a hand, and a vine shot out.

Krey grabbed Nora and tried to drag her, and himself, backward. His injured foot caught on the roof. He halted and cried out.

Nora was on her knees in an instant, pulling him back. "Someone see us?"

"Yeah," he said through gritted teeth. The end of a vine slapped the roof in front of them.

Nora cursed and scampered back. "Can you fly?"

"Doubt it." He tried, shocking himself when he floated several simmets off the roof's surface. "Yes!" he cried, landing on his hands and knees. "Get on!"

She did. He wrapped her in his magic, wincing when he sensed her bruises and torn skin. Flying low over rooftops, he sought another place to continue fighting.

Nora spoke in Krey's ear. "Taima says the army has taken the northwestern portion of trog territory. My father is advancing with them."

Krey ground his teeth. The news confirmed what his gut had been telling him: after perhaps an hour of full-on battle, the Cellerinians were already winning. Trogs simply couldn't prevail against so many soldiers and guns.

"What does Taima say we should do?" Krey asked.

"She's still flying high, trying to figure out if there's a weakness we can take advantage of." Nora stiffened. "Not again!"

Krey looked where she was pointing. In the street below, about fifty Cellerinian soldiers chased a much smaller group of trogs. Shots rang out. One trog fell while the others kept running. A soldier sent out a vine, capturing another trog.

They'd seen similar scenes earlier. When trogs leapt from hiding places to confront the enemy, they quickly found themselves outnumbered and had no choice but to flee. And it wasn't just the trogs hidden in the streets who were in danger. Nora and Krey had also watched soldiers swarm into buildings to root out hidden archers and magic eaters.

There was nothing two ice lysters could do to save the fleeing trogs. More likely than not, the Cellerinians would subdue the group and capture the survivors. According to Taima, a large building outside trog territory was already filling with prisoners of war.

Krey turned, unwilling to watch the scene play out. As they departed, he heard gunshots and a pained cry.

After landing on another low roof, he and Nora tried to assist besieged trogs below. But when Krey took down one soldier and five more rounded the corner, he felt like he was using a watering can on a forest fire.

We're losing Deroga.

———

After a long jog, full of twists and turns, Sarza stopped in front of a ladder. "Here." She began climbing up.

Zeisha turned to Kebi. "Any idea where we are?"

Kebi held up her bundle of papers. "We travel too quickly for me to follow the maps."

Sarza climbed the ladder and moved the piece of furniture that covered the hole in the ceiling. Zeisha followed, stepping into a dark room. The trogs had created dozens of these Extrain-tunnel access points over a century ago, in a brief bout of inter-clan cooperation.

The group rushed through the building, a journey that felt somehow familiar to Zeisha. They stopped in the lobby.

Swiveling her head, Zeisha took in the ancient, ornamental stair-case at the rear of the room and the columns throughout. She drew in a breath. "I know this place. There are people hiding here. Trogs who can't fight." It was the refuge she'd originally been assigned to. "Why did you bring us here?" Zeisha asked, turning to the seer.

Sarza's mouth was hanging open, her eyes glazed.

"Sarza?" Zeisha asked.

When the young woman didn't answer, Zeisha shook her arm. It did no good. A few seconds later, Sarza came out of her trance with a jolt and a loud curse.

"What's wrong?" Zeisha asked.

"This building—the army's gonna burn it down if the Anya doesn't prevent it."

Zeisha grabbed the seer's arm. "There are people on the twenty-fifth floor! Should we move them?"

Sarza's eyes were wide. "No time. Go outside! Now!"

They all rushed through the open front doorway. Zeisha stared down the long, straight street. A group of soldiers was coming their way, distant enough to be blurry—and close enough to arrive in minutes.

Once again, Nora and Krey were forced to flee a rooftop perch. Gunshots and magical stones pursued them.

Taima had assured them the king couldn't see much of trog territory from his current position. As Krey flew over the area, Nora's hope for a victory withered. Everywhere, soldiers advanced, forcing trogs farther into their ancient territory. Fires filled the sky with dark-gray smoke.

Krey flew over a deserted street, between two clans' territories. Suddenly, he dropped about a met, leaving Nora's stomach behind. She yelped.

"Gotta . . . land," Krey groaned. He made a sharp turn toward a third-story window. Nora's knee slammed into the hard edge of the opening as they entered. Inside, Krey fell to the floor. They rolled yet again, throwing up clouds of dust, their bodies separating in the process.

Fresh pain flooded into Nora's back. "What the hell, Krey?" Coughing from the dust, she sat up. She regretted her outburst when she saw Krey.

He was on his side, curled up, holding his injured ankle in the air. Most of his foot was black and blue, and his ankle was swollen even bigger than before. She crawled to him. "Lie back, okay?" She took off her pack, which they'd emptied of ice the last time they fueled up.

Krey's remaining feathers made it slightly fluffy. "Put your foot on this."

He turned onto his back, his face twisting with pain. Nora rolled the pack and set it under his ankle. He lowered his leg, whimpering when it touched the fabric.

"What happened?" she asked. "Ran out of fuel?"

He nodded.

She lowered herself onto her belly. With the way her back hurt, she couldn't imagine ever lying on it again. Resting her head on her overlapped hands, she closed her eyes.

"Nora?"

Her eyes fluttered open. Had she dozed off? In the middle of a battle? She turned her head to face Krey.

His gaze was focused straight above him. His chest rose and fell rapidly. "I could fly on Taima, all the way to your father. No one would see me on her back. She could breathe a bunch of fire to distract everyone. I'd fly down and touch your father and make him end this thing." His eyes were still aimed at the ceiling.

Nora gaped at him, then pushed herself up, grunting as the injured skin on her back stretched. She knelt next to Krey, leaning forward to put her face in his line of vision. His gaze shifted to the side, avoiding her.

"First of all," she said, seething anger thick in her voice, "for such a smart guy, that's an insanely stupid plan. Second, you did *not* just insinuate that you're about to eat brain matter again, did you? Because that's what it sounded like."

Finally, he looked at her. "I know the plan is horrible. I'm hoping you can help me think of something better. And yes—I'm willing to go back to something that disgusts me to save the trogs. I'm willing to risk my very sanity for them. Pardon me for having such an idea. And thank you so much for the guilt trip."

"Don't lie to me, Krey!" she screamed. A spatter of spit landed on his face. As he wiped it away, she continued, "Don't tell me it disgusts you! At least be honest! That's what you promised me!"

"Honesty?" He pushed himself up on his elbows, causing her to sit up straight to avoid being headbutted. Then he sat up all the way, anger apparently smothering his pain. He turned to face her. "I've never *not* been disgusted by eating brains, Nora! But you wanted honesty, so I'll tell you this—no matter how gross it is, I want it. I want it all the time. And when I'm tired or hurting, I want it more, so right now, you have no idea how hard it is to sit here and talk to you instead of flying off and finding some shimshims and tearing them apart until I get the fuel I need!"

His emotion stifled hers. "So why don't you?" she asked in a low voice.

"Because I promised you and Zeisha and Ovrun that when I have a craving, I'll tell you. I was pretty sure you were sleeping just now. I almost decided to eat all my feathers and fly away. But I promised. And when I promise something, I mean it."

Nora closed her eyes and didn't open them until she'd taken a deep breath, let it out slowly, and taken another. At last, she met Krey's gaze. "This right here," she said quietly, pointed back and forth between them, "this is making me trust you again. I think deep down, you want me to tell you the truth."

He stared at her for a few seconds, then nodded.

"Here's the truth, Krey West," Nora said. "You are way too smart and way too strong and way too *good* to ever return to that dark magic."

He swallowed, then whispered, "I know." Another swallow, and then his voice was a little stronger. "But I don't want to lose this battle. I don't want the trogs to lose their city. Their way of life."

"Me either. But if you go out there and attack my father, we won't just lose this battle. I'll lose you too. I still don't have many friends, Krey." Her voice cracked. "I don't want to lose you."

He squeezed his eyes shut, his jaw flexing and nostrils flaring. "You don't know what the cravings feel like."

"I don't." She took his hand. "But if you can make it through this, when you're exhausted and you have an ankle that looks like a giant, mutated grape, you can make it through any craving." She gave him a small smile and was relieved when he returned it. "You're not alone," she said.

He squeezed her hand and nodded.

Nora!

Taima's strong voice made her flinch. *What is it?*

Your help is needed elsewhere.

Okay, send me directions, and I'll tell Krey to fuel up.

No, he is too slow. I saw where you landed. With the king in his new position, Osmius can fly safely. He is on his way to carry both of you while I stay in the air, watching the king. He shall come to your window.

Nora turned back to Krey. "How do you feel about flying on Osmius?" she asked.

His only response was a groan.

The Anya pointed at the front corner of the building. "Take me there," he told Ovrun. He didn't raise his voice, yet it was filled with authority. "Vine eaters, cover me."

Zeisha ran ahead with the other vine eaters, but the Anya's voice stopped her.

"Not you, Zeisha. Stand by me."

He'd told her that at every location. *Stand by me.* She'd tried to insist that she should use her vines to protect him. His only reply had been, *It is not your role.*

Zeisha returned to the Anya, stewing in the same mixture of relief and guilt she'd felt each time. The last thing she wanted was to strangle someone with a vine. But how could she just stand there while everyone else played a role?

Anticipation shone from the other vine eaters' eyes. Ovrun and Kebi had their bows out, and Sarza's hand was on her knife.

Zeisha turned to the Anya, ready to insist she fight with the others. But he spoke first. "I need your help. Right here."

She couldn't argue with that.

Every other time the Anya had accessed the magic of the Well, he'd sat on the ground. Using unfathomable power, he'd twice brought lava from the earth, cycling it like a fountain so it flowed continuously without building up. Twice, he'd created geysers of steam. And once, under his hands, the dirt of the streets and the water that flowed deep below had combined to make thick, tall, earthen walls, bordered by deep trenches.

This time, the Anya remained standing, leaning on his cane. "Take off one of my shoes," he told Zeisha. "Then hold me up."

She had a hundred questions but no time for any of them. Her deft fingers untied and removed his shoe. She placed her arm firmly around his waist. He raised his hands, dropping his cane and leaning on Zeisha.

All across the street, thick dirt lifted from the ground, creating a low line between the Anya and his defenders. The dirt hovered briefly at ankle level, then rose. Compared to lava and steam, it was frightfully unimpressive.

A shot sounded when the dirt was at hip level. The Cellerinians were too far away to aim well, but the sound made Zeisha jump and cry out.

"Shh," the Anya whispered, not moving his hands or taking his eyes off the rising cloud of dirt.

The soldiers continued to advance. They outnumbered Zeisha's team, but only by a little. Another gunshot sounded. An arrow landed in the street, falling short of the Anya's defenders.

"Guard him!" Kebi cried. The street in front of the defenders filled with waving vines, all still attached to the magic eaters' hands. The motion made it harder for soldiers to aim, and the vines acted as a sort of shield. Ovrun and Eira nocked arrows. The street filled with the sounds of pounding feet and battle cries.

Hands still raised, the Anya remained calm. The dirt rose higher, blocking Zeisha's view of the skirmish beyond.

Her breaths quickened. She wanted to scream, *We can't keep them away with puffs of dust!* But her lips remained closed, her eyes wide open.

More gunshots sounded. A female vine eater cried out. Panic rose in Zeisha's chest. The Anya leaned on her, heavier than ever.

The clamor of battle crescendoed—shouts, snapping vines, gunshots, cries. Zeisha fixed her gaze on the wall of dirt, trying desperately to see through it.

Then the dust itself drew her focus. It was turning. Slowly at first, then faster—faster—so fast, it now appeared as a line of dusty, rotating columns. The speed increased further, the dirt spinning so fast that it appeared solid. It extended all the way across the street and down the side of the building they were guarding, not stopping until it hit large buildings on either end. But the Anya had left a narrow opening, wide enough for one person to pass through.

"Return!" the Anya commanded in a shockingly strong voice.

Two vine eaters came sideways through the opening, one hopping due to a wounded leg, the other supporting him. More followed. There was Kebi—*oh, thank God, she's safe*—carrying a young vine eater with a gut wound. Zeisha caught a glimpse of Sarza just outside the opening, fighting fiercely with her knife.

Shouts and shots rang out. Two uninjured vine eaters climbed onto their comrades' backs, peeking over the dirt fence and shooting vines at the Cellerinians beyond. More vine eaters ran through the gap, some of them running past the building to ensure the soldiers didn't circle around and attack from a different angle. Sarza and Ovrun came last, both walking backward, fighting the whole way. As soon as Ovrun was through, the spinning dirt morphed to fill the gap.

Still, it was just spinning dirt. Barely aware of the Anya's continued weight on her, Zeisha watched the shield, expecting soldiers to burst through. Her palms buzzed with magic, her vines ready to emerge.

She heard one pained cry from beyond the shield, then several more in quick succession. She brought her confused gaze to the Anya.

He was directing his defenders to go inside. When he turned and saw Zeisha's expression, he gave her a broad smile. "The dirt cuts them if they try to pass."

A laugh burst from Zeisha's mouth. Shaking her head, she helped the Anya move toward the building.

Ovrun ran up to her. "I got him!" As he scooped the Anya into his arms, more shots rang out from beyond the spinning dirt.

"Get inside!" Zeisha cried, running.

She heard a grunt. Her eyes fell on Ovrun, confused. He'd carried the Anya all morning. Why would he struggle now?

The grunt turned into a moan. It wasn't coming from Ovrun's mouth. Zeisha's gaze shifted to the old man in Ovrun's arms.

The Anya's shirt was red with blood.

38

A recent study showed that children who laugh at least twelve times a day are more likely to achieve success as adults. It also showed that as our nation's educational standards have improved, laughter in class-rooms has decreased.

A group of Derogan teachers wants to get their students giggling. They tell daily jokes and give extra credit to kids who do the same.

-"On the Subject of Laughter" by Genta Ril
The Derogan Chronicle, *dated Cygni 2, 6293*

"Go!" Zeisha screamed.

Ovrun was already running toward the building's doorway, carrying the Anya and leaving drops of dark blood on the dusty street.

Zeisha followed. Just before she reached the building, she gasped. Osmius was approaching, flying low, carrying Nora and Krey.

More shots sounded. Zeisha rushed inside and knelt by Ovrun, who was sitting on the dusty floor, holding the Anya. A vine eater handed Ovrun a shirt. Ovrun pressed the cloth to the man's bleeding stomach. The Anya was awake, his face twisted with pain.

"Zeisha!"

At the sound of Krey's voice, she turned. He was flying into the room. Nora ran in behind him. Zeisha's eyes fell on Krey's swollen ankle. "Your foot!"

Krey landed on his good foot and lowered himself to sit next to her. He was pale, with bloodshot eyes. "I'll be fine," he said. "Are you okay?"

"Yes, but he's not." She turned back to the Anya and rested a hand on his cool, wrinkled cheek. "I'm sorry," she whispered.

His eyes, still clear and vibrant, met hers. "It is my time," he murmured through pale lips. "And yours."

"Shh. Save your strength." Zeisha tuned out Ovrun and Nora, who were both trying to stop the man's bleeding. Her attention remained fixed on the Anya's face.

"Zeisha." Somehow he smiled. "If I had a child—" He paused, his mouth stretching into a grimace, his eyes squeezing shut. After taking a deep breath, he gazed at her again. "I would have prepared them to use the Well. I would have taught them to be gentle. Good. To listen to God." There was that incomprehensible smile again. "You already know these things, child. You are ready."

Zeisha stared at him, trying to make sense of his words. A coughing fit overtook him. Ovrun and Nora murmured in alarm. The coughing stopped, and the Anya gave Zeisha a weak smile.

The peace that had washed over her yesterday swept through her again, dissolving her fear and uncertainty. All she could think was that she loved this man she'd just met.

"Come close," the Anya whispered.

Zeisha leaned over.

"Closer."

She brought her ear to his mouth.

"Remember these words." In a low, clear voice meant only for her, he said, "Listen always. Love always. For you are now the steward of the Well."

Every noise in the room faded to nothing. Heat entered Zeisha through the Anya's hand on her cheek and his breath in her ear, a warmth so rich and substantial, it felt nearly solid. With it came a new sense of power, far beyond any she'd experienced as a vine eater. Her body trembled, unable to contain the rush of strength.

The Anya's voice reached her ear again: "Share this gift with your own child." His hand came up to cup the back of her head. "Or one who is like your child."

Despite her shaking, Zeisha's breaths remained slow and steady. "Thank you," she said, lifting her head to look in the Anya's eyes.

He gave her a soft smile, all trace of pain gone from it. When she returned the smile, his face relaxed. A sigh exited his mouth. It was long and full. Zeisha knew it was final.

The sounds of the room—shuffling bodies, low voices, moans of the wounded—returned to Zeisha's ears. She sat up. Ovrun and Nora were both pressing on the Anya's wound, the cloth and their hands covered in blood. Krey was watching her.

"He's gone," she whispered, laying her hand on the Anya's still chest. His open eyes seemed to gaze at nothing and everything.

Krey's warm hand fell on Zeisha's shoulder. "You're shaking," he said. "What did he say to you?"

Zeisha paused, searching for the words. "He—" She swallowed. "He wasn't the last Anya."

Krey's mouth curved into a slow smile. "You."

"Yes."

He pulled her into a tight hug. When he let go, Nora and Ovrun were watching them.

Nora's eyes dropped to the white-haired man on the floor, then returned to Zeisha. A bittersweet smile on her lips, she said, "I can't think of anyone more perfect for the job."

"Sarza," Nora said, "do you see anything? Have any hints about what we're supposed to do next?"

The two of them, plus Krey, Zeisha, and Ovrun, were huddled together in the lobby where the Anya had died. According to Taima, the line of attackers had moved on. The vine eaters who'd acted as lookouts had returned, confident the building wasn't in immediate danger. To play it safe, Kebi was fetching the trogs on the twenty-fifth floor. They would all climb down the building's back stairs and escape through the Extrain tunnels. The vine eaters were walking to the tunnel entrance now, minus Zeisha and one who'd succumbed to a gunshot wound.

"If I saw anything, I'd tell you," Sarza answered, her voice curt.

"Okay." Nora let out her breath. She didn't want to say the next words, but she had no choice. *If I'm ever queen, I'll have to get used to these hard conversations.* "Taima says the army is in control of nearly all of trog territory."

Everyone's shoulders drooped. A couple of groans escaped.

Nora continued, "Some trogs are still fighting, but it'll all be over soon. The soldiers are disarming trogs and bringing them to a single, large building outside their territory. My father is leading from the back of a wagon that's parked in an abandoned street."

She turned to Zeisha and Ovrun. "The good news is, your team protected most of the residential areas. If my father still lets the trogs live here, at least they'll have homes." She took a deep breath. "I guess our next step—"

"Nora?" Zeisha's quiet voice interrupted her.

"Yes?"

"The Well still wants to help us."

Nora swallowed, trying to squash the bit of hope that sparked in her heart. "What does that mean?"

"I'm not sure. I don't even know if I'm using the right words. But

I'm listening, like the Anya told me to. We need to move. We should be near the king."

Nora felt a wry smile tug at her lips. "I'm supposed to be the one who suggests ill-timed confrontations with my father." She looked between Krey, Ovrun, and Sarza. "We listened to the last Anya. We should listen to this one too."

Krey took Zeisha's hand. "My ankle's killing me, but I think I can fly. It beats walking. Just give me a few minutes to fuel up."

"You're sure you're the only feather eater left?" Zeisha murmured into Krey's ear as they flew low through Deroga's streets.

"Unless the army's got one hidden. They brought three. Nora and I took down two, and Taima incinerated the other."

Zeisha shuddered.

"We need to be quiet," Krey said. "We're getting close."

She knew he must be relieved. It was the fourth time he'd made this trip, having already carried Nora, Ovrun, and Sarza. And he'd been weak at the start.

They flew between two tightly spaced buildings, stopping to hover near an alley. Two soldiers, wearing the blue shirts, black pants, and black jackets of the Cellerinian Army, patrolled the area.

Krey's back swelled with steady breaths that pressed against Zeisha's chest. When both soldiers had their backs turned, he flew at top speed across the alley and through the back window of a gray building. Inside, he slowed and hovered close to the ground, letting Zeisha dismount in a large storage room.

The others waited in a room at the front of the building. Krey didn't take her there immediately, though. He hovered next to her and murmured, "I still can't get enough of you flying with me."

The statement made her smile, but she felt a deep yearning that had nothing to do with him. The Well itself seemed to be calling to her, begging her to connect with its magic. "Let's go," she said.

Krey flew low, leading her through a doorway and into a huge room filled with shelves, many of them collapsed. This must've been a preday store of some sort. It was dusty and smelled of age, dampness, and rotting polymus.

They reached Nora, Ovrun, and Sarza, who were all huddled behind a counter, near a huge, broken-out window at the front of the building. Krey landed and lay down, propping his foot on a crate. He shoved a few diced feathers in his mouth. Eyes closed, he started chewing.

Zeisha whispered, "What's happening out there?"

"Taima has been sending me pictures," Nora said, her voice soft, "and we've peeked out that window a few times. My father is still in the back of an open wagon, conferring with army officers as they come and go. A dozen royal guards are constantly around him. They're probably all mind controlled. There's also a group of soldiers guarding the street, and another group patrolling a larger perimeter."

"Okay." Zeisha took a deep breath, still feeling that strange draw to the Well, but unsure what to do with it. "What's our goal here?" she asked.

Nora was uncharacteristically hesitant. She glanced at Ovrun, who gave her an encouraging nod. "We need to capture my father," she said, "and I need to take his place."

Zeisha's brows rose. "As queen?"

"Just until he recovers."

"If he recovers," Krey said softly.

A *thud* sounded. Zeisha swiveled her head and saw that Sarza had toppled over and was lying on the dusty floor, eyes closed.

Krey jolted, sitting up. Nora knelt by Sarza, trying to rouse her.

"It's okay," Zeisha said. "It's a vision. Sometimes she freezes; sometimes she falls over. She'll be okay."

Nora looked up. "Are you sure?"

"It's been happening all day," Ovrun said.

Nora nodded uncertainly but returned to her seated position. "You remember when we all went to the palace, when Krey . . ." She trailed off, looking at Krey. Her expression softened, which struck Zeisha as odd. Usually when she mentioned anything about Krey's brain eating, she got angry.

"Anyway," Nora continued, returning her attention to Zeisha, "back then, we wanted to take my father from the palace and bring him somewhere private where he could recover. That's what we need to do now. I'm his legal heir. I'll return the city to the trogs and clean up the mess in New Therro as well as I can until he's ready to take his crown again. I . . ." She trailed off, looking down and pressing her lips together. "I don't feel ready." Her eyes found Ovrun, and she took his hand. "But I know I'll have support."

"No!"

The word had come from Sarza, and it was way too loud. In an instant, Nora lurched forward and clamped a hand over the seer's mouth. "Quiet!" she insisted before removing her hand.

Sarza sat up and opened her mouth to speak, but Nora shook her head hard, holding up a hand. Sarza stayed silent, looking like she'd explode with whatever she wanted to say.

Half a minute later, Nora whispered, "Taima says everything's normal out there, despite your outburst." She glared at Sarza. "Don't do that again."

"Listen to me, Nora. You can't forcefully depose your father."

"Why not? Besides the obvious difficulty of figuring out how to do it, I mean."

"Oh, Zeisha could make it happen." Sarza's gaze shifted to the new Anya, and a rare smile took over her face. "You're gonna do some cool stuff." She turned back to Nora. "If you steal the crown from your father today, Cellerin may not survive."

"It wouldn't be stealing! I'm the legal heir!" Nora's whisper had fire in it.

"You're not the legal monarch. Your father is. Most of the country has no idea about his crazy brain magic."

"You know about that?" Nora blurted.

"Yeah. I . . . uh . . . I listened to some of your conversations when

Krey was locked up." She waved a hand, as if brushing away the statement. "Listen, Nora, you take your daddy's crown, and his people will think you're a stupid, power-hungry teenager. Some people will follow you, sure. But others will do whatever they can to return your father to his position. It'll get violent."

"So what are we supposed to do?" Nora asked.

"You're not gonna like it. Hell, I don't like it." All Sarza's breath came out in a sigh that seemed terribly loud. "You gotta negotiate."

"Negotiate? What do we have to offer?"

Again, Sarza smiled. "It's less about offering . . . and more about threatening."

Zeisha sat in a dark corner of the preday store, eyes closed.

Listening.

She had no idea how to use the Well or how it might help in their current situation. Her only choice was to hope something—or, as the Anya had said, some*one*—spoke to her.

She wished she could sit in the middle of a green meadow, warmed by golden sunlight. She'd breathe the scent of sweet wildflowers and listen to a bubbling spring nearby. That, she thought, would've been the perfect way for her to connect with the Well.

Instead, she was on a dusty floor, breathing the mustiness of bygone years and listening for . . . well, she didn't quite know what she was listening for. And she was okay with that. Tranquility flowed through her. Even here, she somehow knew that all was well.

She ran her fingers over the floor. Truth came to her, settling in her mind as if carried there on a soft breeze. The dust that clung to her hands, she realized, was dust from the planet. The oddly sweet mold she smelled was also from Anyari. The air she drew into her lungs was the same air that kept Anyari's species alive.

Even in this old store, I feel Anyari.

As the Anya had performed his magic, making fences of lava, steam, and mud, he'd touched the ground. He'd even placed a bare foot in the dirt at their last location. *How can I touch the ground without someone seeing me?* Zeisha's mind slipped in and out of that problem. There was no anxiety in her pondering. The answer was there, she just had to listen.

An image entered her mind: the Anya, holding his hands up, making the dirt spin. The Anya had used his foot to touch the dirt when he'd made his final shield. But he'd also touched the air. *The Well isn't just in the ground. It's everywhere.*

Zeisha smiled, though she still didn't know what it all meant. She held that picture in her mind, of the elderly man creating his spinning fence. She continued to listen for the voice she'd heard all her life, during prayers and times of quiet. Mind still and ready, she drew in deep, soothing breaths of Anyari's air.

The same air my friends are breathing. The same air the king is breathing.

And suddenly, she felt it. The magic of the Well, all around her. She gasped with the wonder of it. This world was brimming with magic. And it was *meant* to be used. By her. Today.

An idea entered her mind. Her first instinct was to reject it. *Nothing violent! I won't use my magic that way!* A peaceful, yet urgent assurance filled her mind. The power behind the Well shared her desire to harm no one.

This might even be fun.

Eyes still closed, Zeisha stood, drawing in another deep breath. When her eyes slid open at last, she found Krey, Ovrun, Nora, and Sarza all standing nearby, watching her.

"I have a plan," she said, smiling.

Zeisha stood in the old store, eyes closed again, breathing and listening. The Anya had talked a bit while he guided the magic of the Well.

But he'd had decades of experience. She didn't think she could speak a syllable.

Once again, she sensed the Well's power in the air, felt its eagerness to come out of its dormant state. Her mind traveled along motes and strands of magic. Though her eyes were closed, she could sense her friends' locations, even the positions of their bodies, by feeling the air around them. A smile pulled at her lips.

Zeisha had thought she'd need to stand by a window or something. Now she knew she could perform this whole task right where she was. She followed the magic in the air outside, seeking the king and his mind-controlled guards. Each time she found one, she took control of the air around their face. The actions were new, yet intuitive. She listened and acted. It was thrilling.

She reached out to the soldiers patrolling the perimeter, even the ones behind the building where she now stood. At last, she was ready. She guided the air's magic with loving, cautious nudges. The Well responded eagerly, reducing the oxygen in the air around each soldier's head. Not enough to make them unconscious; that would lead to quick death for some. No, just enough to—

Laughter sounded outside. One voice, quickly followed by another, then multiplied by ten and more.

Zeisha had grown up in the shadow of Cellerin Mountain, which was tall enough that some climbers suffered from oxygen deprivation. She'd heard stories of people hiking near the top, unable to contain their laughter.

Not everyone reacted to low oxygen in such a way, but she'd asked the Well to adjust the air around each individual, reducing their oxygen just enough to push them into giddiness.

It worked better than she'd imagined. Laughter filled the street—high-pitched giggles and deep guffaws, like someone was telling the best jokes ever, one after another. Zeisha knew that with the giddiness came a sense of freedom and goodwill, just the combination she needed.

She sensed she didn't need to control the Well's every action. Just as the Anya had walked away from each of his active shields, she could let go and trust the magic.

She opened her eyes. Her four companions stood before her, anticipation on their faces. "You all need to work quickly," she said. "I can't let this go on too long, or it'll harm the soldiers out there."

They all knew their roles. Without a word, Ovrun, Krey and Sarza left through the building's front entrance—two of them on foot and one in the air.

Zeisha turned to Nora. "You ready?"

Nora nodded.

They dashed to the building's back exit. The soldiers in the alley merely laughed as the princess and the Anya took their guns. Nora then ran in one direction, Zeisha in the other. She knew her path was likely to be free of soldiers; Taima had scoped it out in advance. Still, she stayed in the shadows of buildings as much as she could. At last, she stopped, panting, at the top of a hill in an overgrown park.

Zeisha stood under a tree and reconnected to the magic in the air. In her mind's eye, she saw dozens of soldiers, still laughing. She laughed too. *It worked!* Then her laughter stopped, and a rush of gratitude drove her to her knees.

"I am the Anya," she whispered. "This is who I'm meant to be." A breeze, flush with the magic of the Well, flowed across her upraised face.

***

Ovrun sprinted toward the guards surrounding the king. He knew several of them. Merriment caused some of them to clutch their stomachs. Others cried in their giddiness. It was clear that Ulmin, who was also laughing, no longer controlled them. Ovrun ran from one guard to the next, taking their weapons and putting them in his pack. When he reached the king, he asked for the man's gun and daggers. Ulmin Abrios happily handed them over.

When Ovrun finished disarming the king and his royal guard, he moved on to the soldiers in the street. There were fifteen of them, all as disheveled and dirty as Lars had been. Some of them teased him by playing tug-of-war with their weapons, but none tried to harm him. They were all too happy for that.

Ovrun filled his pack. He shoved guns in his pockets and the waistband of his pants. At last, he completed his task and ran inside a building where he'd agreed to meet his friends. He dropped the weapons, keeping just one gun in the back of his waistband.

Krey and Sarza, who'd been disarming the soldiers patrolling the perimeter, arrived soon after. Krey landed and sat against the wall, grimacing. "You okay, man?" Ovrun asked.

"I don't have any more feathers," Krey said. "I don't even think I can use the last few I ate. I pushed way too hard today. And my ankle —" He winced, like even saying the word made it hurt more.

"You need a healer," Ovrun said.

"The sooner this thing ends, the sooner we can find one," Krey said. "Are we sure we got all the weapons?"

Huddling together, they compared verbal notes. They quickly determined that none of them had disarmed one particular soldier they'd seen guarding the street from between two buildings.

"I thought you were getting the people close to the king!" Krey said.

"Only in the street. I thought one of you had him."

Sarza cursed.

Ovrun stood. "It's no problem. I got it. I'll meet you back here."

He ran. As he neared the street, he heard continued laughter. He found the soldier they'd all missed and approached him from behind.

The giggling soldier turned. "Heeeey!" he said, in a voice indistinguishable from a drunk's.

"Hey!" Ovrun said. "Can I have your gun?"

"Sure!" The man held his hands wide, away from the holster at his waist. But when Ovrun grabbed for the weapon, the soldier spun away with the grace of a dancer. Ovrun advanced, and the man leapt back, chortling the whole time.

They continued this strange dance for several seconds. Ovrun was about to attempt a tackle when something pressed against the back of his head, making him freeze. A deep voice said, "Hands up, or I'll shoot."

The soldier in front of Ovrun continued laughing senselessly. Ovrun swore. His own gun was shoved in the back of his pants. Maybe if he was fast enough, he could reach—

The man behind him pulled the gun out.

With a sigh, Ovrun lifted his hands.

"Clasp them behind your head," the voice said.

Ovrun did. Suddenly, the man leapt on him. All the air left Ovrun's chest as he slammed into the street. His chin hit hard, his teeth piercing his tongue. Metallic blood flowed into his mouth. In seconds, the soldier put shackles on his wrists.

"Stand up," the man said.

Ovrun did. The soldier came around to stand in front of him—too far away for Ovrun to kick or headbutt him.

The man shot a disgusted look at his comrade, who was still cracking up. Then he turned to Ovrun, shaking his head. "You're gonna tell me what the hell is going on."

39

Tomorrow, the archeologists at Cellerin Mountain will uncover and remove the artifact they've been seeking. They expect to harness its unique radiation for medical advances. Some people even predict the radiation may contribute to other technologies, such as weather alteration. In the near future, we may not only tame the human body, but the planet as well.

Time will tell if the optimism is warranted. But I get the feeling whatever they pull out of that mountain will truly change our world.

-"Uncovering the Future" by Genta Ril
The Derogan Chronicle, *dated Cygni 5, 6293*

NORA RAN THROUGH DESERTED STREETS, following a map Taima had placed in her mind. Her back screamed with every step. She tried to ignore it.

At last, she arrived at her destination: a wide, empty street. Taima was already waiting. As Nora climbed on the dragon's back, she said, *Thank you for this.*

Taima lifted off then ascended at an incredible speed. Nora held on tight and embraced the thrill that coursed through her.

Once they were above weapons range, it took very little time to get to the street where Nora's father waited. From the altitude where they hovered, Nora squinted at what looked like a toy wagon. Tiny figures scurried in and near it. Her father, she knew, was one of them.

Her heart pounded. Renewed energy filled her, dulling her back pain. *Taima, can you tell if the people down there are still laughing?*

I cannot hear them, but they do appear . . . disorganized.

Okay. Nora filled her lungs with air, then released it slowly. *I guess we'd better go down.*

Taima descended in a gradual spiral. Nora held her breath, fearing every moment that she'd hear gunshots.

As they drew closer to the ground, a welcome sound filled her ears: many voices, laughing. Her heart raced. Her palms sweated on Taima's scales.

Zeisha had promised to restore the king's oxygen when she saw or sensed the dragon descending. Nora craned her neck to see past Taima's strong shoulder. She found her father's gray-streaked hair near the wagon. He wore the same black uniform as his guards.

Ulmin was waving his hands around, shouting questions at his laughing guards. Nora tensed as he reached in his pocket and put something in his mouth. Probably his dark fuel. Nora held her breath, desperately hoping the laughing guards would be resistant to mind control, as Krey said the intoxicated guards at the palace had been.

Her breath came out in a *whoosh* when the guards continued laughing.

Taima descended farther, close enough for the edge of her shadow to fall on the king of Cellerin. He looked up. Nora could make out the O of his mouth.

"Father!" she called. Maybe it was silly or petty, but she could no longer call him *Dad.*

"Nora," he responded. His guards' raucous laughter punctuated the word.

Closer, Nora told Taima.

The dragon descended and hovered, her broad wings stretched over the wide street, ready to take off if anything went wrong.

Ulmin's eyes were glued to his daughter. Again, he popped something in his mouth. Nora shuddered.

"Father," she called, "you and I are going to negotiate for the future of Deroga." Her voice was strong, though her heart threatened to leap from her chest.

The king opened his mouth to answer, but someone else spoke first. "My king!"

Nora swiveled her head to find the source. Nobody should be aware enough to talk to her father coherently. When her eyes fell on the male soldier approaching the king, she drew in a high-pitched gasp. The man was leading Ovrun across the street, holding a gun to his head.

When Taima's great, domed eyes found the armed soldier, she aimed her head upward and shot into the air. Nora screamed, holding on with every bit of her strength. *I'm going to fall!*

The dragon stopped her sharp ascent but continued to rise, flying in swoops and wild zigzags, clearly trying to ensure that the armed man would find her a difficult target to hit.

Trying not to vomit, Nora cried, *Taima, I need to talk to my father!*

That man has a gun! the dragon replied.

I don't think he'll shoot, not while I'm on your back. Please—

He dropped them, Taima said, even as she began a gentle descent.

What? Nora looked down, but from such a height, she couldn't see much.

Taima sent Nora a memory from a moment before. The soldier had dropped the gun he'd been aiming at Ovrun. He'd taken a second weapon from a holster and dropped it too. Then he'd kicked them both away.

Soon, Taima was again hovering over the street. Nora's father had moved several mets away from his loud, gleeful guards. The clear-minded soldier stood near the king, holding a knife to Ovrun's throat.

Nora's breath caught in her chest. *Ovrun, I'm so sorry.* She wanted to kneel and plea for Ovrun's life. Instead, she smoothed the panic and dread off her face. *Taima, can we please land?*

Taima touched down, leaving plenty of distance between herself and the king. Nora raised her voice over all the cackling laughter. "Did you tell him to drop his guns?" she asked.

"Of course. I want to speak with you, Nora. I want you to feel safe."

Her father's expression was as kind as ever. It clawed at her already-hurting heart. Through pure stubbornness, she kept her voice level. "Will you let Ovrun go?"

Her father raised his eyebrows. Then he laughed hard. For a moment, Nora thought Zeisha had reduced his oxygen again. But no —his eyes, fixed on his daughter, held none of the drunk confusion Nora saw in his guards. At last, he calmed. Still smiling, he said, "Don't be silly, sweetheart."

Nora took in the laughter. His words. His expression. He knew Ovrun was her friend, and yet as he refused her request, he was . . . delighted.

For the first time, she recognized the madness in her father. She'd seen it to a lesser extent at the palace over two months ago. She hadn't been ready to acknowledge it then.

And all at once, she knew the truth, as certainly as she knew her own name. Her father wouldn't recover from this. He'd lost himself already.

He's my enemy. I can't save our nation by fixing him. I can only save it by fighting him.

The realization sent crushing pain into Nora's chest, followed by a wave of desperation. *I'm betraying him if I give up on him! I can come up with the right words to pull him out of this; I know I can.*

Except she knew she couldn't. She pushed away the denial that threatened to destroy their whole plan. The truth was right in front of her. She was done avoiding it. Grief and second-guessing could come later. She had a job to do.

But would her father even negotiate? Did he care about anything but his own power?

He was watching her with his head tilted a bit to the side. When he spoke, it was with the gentle, loving voice he'd always reserved for her and her mother. "Dani has told me everything, darling," he said.

Nora gritted her teeth. Dani had only talked because he'd forced her to.

"I know you care about this young man," Ulmin said, gesturing to Ovrun. "You must let go of any romantic ideas; you can do far better than him. But I'll be happy to release him, because I love you. All you have to do is return home with me."

And so we begin. Aloud, Nora asked, "If I say no?"

There was that grin again. "Then I'm afraid the good soldier here will slit his throat."

Nora refused to let panic overwhelm her. "If that happens," she said calmly, "the dragon I'm riding will reduce your good soldier to a pile of ashes." It wasn't an idle threat. If that man drew his knife along Ovrun's throat, Nora would beg Taima to destroy him. She'd regret it later . . . but she'd do it.

Ulmin shrugged. "That would change nothing."

The words stabbed at Nora's heart. Her father used to care about every one of his citizens.

She took a deep breath, ready to make her demands. But her father's gaze shifted away from her, his eyes widening.

Nora turned, then suppressed a smile. In the distance, glowing, orange magma shot into the air. It pulsed rhythmically, like the earth was spitting, refilling its mouth, and spitting again. Zeisha had activated the Well a second way now, just as they'd planned. Several of the king's guards took notice of the spectacle, pointing and guffawing even louder.

"Father," Nora said, drawing his attention back to her, "you will leave this place after signing a decree acknowledging that Deroga permanently belongs to the trogs. You will release every New Therroan soldier from your army. And you will give full independence to New Therro."

His jaw muscles clenched. His skin took on a reddish hue. "Why would I do that?"

"You saw the shields we put around neighborhoods today. We have a lyster who can use the magic of Anyari. That same lyster has reduced all these guards and soldiers to the state they're in now. If you don't meet our demands, that lyster will tear up the nation of Cellerin. Floods and fires and quakes will make your kingdom unrecognizable."

"I don't believe you." His eyes shifted to look behind Nora. His jaw dropped.

She turned. As if on cue, a massive, steaming geyser had risen in the air, twice as high as the pulsing lava.

Zeisha would never use Anyari's magic in violent ways. But Sarza had said they needed a threat. This was the perfect one. It didn't matter how much brain-controlling power the king had; he knew he couldn't overcome the magic of a planet.

"Test me, Father," Nora said. "We'll start with the palace grounds."

Ulmin's gaze returned to Nora. With every one of his rapid breaths, his chest swelled and his nostrils flared. When he spoke, it was with a deep, ominous voice Nora had never heard him use. "No one—*no one*—threatens my land."

The words transported Nora back to her conversation with Krey, when she'd called Cellerin *my land*. His response had remained with her ever since. "It's not *your land*. This nation doesn't belong to the royal family, Your Highness. It belongs to all of us."

Nora was pondering that when her father said three more words: "I'm sorry, darling."

She didn't have time to ask why he was apologizing. Faster than she'd ever seen him move, her father, a stone lyster who rarely used his faculty, lifted a hand and shot a thick, stone spear straight at the glorious, black dragon.

The weapon pierced Taima's chest. Above the awful laughter in the street, a sound arose: Taima's roaring, keening cry. It was the most terrifying, grief-inducing thing Nora had ever heard.

Taima lifted into the air, still releasing that rich, pained scream. Nora catalyzed fuel she hadn't realized she still had in her. A dense ball of ice struck her father, catching him off guard and preventing him from creating another spear.

In seconds, Taima was out of the king's reach. Her scream turned into a soundless groan, penetrating Nora's mind.

How bad is it? Nora asked.

The dragon didn't respond.

Taima? How bad?

There was a long silence, thrumming with tension. Taima at last spoke to Nora's mind. *This injury shall be my final one.* Pain saturated the words, spilling into Nora's heart.

Nora began weeping. Her mind raced to find some way to help. *I know where a blood lyster is!*

The wound is too severe, Taima said.

Nora cried harder. The dragon was right. Healing magic worked best on humans. Even the most skilled blood lysters could only heal small wounds on animals.

Maybe Zeisha can heal you! The amount of power she has now, it—

She has power over the planet, Taima interrupted. *Why would she be able to heal a dragon?*

Nora grasped desperately for a solution but found none. *I'll reach out to Osmius. He'll have an idea; I know—*

NO! Taima's voice remained strong, despite her obvious agony. *If you tell him, he will fly here. The king will control him.*

Then fly to him.

No, Nora. Your task here is not through.

There's nothing more we can do! My father called our bluff! You're

—you're dying, Taima! Drop me in a nearby street. I'll find a way to save Ovrun. You can spend your last minutes with Osmius.

Nora-human. It was the first time the female dragon had ever used that term of affection. Her voice had taken on a gentleness that seemed at odds with her injured state. *This wound shall kill me, but not for hours. I am a dragon. My body is strong. We will not give up yet.*

Nora's heart broke as she anticipated the hours of agony the dragon was facing. But if Taima could show such courage with a spear in her chest, Nora must follow her lead. Through sheer force of will, she stopped crying. Instantly, an idea struck her mind. When she shared it with Taima, the dragon approved.

Hurry, Nora said. *Zeisha will restore the oxygen soon.* She was surprised it hadn't happened already.

Hold tightly to me, the great dragon said.

Nora suppressed a scream as Taima performed a steep, terrifying dive. When she was within weapons distance from the king, she began flying evasively, performing unpredictable turns at remarkable speeds, sending Nora's stomach spinning. Yellow blood flowed from around the spear in Taima's chest, flinging through the air each time she turned. The king shot more stone missiles, but none hit the dragon.

Are you ready? Taima asked Nora.

Nora catalyzed the last bit of her ice. She tightened the grip of her boots and her hands on Taima's scales. *I am.*

Taima turned, nearly flinging Nora off her back. The great dragon dived straight at Ulmin.

Ice flew from Nora's hand, sphere after sphere of it. She was lysting at greater speed than ever before. But her father—by the stone, when had he gotten so good?—also shot one missile after another, his made of stone.

They'd both sacrificed accuracy for speed, but one of Nora's ice balls hit an incoming spear. Another hit her father's shoulder. Nora twisted to avoid a shining stone missile.

The dragon drew close to her target. Sunlight reflected off her golden, compound eyes. She opened her massive mouth. Her razor-edged teeth gleamed, and fire shot past them, aimed at the king.

Nora heard her father roar in pain. Taima pulled up sharply, lest they crash into the ground. She ascended, and when Nora's eyes found her father, she drew in a breath. Smoke rose from his hands as he beat them against the dirt.

Maybe she should've thrilled at the sight. It was what she'd told Taima to do. With his hands injured, Ulmin couldn't make any more stone weapons.

But Nora's heart ached for her father. His hands—the same hands that had caressed her, fed her, held the books he read to her— might never be the same. Could even a skilled blood lyster fully heal such an injury?

Trying to get her mind off what she'd done, Nora asked Taima, *Are you okay?* It was a silly question. A spear was still embedded in the dragon's chest.

One of his spears found my leg, the dragon said. Her voice was weaker than before.

Nora squeezed her eyes shut briefly. *Do you have the strength to take me down there?*

Do not insult me, Taima said, beginning her descent. *I have more strength than you can comprehend, little girl.*

Nora held back tears and laughter.

Taima landed in front of the king. Nora's eyes fell on Ovrun, who was still rigid with fear, the soldier's knife at his throat. Nora hoped he saw the promise in her expression: *I'll get you out of here if it's the last thing I do.*

The street was strangely quiet now. Most of the laughter had died down, though an occasional, hoarse chortle broke through. Everyone wore stupid, exhausted smiles. Nora guessed they were too tired to laugh. *Please, Zeisha. Give me a couple more minutes.*

Ulmin somehow found the strength to stand. His hands were

swollen claws, pressed against his chest. Face dark red, he breathed hard, glaring at the dragon and his daughter.

Nora tried to ignore her rising sympathy. "If you do not agree to our terms, the dragon will burn you again. Then tomorrow, we will begin destroying this land with magic like you've never seen."

His eyes moved behind her again, taking in the jets of steaming water and magma. He sucked air through his clenched teeth and returned his gaze to Nora. His voice was as pain filled as Taima's. "You'd never harm the land. It's your inheritance."

His words tore into her heart. *The value of our kingdom isn't in the land,* her father used to say. *It is in the people.* Now he saw his people as nothing more than fuel for his power.

Nora almost reminded him of that. But she had to speak the language of madness, not logic.

Nausea in her gut, she said, "You're underestimating me, Father." She allowed a grin to take over her face. "Can you imagine how much power is in our planet? Once I start issuing those commands, I'm not sure I'll be able to stop."

Nora had no trouble spouting the lies, because there was an element of truth in them. This was a bluff, but if it hadn't been . . . Nora could imagine herself embracing such limitless power. *And that's why I'm not the Anya.*

Breathing heavily, King Ulmin locked eyes with his daughter. She didn't look away. He lifted his chin and squared his shoulders, regal stubbornness on every line of his form. "I will not give independence to New Therro. They have always been part of Cellerin. They belong to me!"

"Then the dragon will burn your legs," Nora spat. "And tomorrow, the disasters will begin!" From the wagon, one of the guards pointed at her and giggled.

"I won't give them independence!" her father roared. His face screwed up in pain, and he brought his volume down. "But I'll let their soldiers go. They're incompetent anyway. They can stay here when the rest of us leave. They'll have to find their own way home."

Nora stared at him, almost not believing what she'd heard: *when the rest of us leave.* As well as she could from her perch on Taima, she mirrored his determined stance. "You'll leave today."

"The trogs can have their worthless city. I don't care."

He did care; she knew that. But his eyes kept flicking between the magic behind Nora and the dragon she rode. She'd scared him, just like she'd wanted to do. Manipulating her father made her feel ill, but she couldn't stop now. "No deal unless New Therro gets its independence."

Her father's eyes flashed. He turned to the soldier holding Ovrun. "Is the knife sharp?"

"Very." The man's voice was almost a growl.

Ulmin returned his gaze to Nora. "Take my deal, or you can watch your friend die. And you can tell your dragon to kill me too. I'd rather lose everything, even my life, than give up New Therro. It's mine."

There it was again: proof that she'd lost her father. He was risking his entire nation and his own life, just to keep control of a small, troublesome province. Nothing Nora said would change his mind. *This is a negotiation,* she told herself. *And Ovrun's life is on the line. Take what you can.*

"Deroga belongs to the trogs. Forever." Her voice was firm. "You'll release the New Therroans from the army today. And you'll let Ovrun go. In return, we won't use the magic of the planet against you. We'll let the army leave peacefully."

Her father stared at her for a long time. She didn't pull her gaze away. At last, he turned to the knife-wielding soldier. "Let him go." The soldier obeyed.

"Up here, Ovrun!" Nora shouted.

Taima bared her teeth at Ulmin as Ovrun climbed up.

Nora and the king worked out a few final details. It was a business negotiation between strangers, not a conversation between a daughter and her father.

When they'd come to a final agreement, she leaned toward him and spoke in a low voice. "I never wanted your crown, Father. But I know now I'll have to take it. Not today, but soon. Our people deserve better than what you can give them."

He didn't say a thing, but his eyes blazed with some emotion she'd never seen in him before. A sense of foreboding, thick and acidic, filled her stomach. *I don't think I should've said that,* she told Taima. *Let's go.*

The dragon lifted into the air. Once she was well beyond the reach of bullets and magic, she flew in a large, diamond pattern, completing the shape three times. That was Zeisha's sign to release the magic of the Well, returning full oxygen to everyone below.

As they flew, the magma jets and geyser disappeared. The new Anya had completed her mission perfectly. Nora had gotten most of what she wanted.

But her heart was as raw and bruised as her back. She squeezed her eyes shut against her grief. For the unrecognizable man she called her father. For the proud, beautiful dragon she was riding.

Taima dropped her passengers in a deserted street near the building where Krey and Sarza waited. Then the bleeding reptid departed alone to spend the last hours of her life with the dragon she'd loved for two hundred years.

Nora clutched Ovrun's hand and watched Taima fly away.

40

An editor won't examine these words. They won't go to print.

I don't know why I'm writing them.

Today, the world ended.

I was reading in the park, and every person around me turned stark white. Blood gushed from their eyes, noses, and mouths.

They died. All of them.

I went home and found my dead family. I walked through streets full of smashed vehicles and pale corpses.

I encountered another living person. A middle-aged man. He began walking with me. That was hours ago, and he still hasn't said a word. I suppose he's in shock. I suppose I am too.

We're sitting in a stadium now, with a few hundred other survivors. We all found each other through social media.

I'm surrounded by people, and I've never felt so alone.

> *-Journal entry by Dari Beck (known pseudonymously as Genta Ril), dated Cygni 6, 6293*

ZEISHA SAT before a jet of magma. The magical, molten stone lit up the dusk and cast a flickering, red glow on her skin.

She'd traveled to all the residential areas where the Anya had put up shields. At each one, she'd asked the Well to go dormant. Every time, it had sent her a burst of what felt like love and gratitude before doing as she'd requested. Now all the trogs were returning home.

This magma fountain was the only magic of the Well that Zeisha still needed to release. It was the first one the Anya—the *other* Anya, she supposed she should call him—had created. She got the feeling the Well was happy to stay awake a little longer.

Digging her fingers in the dirt, Zeisha sensed power and intelligence.

She sensed God.

She'd tried to remotely "switch off" the shields, but it was impossible. In order to access the magic of the Well on and below the planet's surface, she had to touch the ground nearby. Air magic, the type she'd used to make dozens of people laugh, was different. She could sense and control it for blocks in every direction, connecting to it through her breath.

Zeisha basked in the warmth of the nearby magma. She watched it for a few seconds, but it was bright enough to hurt her eyes. She closed them and pondered the events of the last several hours.

She hadn't expected to be able to limit the guards' and soldiers' oxygen for as long as she did. However, Zeisha found that the Well was remarkably intelligent, adjusting itself continuously. It kept the guards and soldiers in an altered state while ensuring that each of their bodies had enough oxygen to recover fully. Still, she was relieved to liberate them from their giddy imprisonment.

Zeisha accepted the hugs and praise of her friends when they reunited. She cried with Nora over Taima's fate. Before long, they emerged from hiding, having confirmed that the army had released the captive trogs.

First, they sought out a healer for Nora and Krey. After that, they found Eira. She told them of the treaty she and representatives of the other clans had signed with the king. By late afternoon, the Cellerinian Army was departing trog territory.

Through all this, Zeisha had shared in the urgency, excitement, and pain of her friends. But that indescribable peace had remained too, covering her soul with a liquid assurance that all was as it should be.

That *she* was as *she* should be.

She'd been changing ever since she was freed from the militia. The Anya's gift had further transformed her. Zeisha sensed that at a deep level, she'd been made new.

She opened her eyes, shocked to find that the dim light of dusk was gone. The jet of magma dulled the starlight overhead. Zeisha ran her fingers over the ground on either side of her. *It's time for you to go to sleep*, she thought. *I'd like to see the stars.*

A burst of love filled her. With a *whoosh* that might have been a sigh, the magma flowed back into the ground. The dirt closed over it.

Nora was clearly trying to get ready quietly. "I'm already awake," Zeisha whispered.

"You can sleep longer," Nora said.

Zeisha pushed off her covers. "I'm ready to get up."

A whisper came from beside them. "Me too." Sarza, their newest sleeping companion, got out of bed.

The three of them exited into the gray, pre-dawn light, then strolled along the street. Ovrun was walking toward them. He and Nora had a long day of hunting ahead. Once again, the Cellerinian Army had destroyed much of the trogs' food.

Surprisingly, Krey was next to Ovrun. He was limping a bit, but he still greeted Zeisha with a big smile. They all walked to the dining room they'd been using for months now. Until food stores were replenished, they'd have to skip breakfast. But a leader of one of the other clans had given Nora a bottle of juice to thank her for negotiating the truce.

Nora poured the juice into clay cups. "Zeisha, I wanted to tell the woman who gave me this that she should be thanking you. But I know you don't want people to know about your new magic."

"I appreciate that." Zeisha tried the juice. Like the drink they'd had on her birthday, it tasted mildly fermented.

Sarza sipped hers, then drank it down in several large gulps.

Zeisha liked the seer, which was odd, since they seemed to be opposites in every way. Lifting her cup, Zeisha said, "We should all thank Sarza. We wouldn't have met the Anya without her."

"To Sarza," Ovrun said with a smile.

"And to the Anyas," Nora added. "Old and new."

They all drank.

It was a short, subdued celebration. Ovrun and Nora needed to start hunting, and Sarza had an early meeting with Eira.

"Want to walk in the park?" Krey asked Zeisha.

"Sure."

They meandered among the spring-green trees, the gentle light of the morning sun warming them. Tranquility still filled Zeisha, but it was tinged with exhaustion and a bit of sadness she couldn't explain. She squeezed Krey's hand, as if the warm pressure would push away her unwelcome emotion.

Krey squeezed back and smiled. "You were amazing yesterday.

You might be the only person in the world who'd use laughter to win a battle."

She smiled. "I hear you were pretty great too. How's your ankle?"

"It only aches a little. That River Clan healer is talented."

"Good. But let's sit." She gestured to a bench. "You should probably rest it when you can."

He sat and put his arm around her, pulling her close. "I haven't had a chance to tell you yet—I talked to an injured New Therroan soldier yesterday when I was waiting for a healer."

"I bet he was ready to go home," Zeisha said. The New Therroans had stayed overnight in trog territory and would return home that morning. Eira had even convinced the king to loan them a couple of wagons for their wounded.

"He was. We also talked about what comes next." Krey pulled his arm off Zeisha's shoulders and twisted so he could look at her. His eyes were bright and wide, and his words spilled from a smiling mouth. "He said the New Therroan soldiers hate the king even more now than they did before. And Nora earned their loyalty, negotiating for their release from the army. He thinks New Therro will help us bring down the king."

That was all good news. But rather than encouraging Zeisha, Krey's words turned a page in her mind. Everything was suddenly clear. She wished it weren't.

"What's wrong?" Krey asked.

"Nothing—I mean everything—I mean, I don't know." The peace that she'd hoped would stick with her forever had fled. Her stomach was heavy, her heart compressed. "Krey," she said softly.

He took one of her hands. His eyes drifted to her lips.

She drew her hand back and twisted her fingers together. "You know what?"

"What?"

"I love myself again."

Krey's lips curved into a sweet, gentle, strong smile, the one she'd never seen him give anyone else. "That makes me happy, Zei."

She swallowed and gave him a wobbly smile. "I'm starting to know myself too."

"Should I call you the Anya from now on?"

She laughed softly. "Please don't."

"I'll only call you that in private."

Her smile disappeared. She could feel her pulse throbbing in her neck. "I've changed. And not just because I'm the Anya. I've been changing for months."

His grin faded too, like he'd finally sensed how serious this conversation was. *Oh, God, I don't want to hurt him.*

But she didn't see a way around it.

"My entire life has changed," she said. "There's still a lot I need to figure out—about myself and my magic. And I need to do it—" All at once, she was crying. "I need to do it—"

Krey's throat convulsed as he swallowed. She resisted an ill-timed urge to touch it. In a strained voice, he said, "You need to do it alone." A statement, not a question.

Zeisha nodded.

Krey squeezed his eyes shut, but not before she saw the angry pain in them. "But I love you," he said.

"I know," she managed to say. "So do I."

His eyes popped open. "*So do you* what? Love me, or love yourself?"

"Both."

Krey ran both his hands through his hair, standing as he did so. He stepped away, then spun around, crossing his arms tightly over his chest. His eyes glistened with tears, but his voice was harsh. "If you really love me, why this? This isn't love!"

She had to stop crying. *Deep breath. Another.* She stood. "Sometimes love isn't enough." She stepped forward and grabbed one of his hands in both of hers. He didn't pull away. "Oh, Krey, you have dreams as big as this world. And I can't wait"—a sob broke through, but she kept talking—"I can't wait to hear all the stories of the amazing things you do. You want to depose the king and then go on to build libraries and universities. I love you for your dreams—no, really, I do!—but I don't know if I can be part of them. There's this whole world of peaceful magic out there, and I've been trusted with it. That's where my future is." Even as she said the words, it felt like a piece of herself clicked into place.

He snatched his hand away. "So it's just gonna be you and the Well, huh? Hanging out together, doing magic?"

"No, not just me and the Well. I still need friends, Krey. Without —" She had to push the words out. "Without *us*, I'll need friends more than ever. I hope you'll be one of them."

"Zeisha!" The one-word cry nearly cracked her resolve. His trembling hands reached up and cupped her face. He leaned close, his gaze finding her lips and then her eyes, begging her to kiss him. Like that would fix everything.

Oh, how she wanted to. "I'm so sorry," she whispered.

"Yeah." His brows drew together, and he blinked hard. "Me too." He dropped his hands. Shoulders hunched, he turned and limped away.

Zeisha watched him leave. Just before he reached the street, he stopped and turned, fixing his gaze on her again. He raised his hand. His lips moved, mouthing, *Goodbye.*

Zeisha held up her own hand, terribly aware of the many mets between them. "Goodbye," she whispered.

Krey nodded once, lowered his hand, and left.

Zeisha sat on the bench, raised her face to the sky, and let her cries pierce the air. After a long time, her shoulders went still and her tears stopped flowing, leaving her spent and empty.

For several long minutes, she was quiet. Numb. Then a hint of familiar serenity brushed against her spirit. She opened herself to it, and a wave of peace rushed in, deep and rich, flooding every part of her—from her swollen eyes to her broken heart.

Zeisha knew again that all was as it should be.

EPILOGUE

"Five more!" Ovrun told Krey. "You can do it!"

Krey lowered himself for the first half of a push-up, then collapsed in the grass. "No, I can't. I don't know how you do so many. Running is way easier."

Ovrun laughed, extending a hand and helping Krey sit next to him. "I guess that's enough for tonight." He was about to suggest they go to dinner. Then he realized Krey was gazing at nothing, his lips pressed into a frown.

Ovrun dropped a hand on his friend's shoulder. "Hey . . . ready to talk about it?"

Krey shifted his gaze to meet Ovrun's. "About what?"

Ovrun lifted his brows.

A long sigh exited Krey's mouth. "I miss her. I see her every day, but I miss her."

"Of course you do, man. It hasn't even been three weeks."

"Longest twenty days of my life." Krey's brows knit together as his eyes found whatever point they'd been fixed on before. "Everybody thinks I'm sad, and I am . . . but I'm pissed too. I mean, I left my home to save her from people who were stealing her humanity. And this is what I get? She just wants to be alone? To figure herself out?" He shook his head and turned back to Ovrun. "I'm aware that makes me a massive asshole, by the way. I don't want to see it that way. But I can't get it out of my head."

"You're not an asshole," Ovrun said. "But . . . lemme ask you. Would she have been worth saving if she wasn't your girlfriend?"

Krey shook his head, laughing softly. "Don't come at me with logic, man. It's not fair." After a brief silence, he said, "Of course she would've been worth it."

"Do you think she made a mistake? Breaking up with you?"

Another sigh. "I don't. She's changed. I have too. She did what she needed to do." One of Krey's dark eyebrows rose. "But I'm still pissed."

Ovrun smiled. "Fair enough."

Rapid footsteps caused them both to turn. Nora ran up and stopped next to them. Her cheeks were red with exertion, and she was a little out of breath.

Ovrun stood. "Ready for dinner?"

"Actually, I've got food in my pack. Osmius just landed. I wanted to ask you to fly with us." Smirking, she turned to Krey. "You're welcome to join us."

"I'm not in the mood for torture tonight, but thanks."

"Didn't you go on a flight earlier this afternoon?" Ovrun asked Nora.

"That was the plan, but I got busy unpacking a shipment from Cruine."

Ovrun nodded. Everyone in Deroga had been working nearly nonstop, cleaning up the mess the Cellerinian Army left behind. He, Nora, and the other hunters had spent two weeks replenishing meat supplies. Since then, Ovrun had been helping renovate homes on the Silver Clan's new residential street. That was one good thing about the battle—the six trog clans were actually working together now.

A flight through the late-spring air would be a great change of pace. "I'd love to go," Ovrun said.

Nora's smile dazzled him. "We don't have much sunlight left, so let's hurry."

"Well, if you really wanna go fast . . ." He scooped her into his arms, eliciting a scream. " 'Bye, Krey!" he called over his shoulder as he sprinted away with Nora.

Before long, he set her down. They walked briskly, eating fruit from Nora's pack. Just as they were about to turn onto the street where Osmius always landed, Nora halted. Ovrun turned. "Coming?"

She sauntered up to him, a smile on her irresistible lips. Her hands rested on his chest, then slid up to his shoulders. Tickling the nape of his neck, she said, "I've hardly seen you this week. You been avoiding me?"

He let out a low laugh. "Never."

She rested her head on his chest. His arms tightened around her. *How does she manage to make a hug feel so amazing?* Ovrun was still aching to hear her say she loved him, but he wouldn't push her. Even without those words, these stolen moments were indescribably great.

"We better go," Nora whispered.

Osmius didn't say a word as they flew over the city. When dusty wilderness had replaced suburban buildings, Nora asked, *How are you?*

It was several minutes before the dragon answered, *I am lost without her, Nora-human.*

Nora swallowed hard. *She was unforgettable.*

Imagine how unforgettable she is after two centuries.

Nora sent as much love as she could from her heart to his.

The sun had set, turning the land below gray. Above, clouds covered most of the sky.

A sudden urge filled Nora. *Osmius, I'd like to see the palace.*

Why?

She pondered that and at last replied, *Because Cellerin is my home. The palace represents that.* After a pause, she added, *It'll be dark by the time we get there. You can fly over the clouds. I'll peek down through a gap. My father won't see you.*

Very well.

When Cellerin City came into view, Osmius flew higher. Nora held her breath and shivered as they passed through a misty cloud. When they emerged, the stars above seemed close enough to scoop up a handful of them.

They flew past the city, catching glimpses of its lights through breaks in the clouds. Before long, Osmius slowed. *I believe the palace is just ahead. I shall share my sight with you.* He sent his superior night vision into Nora's mind, then came to a halt over a gap between clouds.

In Nora's mind's eye, the edges of the clouds looked luminous. The dragon's focus, and hers, shifted to the land below.

Nora was prepared to gaze at the palace's perimeter fence, the pond, and all the familiar buildings. She saw none of that. The view below was unrecognizable. *Where . . . where are we, Osmius?*

His words were as hesitant as hers. *We are . . . at the palace. I am certain of it.*

"That's not the palace," she said aloud.

"What is it?" Ovrun asked.

Nora couldn't seem to form the words. Through the space between clouds, she saw an unbelievably massive stone dome. It was solid, except for ventilation holes at regular intervals and a larger opening at the very top. As she watched, a piece of stone filled in a bit of the opening. She saw no workers, no scaffolding. It was like the surrounding stone had simply . . . multiplied.

"How . . .?" Nora breathed.

The answer was clear. Her father was a stone lyster. Creating this structure was, by all measures, impossible. But King Ulmin had used brain magic in impossible ways too. He'd discovered the secret to intensifying both his magical faculties.

Another piece of stone appeared.

Nora remembered the words she'd spoken to her father three weeks before. "I never wanted your crown, Father. But I know now I'll have to take it." She'd seen the insane look in his eyes and had immediately wanted to take back her impetuous words.

Her father would do anything—even enclose himself within a dome made of magically created stone—to keep his crown. Nora didn't know him anymore, not at all.

And she couldn't imagine how she'd stop him.

A NOTE FROM BETH

Thank you for reading *The Vine Eater*! Reviews make a *huge* difference to authors and readers. Will you write a short review on Amazon? I can't tell you how much I'd appreciate it. (While you're there, click on my author page and Follow me!)

Want to know the full story behind the Anyarian apocalypse? *The Seer's Sister* is the full-length prequel novel to The Magic Eater's Trilogy. It's available free to my Email Insiders! Subscribe now at carolbethanderson.com.

Curious about what happens next? Keep reading for a sneak peek of Book 3, *The Stone Eater*. Visit Amazon to order it now!

THE STONE EATER: BOOK 3 OF THE MAGIC EATERS TRILOGY

SNEAK PEEK

I hope you enjoy this early peek at The Stone Eater. *Details will change between this version and the final one, but this will give you a taste (pun intended) of what's to come! I look forward to getting the final book of this series into your hands!*

-Beth

FIRST THINGS FIRST.

King Ulmin Abrios never felt truly awake until he fueled up. He reached into the dark for a canister on his bedside table. It had two compartments, separated by a perforated, ceramic disc. Every night, Chef Pryn filled the bottom chamber with ice and the top with fuel.

As Ulmin removed the lid, his heart began to race. That made him laugh softly; he was like a little boy when it came to his first fuel of the day.

His fingers brushed across several soft, delicately thin layers of brain matter, diced into bite-sized pieces. The ice had kept them fresh, and he delighted in how pleasantly cool they felt against his warm skin. From the odor wafting up—sweet with a hint of earthiness—Ulmin could tell this fuel came from a cervid. He'd gotten good at distinguishing between species through smell alone.

He pinched several pieces of fuel and put them in his mouth, resisting the instinct to lick his fingers. *Silly old man*, he thought, laughing again.

He didn't stop eating until the top chamber of the container was empty. With a sigh, he tapped his fingers together, feeling the dampness left behind by brain matter. *Oh, what the hell; life's pleasures are meant to be enjoyed!* Ulmin licked his fingers with relish.

Before getting out of bed, he lit a candle, then fished a piece of ice out of the canister and rubbed it on his neck, sighing in relief. The palace complex was terribly hot. As the day went on, it would only get worse.

Ulmin walked to his sitting room, his flickering candle lighting the way. As he entered, he flipped the light switch. The electricity had been out for a week, but he kept trying, just in case. When the room brightened, his mouth broke into a smile. He blew out his candle, murmuring, "Back in business."

When he'd started creating a stone dome over his palace, Ulmin hadn't considered the fact that it would block sunlight from reaching the solar panels. His was the only building in Cellerin with solar power. The day the large batteries had lost the last of their power, he'd been furious.

He'd instructed a staff member to find workers to move the panels to the top of the dome. To help the workers climb the stone outside, Ulmin had created handholds, footholds, and anchor points for ropes. Only one person had fallen to their death. Not too bad, considering how high the dome was.

Rejuvenated by the brightness of the room, Ulmin exited. After greeting the two stoic guards outside his door, he continued strolling through the residence.

From afar, he saw electric light coming from the kitchen. *Excellent; Pryn is awake—and, judging by the smell, he's cooking cervid sausage.* These days, Ulmin seemed to be waking earlier and earlier. Sometimes he made it to the kitchen before his chef. Mouth watering in anticipation of a delicious breakfast, Ulmin took several more steps.

He slowed. Low voices emanated from the kitchen. Ulmin identified Pryn first . . . then Dani. His sister-in-law. His whole body suddenly tense, he took a few more steps until he could make out their words.

"You know he's controlling everyone in this place!" Dani's voice was barely above a whisper, but Ulmin could hear the shrill passion in it. "You're his friend and his . . . his . . . supplier. He controls you less than anyone else. If anyone's going to stop him—"

"He's my king!" Pryn said, his quiet words matching Dani's in intensity. "I can't stop him; I don't even want to!"

"You can be honest with me, Pryn! I'm not testing you; I—"

Ulmin stepped into the kitchen. Dani stiffened, snapping her mouth closed.

"We can all be honest." The king's voice rang through the small space. "Or at least I thought we could."

His eyes locked on Dani's. Hers were wide. Scared. He shook his head sadly and captured her mind. "Everything is fine," he said, voice soothing and soft. "You're safe and happy here."

Her mouth widened into a smile. "I'm safe and happy."

"That's right." He crossed to Dani and pulled her into a hug. She relaxed into it.

For years, Ulmin had only occasionally used his mind-lysting faculty on Dani. It was a couple of months ago that he'd begun controlling her most of the time she was awake. He'd hesitated to do such a thing, but she hadn't given him a choice. She'd been questioning his decisions. Disrespecting his authority. She'd grown far too comfortable with him.

Now, Ulmin wished he'd increased his control over her sooner. It was for her good. He could sense her serene joy as he held her. So much more pleasant than the rebellious spirit he'd heard in her voice moments before.

He released her and gave her a wide smile. "Shall we eat?"

"If that's what you'd like."

Ulmin's gaze rose to find Pryn watching the exchange. The chef's face broke into a grin. "Cervid sausage, anyone?"

"And maybe a little something additional on the side for me?" Ulmin asked, giving Pryn a wink.

Pryn chuckled. "Always."

Order The Stone Eater on Amazon today!

ACKNOWLEDGEMENTS

A lot of people picture authors sitting at their desks, drinking massive quantities of coffee, typing at the keyboard . . . alone.

Some of that applies to me. I do often use a desk. But I don't drink that much coffee, and what I do drink is decaf.

Most importantly, I don't write alone. My Acknowledgements are always long because *so many people* from all over the world help me produce my books! I may be alone at my desk, but I'm assisted—virtually—by others.

My alpha readers are wonderful souls. I send them a manuscript one big chunk at a time, complete with unlikeable characters, plot holes, and plenty of typos. Their feedback helps me craft a better novel. Thank you times a million to these alpha readers: Becky Brickman, Kim Decker, Brenda Elliott, Brooke Hunger, Stephanie Lynn, Kristin Newton, Becki Norris, Nikki Tuggy, and DeDe Pollnow. Your feedback made a *huge* difference in this book!

I send my beta readers a revised version of the book, and they help me craft a polished story that readers will hopefully love! I can't thank these readers enough for their incisive, useful feedback: Alain Davis, April Mcdermitt; Author Danielle Ancona; Becki Norris;

Bren Elliott; Brooke Hunger; C.M. Irving; Caroline Hannam; Eileen Curley Hammond; Eli Anderson; Elizabeth Belt; J.P. de La Fontaine; Katie Lee; Kim Decker; Kristin W.; Lisa Henson, Capital Editing Services; Marjorie; R. Mark Jones; Michelle Sundholm; Nikki Tuggy; robin; Robin Gonzales; Ruth Zeman; Sarah Joy Green-Hart; Stephanie Lynn; and Tracy Magouirk. This book is what it is because of you!

It can be hard to come up with unique fantasy names! Many of the character and location names in *The Frost Eater* came from creative people besides me. Here are the contributors, with the names they suggested in parentheses: Abigail Swire (Cage), Ana Anderson (Zeisha, Lerenor, & Cerinus), Beth Harris (Cruine), Jamie Brown (Isle, changed spelling to Isla), Julie Simmons (Fayla, changed to Faylie), Kristina Adams (Kebi, Eira and Taima), Marie-Eve Mailhot (Evie), Melissa (Wallace, changed spelling to Wallis), Molly Norris (Brea, Kamina), Melissa Dials (Girro), Megan Koehnlein (Sarza), Vonda Hill (Beck), Julie Simmons (Phip), Carol Breckenridge (Lars), Zarine Arya (Preet), Elizabeth Belt (Osk), Heather (Pryn), Penny Brinker (Dera).

Andrew Hall is a talented photographer, and a photo in his post-apocalyptic series inspired the layers of graffiti in the Derogan suburbs. Follow Andrew on Twitter at @andhphoto.

Thank you to my ARC readers for finding last-minute errors! Congratulations to Lisa Henson of Capital Editing Services, Charlotte Voorspoels, and Clarissa Gosling for tying as winners of my typo-hunting contest.

Mariah Sinclair (mariahsinclair.com and thecovervault.com), once again, this cover knocked it out of the park. Thank you!

Thank you to BMR Williams creating the map!

Thank you to all my Twitter friends for your incredible support. I especially want to thank several people who gave me feedback on Sarza's character: Avery Davis, J.E. Andrews, Meg Kathleen, Normandy Fox, and Patrick Bergen.

My creativity is a gift from God, and I'm so grateful to Him for that (and for all His other gifts)!

Readers, thank you for your enthusiasm! It means the world to me.

-Carol Beth Anderson
Leander, Texas
2020

ABOUT THE AUTHOR

Carol Beth Anderson is a native of Arizona and now lives in Leander, TX, outside Austin. She has a husband, two kids, a miniature schnauzer, and more fish than anyone knows what to do with. Besides writing, she loves baking sourdough bread, knitting, eating cookies-and-cream ice cream, and spending way too much time on Twitter. Beth is the author of the Sun-Blessed Trilogy, The Magic Eaters Trilogy, and *The Curio Cabinet: A Collection of Miniature Stories*.

Find Beth on Facebook, BookBub, and Goodreads, all under the name Carol Beth Anderson. She's also on Twitter and Instagram as @CBethAnderson.